I managed to pull away from him and ran toward the mountain top. He was no more than a step behind me, but where the top of the mountain was as far as he could go, it was just the beginning for me. I plunged over the edge and let myself fall, my wings spreading out and quickly catching at the unbelievable mix of air currents. The fall became a lazy, circling soar, my arms back under my wings, my hair flaring out backward to the caress of the stream.

I tipped away from the ladder of air and beat skyward, glorying in my strength, sending a laugh of victory down toward the tiny figure still standing on the mountain top. He could never match me, never be my equal in a million lifetimes and I would prove it to him over and over until he had no choice but to believe it. He would learn how outrageously he overstepped himself by aspiring to *me*, and in learning he would finally go away. I didn't need him or anyone, not when I could *fly*!

THE WARRIOR REARMED

by
Sharon Green

DAW BOOKS, INC.
DONALD A. WOLLHEIM, PUBLISHER

1633 Broadway, New York, NY 10019

First Printing, January 1984

4 5 6 7 8 9

PRINTED IN THE U.S.A.

1

I sat beside the pretty little blue pond, just in the shade of a nearby tree, trying to rid myself of the gray mood of brooding. Constructive thought is almost impossible in that kind of mood, but it had descended on me the night before and I couldn't seem to shake it. With all the problems I had, I should have been spending my time considering solutions, but all I felt capable of tackling right then was sitting still and breathing in the fresh, clear air.

My mind was so close to being shut down from self-centered consideration, I nearly missed the faint, unfamiliar mind trace. It was near enough to cause me to focus on it immediately, but I hadn't been wrong in my first, fleeting impression: there was a small, frightened animal somewhere in the grass near me. On that planet it could have been something a lot more harmful, but I hadn't been as frightened as I once would have been. I'd been growing on Rimilia, but I still had a far distance to go.

In curiosity I touched the mind of the small animal, automatically soothing its fright, and a bright-eyed head suddenly popped up above the grass to look at me, sharing my curiosity. The animal was only a little above a foot long, fluffy dark-red fur covering it, pointed ears above shiny black eyes, a small button nose and mouth. The sight of it charmed me, and when the adorable little thing saw and felt my smile, it moved toward me in small, delicate hops, landing in my lap after quickly covering the ten feet between us. A purring sound came when I began to stroke the soft, thick fur, the contentment in its mind so strong it nearly acted as a balm on my own agitation. I turned to look at the cool pond water as I continued to stroke the animal, and made sure my gray mood was blocked from it completely.

"So there you are," a voice came a minute later from behind me, breaking into the semi-trance of peace I'd almost fallen into. I wasn't totally startled, and was able to calm the small animal in my lap before it could panic and bolt. The voice had come from Lenham Phillips, a brother empath of mine, and Len's calming thoughts joined mine as soon as he realized there was a mind that needed calming. Len's abilities weren't as strong as mine, and he wore a wry expression as he came up beside me to lower himself into the grass.

"Sorry about that," he said, gesturing toward the animal that had turned its head to look at him. "I didn't realize you had company here. Tammad's been searching for you, and he's getting more and more annoyed the longer he can't find you. I think you'd better head back."

I just turned my face from him without saying anything, sending my attention back to the tall shade trees and wide bushes all about us. I wasn't quite used to seeing a man of my world dressed in the *haddin* of the men of Rimilia, but Len felt as comfortable and natural in the brief body cloth as he had begun to look. The newest addition to his wardrobe was a swordbelt, the wide hilt of the weapon protruding from its top a still-unaccustomed thrill to the blond man beside me. I knew that Len had been given his first lesson with a sword that morning, and although he wasn't as big or accomplished as his teachers, he must have done well enough to please them. Len would have checked the truth of their professed opinions in their minds, and if they hadn't really been pleased his own mind wouldn't have glowed as it did.

"Terry, ignoring me won't change anything," Len said, stirring where he sat. "Tammad agreed to let me try to find you, but if we don't show up pretty soon, he'll come after you himself. You shouldn't have come out here alone to begin with; once he sees you're safe and his worry disappears, all he'll be left with will be anger."

"I don't care," I muttered, tightening my shield even more around my reactions to the thought of Tammad's anger. No matter how strong I grew I still couldn't seem to keep from turning pale and shaky at the thought of facing an irate Tammad. The beast had more than one advantage over me—which brought me right back to my original problems.

"The hell you don't care," Len snorted, reaching a hand out to stroke the side of the small animal in my lap. "You've been jumping from one emotional reaction to another since Tammad rebanded you last night, but indifference wasn't part of the group. Frankly, I don't think you're capable of being indifferent toward him."

The flash of anger I felt had to be two-thirds embarrassment, but that only made it worse. I'd had enough embarrassments on that world to last anyone a lifetime, and all the feeling made me want to do was strike back. Without stopping to think about it I hurled a command at the little animal I held, and not thinking about it made the action more effective. Accompanied by a growl the animal's sharp, white teeth flashed toward Len's hand, causing him to snatch it back with a yelp of startlement. If he hadn't moved so fast he would have been bitten, and he wouldn't have been able to move so fast if he hadn't caught the sudden attack rage in the animal's mind. The little animal, picking up Len's burst of startlement and not understanding why it had briefly been aggressive, hopped quickly out of my lap and disappeared into the grass, ignoring my attempts to call it back. The calm I needed to calm its flurried thoughts was beyond me then, and that made me more upset.

"Now see what you've done!" I snapped at Len, turning my head to glare at him. "The little thing is gone and it's all your fault. Why didn't you leave me alone?"

"*My* fault?" Len demanded, his blue eyes hardening at the accusation. "You coerce it into attacking me, and its *my* fault? Terry, if I didn't owe you for breaking me out of a slave cell in that city, I'd . . ."

"You don't owe me for anything!" I interrupted, not liking the way his mind firmed up behind his stone-hard stare. His thought patterns were more like a Rimilian's than ever, and I wasn't used to coping with that sort of reaction from him. "If I hadn't gotten you and Garth loose that night, you would have been released the next day anyway. You don't owe me a thing. Not a thing!"

I turned in the grass and started to throw myself to my feet, but somehow Len knew I was going to run from him. His hand might not have been as big as Tammad's, but it was still big enough to flash out and wrap around my ankle to hold me down. In desperation I kicked at him, frantic to get loose, but his other hand caught my second ankle and I was down in the cool grass on my face, caught the way I was always caught on that world. I struggled and tried to kick out again, but a single twist forced me to my back, and then Len was kneeling across me.

"That's more than enough," he said, grabbing my arms to hold me still. "If I hadn't had some success in copying that shield you developed, I'd be flat on the ground from that whirlpool of frenzy you've been leaking. You're going to tell me what's bothering you, Terry, and then we're going to talk it over like two adults. Walking around shielded all the time is too much like being unawakened, and I don't want to have to do it any longer."

I stared up at him, feeling the constriction he was talking about, but somehow helpless to do anything about it. My thoughts *were* like a whirlpool, twisting around and around without going anywhere, dragging me farther down into the depths and taking more of my strength the longer I fought them. I stirred against the unyielding grip of his hands, having not the faintest idea of where to begin, but the spinning had enough ideas of its own.

"Len, it isn't true that the Amalgamation would sell me, is it?" I blurted, distantly shocked that I'd had the nerve to put that particular problem into words. "They wouldn't just—hand me over to the first man who had something they wanted, and who decided he wanted me? They'd remember how long I'd worked for them, and that I was one of them, and refuse to turn their backs on me—wouldn't they?"

He stared down at me with no expression on his handsome face, but through my shield and his I had the distinct impression that his thoughts were a blur. His hands left my arms to brush the ends of my hair free of my face, then he sat himself beside me in the grass again.

"Well, I guess I asked for it," he muttered, running a hand through the blond hair that was slowly growing toward the length that Rimilian men wore it at. "Terry, I'd lie to you if I could, but I haven't the strength to hold this shield up much longer. The truth is—I don't know. I know I was there when Murdock McKenzie refused to give back whatever price Tammad paid for you, but you've been involved in this a lot longer than I have. Do you think they'd give up all claims on a Prime just for—whatever Tammad paid?"

"I don't know," I said, shaking my head automatically as I sat up in the grass. "I don't even know what it was that he paid. All I know is that he said they abandoned me—and then closed me in these chains to prove the point."

I looked down at the bronze bands on my wrists and ankles, feeling the one around my neck even if I couldn't see it, knowing they were all beyond a woman's strength to open. The light, small-linked chains marked me as Tammad's property, his beyond argument or offer. I hated being locked in chain; to me it was a measure of things on that world that being five-banded was the highest distinction a woman could achieve.

"So that's why you went so wild when he banded you," Len said, staring at me soberly. "I wasn't that far away when it happened, but I thought you were just being difficult again. Terry, can't you understand that it's *necessary* for a woman to be banded on this world? Did Tammad *say* he was banding you to prove possession, or is that just your own idea?"

"Oh, I just snatched the thought out of the blue," I answered, staring back at him. "The fact that all women on this world are possessions didn't count in the least. Neither did the coincidence that he did it right after I told him again that I refused to obey him or stay with him. Whenever I insist that I'm leaving this world he pretends he doesn't hear me—except for last night, when he trotted the chains out. You must be right, Len. It's all my imagination."

"You're still ignoring the necessity for banding," Len answered, surprising me by not reacting to my sarcasm. "Women who aren't banded are up for grabs in this society; Tammad's just making sure no one grabs without knowing what he's getting into. Don't you care that he's willing to fight to keep you?"

"Why would I care?" I asked with brows raised high. "It isn't as if he could die trying to keep me, or that whoever killed him would then be entitled to claim complete possession of me. It isn't even as if he has one fight already lined up, and wanted to announce his answer to the challenge by five-banding me. These chains are just cultural decorations, best ignored if not forgotten about entirely. Right, Len?"

"Terry, do you really think you're going to change anything by fighting it?" he asked, compassion joining the calm in his voice and eyes. "Everyone on this planet must know how you feel about being a possession, but Tammad also knows how you really feel about him and he won't let you go. He doesn't mind risking his life fighting for you, and the best thing you can do is accept the risk the way he does."

"Accept it?" I exploded, furious that he'd even suggest such a thing. "Accept the fact that he'd be dead and I'd belong to someone else? If he died I *wouldn't* care what happened to me; do you think I could live knowing he was dead because of me? No matter how happy he was to take the risk? You'd better know I won't stand for it, Len. Do you hear me? I won't stand for it!"

I'd exploded so far out of control again, I didn't realize what was happening until it was almost too late to stop it. My shield had thinned further and further until it was totally gone, and all the fury and rage and frustration I felt came pouring out of my mind at Len, covering his shield and bearing down hard. His handsome face twisted as though he'd been stabbed with a knife and his right hand went up in a feeble gesture, as though my mental onslaught could be stopped by physical means. His mind resisted mine for no more than seconds, and then he collapsed back on the ground at the same time that his shield gave way. But his shield fell inward rather than fading, and the oddity of that caught my attention enough so that I suddenly realized what

I was doing. I cut the projection an instant before it touched him, then discovered that I was trembling all over, the infamous cold sweat covering me in a way I'd always considered to be pure fiction. Close calls were supposed to bring on that sort of reaction, along with the pale face and closed eyes that had settled on Len. I took a shaky breath and put a weakened hand to my head, wondering if I looked as bad as he did.

"Len, I'm sorry," I said after I'd wet my lips with a dry tongue. "I didn't mean to—whatever it was I did. Are you all right?"

"I'll let you know as soon as my heart starts beating again," he gasped, opening his eyes to struggle back to an upright position. Once he was sitting again he ran both hands through his hair, then looked at me bleakly. "Do you have any idea what that felt and looked like from my end? I don't believe I'm still in one piece."

"I think I'm afraid to ask," I mumbled, paying a lot of attention to the pond and the bushes and grass around it. My abilities were growing on Rimilia, but not in a nice, slow, acceptable fashion. Anger and fear seemed to trigger that growth, leaving me to find myself doing things I'd never even considered doing—or thought that I *could* do—before it happened. Coping with the abilities was turning out to be easier than coping with the surprises; deciding whether or not I was pleased to have all of it was another matter entirely.

"It was like a—a giant, rushing storm," Len said, and a corner of the fear he'd felt showed briefly in his eyes. "The lightning had substance and the thunder had weight, and I knew that if it touched me I'd be crushed and shattered, both at the same time. Terry, I don't know what you're feeling because you're shielded again, but if that's what's behind the shield, you'd better get it resolved fast, with or without help. The next time you might not be able to pull back."

"Speaking of shields, let's discuss yours," I said, ignoring everything else he'd said. If I'd tried thinking about any of it, especially the not being able to stop part, I'd have gotten a lot more practice in hysteria.

"What about my shield?" Len asked, not really distracted. "I know it isn't as strong as yours, but it's better than anything I thought I'd have. I never even considered a shield until I saw yours."

"That's at least half our problem," I grumbled, feeling an uncomfortable mixture of anger and frustration and disquiet. "We're conditioned into thinking about our abilities only when we're Mediating, and not much even then. Every time I find myself doing something new, it's a shock.''

''It wouldn't be as much of a shock if we also weren't conditioned against experimenting,'' Len agreed, getting to his feet to move the three steps necessary to get to the pond's edge. ''How can we know what we're capable of if we don't experiment?''

I watched him crouch down and put his hands in the water, then raise them dripping to his face, where he held them for a long minute without moving. It was on its way to being a hot, sticky day, but that wasn't why Len had needed the water. I knew why he needed it, but the guilt I'd been feeling was crowded out by outraged indignation.

''Would you repeat that statement?'' I said, letting my stare burn into him as I shifted in the grass. ''I'd like to be absolutely sure I heard right before I kill you dead where you stand.''

He turned a faint frown in my direction, not understanding immediately, then the dawn arrived to erase the dripping frown and fill his light eyes with memory. Not too many days earlier, Len had helped Tammad punish me for the experimenting I'd done, telling me how foolish and dangerous it was for an empath to do something like that. He'd frightened me so badly that I still shuddered when I thought about it; now he had the nerve to complain that we weren't doing enough of the very thing he'd been so dead set against. I opened my mouth to tell him exactly what I thought of him, but he got his parry in first.

''You still haven't said what you were going to say about my shield,'' he interrupted, letting the words come out calm and interested as he wiped his face with his forearm. ''Do you have a suggestion for improving it?''

''The only suggestion I have for you would be anatomically difficult!'' I snapped, rising onto my knees with my fists clenched. ''You put me through hell, and then calmly decide that you've changed your mind? I think *I'll* decide to beat you over the head with something!''

''I haven't changed my mind the way *you* mean it,'' he said, still maintaining that infuriating calm. ''We need to experiment with our abilities, but inside ourselves, not on other people. Experimenting on the people around you is a good way of committing suicide.''

''Len, there *is* no other way of experimenting except on the people around us!'' I insisted. ''Being an empath means interacting with other people; you can't interact all by yourself! And that shield you're forcing didn't do much to keep Garth with you

when you two and Tammad were captured, now did it? You had
to work directly on the men who captured you, didn't you? You
took a chance to get what you wanted, and it paid off without
anyone knowing you did anything, now didn't it?''

"I was lucky," he said, his tone as flat as the look in his eyes
was decisive. "I could just as easily have gotten caught—and
lynched for it. It's a risk I won't take again until I get a lot better
with this sword I've been given, and maybe not even then. Now,
what did you mean about my 'forcing' my shield?''

I stared at him for a minute without answering, wishing I
could deep probe him without his knowing about it. Was he
really that afraid of using his abilities, or was he trying to talk
me out of using mine? We both knew I was a lot stronger than
he; was he just trying to keep me manageable by scaring me? I
didn't know what difference the answer would make, but I
would have enjoyed knowing the truth.

"The shield you're projecting is almost a physical effort," I
said at last, settling back on my heels. "You're pushing up on a
cloud of confusion to hide your thoughts and feelings, rather
than using an actual shield. Try relaxing completely and then
sensing around yourself. Do you feel something hovering just
past awareness, something your mind is automatically pushing
away and keeping unformed?''

Len frowned where he crouched by the pond, as he searched
around inside himself, his search a struggle I could feel as I
reached toward him with my own mind. I couldn't help him with
the struggle, it was something he had to do for himself, but
guiding him was another story.

"You're pushing too hard," I said in a murmur, passing on
some calm to ease the tightness and anxiety he was falling into.
"Relax a little more and let the sensations come to you rather
than chasing after them. Softly, gently, relax and become *aware*.''

"I think I have it," he gasped after another minute, the sweat
of non-physical exertion mingling with the drops of pond water
on his face. "It's like a sheer bubble I've been keeping at arm's
length without knowing it. It doesn't take any effort to keep it
away; the effort comes in when I think about bringing it close.
Just as if it were on a spring.''

"You don't need effort to bring it close," I denied, remembering my own first tries with the shield. "If you try to force it
close you'll lose your grip on it. Just *let* it come close, as if you
were allowing the sensation of sweet, fresh air touching your
skin to enter your awareness. It's hovering there, waiting for
permission to ease close. Give it permission, Len.''

His handsome face had tightened because of the struggle, matching the fists his hands had become where his arms rested across his thighs. His entire body showed a forced rigidity—until suddenly it was completely gone, and a look of surprised pleasure covered his face.

"It's easy!" he exclaimed with the delight of a child, his mind now tightly enclosed by a smooth, shining, impervious sphere. "You don't have to hold it up, you don't have to force it; it's the next thing to a magical wish. Decide that you want it and it's *there*."

"It sure is," I said, for the first time able to examine a shield from the outside. It seemed totally untouchable, and I began to wonder how smart I'd been in helping Len form it. If I couldn't figure out some way of breaking through it, I'd never be able to touch him mentally again without his permission. The thought was beginning to bother me, but suddenly I pushed it away with disgust. The day I became convinced I had to reach and control everyone in range was the day I needed to be stopped permanently.

"It's beautiful," Len breathed, bringing my attention back to the calm pleasure he showed. "Just as beautiful and natural as you are, Terry. I can understand why Tammad would risk his life to keep you. If he weren't around, I'd take a stab at it myself. I still haven't forgotten how good you were in the Hamarda camp."

For the second time that day I opened my mouth to shout at him, but that time I didn't need anyone else to interrupt me. I'd run out of words to say to that particular sentiment a long time ago, leaving me with nothing but a very strong awareness of how much I was wanted for what I could *do* rather than what sort of person I was. I stared at him for the briefest instant before standing up and turning away, but I hadn't gone more than four steps before he was right behind me, his big hands on my arms pulling me to a halt.

"You ought to know by now that being told how desirable you are isn't something you can run away from on this world," he said, his tone more amused than annoyed that that was exactly what I'd tried to do. He turned me around to face him again, but his grin faded and died when he saw the silent tears rolling down my cheeks. I may have hated that world and its ways, but in that one respect it was no different from any other world in the Amalgamation. Everyone wanted me—but not for the right reasons.

"Terry, why are you crying?" Len asked, gently pulling me closer to his chest and putting his arms around me in comfort. "You know I won't touch you without Tammad's permission,

and neither will any other man around here. I was just trying to
tell you how I feel, in the way that's most natural in this culture.
It's supposed to please you—not make you cry."

His hand coaxed my head down onto his chest, but I stood
there stiffly even as the flow of tears increased, beyond all
comforting and consolation. The pretty green and gold day had
become covered over with the dingy gray of personal disillusion-
ment, one I couldn't bring myself to accept. Even Len—who
should have been an exception—wanted me only for my abilities.
Len's breath drew in sharply as his mind touched mine, and then
his hand was at my face, raising it to the concern in his eyes.

"Why are you hurting like that?" he demanded, his new shield
quiveringly ready to snap tight. "Nothing I said should have
caused you such pain! Terry, tell me what I did to hurt you!"

"You didn't do any more than anyone else," I whispered,
pushing at him to make him let me go. "You and Tammad and
Daldrin and Garth, and everyone else in the whole damned
universe. Let go of me, Len, I've got to be by myself for a
while."

"You've been by yourself long enough without it doing any
good," he said, tightening his grip to hold me where I was. I
struck at him with my mind, but his shield was suddenly there to
bounce me off harmlessly. "And that won't do you any good
either," he said, referring to the shake I'd given his shield.
"You weren't faking that pain, and I'm going to know what
caused it. Now."

"Sure," I nodded, ignoring the way his hand wiped at the
wetness on one of my cheeks. "As if it'll make any difference.
Tell me why you suddenly find me so desirable, Len."

He hesitated briefly as he looked down at me, trying to see
into me with his eyes rather than his shielded mind, then gave up
the useless effort.

"I've always found you desirable," he said, making it sound
like a comment on the weather. "When I finally got to use you
that night it didn't end those feelings, it reinforced them. If you
expected me to lie about the pleasure I felt, or act ashamed and
pretend it never happened, you're living in a dream world. I
enjoyed having you under me, moaning and squirming and
trying to pretend that you weren't having just as good a time as I
was. If it were my choice I'd do it again, here and now or
wherever else we happened to be. Your mind welcomed me as
warmly as your body did, and that was something I'd never had
before, even during the times I'd taken a woman when awakened.
Why shouldn't I find you desirable?"

I looked away from him as I felt my cheeks flare with heat, wishing he hadn't been so cold-bloodedly graphic. In point of fact he'd raped me that night, just as Garth had, and as far as I was concerned, it didn't matter that he'd taken the trouble to make me enjoy it. But according to the laws of that world it hadn't been rape, and my own opinion to the contrary didn't matter; even if I *had* responded to him, even if he hadn't hurt me as he could have; it still wasn't right.

I said, "It strikes me as odd that you didn't mention how desirable I was until after I helped you with that shield. Someone with an overly suspicious mind might have jumped to the conclusion that my desirability lay more in what I could do for you that way than in any other area."

"Why, that's utterly ridiculous," Len laughed, but the laugh seemed a shade too hearty, and his shield stayed tightly in place. "If you won't take my word for it, just ask any man around here. You're a beautiful woman, Terry, and attractive even beyond that. Why else would so many men be interested in you?"

"So many men," I echoed, seeing the difficulty he was having in keeping his gaze on mine. "Men like Garth, who considers important women a personal challenge, or like Daldrin, who had a taste of what a female empath could do for him in the furs, or Tammad, who needs an empath he can control, to help him build his shiny new world. Are those the admirers you're talking about, Len? At least you've added your name to a distinguished roster."

"All right, maybe I *was* thinking more about you as an empath than as a woman," he suddenly admitted, his gaze now steady as he let me go. "But you can't be serious about adding Tammad's name to that list. Terry, he's crazy about you, and you damned well ought to know it. What more does he have to do than he's already done?"

"Ah, all those wonderful things he's done," I nodded, folding my arms. "Like kidnapping me from Alderan, and dragging me along with him against my will, beating me to make me obey him and trying everything he can think of to get me to work for him. But he's succeeded in one thing I can't deny, and that's hooking me good and proper. That's why I can't believe anything he tells me."

"Come on, Terry, you're a trained Prime," Len protested, a mixture of frustration and upset in his eyes. "Are you trying to make me believe that you can't read Tammad well enough to know whether or not he's lying to you? Even *I* could do that!"

"That's because you're not in love with him," I muttered,

turning away to stare at the faint footpath leading away from the pond and through the trees, back toward Aesnil's palace. "If you were in love with him, everything he said would be weighted down with the lure of possible truth, a truth you couldn't quite make yourself believe in. If you believed him and it *was* true, your life would be paradise from then on through forever. But if you believed him and it wasn't true, the—*horrible*, unending pain—I've already had a couple of tastes of that, Len. I think another taste would kill me."

I didn't realize I'd closed my eyes until his hands came to my arms, silent compassion and a pain-sharing flowing from his mind to mine. It seemed particularly odd that I, who could generate trust in anyone around me, couldn't find any of that precious quantity for the one man in the universe I would give my life for. I tried to hold back my reaction to that feeling, but I'd held it back so long that it was overwhelming. Too much of it exploded from my mind—right at Len, who was wide open and entirely off guard. His strangled, tormented cry spun me around, just in time to see him fold bonelessly to the ground, his hands falling limply away from his head where he'd frantically pulled them. I stood rooted for one eternal instant, then turned and ran back up the path.

My race through the bushes and trees was one big blur of green and brown, punctuated by the reaching out of branches and roots, tearing at my gown and tripping my feet. The stroll out to the pond had taken about ten minutes; racing back at top speed took hours longer. I was on the verge of collapsing along with my lungs when I burst through the small side door of the palace, startling the guards so badly that they nearly drew on me before they realized I wasn't attacking. I tried to speak through the heaving and gasping of my body, discovered it was impossible, then tried again anyway, waving my arm back in the direction I'd come from and mewling incoherently. The idiots didn't understand the gestures or any of the single words I managed to force out, and when heavy, hurried footsteps brought more men on the scene, I found out why. The newcomers were Tammad's *l'lendaa*, led by Loddar, a man of enviable composure. His immediate appearance with the other warriors from Tammad's city let me know they'd probably been looking for me, and he stopped in front of me to put his hands on my shoulders.

"Calmly, *wenda*, calmly," he soothed, speaking the Rimilian language with deliberate slowness. "Neither these other *l'lendaa* nor we understand the tongue of your people. You must speak in our tongue if we are to assist you."

"Out . . . by the pond," I gasped, this time speaking Rimilian in between panting. "Lenham . . . I have caused . . . him harm. You must . . . help him."

Loddar frowned, but he turned to look at one of the three men stationed at the door.

"Do you know the location of this pond she speaks of?" he asked. "I would have her guide us to the place, were my *denday* not awaiting her return. The man in need of aid is a brother of ours."

"The pond is easily found," answered one of the three, a man as large and blond as all Rimilian males were. The three guards wore baggy trousers and loose shirts and leather sandals rather than the simple *haddinn* of Tammad's *l'lendaa*, and all three were sweating. "You need only follow the clear path into the small woods, which lies beyond the garden without this door. The path will lead you to the pond."

"My thanks, *l'lenda*," Loddar nodded, then turned to the four men with him. "Do you hasten to this pond and search out Lenham," he directed in a low voice. "When you have returned with him, bring word to the *denday* of how he fares."

"Plittar," answered one of the four for all of them, a casual word carrying the general meaning of "anything you say," with uncaring shrug appended, a word never used to a *denday*. They turned then and left the palace, stretching their stride but not really *hurrying*. If I'd had the breath I would have screamed at them to move faster, and then I remembered I didn't need to shout or scream. I reached out to their four minds and planted a strident sense of urgency in front of their attention, and had the pleasure of hearing their steps turn into a trot before Loddar's voice brought me back to the palace corridor.

"Is that where you had taken yourself, *wenda*?" he was asking, the disapproval he felt carefully missing from his tone. "You did not ask the *denday*'s permission before departing, nor were you properly escorted. Tammad will not be pleased."

I could have answered him if I'd had to, but I used my continuing need to take deep breaths of air to maintain a momentary silence. Loddar had been better to me than most people on that world—not good, but better—and didn't really deserve the sort of answer I'd been about to snap at him. I drew in three breaths, then a fourth, then finally nodded at him.

"You are surely correct in all that you say," I agreed, keeping my tone as unaccusing as his had been. "Now, as there are other matters awaiting me, I must leave you."

I began to turn away from him, prepared to leave things as

they stood as long as he did, but he didn't leave them that way long. Even before I was fully turned away, his hand came to my arm.

"*Wenda*, there is no more than one matter awaiting you," he said, his still-calm tone tinged with the beginnings of annoyance. "Tammad awaits you, and will be kept waiting no longer than the time required for me to take you to his chambers. What awaits you beyond that is for the *denday* to speak of."

I turned my head back to look at him, letting no expression show on my face. The first and easiest step was to soothe his annoyance, and then I was able to work. His strong sense of duty needed accomplishment-already-attained to weaken it, but once that was done the unconcern and indifference were slid in its place without his fighting them. Loddar's emotions were of a chore successfully accomplished, and his uncritical, reasoning mind followed right along, accepting the feelings as natural and unarguable. His hand left my arm as he turned away, already forgetting about me, looking toward the doorway out as though considering the idea of following the men he'd sent after Len. I turned again in the opposite direction and walked up the corridor, aware of the stares and fear coming from the three door guards, but too weary and disgusted to worry about them. The guards had undoubtedly heard stories about me from others of the palace guard, about my secret powers and how I'd used them for their *Chama* Aesnil. That fearful people often removed the object of their fear with violence made the situation a dangerous one, but at that point I couldn't have cared less. I was so upset and confused, it was a miracle I'd been able to work through it.

The palace corridors were large and airy and beautiful, but I saw little more than my own inner turmoil as I walked, my outer awareness touching only the route I took to the destination I'd decided on. Tammad was probably in the apartment which had originally been mine, and he was the last one I wanted to see just then. I needed a quiet place to sort out my thoughts and try to understand what was happening to me; quiet was not what I'd find around Tammad. I walked the smoothly polished stone of the corridors, passing silent guards and hurrying slaves, ignoring them all as I ignored the walls and rooms and courtyards I passed. I was intent on only one room, a room I'd appropriated once before, and it was a good distance away from the entrance I'd come in by.

Reaching the room and slipping inside was both a relief and a surprise, the surprise centering around the fact that I'd met no others of Tammad's men on the way. I didn't know how many of them he'd sent out looking for me, but even the ones who hadn't been sent out would have known enough to stop me if they saw me. I leaned on the door to make sure it was closed, then walked toward the lightly curtained windows.

The room wasn't as large as the suite Aesnil had given me, but the pale yellow fur carpeting on the floor was thick and soft, the number of fat brown cushions scattered around and piled nest-fashion more than adequate, the wide, deep pile of bed-furs invitingly comfortable, the windows wide and tall and streaming yellow sunshine behind the sheer yellow curtains. It was a warm, attractive room, designed to please the senses, but there was no pleasure in me as I walked through it and stopped in front of the windows. Putting a hand out parted the sheer curtains enough to let me see the chasm the room looked out over, a drop of more than a hundred feet through empty air to a bottom I couldn't quite see. I felt as though I were falling through all that air, helpless to stop or change direction, a victim of forces totally beyond my control. Abruptly I turned away from the windows, hurried with head down to the nest of brown cushions, then let myself drop into the middle of them.

"What if he's dead?" I whispered aloud, closing my eyes against the terrible pain the question produced inside me. "What will I do if I killed him?"

The empty room gave me no more of an answer than my own mind did, the total silence increasing the illness I felt. Len had been trying to help me and I'd hurt him, possibly even destroyed him. I didn't know what to do with the power that was growing so strong within me, didn't know how to control it to keep the people around me safe. If I hadn't had so many things upsetting me I might have had a chance to learn, but it had been so long since I'd felt anything remotely like calm, I almost couldn't remember what the emotion was like. Everything worked against me on that world, the people, the dangers, the involvements, everything! I picked up a cushion and hugged it to me, watching the window curtains begin to move to the urgings of a breeze, more miserable than I'd ever thought it possible to be. If Len was dead I'd have to kill myself—if I could find the nerve to do the right thing in the midst of all the blunders I'd made. I lay back and put the cushion I was holding over my head, hiding myself from the sort of world I'd never wanted to be a part of.

I didn't fall asleep, but time passed in long strides without my noticing it, more than an hour slipping away behind non-thinking semi-oblivion. It would have been good continuing on like that forever, but the sound of the door opening dragged me back to unpleasant reality. I knew instantly that it was Tammad who came in, but didn't move or speak even to demand how he'd found me. His emotions were a blend of relief and annoyance and concern and a few other things I couldn't resolve, and all I could feel was disgust with myself. After all that had happened, the first thing I did when someone else showed up was reach out to touch them with my mind. I had long since begun sweating under the cushion over my head, but I didn't move it away even when Tammad stopped in front of me, cutting off some of the strengthened breeze from the windows.

"Terril, what do you do here?" his voice came after a minute, his mind working toward making his tone sound calm. "Lenham has awakened with a great ache in his head, yet his first words were a questioning concerning your well-being. For what reason was he concerned with your well-being?"

"For the reason that he's a fool," I mumbled into my cushion, resisting the urge to stir in discomfort. "If he weren't a fool, he'd never come near me or think about me again."

I was sure he hadn't heard my nearly private comments, but a surge of anger flared in his mind, and then the cushion was suddenly gone. I blinked back the brightness to see him crouched in front of me, forever broader and more well-muscled in reality than any memory made him. Standing straight he was more than a head taller and nearly twice as wide as I, his long, shaggy-blond hair so perfectly a part of him—and so perfectly misleading. With leather wrist-bands and sword belted at his waist and dark green *haddin* he was the picture of a backward, thoughtless barbarian; backward and barbarian he might be, thoughtless he certainly was not. The thoughts in that shaggy head were more intricate than even I knew, and I seemed to know more of his plans than anyone else on the planet—or in the Amalgamation.

"That something disturbs you is more than clear, *wenda*," he said, reaching out a broad hand to smooth aside my sweat-dampened hair. "We will first speak of what disturbs you, and then we will speak of what occurred between you and Lenham. I do not care to see you so distraught."

"Distraught is becoming a way of life," I answered, wondering for the thousandth time why those light blue eyes of his affected me so strangely. The weight of their stare seemed to press me down to the size and ability of a helpless child, especially when he was angry. It was true that he was more dangerous than any being I had ever met, but there was more to it than that, considerably more.

"That is scarcely the response I sought," he said, putting a little more stern into his tone and stare. "There has been enough of misunderstandings and unvoiced distress between us, *hama*. You will learn to speak freely to me, so that we may see to your unhappiness together. Now, tell me what disturbs you."

"Wasting my breath repeating things disturbs me," I said, hating myself for the faint tremor in my voice. "I don't want to be banded, I don't want to be held here against my will, I don't want to be fought for, I don't want to be used, and I don't want to stay on this world. Now that you know what's disturbing me, go ahead and fix it."

"*Wenda*, what battles a man fights is for his consideration, not for the consideration of his *wenda*," he said, the reproof in his voice milder than the annoyance in his mind. "That this Daldrin and I choose to face one another is of concern to no other save ourselves. The choice belongs to *l'lendaa*, and we are *l'lendaa*."

"Of no concern to anyone else?" I screeched, sitting up amid the cushions to stare at him. "Have you two changed the reason for the fight and forgotten to let me know? The last I heard it was winner take all, with me as the all. Are you saying that I'm now free to decide on my own future, no matter who wins?"

"I have said nothing of the sort," he returned, still somewhat patient but only just barely. "You are my woman and will remain such, no matter that your humor changes with each turn from darkness to daylight and back again. I now know your love for me is as deep and complete as mine for you, therefore will you remain beside me as long as life is left to me. And this Daldrin has not yet even drawn sword from scabbard; why do you insist upon seeing me as bested?"

I opened my mouth to answer him, closed it again, then blew out a breath of vexation. How do you answer a black and white question when any possible answer has to be gray? The barbarian's expression was calm and reasonable, nothing to jeopardize the calm and reasonable stance he'd taken; if not for the gleeful satisfaction in his mind, he might have had me cornered. Instead of letting myself be cornered, though, I decided to counterattack.

"What makes you think it's you I'm worried about?" I asked, pleased at the immediate disappearance of his satisfaction *and* glee. "If not for Daldrin's sense of honor and willingness to help, I would have had a lot more trouble here than I did have. You demanded what was yours by right and got chained up for your trouble. He kept quiet and got done what had to be done."

A thick physical silence descended as those blue eyes stared at me, but the level of mental noise increased almost to ranting

range. Outrage was the most prominent feature of the group,
interlaced with anger and jealousy—and a good deal of confusion.
I kept my eyes on his, pretending I didn't know what he was
feeling, hoping he would decide I really wasn't worth fighting
for after all. A decision like that would have made my efforts
worthwhile, but I must have forgotten for the moment who I was
dealing with. The level of frustrated annoyance in his mind rose
higher for a minute, then his usual calm was forced through to
cover everything else.

"You seek to make me believe your concern is for this
Daldrin?" he asked, considering me in a way he hadn't done
earlier. "Perhaps, then, your feelings for him are stronger than
any you possess for me. Perhaps it would be best if I were to
unband you and sell you to him."

"Sell me to him!" I blurted in outrage, knowing he was
deliberately pushing me off-balance again but unable to stop my
reaction. I tried to vocalize the outrage, found myself gibbering
like an idiot, then lapsed into seething silence when I saw the
barbarian grinning at me.

"You seem to dislike the possibility of being sold to another,
wenda," he said, reaching toward me again to touch my face
and the side of my neck. "Should it truly be your desire to
remain mine, you must continue to interest me. You have done
little lately to command my interest."

"I would love to tell you what to do with your interest!" I
snapped, pushing at his hand as I moved away from the caress.
"How dare you talk about selling me as if I were a—a—
possession! I'm a Prime of the Centran Amalgamation, and
happily not a native of this backward, barbarian world! I demand
that you take me back to my people immediately!"

"Why do you insist upon giving yourself unnecessary pain,
hama?" he asked with a sigh, no longer grinning. "You are
indeed my possession, mine to do with as I please no matter your
origins. Should I choose to sell you to another, that choice, too,
is mine. I, however, do not choose to sell you to another,
therefore will there be battle between this Daldrin and me. You
had best accustom yourself to these truths, *wenda*, else happiness
will never find you."

He continued to crouch in front of me, his eyes filled with
compassion, his mind seriously concerned. He believed everything he said and really wanted me to accept it, but the situation
was something I would never accept.

"I won't be owned," I grated, feeling my right fist clench
against the cushion it leaned on. "I won't be ordered around or

sold or used, and I especially won't be fought for. You can't
ignore the fact of what I've become, something beyond a woman
you can control.''

"You now consider yourself something other than a *wenda*?'' he
asked, raising one eyebrow. "Was this not what you originally
wished to be considered, no more than an ordinary *wenda*? Was I
not condemned for seeing you as more? First I am reviled for
seeking the possession of a Prime, and now I am reviled for seeing
no more than a woman? Do you attempt to try my patience to its
limit, woman?''

His blue-eyed stare had hardened considerably, a perfect match
to the greatly increased annoyance in his mind. I stirred against
the cushions in faint discomfort, but refused to back down.

"Don't pretend you don't know what I'm talking about,'' I
answered wondering if I sounded as defensive as I was beginning
to feel. "You know very well that I wanted to be seen as a woman
rather than as a tool, something you still haven't managed to
accomplish. I did *not* want to be owned and ordered about and
fought for as though I were a prize *seetar*! It's a manner of
treatment I won't allow no matter how you try justifying it!''

"You speak as though you mean to defy me, *wenda*,'' he said
very softly. Those blue eyes were directly on me, totally lacking
the softness his voice held. "Do not mistake my attempts to aid
you in your distress for license to do as you will. The *darayse*,
the non-men of your land are not to be found here in mine; here
wendaa do as they are bidden, just as you will do. You may
speak of disobeying me if you wish; do not think to attempt the
reality.''

"Why, you miserable barbarian!'' I said, suddenly seeing the
light. "You weren't ignoring what I said about going home and
not obeying you or working for you, you were humoring me!
The poor, helpless little female is upset for some strange reason,
so the big, strong warrior, in his generosity, decides to spoil her
a little. Let her ramble on about what she will and won't do, let
her fool herself into believing she's a real person. She won't be
punished for any of it—unless she forgets her place so far that
she tries to do what she's been talking about!''

I struggled to my feet among the cushions, then looked down
at him where he crouched, wanting to add to the flood of words,
but too furious to do so. I turned my back on him instead and
strode to the windows, seething so hotly I was sure the lightly
fluttering curtains were in danger of catching on fire. On top of
everything else, he'd been *humoring* me, as though I were
someone who had temporarily lost her sense of what was right,

but was sure to regain it in time if handled gently and with understanding. I was so furious my emotions were beyond description. I stared out at the slightly dimmed sunshine and didn't even see it.

"Why do you persist in anger?" he demanded after a minute from right behind me. "You are not unaware of the doings of this world, you are not unaware of the fact that I mean to keep you. Why must you be forever challenging my authority over you, forever denying my right to do as I must and should? Why have you not yet learned that your strength and abilities entitle you to no more?"

"You dare to speak of what I'm entitled to?" I snapped, jerking around to glare up at him. "I'm a Prime of the Centran Amalgamation, entitled to anything I damned well please! *Everyone* knows that, with the single exception of the barbarians of *this* miserable world! You have no right keeping me here and forcing me to obey you, and it would serve you right if I decided to take over instead of simply leaving!"

"Again you speak of challenging me?" he asked, folding those massive arms in annoyance as he stared down at me. "I have no interest in further indulgence in such foolishness, *wenda*. You are able to face me with neither sword nor dagger nor empty hands, a fact which has already been well proven. You are meant to obey me, not I you, and this, too, has been proven."

"Has it really?" I murmured, suddenly tempted beyond denial. I'd found the idea of controlling Aesnil impractical due to the fact that she would be out of my reach so much of the time, but Tammad was another matter. He usually insisted on having me near him most of the time, an arrangement which would make no one suspicious. I had no interest in running the rest of those barbarians through him, but I had a great interest in returning to my embassy where transportation to a civilized world would be available. After that I could find a place to stop and breathe, and think of a way to get them all to leave me alone.

"I don't understand why you keep saying you want me here," I said, looking up into his eyes and reaching toward him with my mind. "What you really want is to return me to my embassy, isn't it? You have Len to read people for you, and Garth to do whatever you plan for him to do, and Gay King to please your body. All you have to do is go and get her, which can be accomplished easily after you leave me at the embassy. Isn't that what you really want?"

A frown had formed on his broad face at the first of my words, his mind immediately beginning to deny those words. I let the denial slide past me, not even touching it, waiting for the faint agreement I knew would come when I mentioned Len and Garth and Gay. The agreement wasn't as strong as I thought it would be, but strength wasn't necessary. Just having the agreement did the trick, letting me grab it and increase it as I smiled.

"You see how nicely it will all work out?" I pressed, expanding his agreement by force against the frown he still showed. "Len *wants* to work for you and so does Garth. Gay is dying to please you, and will never refuse you no matter what you tell her to do. Since you have all that, it would be foolish to keep one small, useless *wenda* on top of it, now wouldn't it? A wise man would rid himself of her as soon as possible, wouldn't he?"

His agreement writhed in my mental hands, fighting to change to denial. He stood with eyesight directed inward, his teeth clenched, his no-longer-folded arms tense at his sides with straining fists. I felt the sweat break out on my forehead as he fought me, shocked that he was able to resist as much as he was doing. The last time I'd fought his mind I'd won easily, brushing aside his mental strength the way he would brush aside the physical strength of someone not quite his giant size. Mentally I was his superior; how was it possible for him to resist me like that?

"Just think how good it would be to have no one around to oppose you!" I gasped in desperation, trying to thrust delight in to bolster the wavering agreement. "Everyone around you doing exactly what you say, more than pleased to obey completely! The one bane of your existence would be gone, and you'd never have to see her again!"

Red-hot rage suddenly exploded in his mind, crashing through the wavering agreement I held, shattering my grip and back-blasting into my wide-open mind. I choked and clutched at my head, barely feeling it when my knees hit the carpeting, wrapped in a yellow-red blaze of pain that didn't even let me scream. I writhed in the conflagration, fighting to breathe, and just as quickly as it had come it was gone, leaving behind a booming throb of an ache interspersed with stabbing pains. My body wilted with the withdrawal of that unbelievable pain, and I would have collapsed to the carpeting completely if two strong arms hadn't caught me. Somehow, unbelievably, I'd lost to him again, and the magnitude of that loss was unbearable. I tried to shout against the words coming at me behind the thunder of surf, but I lacked the strength even to moan. Blackness developed due to the frenzy of the attempt, and gathered me in completely.

2

Consciousness came back slowly and reluctantly, as though afraid to face again the pain it knew was waiting. I moaned as the ache welled up behind my closed eyes, making my head echo with the throb, vaguely wondering what it would be like if my shield weren't closed tight. I became aware of a dampness across my forehead and fought my arm up to grope in an attempt to find out what it was, clumsily encountering a length of folded cloth. I began to pull the wet cloth away with a grunt, but another hand came to keep me from doing it.

"You'll be better off leaving it there," Len's voice came, soft with the knowledge of what loud noises would do to me. "You may not think it's helping, but it is."

I forced my eyes open to look in the direction his voice came from, blinked back the blurriness, then finally managed to focus on him. He sat looking down at me from no more than a foot away, his brand-new sword gone, his face wearing a wry expression. Looking around showed me a silver and blue room, one of the rooms of the suite Tammad and I shared, definitely not the last sight I remembered before tuning out. It came to me then that I was lying on the wide pile of furs the barbarian and I used as a bed, with Len sitting on its edge to my right. My eyes flickered again to the rest of the room, searching for something I didn't want to think about, and Len made a sound of subdued amusement.

"If you're looking for Tammad, he's in the next room," my brother empath informed me, his voice as dry as the desert air. "Bite off a little more than we could chew, did we?"

His eyes and tone told me that his poor opinion of me was back in full force, but that was hardly unexpected. I closed my eyes and put an arm over them, then took a deep breath.

"I can't decide whether I have a greater dislike for your old personality or your new one," I told the darkness in a very soft croak, feeling the reverberation of every word. "Your new personality is unspeakably patient, but the old one gloats."

"I'm not gloating," he denied, trying to shed some of the dripping satisfaction in his voice. "I'm just wondering what you tried to do this time—and curious as to why it backfired."

"What I tried to do was get that barbarian to take me back to the embassy," I admitted, making no effort to keep the disgust out of my voice. "Not only didn't it work, it also exploded in my face. As far as the why goes, your guess is as good as mine. Last time I looked, I was stronger than he was."

"And this time he walked all over you," Len agreed in a thoughtful voice. "If anyone had asked me, I would have bet against this sort of an outcome. Are you sure that's all you did, try to force him into taking you back to the embassy?"

"Of course I'm sure," I said in exasperation, pulling my arm away from my eyes so I could half-glare at him. "Even if I were into world conquest, this is hardly the world I'd want to conquer. All I want is to go somewhere where I'll be left alone. Is that so much to ask?"

"I'm not the one in line for the question," he said, suddenly trying not to look sympathetic. "Some men, like me, for instance, would let you go wherever you thought you had to, and then spend their time kicking themselves and worrying about you. Tammad belongs under a different heading, the one that reads, 'We'll work it out together.' Why don't you try remembering exactly what you said and did."

I was tempted to accuse Len of avoiding my question, but my head hurt too much and it was fairly obvious that that was exactly what he was doing. Instead I dragged out the data on the episode I'd gone through with Tammad, including the details of his strange resistance, and gave them all to Len. His silence at the end of it gave me a chance to exercise some vestige of pain control on myself, which seemed to go a short way toward returning me to normal. I was able to get rid of the damp cloth and drag myself to sitting before Len pulled himself out of the deep thoughtfulness he'd fallen into.

"I think that may be it," he muttered under his breath, looking at me with those pretty blue eyes. "In fact, I'm sure of it."

"Well, I'm glad that's settled." I smiled, pushing back the dampened hair from my face. "Now let's have a contest to see which of us can stand up straight first without falling."

"Terry, stop being an idiot," he snorted, surprising me by having heard what I said. "I think I know what happened to make Tammad stronger than you, even though he really isn't."

"Scientific curiosity aside, Len, I'm not sure I want to know,"

I said, looking away from him toward the windows. "I had exactly one advantage over Tammad, and now even that's gone, right along with my last chance to get out of this place. What difference does it make *why* he beat me? It won't change the fact that he did."

"Whys are more important than you seem to understand, Terry," he said, putting his hand under my chin to turn my face back to him. His expression was more serious than was usual with him, but his eyes were warm with compassion. "I think Tammad was able to beat you at your own game because you weren't simply trying to make him take you somewhere, you were trying to make him give you up. Hasn't it come through to you yet that he loves you far too much to give you up?"

"That can't possibly have anything to do with it," I denied, disturbed over the idea. "You'll see how deep his love goes when I refuse to help him with any more of his plans. And I didn't ask him to give me up. I never would have presented so radical a concept with the sort of precarious hold I had on him. It would have been stupid."

"Stupid comes in a variety of flavors," Len answered, beginning to look impatient. "According to your own account, the first thing you told Tammad was that he wanted to take you back to the embassy. He obviously didn't agree, but he also didn't fight unreasonably hard. You weren't satisfied with the reaction you were getting, so the next thing you told him was that he was foolish trying to keep you, and would be smart if he got rid of you as soon as possible. His reaction to that one should have told you that you'd gone too far, but instead of calming him and withdrawing, you had to add the crowning touch. You had to tell him he'd never see you again. I'm not surprised that he exploded; I'm surprised he didn't blast you flatter than he did. With you wide open and him pouring out rage and fury, you're lucky he didn't burn you out completely. If you'd used your head, you would have known what his reaction would be without taking the risk of testing for it."

"What do you mean, testing?" I demanded, suddenly suspicious of where his facile logic was taking me. "I was trying to get myself out of this place, not making nebulous and fatuous tests of some sort."

"Sure you were," he scoffed, leaning down to one elbow on the bed furs away from me. "Terry, when an ordinary woman tests a man's desire for her, she uses words or actions to see what he'll do. When a female empath tries the same thing, she shoves at his emotions to see how easily she can change them.

You knew you would be wide open if he exploded, but you didn't expect him to explode. You expected him to accept me and Garth and Gay in place of you, and expected the substitution to be easy. You tested him despite the danger of being burned out because you still don't believe he really loves you.''

Len was staring directly at me, his eyes searching deeply as his mind poked at my shield, both trying to find a way within. I avoided his stare while ignoring the poking, then shrugged in an aimless sort of way.

"I've already told you how I feel about that," I said, trying not to sound as defensive as I felt. "Everyone in sight keeps assuring me how great his love is, but all I know for sure is how *I* feel. And that has nothing to do with what he feels for me."

"I don't believe you can sit there and say that!" Len burst out, straightening again near my right shoulder. "After everything that man has done, how can you still doubt him?"

"What sort of everything are you talking about?" I asked, watching the billowing curtains at the window. "The way he kidnapped me, the way he refuses to let me go, the way he insists I obey him and beats me if I don't? Or maybe you mean the way he keeps trying to get me to work for him? Those last items really make me feel wanted and loved."

His big hand came again to my face to turn it back to him, and I could see forced calm fighting with exasperation in his expression.

"How about the way he came after you to the Hamarda camp and here?" he asked, trying to keep from shouting. "Those Hamarda were ready to accuse him of slave stealing when they found you gone, but he didn't care. He was ready to kill any or all of them who tried to keep him from following you immediately, and would have fought them singlehandedly if the rest of us hadn't calmed him down. By the time we got here, he was closer to being frantic than I've ever seen him. Instead of using the diplomacy he's so good at to free you, he marched right in and up to that Aesnil woman and *demanded* your release. Only a man in love could have acted like such a damned fool."

"Or a man desperate to regain an object of irreplaceable value," I pointed out, this time holding his gaze. "If you've forgotten I'm a Prime, Len, he hasn't."

"Damn it, Terry, you're making it all one way!" he shouted. "He's been jumping around like a madman, but you insist on looking at him with your eyes closed! What about the way he's been civilizing you, teaching you not to be such a spoiled brat? Doesn't that show you he means to spend the rest of his life with you?"

I could feel myself stiffening in reaction to that comment, but Len didn't notice it because he wasn't able to reach my mind. I pulled a section of my gown out from under me, then moved a short way away from him.

"So that's the way you see it, is it?" I asked icily. "Everything that that barbarian does to me is simply him *civilizing* me! Okay, Len, have it your own way. I'm nothing but a spoiled brat in need of adult teaching. But I think I've had enough of it for one day. Why don't you take your maturity and get out of here."

I slid off the bed and stood up, turning my back on my loyal brother as I walked toward the windows. It was amazing how everyone always found a good reason for the things Tammad did to me, but the things I did in return were invariably considered the tantrums of a child. I'd heard the contention so often, I was seriously considering believing it myself.

"Getting all huffy and offended won't accomplish much, Terry," Len's voice came after me, annoyed rather than contrite. "It's time you stopped acting like a sullen child and got around to making an adult commitment. The people of this world are offering you a life with meaning, and all you have to do to accept it is offer your abilities in exchange. Garth and I have already accepted; the longer you wait to do the same, the bigger the fool you make of yourself."

I raised one hand to my head as I stared out through the moving curtains, wishing there were less heat and humidity in the breeze that rippled them. I still had enough of a headache to find the heaviness of the air painful, a dull pain which fit in perfectly with Len's laughable suggestion. I knew all about the meaning of the life I was being offered, a meaning considerably different from the one Len and Garth saw. They'd found freedom on that world of barbarians, but they were men on a world run by men. I was nothing but a woman, a mere *wenda*, one whose sole purpose was to give pleasure and obedience and comfort to those men. Hand over the power of my abilities for the priceless gift of a life like that? Sure, why not.

"It's comforting to know your stubbornness was undamaged by what you went through," Len said dryly. "Tammad, especially, will be relieved to learn that. Ever since he found out you weren't badly hurt, he's been anxious to discuss your little experiment with you. You ought to find the time most absorbing—as well as instructional."

I closed my eyes as I cursed feebly under my breath, half sick at the thought of having to face that barbarian. He'd punish me for trying to control him, as strictly and horribly as he always did. He continued to want to use my abilities as a Prime, but refused to accord me the privileges those abilities made mine by right. He violently resented the thought of being controlled in any way, most especially by the power of the mind. The thought of what he would do to me this time made swallowing difficult and weakened my knees. I hated myself for being such a coward, but he never failed to affect me that way.

"Terry, why do you keep fighting him?" Len demanded, but gently, from right behind me as his hand touched my shoulder. "You're afraid of what he'll do and you're right to be afraid, but all *he* wants is to be gentle with you. His greatest joy is to share laughter and love with you, but you refuse to allow him that. He's a man and you're a woman; why can't you relax and let nature take its course?"

I felt my head drop even lower than it had been, wishing it were as simple as Len was trying to make it. We weren't discussing a man and a woman, we were discussing a barbarian and a Prime, a man who would use anyone and anything to achieve the goals he had set himself, and a woman who was tired of being used. Nature didn't intervene in affairs like that; nature wouldn't dare.

"I can see Tammad was right the way he usually is," Len sighed, taking his hand off my shoulder. "He maintains that if a man and woman are right for each other, no one can prove it but they two. If it can be worked out, it's now up to you and him. I'll see you later."

Len's footsteps moved away from me across the floor, his bare feet whispering against the carpet as he made for the door. I was suddenly aware of the fact that I wasn't wearing sandals any longer, and that foolish revelation somehow made me want to turn and call out to Len to keep him from going through that doorway. I was half turned and ready to call out when I realized that delaying the inevitable would not stop it from *being* inevitable. Tammad could not be kept a room away from me forever, not by any power then at my disposal. I turned completely back to the windows then and just stared out, waiting for the inevitable.

If I thought I'd have something of a wait, it didn't take long to disillusion me. Len could barely have cleared the doorway when other feet, heavier feet, made their own sound across the carpeting coming in. Before I knew it he was standing right behind me, and I didn't have to open my shield to know him. There was usually something electrical in the air when he was around, and that time was no different from any other.

"I see, *wenda*, that you have recovered," he said after the briefest of hesitations, his voice filled with its usual calm. "You suffer from no other ill-effects, no hurt you have neglected to mention to Lenham?"

"I have a headache," I answered, still not turning around. "Compared to the condition I'm usually in on this planet, that's equivalent to being in the best of health. You needn't worry that you'll have to put off the beating."

"Good," he said, and his immediate agreement made my eyes widen. "When I might be able to beat you was, of course, my sole concern."

I snapped my head around to look up at him, but no expression showed on his rugged, masculine face. I opened my shield and probed at his mind, then wished I hadn't. There was no light-hearted, good-natured humor behind his comment, just a thick, dark cloud of anger and more anger. I winced at the intensity and strength of it, and he slowly nodded his head.

"It is as I thought it could not be," he said, folding his arms as he stared down at me. "Not only did you attempt the outrage of invading my thoughts, you now have the temerity to attempt the same again. Woman, does my rage mean nothing to you?"

"Touching your mind is like looking at you," I answered in an unsteady voice. "If you don't like it, of course I won't do it again."

"Ah, you now understand that the action displeases me, and will therefore refrain from indulging in it," he nodded, his eyes still not moving from my face. "How obedient a *wenda* you have become, and how easily the obedience was brought forth. I hesitate to estimate the length and breadth of your obedience when once you have been punished."

A thrill of fear washed through me at that, but not the simple sort of fear brought on by the presence of a hungry predator or a danger-filled, imminent accident. The barbarian was worse than any predator, more dangerous than any accident, and he had just given me his word. I backed up right into the central window brace, my knees weaker than they had been, and his right hand shot out to my left arm to steady me.

"I hear no words from you, *wenda*," he said, his voice still as unwarmed as it had been. "Have you no interest in estimating how deep your obedience will be once you have been punished?"

"There's really no need for that," I quavered, stepping back, too aware of that giant-sized hand on my arm. "I am, after all, a civilized woman, and capable of understanding when I've committed a breach of etiquette. I'm sure you know you deserve an apology, a deeply sincere apology, one which will be immediately forth—''

"Silence," he quietly interrupted, cutting off my half-hysterical babble, gently drawing me toward him. "There is no matter of etiquette between us, no matter so light and unimportant that simple words of apology will suffice. Once before you entered my mind unbidden, not to soothe or share but to tamper, and much did I believe that the punishment you received then was enough to keep you from attempting the same again. It appears I was mistaken, but will take care that the same mistake does not appear a second time. Should this current punishment not deter you, you have my word that I will see myself collared and sold as a *wenda-graj*.''

Half-hysterics became full-blown panic, but shaking my head and stuttering incoherently didn't keep me from being drawn gently but firmly away from the windows toward the middle of the room. If the barbarian promised to have himself sold as the equivalent of a ladies' maid if I ever touched him mentally again once he was through with me, I might not even survive whatever he was going to do. At that point I wouldn't have minded not surviving, but I was very much afraid that survival would be part of the punishment. I looked up at that massive body in front of me, looming like an avalanche in the making, the hard blue eyes unwavering, the face expressionless, and discovered how close it was possible to come to fainting from fright without actually doing it.

"Please don't," I begged in a whisper, pushing feebly and uselessly at his hand on my arm with my free hand. His grip wasn't hurting me, he hadn't even raised his voice, and those two facts together had me more desperate than almost anything else. "Please don't punish me, please!" I begged. "I know I did wrong, more wrong than I can say, but I won't do it again, I swear I won't! I swear it!"

"I am well aware of that fact, *wenda*," he said, turning toward the door as he pulled me along. "We will begin by having you cut and trim the switch to be used on you, and then, after the switching, there will be other things for you to do. Your punishment will consume much time in the giving, even more in the receiving."

"No!" I choked, wild at the thought of those other beatings he had given me, ones where he hadn't been nearly as angry as he was right then. In other frightening situations I had struck out with my mind, but just then such a reaction was impossible. I felt paralyzed in the very center of me where my talent lay, frozen and half dead and totally incapable. I couldn't have struck at him even if my life had literally depended on it, or, even more importantly, my sanity.

"Wait, wait just a minute!" I babbled, suddenly realizing it was time to admit I had lost. "What I've said to you till now—I've changed my mind! I'll do anything you want me to do—anything!"

He stopped that inexorable progress toward the door, and though he still held my arm, I could have fainted from relief. I'd have to work for him now, reading people and helping him influence them, but that was better than—I shuddered to think of it. He turned his face toward me, and it wore a faintly surprised expression.

"This is truly unexpected, *wenda*, this decision you have made," he said, looking down at me. "I had not thought to see you moved from the stand you had taken. And yet, it occurs to me that I may not accept such a decision from you, for it would seem that you were coerced from your sworn word, which is a dishonorable act. I would not care to be thought of as dishonorable."

"No, no, coercion has nothing to do with it!" I assured him quickly, desperate to keep him from turning toward the door again. "The decision was freely made, based on an estimation of what was due you after my invasion of your—privacy. It's the least I can do."

I looked up at him anxiously, wishing I had the nerve to peek at his mind, totally unable to tell what he was thinking from the expressionlessness he had slipped back into. He thought about what I'd said for a minute, then nodded his head.

"Very well," he said. "As the decision was freely made, I shall accept it. You will now do exactly as I wish."

"That's right," I agreed, relieved that the bargain was accepted and completed. "I know your plans for unifying your people call for the assistance of an empath, and now you've finally got one where you want her. So where shall I begin? With Cinnan and Aesnil? It won't be easy, but I'm sure I can do it. Cinnan already feels brotherly toward you—so—"

My words trailed off and died, due entirely to the fact that he was slowly shaking his head. I couldn't understand what he was disagreeing with, unless I had his objectives in the wrong order.

"I hope you don't mean you want to return to the Hamarda first," knowing my expression showed the distaste I was feeling. "Being there with you won't be the same as being there alone with them, but I don't know how well I can handle my own emotions in the middle of. . . ."

"*Wenda*, I have no knowledge of what you speak," he interrupted, his voice and eyes oddly free of confusion. "The need I have for one the power is no longer a need, for Lenham sees to it. You have denied me the use of your power, greatly disturbed over the matter, therefore I do honor your denial. I shall not again set such tasks to your hand."

"But—then—what have we been talking about?" I asked, honestly puzzled and definitely uneasy. "Aside from my abilities, what else is there?"

"Such a question seems foolish to one who is able to look upon you," he answered, letting his eyes move over me in that intrusive, possessive way he had. "You will do exactly as I wish—in all things."

"But—that wasn't what I meant!" I protested in shock, unconsciously trying to take a step back from him as my eyes widened. Somehow I'd managed to forget that he was still holding my arm; stepping back didn't take me very far.

"It matters little what thing was in your mind, *wenda*." He shrugged, holding me easily less than an arm's length from him. "It was in all things that you pledged yourself in obedience, therefore is the choice of area mine. Should you wish to attempt the reclaiming of your word, we may discuss the matter after the first of your punishment is done."

"No!" I said immediately, then calmed somewhat when I saw he wasn't beginning to move toward the door again. "No, a discussion later won't be necessary. We made a bargain and I'll hold to it."

"Excellent," he commented in distant approval, finally letting go of my arm. I reached over and rubbed at the place even though I didn't have to, reflecting that I had been extremely fortunate. After all, what could he ask me to do that I hadn't already done in the past?

"It pleases me, *wenda*, that there is to be no delay in the eager service I am to receive from you," he said, folding his arms as he looked down at me. "There has been little from you in the way of eagerness of late, not to speak of service. The difficulty you insisted upon would not have been permitted much longer in any event; seeing to it now merely ends an unpleasant episode sooner than expected."

I parted my lips to argue his distorted version of recent happenings, prepared to bitterly defend my position, but his right hand snapped up, silencing me with surprise.

"No words!" he growled, his distant approval and satisfaction long gone. "I have had too many words from you of late, all of which have done no more than convince you you might disobey me with impunity! You may not speak again till you have my permission to do so!"

I closed my mouth again with a snap, angry that he would dare speak to me that way, but determined to see the thing through. Silence he wanted, and silence he would get.

"Better," he grudged with a slow nod, refolding his arms. "You now pout as would a berated child, yet is it done in silence. Let us continue further to the point of eagerness and service."

He stepped closer then and put his arms around me, but not to hold me. His hands tugged the gown sleeves off my shoulders, urged the whole thing down to my waist, then let it go to fall to the floor around my feet. My first reaction had been to consider holding onto the gown and not letting it be taken, but that would have been foolish. It was hardly the first time the barbarian had stripped me naked, and I could still think of no way in which he might be stopped. After a first, abortive movement I merely stood there, telling myself the action meant nothing, but still feeling the discomfort of embarrassment in my cheeks.

"Considerably more acceptable," he said, stepping back to look at me again. "The sight of a woman in his bands gives a man great pleasure. Step entirely out of the garment and give it to me."

I frowned as I reached down and picked up the gown, not understanding why my doing such a silly thing was beginning to give him such intense pleasure that it crowded at my mind. I had the gown taken from my hand, watched him walk to the window with it, then watched him toss it out. The gown had a long way to fall before it hit the ground, but it didn't take nearly that long before I understood what was happening. I had dressed *myself* in that gown that morning, a gown that had been given to me by Aesnil. It had now been permanently taken away from me, and whatever clothing I had in the future would undoubtedly be given me by Tammad. The gesture made me feel more stripped naked and dependent than I had in a long while, and when the barbarian turned back from the window, he must have seen it in my expression. He smiled faintly, satisfaction joining pleasure, then went to the pile of cushions and sat himself among them, next to a small wooden table holding a tray.

"Why do you stand with your hands before you?" he asked me, the amusement in his voice stinging terribly. "Come and place yourself before me, your arms at your sides, so that I may have the pleasure of looking upon my belonging.''

It took a great effort to force myself to motion, an even greater effort to put my arms down. When I stopped in front of him, the whirling of my emotions was nearly enough to make me dizzy. I didn't *want* to be looked at like that, like nothing more than a barbarian's possession, like something to be owned and *used*! The presence of the bands on me, around my wrists and ankles and throat, was pure indignity, tightening my hands into fists at my sides.

"Again I see nothing of eagerness in you," he said, annoyed. "It is clearly foolish to be patient with you, *wenda*, for patience does no more than encourage your disobedience. Be informed that my patience is now at an end. Kneel before me."

I felt another frown take me as I slowly went to my knees in front of him, seeing the anger in his eyes and feeling it push against me. He was unhappy with the way I was reacting to being put on display, but what else did he expect? He stared at me briefly from the crosslegged position he had taken among the cushions, and then his hand flashed out to take me painfully by the hair.

"Again I feel the tendrils of your mind slipping close to mine!" he growled, ignoring the gasp of shock and pain torn from me. "Though to you it is ostensibly the same as looking upon me, to me it is unconscionable invasion. It seems you require a more constant reminder to induce proper behavior. Kneel and bow in the manner you were taught among the Hamarda."

My fists flew to my forehead as his hand forced my head to the carpeting, my heart thudding loud enough to be heard at the other end of the room. I *hadn't* been probing him, merely picking up the strongest of his emotions, but I couldn't have told him that even if he hadn't insisted on my silence. Being defiant when he wasn't angry seemed to come naturally to me, just as naturally as fright when he *was* angry. No, it wasn't simply fright that I felt, though fright was a part of it; the emotion was much more complex, and I couldn't seem to resolve it. I heard him stand up and walk away from the cushions, pause somewhere else in the room, then return.

"I will have eager service from you, *wenda*, and I will have it now," he said, sitting down among the cushions again. "Should I find myself displeased with your service, you will be immediately punished. Raise yourself again so that you are merely kneeling."

I straightened myself again as he had commanded, flinching away from the renewed calm he was projecting. He was too close, and his mind was too strong, for me to be able to stay away from him completely. I decided I had to explain the problem no matter what he had said about my not speaking, but sight of what he was holding put the words right out of my mind.

"This cloth about your eyes will keep memory of required obedience clearly before you," he said, finishing up the folding of the dark cloth in his hands. That, in itself, was bad enough, but the length of thick leather on the cushion to his right made things considerably worse.

"You can't be serious!" I blurted, staring in horror at the cloth and leather. "Tammad, this is all insantity! I can understand your being angry and wanting to punish me, but can't you see how useless this all is? Things will never be the way you want them to be, no matter what you do to me! Blindfolding me and then tying me the way the Hamarda did won't change any of the important things standing between us, the things that will always keep us apart! None of this is from *my* world, none of it something I can *relate* to! Please let me go back to my people!"

He stared at me in silence for a moment. The words I had spoken were true representatives of the way I felt, and he seemed to know that. I'd tried playing the game his way, tried easing the feelings of invasion he'd had, but it had all been for nothing. There was a certain point beyond which I couldn't go without being truly humiliated, and that was it. His stare and silence stretched out a bit longer, then his hands came to my arms to draw me gently into his lap.

"Terril, though the difficulty seems truly great for you, you must strive to understand and accept the realities about you," he said, his soft voice calm. "You cannot be returned to your people for you are already among your people, here on Rimilia. You are my belonging and will remain so, therefore must you learn to obey me properly. This matter of your agreement to do as I wish was merely idle foolishness, merely a manner in which I might measure the depth of your failure to understand what place you stood in. You will obey me whether there is agreement within you or not, *wenda*, for only through obedience will you survive here if I do not. Should another take you and band you, he will not feel the patience my love for you brings far too often than is wise. I will not see your life lost through lack of proper action on my part."

He turned me around in his lap then, ignoring the stumbling, tongue-tied arguments I tried to put forward, then placed the dark cloth around my eyes. I *didn't* understand what was going on, didn't *want* to understand, but when the dark cloth cut off all light and vision the understanding began to creep up on me, until I thrust it away again. He was wrong about where I belonged and about obedience and survival, and what did he mean by saying he might not live? What did he know about his meeting with Daldrin that he wasn't telling me? He tightened the blindfold with an extra knot, pulling my hair slightly, leaving me with no more awareness of things than that and the bare thigh my own bare flesh rested upon. I felt again as though I were falling through empty air, helpless in the grip of gravity, and reached up to tear the blindfold away. Instead of reaching the cloth, however, my hands reached only his.

"You may not remove it," he said, his hands everywhere that my hands tried to go. "You must also learn not to impose with your powers, for that sooner than any other thing will end your life. Your reality is here, *hama*, among those who are larger and stronger than you. You must learn quickly, else you will find no other thing than punishment."

I shook my head, about to protest what he'd said, but I wasn't given the chance. The hands that had kept me from removing the blindfold were suddenly at my waist, lifting me from the thigh I sat on and placing me belly-down over the other. I struggled, not knowing what was happening, but a big hand in the middle of my back kept me from rising again.

"You were also mistaken in believing I intended to do as the Hamarda," he said, his mind throwing off the distaste of the suggestion. "I do not bind females in leather, merely do I punish them with it for the disobediences they commit. I shall take care not to bring further harm to your back, yet must you recall that you were instructed to remain silent."

I barely had time to understand and believe that he was going to punish me before the first stroke came, sharp and stinging, across my bottom. Five strokes came in all, five hard, measured, punishing strokes with the strength of his arm behind them, each one causing me to cry out in pain. Tears welled under the blindfold and wet the cloth, tears that would have otherwise run down my cheeks. He was actually *punishing* me, and despite the fact that he had done it before, I found myself shocked. Didn't he know I was the one who had helped him survive Aesnil's arena? Didn't he realize I was growing stronger every day? When he was done he lifted me off his thigh and set me back on the carpeting on my knees, and then his hand came to my chin to raise my face.

"This time your punishment was light, *hama*," he said, undoubtedly watching as I rubbed at the stinging ache in my bottom. "Should you disobey again the punishment will be greater, and of longer duration. The switch is not the sole implement capable of teaching you your place. Do you understand?"

I bobbed my head spasmodically, still sniffling, hating myself for not daring to say a word. I didn't *want* to obey him, but he was going to make me do it anyway.

"Good," he said, taking his hand back as I heard him shift around on the cushions. "I presume that this tray of food here was brought for the two of us, but I have as yet to sample from it. Have you eaten?"

This time I shook my head, not even certain I knew what tray of food he meant. I'd seen a tray on the small table near the cushions, but I hadn't the faintest idea when it had been brought or what it contained.

"I find myself scarcely surprised," he said, his tone going dry as he shifted in place again. "Despite my constant urgings to the contrary, your interest in food continues poor at best. With this consideration, as well as my present hunger, in mind, I shall permit you to feed me first."

I nearly blurted out my surprised dismay in words, catching myself just in time to avoid that leather. I was supposed to feed him while I was blindfolded? How was I supposed to find the food—or him?

"Take each serving carefully from the tray so that it does not spill," he instructed, his attention so clearly on me that I could feel it. "I wish to eat the food, not have it draped about me."

His faint amusement took nothing away from the implied threat—or promise—and I sniffled again as I crawled slowly across the carpeting, one hand groping blindly for the location of the tray. A small voice inside me urged me to refuse to serve him, to stand up and pull the blindfold off and then walk out of the room with my head high, but that small voice was insane. If I tried to refuse him he would catch me and beat me again, a lot harder than he had the first time. The humiliation of crawling around on the carpeting was terrible, but the humiliation of being beaten was worse—and more painful.

Just as I thought I'd never find the tray my hand touched it, banging the wood and rattling some of the bowls. I steadied it quickly and pulled myself closer, then rose up on my knees to grope for the first of the bowls. I took it off slowly, two-handed, to make sure I didn't spill or drop it, and then jumped and gasped when fingers came out of the dark to touch my breast.

"Gently," the barbarian's voice cautioned, a faint hum beginning in his mind. "The contents of that bowl were nearly spilled. Do you wish another taste of the leather?"

I shook my head convulsively even as I shuddered, the fingers on my flesh sending tremors through me. He couldn't touch me *now*, not when I had to be so careful! It wasn't fair!

"Now you must find where I am," he said, blessedly withdrawing his hand. I took a deep, raggedly uneven breath and reached out with my right hand, slowly and carefully searching for his face. My fingers first encountered his chest, hard and hair-covered, then slid up to his strong, corded neck. Above that was his chin and cheek, and when I reached them I, too, was reached. I gasped a second time and straightened uncontrollably at the touch between my thighs.

"Ah, melon wedges!" he observed, pretending that he looked in the bowl rather than at my violently shaking head as his fingers explored me. "They are properly for the end of the meal, yet have I developed a fondness for them in my short time here. You may begin with them."

With that the touch was gone as suddenly as it had come, leaving me shaking and desperate to cover myself all over. All I could see was darkness and more darkness; being touched like that, without warning, made me feel more helpless than I ever had in my life. It was as though dozens of people stood about, any of whom might touch me without my knowing who it was. I couldn't stand being done that way—but also couldn't think of a way to stop it.

I could feel my arm trembling as I took one of the wedges and reached it toward him, but his teeth took it from my fingers without anything else happening. I fed him a second wedge and then a third, but when I reached out with a fourth, his hand was at my thighs again.

"You have lost the proper direction," he told my gasp, the hum in his mind making it worse. "I do not care to stretch my neck to reach the wedges. Try again."

This time the touch didn't disappear, not until I'd found where he was again and had fed him the wedge. By the time I was down to the last two wedges, I'd been touched twice more and was a nervous wreck. He kept me from feeding him the last two wedges by feeding them to me, and they were more distasteful than I could possibly have imagined. Being deprived of sight is supposed to heighten the other senses, but I didn't find a new,

deeper flavor in the normally tasty wedges. I couldn't rid myself
of worry over what he was *really* feeding me, to find any
enjoyment in the things at all.

"I will now have the spiced meat chunks," he announced
after the last of the melon wedges was in my mouth. I managed
to find the tray again by the time I had finished chewing, but had
to resort to sniffing before I located the bowl with meat chunks.
My success was rewarded with two hands of fingers at my
breasts, and the meat chunks would have ended on the carpeting
if he hadn't grabbed the bowl and steadied it. His chuckling was
like a file across raw and bloody nerves, and I half wished that I
had dropped the bowl. His caresses were beginning to be more
painful than pain, and I didn't know how much more I could
take.

Unsurprisingly, I didn't last beyond less than half the meat
chunks. The more concerned I became about locating the
barbarian's position accurately, the worse I did. His hands were
on me almost constantly, one between my thighs, the other on
my knee, or side, or breast or neck. I had been reduced to
whimpering, needing him so badly I was almost ready to beg,
and then he broke me completely. His toying fingers suddenly
thrust deep within me, tearing a moan from my throat as inde-
scribable sensations coursed through my body. I dropped the
bowl and threw myself on him, finding hard-muscled arms under
my hands and a hair-covered chest under my face. I kissed at
him and thrust my body at him, mewling and begging without
words to be taken. I was sure he'd been waiting for that, waiting
until I begged before taking me, and was more than ready to be
taken. Considering that, I couldn't understand why his hands
suddenly came to my arms, forcing me away from him.

"Forshame, *wenda*!" he said sternly, shaking me enough to
stop my struggles. "Is this the way in which you see to the
feeding of he to whom you belong? By throwing down the food
he wished to consume? By blatantly and deliberately disobeying?
You must be taught better."

No! I screamed, but only inside as he draped me over his thigh
again. Outside I was crying, sobbing against the punishment he
would give and the way he had tricked me. He'd been waiting all
right, but not for me to beg to be used. He'd been waiting for me
to ignore his orders and do as *I* pleased, just as I usually did.
He'd let me get away with it more than once, but that time I
didn't get away with it. The first stroke of the leather was the
first of eight, harder than the first five and with more anger
behind them. I was screaming by the third and hysterical by the

eighth, and not only because of the pain. He wasn't going to let me do *anything* out of the way, and the humiliating punishment had been designed to teach me that. It was something I didn't want to learn, but that wasn't about to stop him.

This time when I was placed back on my knees, he held onto my wrists with one big hand. The tears were streaming down my face despite the cloth, and I choked on a sob when he touched me again, deeply and possessively, proving that even the beating hadn't destroyed my need. He then let go of my wrists and thrust a bowl into my hands, a bowl that smelled of fried meat strips and vegetables. Wordlessly, still sobbing, I put my fingers into the bowl and carefully fed him, as completely cowed as he undoubtedly wanted me to be. It was *his* wishes and needs which were important, not mine, and I had been taught that the hard way.

He finished the meat and vegetables to the last, also finishing two other dishes, one a roast fowl garnished with nuts, the second a grain pudding of some sort. My fingers were sticky and my arm ached from constantly being raised, and my insides were beginning to rumble with emptiness. I'd been given nothing beyond the two melon wedges, and I didn't have to ask why. My portion of the meal lay on the carpeting where I'd thrown it, handily available if I got hungry enough. I grew ill at the thought of his insisting that I eat it, knowing I would throw it up again if I had to stuff it down, but he spared me that. He poured himself a goblet of wine, the tangy smell of it making me faintly dizzy, then relaxed back among the cushions with a sigh of contentment.

Without having any more bowls to handle, there was nothing for me to do but kneel where I was, listening and thinking and feeling. My knees and bottom hurt, my insides throbbed and burned, I felt sticky and naked and so badly used that I couldn't stop the tears welling in my covered eyes. It didn't matter whether I deserved the punishments I'd been given or not; I felt so miserable from them that I didn't know what to do. He had blindfolded me, and punished me twice, and made me want him so badly I could have died. Now he had left me entirely alone in the darkness he had forced on me, alone and empty and unwanted. That was what I felt the most, unwanted. Nobody wanted me except to use me, and I still couldn't believe he was any different. He may have had Len, but Len wasn't a Prime.

"*Wenda*, why have you begun weeping again?" he asked, touching my face so suddenly that I jumped and lost control due to the startlement. A large, ugly corner of the misery and desolation I was feeling flared out at him, causing him to cringe inside and grunt aloud from the impact before I had it under control again. His hands fumbled clumsily at my arms, as though he were fighting to keep from shuddering or trembling, and then he had gathered me to him, holding me tight against his chest. I lay unmoving in his arms while he fought his twisting emotions, doing nothing to help him regain the calm he struggled for. It was a hard struggle, but his will was too strong for his own emotions to deny him for long. He gained control, and then he gained calm, and then his hand came to stroke my hair.

"Ah, *wenda*, what am I to do with you?" he sighed, holding me tight with one arm while he stroked my hair with the other. "It is my duty to teach you obedience and proper behavior, yet when I do so you become like a small child, bewildered and desolated by a punishment you have no understanding of. When I recall this and withhold punishment from you, you view the lenience as an attempt to coax the use of your powers from you, and grow bolder in your defiance. How am I to deal with you?"

I didn't know what he was talking about and I didn't want to know; I just kept trying to ignore how his holding me made me feel. I could have been so happy belonging to him, so happy just being held in his arms. Instead I had to be a political pawn, traded and fought for and bought and sold and *used*! The sobs joined the tears then, shaking me deeply, and his upset came so close to breaking out of his control that he nearly crushed me. He didn't have to guess at what I was feeling, he *knew*, beyond doubt and beyond argument, and he was having trouble coping with it. I snapped my shield closed and buried my face in his chest, retreating deep inside until I could cope with it myself. He held me for quite some time, his stiffness and uneven breathing telling me almost as clearly as reading that he was making no progress in controlling himself, and he finally had to admit it. His hands went to the blindfold and pulled it off me, his lips came to my hair very briefly, then he was up on his feet and striding away, to the doorway and through it. I blinked back the glare of bright sunlight as I watched the door close, then slowly lowered my cheek to the carpeting. I didn't know where he was going, and I didn't have enough strength left to care.

It has never failed to amaze me how someone else's energy expenditures can drain your energy if you watch them when you're tired. It could not have been more than two minutes after Tammad left that the door opened again, admitting Len and Garth. The determination in their expressions fairly screamed of battle to come, an involvement I wasn't anywhere near up to. I pulled a few cushions closer to me to do what I could about my nakedness, then resolutely turned my face away from their advance.

"Don't turn away like that, Terry," Len growled, rapidly closing the gap between us. "It won't do you any good! I want to know what you did to Tammad!"

What I did to Tammad. I seriously considered raising my head to look at Len as if he were crazy, but it wasn't worth the effort. My looking at him would not have turned him sane. So far Garth hadn't said anything, but his churning confusion told me he was more than ready to add his oar. Garth R'Hem Solohr was an Alderanean, tall and broad-shouldered and dark-haired, a Kabran Colonel and a member of one of the oldest families on Alderan. Being a Kabran he was also a military man, as well versed in the art military as are all Kabrans, who make up more than sixty percent of the Alderan population. Tammad had brought him to Rimilia with a specific purpose in mind, but I hadn't yet found out what that purpose was. Unless it was to join Len in bothering the life out of me, an achievement they weren't far from accomplishing. Len stopped a foot away from me on my right, but Garth the military tactician moved around to my left, accomplishing encirclement with very little effort. I sighed to myself and considered putting the blindfold back on, but wasn't given the chance to do so even if I had decided on it.

"You heard me, Terry," Len snapped, looming over me. "What did you do to Tammad?"

"I beat him unmercifully," I mumbled into the carpeting, closing my eyes. "He begged and pleaded, but it did him absolutely no good. He earned a beating and he got it."

"Well, somebody got it," Garth put in, and a minute later I jumped at the touch of his hand on my bottom. He was crouched down next to me, inspecting the results of what Tammad had done, feeling absolutely no compassion at the sight.

"Maybe Terry would like a few more stripes to join those," Len suggested as he also crouched down, adding his own light touch to Garth's. "We'll both be glad to arrange it, Terry. All you have to do is continue being stubborn."

"Len, Garth, you're hurting me!" I gasped, finding it impossible to crawl away from them without dislodging the cushions I'd arranged so quickly. "Please stop touching me!"

"We'll stop as soon as you tell us what we want to know," Len answered ruthlessly, aware of the full agreement visible in Garth's mind. "Tell us what you did to Tammad."

"I didn't do anything to him!" I answered in desperation,

taking care not to squirm. "He did to me, just as he always does! Please let go!"

"That doesn't make any sense," Len pursued, neither of them moving an inch. "Tammad's emotions were totally out of control, so far out that I nearly didn't recognize him. He told us to take care of you, then just about ran out of the apartment. What could have caused that?"

"I don't know!" I insisted, then yelped as Garth leaned harder. My tone had annoyed him, and he was just short of replacing the touch with a smack.

"I think you'd better tell us everything that happened," Len decided, shifting from his crouch to a sitting position next to me. "Go through all of it, and don't leave *anything* out."

Len had taken his hand back, but Garth still had full possession of my embarrassment, which left me very little choice. I told them everything that had happened, getting swatted only once, very early on, when I tried to close my mind to Len's probing. If my narrative hadn't been open to immediate verification I would have glossed over certain parts, but my tormentors refused to allow that. They had grown impossible to deal with, and at the end of it I lay belly down between them, Garth's hand on my thigh, Len's hand toying with a lock of my hair, both of them ignoring the mist of tears in my eyes as they discussed the mystery.

"I still don't see what could have disturbed him so deeply," Len said, vexed and not bothering to hide it. "He was doing so well with her. Why did he stop?"

"Maybe she didn't tell us everything," Garth suggested, stroking my thigh in an absentminded way. "Whatever was left out would have to be the reason."

"She told us everything she knows," Len disagreed, moving one finger down to touch the swell of my breast. "That whack you gave her did more than force her shield back open. It won't last permanently, but right now she has us in Tammad's class, and she doesn't dare lie to *him*. If only she hadn't closed her shield when she did."

"Please, can I get up now?" I asked in a very small voice, appalled and nearly in shock over the way I was reacting to them. Sarcasm was my usual mode with these two Centran men I'd known so long, but somehow they'd managed to intimidate me. After the session I'd had with Tammad I shouldn't have been surprised; he always intimidated me enough to last a good long while.

"I think you'd better take care of her," Len said to Garth,

withdrawing his hand and moving away a bit. "Tammad was specific about that, and I can see how badly she needs it. I'm not in the mood right now to do her much good."

"Even I can see what's bothering her," Garth chuckled, squeezing the thigh he held. "Tammad got her all ready, then decided to go for a walk. Maybe he's paying her back for doing the same thing to him with Gay."

"She already paid for that," Len laughed, reaching over to run the back of his hand down my cheek. "She must have screamed loud enough to deafen rocks when he switched her for it. You did a lot of standing up after that, if I recall correctly, Terry."

"Len, Garth, please let me go," I begged, looking down at the carpeting in front of me as the tears ran down my cheeks. I couldn't seem to find the nerve to look up at them, and I was afraid of what they would do.

"Terry, Tammad wants you taken care of," Garth chided gently, his hand gone from my thigh. "Are you going to disobey Tammad and refuse to do as he wishes?"

I closed my eyes and shook my head vigorously, making sure they knew I wouldn't disobey. The last thing I would do was disobey, but I was still frightened.

"Although you've done some pretty rotten things to us, I know you're a good girl," Garth said in a warm, approving voice, and I heard a stir, as though he were lying down next to me. "You're going to obey Tammad, and you're going to obey me. Open your eyes now, and come closer so that I can hold you."

I opened my eyes to see that he had indeed put himself on the carpeting next to me, among the cushions, but he was no longer wearing his *haddin*. I trembled as I inched closer to him, and the stream of tears from my eyes increased.

"Oh, now why are you crying, good girl?" he asked gently as he took me in his arms, smiling down at me. "Good girls shouldn't cry when they're being good."

"I'm naked," I sniffled, looking up at him only because his hand was under my chin. "I'm naked, and you're looking at me, and I'm afraid of what you're going to do."

"Yes, you are naked," Garth chuckled, deliberately looking at every part of me. "You're beautifully naked, and if you were mine I would keep you this way most of the time. Would you like that?"

"No!" I wept, burying my face against his chest. "I'd hate it! I'd hate it!"

"But you'd still do it," he said, running one hand over me very slowly. "You'd do it or you'd regret it. Tell me why you'd do it, Terry."

"I'd do it to keep from regretting it," I sobbed, feeling terrible all over. "Please don't look at me."

"Oh, but I enjoy looking at you," he laughed, stopping the movement of his hand at my thighs. "I enjoy looking at you and so does Len, and so does every man around here. But what I enjoy more is touching you. You're trying to keep me out, Terry, and you know what happens to bad girls. Relax your leg muscles."

"Please don't do anything to me," I begged, immediately obeying him. "Garth, please don't—Oh! Ohhh!"

I suddenly felt as though I were on fire, shuddering and airless and dying. Garth held me to him with one arm as I choked and struggled, his laughter low but deeply amused.

"Are you sure you don't want anything done to you, Terry?" he murmured, looking down at me. "Give me a kiss now, and think about the question."

I quickly raised my lips to him, and his kiss cut off the sobs escaping me. The kiss was hard and insistent, almost ruthless, and it made me feel worse than I had before. I writhed against him, tortured and teased by his hand till I thought I would die, but I didn't dare end the kiss until he was ready to end it. He tasted me deeply with his lips and tongue, over and over, and then finally, at long last, moved away again.

"Well, have you decided?" he asked, his light eyes dancing as he looked down at me. "Now, wait another minute before answering, and then tell me your decision."

I writhed helplessly as I waited that extra minute, not wanting to speak but knowing I had no choice. Then, forcing the words, I choked, "I do want something done to me, Garth, but not by you! Not by you!"

"You want Tammad," he said, still smiling pleasantly. "I know that, Terry, but Tammad asked me to take his place. Now I'd like you to ask me the same."

"I—want you to—take Tammad's place," I whispered, saying the words not only because I had to. I was slowly but definitely beginning to feel a terrible need for Garth, one that would soon be beyond control.

"And so I will, Terry," he laughed, kissing me lightly and quickly. "But first I want you to stand up and show Len and me your body, with nothing to hide our view. Go ahead, and wiggle a little."

I scrambled to my feet with a sob, dying from embarrassment and need, but they had to see my body. I showed it to them, around and around three times, my arms up above my head and bent at the elbows, my cheeks wetter and wetter. Garth lay at his ease and grinned, but Len did nothing more than stare at me with a sheen of sweat on his forehead. At last Garth gestured me back to his side, put me flat on the floor, then began tasting me. I screamed so loud he finally stopped, separated my thighs with his hands, then plunged deep within me. I screamed again, at the presence of blessed relief-to-be, then immediately found myself overwhelmed. Len was in my mind, sharing it with Garth, taking everything there was as Garth took all my body had. It went on a very long time, draining every ounce of strength within me, and when Garth finally withdrew and moved away, I curled into a ball on its way to being sound asleep. As I fell asleep I heard laughter, but I didn't know what it was about nor cared.

3

"That miserable cretin!" I snarled, staring around the empty, jumbled room in a towering rage. "That insufferable sneak! That lowlife! I'll kill him! I'll kill them both!"

I hadn't been awake very many minutes, but remembering what had happened before I fell asleep didn't take many minutes, and I knew what had been done to me. Garth and Len had taken advantage of me, and when I thought about how servile I'd been, it made me sick! That little extra had been Len's doing, his idea of a good joke with Garth playing along!

I stalked over to the windows and pushed a curtain aside, seeing the fading, late afternoon sunlight turning patchy with small clouds, wishing I had Len and Garth there to throw out into it. Len had gone far with his experimentation, but he seemed to have changed his mind about experimenting on himself. He must have gotten the idea when he saw how tired and weak I felt, obviously in no condition to defend myself from anything. It had to have started when they first began pushing me around physically; I'd still been groggy from what Tammad had done, and reviving my emotions toward the barbarian would have been simple. I remembered wondering why I felt so brow-beaten by them, but I shouldn't have wondered. Len was encouraging the feeling without my even suspecting it! Once that receptivity was established, a touch of fear made the need for absolute obedience a shoo-in, all of it generously laced with humble submissiveness and heightened physical need. I crumpled the sheer, delicate curtain in my fist, fighting the urge to pull all the curtaining down and stomp on it. I'd get even with them, somehow, somewhere, I'd get even, *damned* if I wouldn't!

"*Wenda*, what has happened here?" Tammad's voice suddenly came, and I turned to see him standing in the doorway, staring around at the wreck I'd made. "Has a storm blown through, or have you been attacked by savages?"

"Attacked by savages is more like it!" I snapped, ignoring the mess he was looking at. I'd thrown just about everything that could be thrown, the cushions, the tray and bowls, the small tables. "And they said it was what *you* told them to do!"

"Lenham and Garth caused this chaos?" he asked, in disbelief. "Did they find it necessary to pursue you about the room, battling each step of the way, before they were able to see to your needs? Are they less than the men I thought them?"

"They're not men at all!" I snarled, dropping the curtain to take a step toward him. "Garth forced himself on me while Len twisted my emotions to suit their mood! You're quick enough to jump on *me* when I tamper, but with Len doing it it's perfectly all right! But why shouldn't it be? Len's male and I'm not!"

I turned back to the window and pulled the curtain aside again, my hand trembling from the fury I felt, the frustration and rage so thick that I had no idea Tammad had left the doorway until his hand gently touched my shoulder.

"No, it is *not* proper that Lenham has done such a thing to you," he said, calm and quiet dominating him as always. "That you invite such treatment by treating others so has no bearing, for I will not see it done to *anyone* about me. As you were punished, so will he be punished."

I turned back slowly to look up at him, not really believing what I'd heard even with the verification so clear in his mind. My expression put a grin on his face, but very little amusement reached his pretty blue eyes. Beneath his usual calm were sharp, uncontrolled flickerings of somber determination, fading the grin after no more than a moment of life. He touched my face with one big hand, then took my arm.

"There is a decision I have come to which you must be made

aware of," he said, drawing me away from the windows and toward our fur-pile bed, the only thing in the room I hadn't thrown every which way. We both sat down half facing one another, I wondering what painfully hard decision he had made. I could feel the pain of it even through the calm of his control, a pain he was making no effort to rid himself of.

"*Wenda*, it has come to me at last that my thoughts have been more concerned with myself than with the woman who is my beloved," he said, stroking my arm once before taking his hand back. "My love for you is very deep, and when I learned that your love for me was the same I thought we would face eternity together, yet now I know this cannot be. My love has failed to convince you of its reality, and this lack brings you greater pain than I had thought it possible for a woman to bear. I have felt the pain, and now know my failure for what it is; it is for this reason that I have decided to give you up."

The bleakness of his thoughts was loss-sharp and tears bitter, and for a minute I sat stunned, not knowing what to say. He wasn't simply trying to impress me with well-advertised nobility, he really *meant* it. He was going to give me up.

"Well," I said at long last, taking a deep breath to calm the quaver in my voice. He was staring straight at me, watching for my reaction, but I wasn't sure exactly what that should be. "So you've decided to return me to my people after all. It's— undoubtedly the best decision you could have made. We never were really right for one another."

I stood up from the bed and turned away from him, wrapping my arms about myself to fend off the chill of still being unclothed. It was his fault I wore nothing, and I'd be well rid of him. The only thing I still didn't know was when he was taking me back.

"Terril, you misunderstand," he said from behind me, a faint puzzlement touching him. "I said nothing of returning you to your people. Among my people, seeing to the well-being of *wendaa* is required of a man. Should he know that returning her from whence she came will bring greater hurt upon her than keeping her where she is, he cannot, in honor, return her. Should he have no feelings for her himself he will see her with another, yet he will not return her. Though I have deep feelings for you which often cloud my reason, I am nevertheless able to know what fate awaits you among your own people. I will therefore find another, upon my world, to band you."

Again I couldn't believe what I was hearing. I turned back to stare down at him where he sat, so deep in shock that my mind had ceased to function. All I could make of what he'd said was that he was going to sell me. He was going to *sell* me!

"*Wenda*, how pale you have become!" he said in concern, standing quickly to put his arms around me. I slumped against him dizzily, barely knowing where I was, my inner voice demanding that I do something—anything!—to get myself out of that nightmare.

"You can't mean that!" I husked, my voice producing itself without benefit of mind to direct it. "You can't just—sell me, as if I were an animal or a piece of clothing! You *can't* sell me, you *can't!*"

Even as I said it over and over again, I knew well enough that he could do exactly that, sell me or give me away or any damned thing he pleased. Women were possessions on that world, and selling them was not only legal, it was routine.

"Hush, *wenda*, and do not concern yourself," he soothed me, stroking my hair as he held me to his chest. "You need not fear the one I shall choose, for he will be worthy of you in all ways. I will begin looking about here, among Cinnan's *l'lendaa* and *dendayy*, and perhaps will need to look no further. It is happiness I seek for you, *hama*, and I will find it."

"No," I moaned, shaking my head in a metronome sort of way. "You can't do that to me, you can't. It's too barbaric."

"It is our way and will prove to be the proper way," he reassured me, concern still coloring his thoughts as he took me back toward the bed furs. "There will be a great emptiness in my life once I have found another to band you, therefore must I fill my memories to overflowing with the taste of you before that time. I shall use you at every opportunity, *hama*, against the time I may no longer use you at all, this instance being the first."

He took me down to the bed furs with him, his arms tight about me, his lips blocking off the incoherent sounds I was making. I still felt mentally numb, totally overwhelmed by what he had said; little wonder I was unable to consider and protest what he was doing. His hands caressed my body, relishing my nakedness, his mind humming and completely devoid of impatience. He fully intended taking his time, and that's what he did. My body took a long while to acknowledge the presence of his hands and lips, but such an acknowledgment was inevitable. He had trained me to respond to him, and my body finally recalled that training, despite the absence of the mind that carried such memories. True awareness of what was happening came to me only when he spread my thighs and entered me, plunging deep in his usual manner of full possession. Even as I squirmed involuntarily to his presence within me, I blankly wondered what had happened to his swordbelt and *haddin*; I hadn't even seen him take them off. He gathered me close to his chest and began to stroke slowly, his mind savoring the pleasure he felt and experiencing every bit of it as if it were the last time he would have me. I moaned and tried to struggle out of his possession, blurrily convinced that he should be listening to my words rather than using my body, but I would have had as much success freeing myself from a landslide, if not more. He tightened his hold enough to keep me where he wanted me and continued caressing me internally, his lips touching me wherever they were able to reach, one hand roving freely. I moaned again and lost the moan to a kiss, but I, myself, was not fully lost to the sensations being given me. Normally I would have been, but normality was a good long way behind me.

It took a long while before he was done, before he had everything he wanted. He seemed to know from the very beginning that my mind would not be giving him a deeper echo of what my body did, and he made no effort to try forcing it from me as he had in the past. He merely used me with very deep pleasure and endless patience, then kissed me as deeply before withdrawing. Rather than just lie beside me, he held me in his arms, stroking my hair and idly touching my body.

"We have been asked to share the darkness meal with Cinnan and Aesnil," he murmured, somehow knowing that my mind had been settled to a large degree by what had been done to my body. "You will serve me properly, as a *wenda* should, giving a pleasing impression to those warriors attending who observe you. Should there be one suitable among them, I do not wish him disinterested by unseemly behavior. I will see that he is fully informed of all of your faults before he bands you."

"No," I protested, distracted by his fingers gently squeezing my flesh. "You can't allow someone else to band me as if I were a native of this world. I won't allow it. I won't obey either of you." Suddenly that seemed to be my way out, and I repeated triumphantly, "I won't obey either of you!"

"You will obey, *wenda*," he chuckled, as though amused at the feeble protests of a very small child. "You will obey your *l'lenda* as all women do, else will you face his displeasure. You may rise now and straighten this room, then will you be taken to the bathing room and prepared for the meal. Your beauty will not be hidden beneath streaks of dirt and disarranged hair."

"I won't be prepared as if I were a sacrificial offering," I argued, desperation allowing me the defiance. "You may be able to force me to obey you in other things, but you can't force me to be pleasing to other men. This is where I draw the line, and I'll stand behind it."

"Have you not yet learned that you will be no other thing than pleasing to *l'lendaa*, simply because they are *l'lendaa*?" he sighed, moving his hand to my thighs. "Are you able to deny the manner in which you are touched? You gasp as I delve within you and cause you to squirm helplessly about, and this so soon after you were well and completely used. Are you able to resist my demands, are you able to force me from you? No more will you be able to deny any other *l'lenda*, no matter what stand you have vowed to take."

"Stop," I gasped, truly unable to resist him. The circular motion of his thumb drained the strength and will from me, a sorcery I had never been able to fight.

"Am I bound to obey you?" he asked, the amusement returning to him as he continued his ministrations. "Must I cease in obedience to your word?"

"Please stop!" I begged, writhing in obedience to his hand and will. "Please stop, please, please stop!"

"Much more acceptable," he said with approval, slowly withdrawing his hand from me. I went boneless with relief as he did so, ashamed that I had had to beg but glad that I had done so, and then I gasped again, this time in surprise. Rather than let me lie collapsed on the fur, recovering, he lifted me from the fur and threw me face down across his knees. The leather he had used earlier was not available, so he had to make do with his leather swordbelt, minus its scabbard. This time it was a full dozen strokes which fell, one after the other, bringing my screams quickly and making them loud. The tears streamed down my cheeks as he finally let me crawl out of his lap, but I wasn't allowed to crawl far. He took my arm and turned me back to him, then raised my face with one hand as the other wiped at my tears.

"You were instructed to put this room in order," he told me gently as I looked up at him from all fours, replacing the tears he removed. "Your disobedience did not go unnoticed nor unpunished, nor will it again. Do you still wish to disobey?"

I stared at him very briefly before shaking my head, his swordbelt having removed all the defiance from me. I still felt defiant, but the throbbing ache in my thighs, bottom and lower back precluded doing anything about the feeling. He leaned forward and brushed my lips with his, showing me that he was pleased with the answer I had given him, then he let me go entirely. I climbed off the bed fur amid sniffles and began to clean up the mess I had made, wincing from my punishment but doing the best I could. If I hadn't done so, I knew what I would have gotten.

Cleaning up the wreckage took longer than making it, but once it was done it was time to leave for the bathing room. For one frantic moment I thought I would be marched there naked, but the barbarian produced a yellow cloth wrap from the closet in the next room, and gave it to me to put about myself. He also chose the gown I would wear afterward, a pale, sheer lavender, then escorted me and the gown to the bathing room and its waiting female slaves. The three slaves listened to his orders with their foreheads to the floor at his feet, waited until he had left and closed the door behind him, then scrambled up to pull the wrap away from me and hurry me into the water. It didn't matter what *I* wanted, only what *he* wanted, but that was the least of my problems. I told the slaves to let me soak for a while, turned the suggestion into an order in their minds, then leaned back to let the water ease my hurting body while I fought to straighten my thoughts.

As unacceptably unbelievable as it was, the barbarian really intended selling me. It made no sense of any kind, but that was what he was going to do. Despite the fact that he needed my abilities to help him consolidate his people, despite the bargains and agreements he had made with the Amalgamation, he was going to let someone else, some other barbarian, band me. For me, accepting the truth of that intention was like running through hip-deep mud, more nearly impossible than simply difficult. I just could not see myself being banded by anyone else, and that was an attitude I had to overcome. If I didn't believe it I would do nothing to try to stop it, which would surely seal my fate.

I splashed some water over my shoulders and finally let myself wonder *why* he was doing it. Objectively it seemed to be a stupid move, but stupidity was a crime he wasn't usually guilty of. He had to have something in mind, something that would benefit him more than my presence. To believe that he was doing it to insure my happiness was a belief I couldn't allow myself. If I ever did, it would crumble the world, and I would never stop crying.

I was left to brood long enough to lose track of time, but the slaves couldn't be kept away forever. They'd been commanded by a warrior and a master, and they had to obey those commands or face the consequences. I hated the thought of being prettied up for show, but my very recent experiences with the barbarian had convinced me that open defiance wasn't the way to win against him. He had to find someone who was interested before he could sell me, and that was the key point I had to work on. How I was going to discourage interest with him literally looking over my shoulder I didn't know, but I'd have to think of something. If I didn't, it was totally my loss.

The slaves bathed me more thoroughly than I appreciated, then helped me out of the water and into a large drying cloth. The next room outward was less steamy than the bathing room, and gave my towelled hair a better chance to dry while the slaves rubbed lotions into my skin. The three of them giggled over the fact that I couldn't sit without feeling swordbelt echoes, and I nearly fed them a replay of what the beating had been like before remembering that they were slaves who knew about such things from first-hand experience. I thought about having to live that sort of life forever, always forced to obey, always subject to punishment, and shed a few tears for all of us. The slaves, thinking they'd embarrassed and hurt me, immediately began pouring out sympathy and comfort, patting my shoulders and making soothing noises. Their misinterpretation of my feelings was hardly surprising, but the tender little scene tickled something at the back of my mind. It had to do with misinterpretation, but I didn't yet know how misinterpretation could help me. All I could do was wait and see.

The slaves were very thorough in their preparation of me, and by the time they were finished I was finding it necessary to consciously fight off depression. My hair had been brushed until it shone, my face had been delicately pinched, and my body wore so subtle a fragrance under the sheer lavender gown that men were guaranteed to come closer to confirm it. I was being presented as a *rella wenda*, a silk woman more suitable for showing off and using in the furs than for normal, everyday chores, a dark-haired, green-eyed woman on a world of blue-eyed blondes. It was one way of saying that without my abilities I was just about useless to the men of that world, and also told me that Tammad had not changed his policy of always telling the truth. Any man who chose me would be told what I was, head to toes and through and through. If I hadn't already hated that world, that was the point I would have started.

Leaving the bathing room for the corridor brought a double surprise, the first being that it was already dark. Torches hung flickering on the walls all around, their flames writhing to the heavy caress of the stiff, warm wind blowing all about. The skies were dark and starless, as though obscured by clouds.

"You are more than lovely," Tammad said, coming forward out of the group of men he waited with to stop and look down at me. He and the others were my second surprise, as I hadn't thought to find so large an escort. Most of the others were the barbarian's men, but a handful undoubtedly belonged to Cinnan.

"Clearly worth the extended wait," said one of the men I didn't know, coming forward to stand next to Tammad as the others clustered around. "You will have little difficulty in finding one to band her, Tammad, yet not as she is. Few will approach you to discuss a five-banded woman."

"I—seem to have overlooked that point," the barbarian answered, his tone calm and controlled while his mind surged and billowed and fought to break through his restraint. His hands lifted toward my neck after a hesitation so brief I wasn't sure there really had been one, and with one surge of his muscles the small-linked, bronze chain was gone from about my throat.

"Ah, considerably better," said the man beside Tammad, and suddenly it seemed that a restraint had been taken, not from me, but from him and the others. The minds of the tall, blond *l'lendaa* had been humming as always, but as soon as the band was gone from me the hum became a growl. I shivered at the unbridled desire in the minds all around me, desperately fighting to keep from being overwhelmed, and took an involuntary step toward the barbarian. As his arm came up to circle me the growls eased off, dying down again to nothing but humming. I shivered a second time, leaning against the warmth of his body, and his arm tightened even more.

"The air has grown damp, and I do not wish to see the woman become chilled," he said to the others, his tone still even and cordial. "Perhaps it would be best if we took no more time before proceeding to the apartments of the *Chama*."

"Certainly," agreed the man beside him, so amenable he was nearly jolly. "Those who await us will be pleased to have their wait shortened."

His sparkling blue eyes touched me briefly with amusement, and then everyone was turning in the same direction and moving off, the barbarian and the other man leading the way, me between them. I'd had a lot of shocks that day, but apparently shocks don't become easier to weather with increased frequency. I'd really thought I knew what it would be like to be offered for banding to the men of that world, but the reality had turned out to be like nothing I had ever experienced. They would not politely contend for my attention the way a group of Centran men would, there would be no civilized courting and pretty words and gifts. They would offer Tammad a price and wait to have it accepted, and then I would belong to them entirely, a possession they could do whatever they pleased with. It was out and out slavery no matter how many times the contention was denied, no matter how much tender concern filled buyer and seller. In only one way was the object of sale considered, and that one way was her relationship with her current owner. As the barbarian had said over and over, a woman who didn't care to be with the man who possessed her, might be just the woman the next man was looking for. For him she would sew beautifully and cook deliciously, and be even more delicious in the furs. If, on the other hand, she did want to be with the man who was selling her, a change of ownership could prove to be more trouble than it was worth. The woman would cry, and do her work half-heartedly, and make the new man force her to feel something in the furs. It could be unpleasant as well as annoying, and many men would not—

My train of thought came to a dead stop, and would have stopped the movement of my feet as well if the barbarian hadn't had his arm around me. I had to quiet the surge of elation that told me I'd found my answer, the one way to discourage other men even with the barbarian watching me every step of the way. Misinterpretation *had* been the key, and I'd been blind not to see it sooner. If I handled it right it would work, and I *had* to handle it right; one mistake and I was done. The elation I'd felt faded to grim determination, but it was better that way. Elation has too much self-delusion in it, and what I needed right then was reality.

The walk to Aesnil's apartment was much too long, but all the men were in a chuckling good mood by the time we got there. The corridors of the palace were designed to pick up every stray breeze in the hot, usually windless climate and intensify it to cool the inhabitants of the place, and the stronger air movement that had developed turned the place into a thing one step down from a wind tunnel. As soon as we left the sheltered area around the bathing room, invisible hands grabbed my gown and hair and tried to toss them off every wall and over every balcony. I snatched at the gown and tried to fight it down from my face, struggled to get the wide butterfly sleeves untangled from the skirt, pawed at the hair that whipped around my head and blinded me, too distracted to notice immediately that a silence had fallen over the conversations that had been going on around and behind me. The first thing I noticed was the return of the mental growls, and then the soft laughter came through, telling me every eye was riveted to my struggle. I know I blushed from disheveled hairline to bare toes, and the increase in laughter told me the men knew it, too. Not one hand came to help me fight the stupid gown down, not even Tammad's, who was enjoying the show as much as the others. I did some growling myself as I quickened my pace toward the next sheltered area, but a lot of good it did me. By the time we reached our destination, every man with me knew beyond doubt whether or not I had a royal birthmark—anywhere.

Aesnil's reception room was all red and silver, red-cushioned and draped, and silver carpeted. A short, broad-stepped dais stood directly opposite the double entry door, back against the far wall to allow enough room for the *Chama*'s guests to seat themselves on the fur carpeting and among the cushions laid on for them in front of the dais. The wide, well-cushioned area was occupied by no more than ten men, all of them strangers and therefore undoubtedly allied to Cinnan, who lazed above them on the broad step just below the dais top. As the *denday* who had banded the *Chama* Aesnil, Cinnan had a lot of power among his people, but the easy laughter he contributed to the conversation of the men on the floor below him showed nothing concerning that power. He was a man to whom power meant very little, therefore he felt comfortable with it. Unfortunately for a lot of people, the *Chama* did not view power with his eyes.

The *Chama* Aesnil lay stretched out on her side on the top of the dais, her long blond hair carefully brushed, her red gown neatly accenting her curves, her eyes down and deeply involved with the way the fingers of her hands pulled at one another. Even from the doorway I could feel her misery and fury, but not many people in her palace or country would have doubted she deserved to be miserable. Finding power a tasty dish, Aesnil had gorged herself on doing exactly as she pleased, sending innocent men to the *vendra ralle*, the arena, to fight for their lives, handing down decisions based on favoritism, and refusing to be banded by the *l'lenda* who had been chosen for her by and from among her *dendayy*. She had also blackmailed me into working for her, and had captured Tammad and Cinnan and declared them *vendraa*. I hadn't had the easiest time in the world with her, but my feelings for her were friendship and love compared to the way the men felt. Cinnan had gotten some of his own back the day before, when his men and Tammad's had freed them from the *ralle* and they had caught up to Aesnil and me, but he had a lot of things still pending between himself and the woman he'd banded. The last time I'd seen her she'd been determined not to give Cinnan any satisfaction he couldn't simply take, which was bound to make things worse for her. When we appeared at the door Cinnan looked up with a broad grin of welcome, but Aesnil stayed as she was, unmoving and uncaring, leading me to wonder how successful she'd been.

"Tammad, welcome!" Cinnan called out, raising one arm in a gesture of expansiveness. "Take a seat where you will, and honor me by joining my repast. We have not yet celebrated our recent good fortune."

"The honor is mine, brother," Tammad answered, leading the way to a place among the cushions to Cinnan's right. "A simple crust is a feast, when one shares it with friends."

"And a feast not enough, when taken among enemies," Cinnan agreed, completing what was obviously a well-known homily. He waited until Tammad had lowered himself to the silver fur carpeting and I had knelt beside him, then said, "I see you have done as you intended. The woman is no longer five-banded, therefore offers may be made for her. Has she displeased you after all?"

I quickly put my head down, as though deeply ashamed, nearly caught off-guard by the abrupt, unexpected beginning of the game I'd decided to play. Now that the first move had been made I wasn't at all as sure as I had been that it would work, and small, invisible feet tiptoed up my nerve ends as my heart thumped a few beats. I could feel Tammad's eyes on me, and his hand came to smooth down the blown-away mess my hair had become.

"She has not displeased me, Cinnan," he said, his voice gentle and calm. "I have merely decided that she would be best off with another, and take the steps required. The doing is for the *wenda*'s sake, that and her happiness."

"I see," Cinnan acknowledged, faintly puzzled by the misery and disappointment I'd trickled to him and his men. They'd be convinced I didn't agree with what was being done, but they'd also be convinced they could tell it just by looking at me. If any of them got the least idea I was using projections, I was dead; needless to say, I was being very, very careful.

Cinnan clapped his hands and serving slaves began entering, males and females wearing the *Chama*'s red and carrying food and drink. There was a rumor that Cinnan intended freeing as many slaves as he could and making them servants instead, but that was too big a job to be done quickly. It was said he would get to it as soon as he had Aesnil settled down, another big job that would not be done quickly. A male slave in tight red-leather trousers carrying a tray of silver goblets stopped in front of Tammad, but before he could take one I reached up slowly and got it for him. The look I gave the barbarian said I was remembering his instructions and obeying him reluctantly, but the emotions I projected to everyone else said I wanted desperately to serve Tammad, but was being very careful not to be too pushy. The barbarian grinned faintly at me where I knelt in front of him, knowing it wasn't servility but the beating with his swordbelt that kept me from sitting, but none of the others in the room knew the same. With or without help they would all misinterpret whatever I did, hopefully getting the message that buying me would be a waste of time and *dinga*. They would picture me as being hopelessly and helplessly in love with Tammad, a woman ruined for any other man—if everything went right. If it didn't, I didn't even want to think about what would happen.

Naked female slaves came around with pitchers of wine, and I held Tammad's goblet with both hands till it was filled full, then hesitantly handed it to him. The wine was that vile *drishnak* which I wouldn't have touched for anything imaginable, and Tammad saw my hesitancy as taking care not to spill any of it on me. The others, however, got the impression that I wanted to take some of the drink that would so soon be inside my love, but simply didn't dare. The combination of longing and intimidation was difficult to handle, but it was the only way to get the message across.

After the wine came the food, spiced meat chunks and stews and roast fowl and fried vegetables, and on and on. The first mouth-watering smells nearly doubled me over with hunger, but I overrode the hollowness due to how little I'd eaten that day and did nothing but feed Tammad and concentrate on my projections. Friendly conversations and a lot of laughter had been coming from the men in the room, but I'd been too busy to keep track of them more closely than just before a specific projection. That was the main reason for my startlement when one of the *dendayy* suddenly appeared right next to us, crouching beside me and in front of Tammad.

"I am Gallim," he said to Tammad, his blond handsomeness growing with the friendliness of his grin. "I would look more closely at this *wenda* you offer for banding."

"Certainly," the barbarian agreed, as calm and casual as though he were offering a *seetar*. "Her name is Terril."

"A lovely name for a lovely *wenda*," Gallim murmured,

looking down at me from his crouch. His mind was humming deeply, more than interested, and I felt the tendrils of panic curling around me. Why hadn't he believed my projections?

"She seems fearful," Gallim observed with a chuckle, putting one large hand to the side of my face. "How is she in the furs?"

"For the most part adequate," Tammad answered, grinning at the furious glare I couldn't help sending him. "Though her cheeks redden modestly, her shyness does not keep her from being as helpless in the furs as any man might wish. It is only when her temper is high that she must be taken with more than normal effort. You see how deep her fearfulness is, that it has already departed."

The two of them laughed softly, showing me that I'd been tricked. Gallim's mind had been no more than calm and faintly curious, but seeing my supposed fear disappear had given him immediate and deep satisfaction. He'd been suspicious of my seeming subservience, and had come over to find out for himself.

"She seemed to be filled with too little spirit to attract a *l'lenda*, not to speak of a *denday*," Gallim said, his twinkling eyes still on me. "She is, however, a truly well-rounded morsel, made to be touched by men."

His observation seemed to be a cue for his hands, which rose quickly to the sheer lavender covering my breasts. I gasped as his fingers closed gently on my nipples and I began to pull away, but suddenly Tammad's hands were on my arms, holding me still. I writhed in the double grip without being able to free myself, furious and ashamed, growing even more furious when Gallim breathed a satisfied, "Ahhh." The motions of his fingers had managed to harden my flesh despite the denial I was filled with, and his initial satisfaction grew even higher.

"It will indeed take an effort, but I now know she may be reached," he told the barbarian, taking his hands back. "Perhaps she had best be fed now, for she seems somewhat pale."

"Her pallor is from another source," the barbarian said, "yet your impression agrees with mine. I foolishly expected her to speak of her hunger before this, yet her stubbornness is apparently too great. Take the food and eat, *wenda*."

He released me and pushed a bowl toward me, either not seeing or ignoring the way I was trembling. I hated him so much right then I could have killed him, with my bare hands or any weapon I could find. Gallim straightened out of his crouch and began moving away, and I blundered against his legs as I jerked myself away from Tammad, trying to get to my feet to run out of there. It was like stumbling against a tree in the forest, painful to you but nothing to the tree. Gallim turned back to see what was happening, but it was already over. Tammad had moved with his usual speed, and I'd been pulled back to be held in his arms.

"No, *wenda*, do not struggle," he whispered, stroking my hair in an attempt to calm me. "I will release you when you have regained control of yourself, not sooner. It is unseemly for a guest to act so beneath the roof of his host, even more unseemly for a *wenda* to do so. Calm yourself and I will release you."

"You let him touch me!" I choked, beyond reasoning with as I struggled to break loose. "You let a stranger touch me and you didn't give a damn! I hate you!"

"*Wenda, wenda*, he is not a stranger," the barbarian sighed, struggling to hold back some emotion he refused to let me see. "Should he find an approval from me to match his desire for you, you will become his belonging. He will then have the right to do more than put a hand to you."

"No!" I whispered, choking on the word as I closed my eyes and shook my head violently from side to side. "You *can't* sell me to him, you *can't!*"

He held me even more tightly against him, trying to quiet me, but I couldn't even quiet myself. The last time I'd felt so abysmally lost and frightened, I'd been a slave among the Hamarda. I'd been afraid I was going to be killed then, but I'd since discovered there *are* things worse than death. I was petrified at the thought of being sold to a stranger, so completely out of control I could no longer even think about the plans I'd made. My gown twisted against the barbarian's body as my struggles grew wilder, and the background conversations and laughter died away.

"Tammad, what ails the woman?" Cinnan asked, more concerned than annoyed. "What words does she speak?"

"She is upset," Tammad grunted in answer, hard put to hold onto me without hurting me. "The words she speaks are in her native tongue, filled with anguish I am unable to ease. It is one reason among many that I seek another to band her. Perhaps another man will find it possible to ease her pain."

"You may place her in our second sleeping room if you wish," Cinnan offered, compassion strong in his mind. "It is unoccupied now, and will provide what privacy the woman requires to collect herself. It lies through that door."

Tammad nodded and stood up among the cushions, taking me up with him then lifting me off the floor. I kept trying to hit him in the face with my fists, but he refused to allow me to do that. I was carried around to the right of the dais, through soberly sympathetic men, and into a small room. The room was dim with the light of only two candles illuminating it, and the barbarian looked around for a moment before taking me over to the pile of bed furs and putting me on it face down. Instead of moving away as I expected him to, he put his knee in my back and pulled my wrists behind me, an instant later producing a snapping sound. I knew what he'd done and I grew even more furious, pulling at the wrist bands he'd connected with a bronze clip, having no success whatsoever in parting them again. He reached down to my ankles and did the same thing to the ankle bands, then left me like that, face down and bound hand and foot, and left the room. He was punishing me for disobeying him about my behavior, I knew, but I just didn't care. Even if he came back and beat me, I still wouldn't care. I squirmed around, finding it impossible to get comfortable, and worked on believing that I didn't care.

Less than a minute later I heard muffled sounds from the outer room, and suddenly became aware of what was happening out there. My outburst must have given Aesnil ideas; the sounds I heard were the vocal evidence of her own outburst, full of reproach and bitterness. I probed to find out who she was shouting at, and was startled to discover it was Tammad. The minds of the men in the room were embarrassed, except for those of Tammad and Cinnan. Tammad was his usual calm self with an undercurrent of annoyance darting through, and he wasn't saying anything in answer. Cinnan, however, spoke for them both and with cold anger. He seemed to be lecturing Aesnil, or at least just beginning; the *Chama* didn't give him a chance to finish. She interrupted after no more than a dozen words, her own words cold and filled with the bitterness in her mind. Whatever she said shocked the other men in the room, and filled Cinnan with frustrated desperation. Tammad was no more than puzzled, but everyone listening seemed to understand that Aesnil meant what she said. When her short speech was done, her mind trace faded away toward the other side of the room, most likely into the other bedroom. The men all remained silent for a moment, embarrassment and upset clear in their thoughts, then they spoke brief words of good-bye and began leaving the room. Tammad was prepared to do the same, but Cinnan spoke, probably asking him to wait, and once the room was empty except for themselves, Cinnan spoke to him.

From Cinnan's tone of mind as he spoke, he wasn't as relaxed and unconcerned as he had appeared when we'd first arrived. He seemed very much like a man who had thought he'd solved all of his problems, only to suddenly discover that his solution had generated new problems which might turn out to be worse than the old ones. Tammad listened with a good deal of sympathy, making occasional comments that were more observations than suggestions, then stopped to think about a question Cinnan asked. There was a certain faint reluctance in his thoughts, but he didn't hesitate long before agreeing to Cinnan's request. Cinnan was pleased and grateful at Tammad's decision, and the two spoke no more than another moment before separating, Tammad fading out quickly, Cinnan remaining in range.

I put my cheek down on the top fur of the bed pile, disgusted with how tired I was. Between the work I'd done projecting to the twenty-five men who were now gone and the eavesdropping of a minute earlier, I was just about played out. I wasn't tiring as quickly as I used to, but I couldn't understand why mental work was so draining. It wasn't like running or lifting things that were heavy—or maybe it was. Just as the bottoms of my feet had gotten used to my going barefoot, it was possible I needed to build up calluses and muscles in my mind, to increase my strength and endurance. It wasn't an unreasonable supposition, but building up my mind would not be like building up my body. I wasn't supposed to use my abilities, especially around Tammad; doing it anyway while hoping he didn't notice wasn't a practical consideration. It would be like lifting weights under his nose while pretending to be napping. I moved in annoyance then pulled at the bands and link, adding frustration to what I already felt. Simply picking up emotions was like raising and lowering my arms during gesturing, but that was as much as I could do without being detected.

"You still seem disturbed, *wenda*," Cinnan's voice came unexpectedly, startling me with his undetected entrance into the room. I struggled around on the bed fur to watch him come closer, annoyed with myself for not keeping track of him. He carried a bowl of something with a wooden spoon handle sticking out of it, and stopped next to the bed furs to crouch in front of me.

"We will see this food within you, and then you may tell me what disturbs you," he said, reaching a hand out to smooth my disarranged hair. "Often, a woman finds it difficult to speak to the man who possesses her, less difficult to speak to another who is willing to listen. I will listen, *wenda*. and we will rid you of your upset."

"Just so easily?" I returned, pulling my head away from his big hand. "With no more than a single discussion, every point of distress plaguing me will be seen to? How powerful you have become, Cinnan, and how awesome."

"Woman, I do not care for your tone," he said, his gaze hardening in response to my sarcasm, his mind hardening to match. "A warrior, should he be so foolish, may spurn the aid of another with such words, yet a *wenda* has neither the strength nor the weapons to answer the insult so generated. To answer courtesy with insult will bring you no more than a strapping."

"Where you see courtesy, I see no other thing than condescension," I said, putting my cheek back down to the fur in weariness. "Leave me be, *l'lenda*, for there are none upon this world who may aid me."

"Your distress seems weighty indeed," he mused, bringing more of his attention to the discussion and away from the distractions his mind had been filled with. "I had not intended condescension toward the one who assisted in my survival in the *ralle, wenda*. Should it be within my power, I would return that timely assistance, and sweeten your life as mine was sweetened. Is there nothing I may do to aid you?"

"Certainly," I said, watching his broad, handsome face as his light eyes watched me. "Unbind me and return me to my people, and all debts between us will be done. That is the only assistance now capable of sweetening my life."

"Ah, *wenda*, there would be little assistance to you in such an action," he sighed, shifting slightly in his crouch as upset touched his mind. "Even were you mine to take where I willed, allowing you to flee whatever distress holds you would not eliminate that distress. It would follow though you fled to the farthest corner of the world, hold you though you fought with the very last of your strength. You must battle it now and find victory, else will you never be free of it."

"There is little likelihood of victory when I must battle *l'lendaa* without number," I shrugged, or at least tried to shrug. "As you, yourself, are *l'lenda*, I was foolish to speak of it. Now leave me be, for I am weary and wish to rest."

I closed my eyes to dismiss his physical presence, but could hardly miss the sharp flash of frustration and annoyance that lit his mind. I knew I'd never get anywhere with him and was tired of wasting my time, but he wasn't prepared to be reasonable.

"What foolishness do you speak?" he demanded, putting his hand to my face to shake it, trying to get me to look at him again. "*L'lendaa* do not battle *wendaa*, they do what they may to assist them! Do you truly believe there are *l'lendaa* hereabouts who would not assist you?''

"Certainly not," I answered, opening my eyes as he wanted me to. "Every *l'lenda* within reach would eagerly offer me the same exceptional assistance offered every other *wenda*, the same, noble assistance you, yourself, offered Aesnil. I consider myself truly blessed."

He stiffened and drew his hand away, but instead of feeling anger or insult, bleakness seeped out of every corner of his mind.

"It was my wish to give nothing but love and happiness to Aesnil," he said, the bitterness in his voice turning his mind raw with pain. "When I was chosen to band her my heart soared, for my desire for her was like a fire in dry woods, consuming all it touched in mindless need. I was content to be no more than he who banded the *Chama*, he who directed her *dendayy* in accordance with her wishes. And then did she direct that I be captured and sent to the *vendra ralle*."

He put the bowl down, forgotten, and rose to his full height, his eyes seeing something other than the room as he began to pace. I flinched at the tortured emotions his mind poured out, regretting having broached the subject, but knowing it was far too late to stop it.

"How great my fury was, I have no need to speak of," he said, walking out of my line of vision toward the room's wide windows. "Had it been a man who had done me so, I would not have rested till his blood covered my sword. And yet—When I found her there, behind the *ralle* in the guard room, her life about to be taken by the swords of the three *vendraa* who had caught her—it was they whose blood I wished to see on my blade. My love for her is as great as ever, yet I cannot allow myself to forget what was done to me, nor am I able to allow her to continue in her previous actions. I gave her pain and humiliation, yes, yet far less than she had earned. She will continue to be punished till she is able to grasp the enormities she has committed, grasp them and regret them. It is a duty I cannot refuse to attend to."

He was silent then, his mind still in a turmoil but slowly settling down, and then he was suddenly on the other side of the bed furs, leaning across it to put a fist in my hair and turn my head to him. I gasped more in surprise than in pain, for he wasn't really hurting me, and looked up into his eyes.

"And another duty I have been given is to see to your feeding," he said, his light-eyed gaze directly on me. "Though

you seek to distract me with argument and insult, I will not
be distracted. Will you eat, or must you be punished and then
fed?''

His mind wasn't really like that of Tammad, but he seemed to
share the ability to put aside his personal problems to concentrate
on whatever job was at hand. He wasn't simply threatening me
to make me obey, any more than Tammad would have been
simply threatening, which gave me very little choice.

''I have had enough beatings at the hands of *l'lendaa*,'' I said,
trying to sound saintly-brave but too tired to argue. ''I will
therefore do as you wish.''

''A wise choice.'' He nodded, releasing my hair so that he
might reach lower with both hands to the clip at my wrist bands.
''As for the rest, you have clearly spoken an untruth.''

''What untruth?'' I asked, now free enough to sit up. ''Of
what do you speak?''

''I speak of your observation upon the subject of beatings,''
he said, walking around the foot of the bed to get to the bowl
he'd left on the other side. He crouched down to pick up the
bowl, then grinned faintly. ''It is apparent to any man who
speaks with you that the number of beatings given you has not
been nearly enough. Had it been otherwise, the edge would
surely have been taken from that weapon you use in place of a
tongue.''

He pushed the bowl into my hands then stood again, folding
his arms in that unspoken-threat-while-waiting manner that seemed
to be part of a *l'lenda*'s nature. The glare I sent him only
broadened his grin, but he didn't speak and neither did I. Being
that close to even cold food had turned me ravenous, giving me
something more important to do with my mouth than talk. I took
the spoon and began using it, ignoring the smug satisfaction
coming out of Cinnan's mind.

I had gulped down almost the whole bowl of stew before
Cinnan turned away from me to take his weapon off and put it on
a table, then turned back to me.

''As you are to spend the darkness with me, you may now
remove that gown,'' he said, putting his hands to his *haddin* as
he began returning to the bed furs. ''Tammad has agreed to see
to Aesnil, therefore will I see to you.''

''What a surprise,'' I muttered, angrily. I wasn't surprised,
not even slightly, showing I'd known the truth from the very
beginning even if I hadn't admitted it to myself. It was the way
that world worked, the world that Len and Garth liked so much.

''What words do you speak, *wenda*?'' Cinnan asked, stopping next to the bed furs to look down at me. "I am unfamiliar with your native tongue."

"It was nothing," I said in Rimilian, not looking up at him. "I should by now be used to Tammad's pursuit of duty."

"It was scarcely his pursuit of duty," Cinnan said, scooping his arms under me and throwing me to the far side of the bed furs before sitting down. "It was a favor I asked of him, brought on by Aesnil's announcement that she will no longer be the *Chama*. A *Chama* cannot be given as host-gift to another by the man who bands her, though an ordinary woman may be. She must learn what it is she thinks to be, and compare it with that which she has always been. Perhaps she will even speak to Tammad of that which troubles her."

I turned my head to look at him as he stretched out on the bed fur, feeling the way he took his own troubles and firmly put them aside until he saw the results of his plans and efforts. His eyes moved over me, appreciating what he saw, and none of it made the sort of sense I could deal with.

"Among my people, a man who feels love for a woman does not give her to other men," I stated, not caring that I sounded accusing. "He also does not take other women to his furs, enjoying them in her absence. When a man does behave in such a way, it is clear to all that he feels nothing of the love for her he so loudly professes."

"What foolishness!" Cinnan laughed, surprising me by not being angry. "If a man tastes of no more than one woman, how is he to know that he prefers that one woman above all others? If he gives her to no man as host-gift, how is he to know she prefers him above all others? As to enjoying the woman in his furs, is he expected to be so boorish as to give the woman insult by dismissing her presence, or making her use a matter of duty alone? The woman is another man's beloved, else he would not have given her as host-gift, or asked that she be seen to. Is she to be treated as *ahresta wenda*, one who is used only out of pity? How uncivilized a man must be to behave so."

He reached over and drew the top of my gown sleeve down to my left elbow, running his palm slowly over the arm he had exposed. The deepening hum in his mind disconcerted me so badly that I barely felt the automatic outrage which developed over having Centran ways called uncivilized. It wasn't the first time those over-blown barbarians had looked at Central and its doings critically, and it scarcely mattered that they didn't know what they were talking about.

"Then perhaps you would be so good as to consider me

uncivilized," I told him stiffly, shifting back away from his hand and raising the sleeve again. "I dislike being given to other men for their use, no matter that the view is considered ill-mannered. I, myself, do not see it so, quite the contrary. Were I to keep silent regarding my opinions, you would have little pleasure from me."

"And now that you have not kept silent, I will have much pleasure?" he asked with a chuckle, for some reason amused. "*Wendaa*, it seems, are much alike no matter their origins. Your words put me in mind of a *wenda* given me as host-gift when I visited one of our far, outlying provinces, a *wenda* taken elsewhere in battle, one who considered herself a warrior. She had worn the bands of men only a short while, and swore to have my life if I should use her. As wild and spirited as she was, her words were not idle."

He chuckled again and pulled the sleeve off my right arm, then grinned wide as I hastily pulled it back up.

"Out of curiosity, I agreed to leave her untouched," he continued, raising up on one elbow and turning toward me. "Though she attempted to conceal it, her disappointment was more than clear. Her concept of honor had forced her to speak as she had, a concept which had no bearing on her true desires. I then fetched a dagger and put it in her hands, gave her what moments she required to prepare herself, then proceeded to take her. She was unable to use the weapon I had given her, for I did not allow the use of it. In such a way was she taught that her use was not hers to give or withhold, no matter the ways of the people to whom she had once belonged. Once taught this lesson, she was magnificent in use, as are all women. Do you wish me to fetch a dagger?"

His stare was so direct that I had to look away, despite the fact that I felt disgusted with myself for doing it. If my ankles hadn't still been linked together at the bands I might have tried running, but that would probably have been as useless as struggling. I'd been told my opinions didn't matter in the least, not on any subject men had already decided about, the standard outlook of Rimilians. I stretched my mind out to see how far I could reach, testing the strength I had left, but that was another dead end. Cinnan was the only one I could pick up, which meant he was bound to notice if I tried tampering. I'd never be able to hold him, he'd still have his way, and then Tammad would find out. I shivered at the thought of what the barbarian would do to me, then shook my head in answer to the question Cinnan had put.

He was quietly awaiting an answer, feeling nothing of impatience, but when the answer came he felt a faint stirring of upset.

"*Wenda*, it is wrong of you to fear me," he said, his voice concerned as his arms circled me to draw me close. "Would Tammad have allowed me your use, were I the sort to bring you harm or pain? I had thought your reluctance haughtiness, yet now see I was mistaken. I will bring you only pleasure, for this you have my word."

"Is pleasure not pain when it is brought about by force?" I asked, doing no more than resting my cheek against his chest. "Though I cannot hope to match your abilities, *l'lenda*, I do not fear you. I have abilities of my own which *you* cannot hope to match. I will not be bested by this world of yours, for that you have my word."

"*Wendaa!*" he growled, annoyed. "There is no soothing their fears when stubbornness jumps in the breach! I see you, too, fancy yourself a warrior, but of another sort. Very well, then, warrior, let us proceed in such a manner. You have been told to remove your gown. Must the command be repeated?"

His hand was on my throat, raising my head to force me to look up at him, making sure I knew he was all through playing games. It was an attitude I'd been trying for, one I'd forced on him without the use of my abilities. If I were going to be raped, I wanted it over with as soon as possible.

"You hold me with the strength of a warrior, then condemn me for disobeying?" I asked, raising an eyebrow. "Do you seek to guarantee my disobedience?"

"Disobedience is clearly no unfamiliar state to you," he growled, letting go of me as his annoyance increased. "See to yourself quickly, else I shall find other things to do with you."

His thoughts were just short of the sort of hardness which meant real trouble. I wasn't trying to get myself a beating, so I squirmed around pulling the gown up, yanked it over my head, then turned to lay it down on the carpeting out of the way. That was when I saw the flash of lightning outside the windows, a silent triple-crackling that lit the darkness in jagged lines before disappearing as quickly as it had come. I stared at the darkened windows, sure it had been heat lightning, and then, from very far away, a rumbling answered the signal of light, speaking of its impending approach.

"The storms will be here by daylight," Cinnan said, obviously having followed my stare. "It is the time of their usual coming, and they are expected. Do you fear the fury of such storms?"

"No," I lied, quickly turning my back on the windows. "I merely find rainstorms filled with ill fortune for me. I simply dislike them."

"I see," he answered, putting his hands on my shoulders to urge me down flat beside him. He remained leaning on his left elbow, looking down at me where I lay.

"Well, why do you hesitate?" I snapped after a minute of being stared at and not touched. "Do you seek to make me feel *ahresta*?"

"I do not hesitate," he said with a very faint smile, still making no effort to touch me. "I am not in the habit of taking a woman in my arms while annoyance fills my mind. I will not have any woman feel slighted when held by me. I would not give her such hurt."

I felt my hands curl into fists at my sides, underlining my need to scream out that it wasn't fair. I *would* have shouted it, but he would have laughed at me, giving back what he had gotten. He'd realized that I'd gotten him annoyed on purpose, and he was trying to punish me for it.

"You may calm yourself or not as you wish," I said, staring up at him with all the furious outrage I felt. "In the end, it will make no difference at all. I have decided that you will have no pleasure from me."

"Have you, indeed, *wenda*," he murmured, reaching a hand out to touch my face gently. "I believe you have already been told which decisions are yours and which are not. Tammad has asked that I see to you and I shall do so, with proper care and tenderness as well as the thoroughness he expects. It is my duty to do so."

"Alas, Cinnan *denday*, your duty is fated to be left undone," I countered, ignoring his hand as I locked eyes with him. I knew he'd never leave me alone of his own accord, and I couldn't stand being pushed around any longer. With the last strength I possessed, I forced my way into his mind and planted doubt so deep he was rendered impotent, for that night at least and hopefully into the morning. His fury finally drove me out, but not until it was too late to do him any good. At first he didn't understand what I'd done, and his anger moved him to try using me harshly—until he realized he couldn't use me at all. The shock in his mind was so strong it reached through the waves of exhaustion rolling over me, telling me he'd never had that experience before. He sat at the edge of the bed furs, trembling from the shock, and I couldn't have done anything to ease his difficulty even if I'd wanted to. Expending the last of my strength had acted as a drug on me, sending me helplessly down into sleep. Even as my eyes closed I felt the stirrings of elation, knowing I'd won after all, knowing Cinnan would be unable to touch me.

The night was peaceful and quiet—but in the morning he told Tammad what I'd done.

4

I knelt to the side of the room, beside a wall, trying to make myself as unobtrusive as possible, flinching every time the lightning and thunder struck. The men in the room were laughing and talking over the storm sounds, drinking the drinks and eating the food they'd been served—that *I'd* served. It still hurt to move, but even more painful was opening my shield and picking up the barbarian's continued anger, the fury he'd been feeling ever since Cinnan had told him what I'd done. Because of the storm, he hadn't been able to make me cut the switch myself, but that hadn't stopped him from using one cut by someone else. I'd been feeling justified in my efforts until I'd come face to face with him, and after that I'd just felt more frightened than I ever had before. The barbarian seemed to consider my efforts toward self-defense a personal affront to *him*, and his rage had nearly knocked me over. Explanations had been out of the question, just as impossible as trying to control his anger. In order to touch him I would have had to open my shield, but I'd had enough pain waiting for me. I didn't have to go looking for any more.

A triple crash of thunder rocked the room, drowning out the conversations and sending me huddling closer to the wall. The reception room of our suite was large enough under most circumstances, but right then I could have used five times the distance between me and the windows. Slaves had replaced the sheer curtains with heavier, glazed cloth of some sort that seemed to be waterproof, but the cloth was still transparent enough to let me see the storm as well as hear and feel it. Thunderstorms had disturbed me for as long as I could remember, but the storms of Central were nothing compared to the violences of Rimilia. Even my shield seemed like no more than fine netting before it, through which flashed every troubled thought on the planet.

"Bring the pitcher of wine, *wenda*," the barbarian called after the thunder had subsided to mere rumbles and growls, backdropping the thud of trampling rain. "My guest has emptied his cup and wishes to have it refilled."

Without looking up I forced myself to my feet, took the pitcher from the small table it stood on, then walked with eyes down to where the men sat among the cushions. The barbarian was hosting an informal midday meal for Cinnan's *dendayy*, a small party to which no slaves had been invited. My serving all of them wasn't considered slavery, but then that was their opinion.

"Kneel here and serve me, *wenda*," I heard from the man closest to the barbarian, the one who sat immediately to his left. I hesitated visibly when I heard the voice, recognizing the tones of Gallim, the *denday* who had been interested in me the day before. I'd seen him when I'd served him earlier, but he hadn't been sitting right next to Tammad then. Having to keep my shield closed was handicapping me, nearly to the crippling point. I knelt slowly and tried to give my attention to his goblet, but he wasn't holding it out.

"The gown you wear this day enhances your loveliness, *wenda*," Gallim said, his voice warm and friendly. "Always have I felt that that color should be reserved for glorious flowers and desirable *wendaa*."

He paused, obviously expecting some sort of answer from me, but the answer I would have made was on the barbarian's forget-it list. The gown I wore was pink, his preference, not mine. I kept my eyes on Gallim's silver goblet and didn't say a word.

"Modesty is becoming in a *wenda*," Gallim finally said when it was clear I had nothing to say, approval strong in his voice. "Raise your eyes to mine, little one, so that I may take pleasure from their beauty. Rarely does a man see eyes of such a green."

I had no interest whatsoever in looking at him, but I also had no choice whatsoever. I raised my gaze from his goblet to his face, then discovered that I couldn't quite meet his eyes. He was looking at me with that direct stare of the Rimilian warrior, deep, penetrating, evaluating and appreciating. I found a point beyond his left ear, and just stared at that.

"She is truly a great beauty, Tammad," he said, putting his hand out to touch my cheek with his fingertips. "It is clear, however, that she has recently shed tears. May I ask what caused them?"

"She was soundly switched, Gallim," the barbarian answered, his voice as calm as ever despite the increased pressure I could feel against my shield. "She shamed me before Cinnan, shamed him as well, and disobeyed my strictest commands. These are common failings with her, ones the switch has not yet cured her of."

"Unhappiness is a common cause for disobedience," Gallim said, as though agreeing in some way with the barbarian. "I will not ask in what manner she shamed Cinnan, for the question would be improper if put to any save him, yet I would put the other question. In what manner were *you* shamed?"

"The woman was given to Cinnan in return for a host-gift," Tammad said, shifting somewhat among the cushions. "Rather than give him the pleasure I wished for him, she gave him insolence and refusal. Were she truly one with me, my feelings would be understood and respected by her, shared in deed though thought disagreed. Those words, first spoken by our fathers' fathers, are truth."

But what about my feelings? I demanded silently, keeping my eyes to Gallim's left. Don't my feelings count for anything? Why can't my feelings be understood and respected? Because I'm not a *l'lenda*? Because I'm only a woman?

"Indeed," murmured Gallim, sparing me enough attention to move his fingertips down my face again. "And yet the truths of a man are often not the truths of a woman. She will, of course, be offered to Cinnan again."

"Of course," agreed the barbarian, the hardening of the calm in his voice making me ill. "He has agreed to honor me when this meal is done."

"I feel sure she will not again attempt insolence nor refusal," Gallim said, his voice warming even further with confidence. For my part I just closed my eyes, hurting much more than the beating accounted for. Another clutch of thunder struck, dinning and vibrating beyond sound, and Gallim's hand came to mine on the pitcher.

"Perhaps you had best pour the *drishnak* now, *wenda*," he said, tightening his hold on my hand to steady the pitcher. "I would prefer seeing it in my cup rather than upon the carpeting."

Controlling the trembling seemed to be impossible, most especially as I couldn't be certain about its cause. I didn't care that he was giving me to Cinnan again as a further punishment, at the same time refusing me the right to defend myself. Why would I care? It wasn't as though I wanted or needed *his* arms instead of a stranger's, it wasn't a thing to make any great difference. With

Gallim's help I managed to fill the cup with *drishnak*, then prepared myself to rise and go back to the wall I'd left.

"Remain where you are, *wenda*," the barbarian directed, stopping me even before I'd gotten the skirt of the gown out of my way. "As my guest enjoys your presence, you will remain before him. And you may refill my cup as well."

I didn't so much hesitate as brace myself against the latest salvo of thunder, then reached the pitcher to my left toward the goblet being held out to me. Gallim's hastily replaced hand kept me from spilling more than a few drops on the carpeting, but neither he nor the barbarian remarked upon the incident. I set the pitcher down on the floor in front of me, folded my hands, then stared down into the tawny depths of the *drishnak*.

Not thinking wasn't hard, but not feeling the thunderstorm was a different matter. The men took their time with the meal, doing more socializing than eating and drinking, occasionally calling me over to fill their goblets. That is, they filled their own goblets from the pitcher I brought, preferring to serve themselves rather than risk the unsteadiness of my hands. I felt besieged from all sides, hammered on, beaten, and in pain; I kept my eyes away from the men I approached, knowing they were looking at me in that way *l'lendaa* had, knowing I couldn't even half-cope with acknowledging those looks. They were all so big and sure of themselves, looking at me as though considering what it would be like to have me in their houses and furs. I shuddered as the last one returned the empty pitcher to me, hating to be looked at like that even as I turned away from the looks. I was on display as available merchandise, hating that even more.

"Ah, Cinnan joins us!" called out one of the men, and I turned to the door that had just opened. Cinnan stood there, tall and broad in his blue *haddin* and well-worn swordbelt, a nod and a smile for everyone in the room—except me. When his glance passed me it took no note of me at all, as though I were invisible or beneath his notice. I felt no insult at being treated that way, just a sad regret that it wasn't likely to last very long.

"Cinnan, you are most welcome to my apartments," the barbarian said, rising to his feet as Cinnan passed me and approached him. "Will you join our meal for a short while?"

"My thanks but no," Cinnan answered, clapping Tammad once on the shoulder. "It was not my intention to disturb you as you made the acquaintance of my brother *dendayy*. I would not have come so early, but other matters press."

"Another time, then," the barbarian agreed easily with a nod, then his eyes came to me where I stood in the middle of the floor. "Step forward, *wenda*, and present yourself to the *denday* Cinnan. As he has agreed to honor me, your presence will be required."

"As it is you he honors, no doubt your own presence would be more fitting," I said, not really believing I'd said such a thing even after the words were out. The pain of the storm had put me into a strangely detached mood, and even if I didn't believe it, I discovered I also didn't care. With that in mind I added, "I feel it would be rude of me to impose upon one who is so pressed for time."

Even as the men in the room erupted into laughter, I could feel my shield thickening almost rigidly with the increased pressure from beyond it. Tammad's expression hadn't changed, Gallim stared at me with disbelief in his light eyes, and Cinnan's expression was quizzical, but I thought I knew where that increase of pressure was coming from; the barbarian never had appreciated my sense of humor. Tammad stirred where he stood and parted his lips to speak, but Cinnan beat him to it.

"Allow me to apologize, *wenda*," he said, speaking loudly enough to be heard over the amusement of his *l'lendaa*. "It was not my intention to insult you by suggesting that there were other, more important matters awaiting me. No matter is of greater importance than the honoring of a brother through his *wenda*, nor the *wenda* herself. Come now, and allow me to apologize in a more—complete manner."

He put his hand out toward me, a faint grin showing on his face, the chuckling of the other men in the room nearly drowning out the rain noises. I didn't have to look toward the barbarian to know that he hadn't moved or changed expression, nor had he any intentions of doing so. He had already given me to Cinnan, so what more was there to say? My hesitation was no more than a deep breath long, then I moved forward to where Cinnan stood.

"Why the hell not?" I said, thrusting the empty pitcher at Tammad, who took it without stopping to think about what he was doing. "Who knows? Maybe I'll even enjoy it."

"What does she say?" Cinnan asked the barbarian without looking at him, his full attention on me. I looked back up at him with something like drunken belligerence, an action which made him blink.

"Her tongue is at times too barbarous to translate," Tammad growled, throwing the empty pitcher behind him with a gesture that matched the pressure on my shield. "No matter the meaning of her words, she will accompany you."

"I was certain of it," Cinnan smiled, putting his hand on my arm as he turned to the door leading to the next room. "Come, *wenda*. I already anticipate holding you in my arms."

There was nothing I cared to say to that, nothing that would have done any good. I let Cinnan urge me along with him without resisting, and a minute later he was closing the door to the sleeping room behind us. He released my arm, giving me the opportunity to walk to the center of the room alone, something I did immediately. The thunder roared again outside the windows, sounding much louder in the nearly empty room, making me hug myself in an attempt to keep from moaning.

"Turn and look upon me, woman," Cinnan said from directly behind me, having come closer without my knowing it. I turned slowly and looked up into his face, seeing the frowning, narrow-eyed inspection I was getting. "Are you ill?" he demanded, brushing the hair back from my face with one big hand. "Why do you seem so strange?"

"In my eyes, I am scarcely the one to be considered strange," I told him, then looked down from his stare. "No, I am not ill."

"Then you will find no difficulty in speaking to me of why you did to me that which you did," he said, his voice hardened. "To treat a man so is despicable, low and vile. Surely you knew you would be punished for the doing?"

"Perhaps I no longer cared." I shrugged, beginning to turn away from him again. "I have recently discovered a great many things I no longer care about."

"You speak of my brother Tammad," he stated, putting one hand on my shoulder to keep me from turning away completely. "He has spoken of how great the rift between you has grown, so great that he feels it best to allow another to band you. Though you seem more than eager to be free of him, a point he counts in favor of his decision, you have shown no interest in any other who would band you. A woman does not often act so, and I would know the reason behind your actions."

"I am not a woman of your world, therefore you may not judge me," I returned stiffly, still not looking at him. "As to the reason for my actions, they concern no one save myself. Even were I to speak of them to you, you would be unlikely to understand."

"I see," he answered, his voice containing something of the stiffness mine had had. Then he took his hand from my shoulder and said, "In that event, we need pass no further time in talk. Take yourself to the foot of the furs and await me there."

My mind darted around briefly, looking for a way out, but without the use of my abilities there was none. Too few steps took me to the foot of the bed furs, where I stood like the condemned awaiting execution. Cinnan waited until I got there before taking off his swordbelt and unwrapping his *haddin*, then he followed me over and stopped to look down at me. As soon as he was close enough I could feel the trembling begin again, the same thing I always felt with one of these *l'lendaa*. They were so damned big; how was it possible to say no to one of them and make it stick?

"For what reason do you fear me, *wenda*?" he asked, reaching out to slide the gown top off my shoulders and slowly down to my waist. "Do you continue to fear that I will cause you harm, despite my word to the contrary? Your hesitation would be more fitting in one who has never been touched."

I looked away from him as he urged the gown down past my hips, unable to answer his question. To him there was nothing wrong in what he was doing, on the contrary it was a duty expected of him. If I'd tried telling him how I saw it, he would have laughed or thought I was crazy. When he understood I had nothing to say, he bent to lift me off the floor, then lay down on the furs and took me in his arms.

"It is clear you must be shown the truth of my words," he murmured, beginning to move his hands on me. His sliding palm touched a still-aching welt just as the thunder crashed again, and I cried out in pain and clung to him, too scattered to continue keeping my reactions to myself. His arms tightened immediately in comfort, holding me to him, trying to calm the shaking.

"It is beyond me why certain *wendaa* must beg for punishment," he said, his voice uneven as he held me close. "As slight as you are, a strapping must be nearly unbearable, no matter the care taken with it. Is obedience so impossible to you that you must choose pain over it?"

"From some men, pain is preferable to pleasure," I gasped, my head whirling. "Pain will drive away the memory of his arms, the need for his body. From pleasure comes naught save an even greater pain, one impossible to guard against. With pain, one may hate without tears."

"Ah, *wenda*, how is it possible to find no more than tears in pleasure?" he asked, something of pain to be heard in his voice. "What is this thing which stands between you and my brother, the thing which brings pain to you both? Speak to me of it, and perhaps I may aid you as you and he gave aid to me."

I hate your world, I wanted to say, still trembling against him. If not for this world and its people, he wouldn't have lied trying to make me work for him. If not for this world and its people, I would not be handed about among strange men, expected to please them. If he were a man of Central, he would be jealous of other men touching me, even if he didn't have the backbone to do anything about it. He'd want to keep me for himself and he'd *care* if I slept with anyone else! He'd never arrange it himself, not ever!

"*Wenda*, I do not understand your words," Cinnan said, and I realized he was trying to hold me still as I struggled in his embrace. I also realized I'd been muttering aloud, but that part didn't matter. I'd been muttering in Centran, and Cinnan didn't speak Centran. I didn't know what was wrong with me, but it felt damned close to being drunk.

"My words—mean nothing," I got out, well on the way to feeling suffocated. "Release me now, for I am no longer able to bear this."

"You must bear it, and more," he said, his voice as implacable as his arms were impossible to escape. "You have shamed my brother once, and I will not allow you to do the same a second time. You will serve me, *wenda*, and will find pleasure in the doing."

I tried to add argument to my struggles, but his lips bottled up the words and refused them exit. With the way I felt, I would have sworn he'd be able to do nothing more with me than commit rape, but being somehow drunk had made me forget what *l'lendaa* were like. He began working on me immediately, his hands touching just so, his lips and tongue teasing, all of them caressing and heating; despite the pain of the storm and the beating I'd had, despite the drunkenness swirling me around, in no time at all I was lost to what was being done to me. It wasn't fair for *l'lendaa* to have that sort of power, to be able to raise a woman's needs and make her a slave to them, and I told Cinnan so as I kissed him. He chuckled softly and moved his hand on me, and I moaned and threw my arms around his neck. There was no doubt about the fact that he had me, but he wasn't surprised; he fully expected me to react the way he wanted me to, and would have been surprised if I hadn't.

Cinnan chucklingly shared the pleasure he made me feel, typically taking even more than he gave as most Rimilian men did, but as far as he was concerned he was only beginning. I couldn't have disagreed with him on my own, but I wasn't making many of my own decisions just then. I became more aware of being held by him, his arms tight about me as he stroked deep to satisfy us both, the satisfaction somehow becoming less and less with each passing minute. In its place the storm intruded, searing fireworks and deafening explosions battering harder and harder in an attempt to shatter my shield and mind. I had been sweating from Cinnan's efforts and my own, but the sweat increased and turned clammy, making Cinnan's massive arms and body under my hands and against my flesh fire hot. My head throbbed and I couldn't breathe, and when I moaned with the heavy pain settling all about me Cinnan chuckled again, thinking my moan was one of pleasure. He leaned down to kiss me without breaking the stride of his lazy stroke, not yet ready to build toward full passion again, but I knew I'd suffocate during one of his sustained kisses. Desperately I jerked my face away, gasping for the air I needed so badly, and the laziness in the body above me suddenly disappeared.

"*Wenda*, what ails you?" Cinnan's voice came, a frown to be heard in it. "You have become pale, and your body trembles in my arms. Where is the pleasure you felt but moments earlier?"

I closed my eyes as I simply dragged in air, unable to answer him as the pain flared through me. It felt as though I were being flogged to death, whips striking from all directions around me. Cinnan's hand came to my sweat-soaked hair, smoothed it once with a gentle motion, and then he withdrew from my body. I immediately began shivering violently, feeling the withdrawal of his body's warmth as almost pain, barely knowing it when he gathered up the fur we'd been lying on and wrapped me in it. My eyes opened with a good deal of effort as the shivering began subsiding, showing me a sober, worried-looking Cinnan who held the fur about me. He smoothed my hair again in an almost unconscious gesture, then backed off the bed furs and turned toward the door to the other room. He was still four hurried strides from it when it opened, admitting a quickly striding Tammad.

"Cinnan, excuse the intrusion," the barbarian began, "yet there is a matter of great—" His words broke off as he realized Cinnan was on the way out rather than being intruded upon, and his calmly worried expression changed to a frown. "What occurs here?" he demanded, a heavy edge to his voice. "What has she . . ."

"This is scarcely likely to be her doing," Cinnan interrupted with an impatient gesture, stopping in the middle of the room as Tammad came up to him. "The woman has taken seriously ill, and I had intended fetching a healer. You will, of course, sit with her till his arrival."

"Ill?" Tammad echoed, jerking his head around in my direction. "It was her assistance that I came for, as word has been brought me that Lenham has collapsed to unconsciousness after being taken by great pain. In what manner is she ill?"

"I know not," Cinnan answered, following as Tammad quickly made his way over to me. "She was excellent in use, far better than I had expected, this despite her great initial reluctance. She glowed beneath me, filled with pulsating life—and then the life drained from her, and all pleasure as well. She became as you see her now, and I knew not what to do."

"Terril, speak to me," the barbarian urged, sitting down in front of me where I lay curled in the fur, sweating and in pain. "Tell me what has touched you and Lenham so cruelly, so that I might see to it. Have you been taken by the same thing? What is it?"

His hand wiping the sweat from my forehead trembled slightly, almost in time to the storm sounds beyond the window. I tried looking up at him, but couldn't seem to focus my gaze; even holding my eyes open was painful. I licked dry lips from an even drier tongue, finding it difficult to answer even after making the decision to try.

"The—storm," I whispered, too deeply wrapped in stabbing nails to even wonder if he could hear me. "The storm—such pain. Can't hide from it. Can't stop it."

"What does she say?" Cinnan demanded, leaning closer. "Why must she continually speak in that barbaric tongue?"

"I much doubt that she realizes which tongue she speaks in," the barbarian muttered, his hand searching for one of mine through the fur so that he might squeeze it gently. "She has told me that the storm brings her pain, and that she is unable to halt it. It is undoubtedly through her power that she is tormented so, yet I spoke of easing her. How am I to keep my word, Cinnan? How?"

"Tammad, brother, do not torment yourself," Cinnan answered gently, putting a hand on the barbarian's shoulder. "A man may do no more than his utmost, especially against those things he has no understanding of. It is possible I may be of assistance to you, yet I must first speak with Aesnil. I will return as soon as may be."

He walked out of my line of vision for a minute, and when he reappeared going toward the door he wore his *haddin* and swordbelt again. The barbarian lay down beside me and took me in his arms, but even *his* presence didn't do anything to help. The pain just went on and on, doubling me over and making me sick to my soul.

It's impossible to know how long Cinnan was gone. The

passage of time is always subjective, even with timepieces around. It had finally occured to me to wonder why I was still conscious when the door to the room opened, admitting Cinnan and a number of other men. They all strode quickly to the bed furs, and Cinnan clapped Tammad briskly on the shoulder.

"Bring the woman and come with me, brother," he said, his voice sounding eager. "I may have found the answer to her difficulty."

"How?" Tammad demanded, only glancing at Cinnan before lifting me and the fur off the bed furs. Being moved that abruptly hurt, but I hadn't the strength even to moan.

"The inner fortress," Cinnan answered, moving fast to keep ahead of Tammad. "I spoke with Aesnil, and discovered that there are chambers deep within which have no direct contact with the outer world. Should it be possible to shield the *wenda* from the storms, the place is there."

"Cinnan, brother, you have more than my thanks," the barbarian answered, his voice soft and even despite his hurry. "Should this take the pain from my woman, my debt to you will be unrepayable."

"Do not speak foolishness, Tammad," Cinnan laughed, shaking his head. "What else might one do than assist a brother? And I have already been repaid, with a sight I scarcely expected to see. When I spoke with Aesnil, the *wenda* appeared *concerned* over this one! She immediately offered the use of the fortress, and her own services as well! Perhaps she will become the woman of my heart sooner than I had expected."

The barbarian grunted and said something else to Cinnan, but I couldn't follow the conversation any further. We were outside the apartment and hurrying through the corridors, practically in the middle of the storm despite the coated cloth hanging across every normally open area. The crash and crackle of the thunder and lightning were the only things left in the world, black pain and yellow pain and every color in between. I strained and fought against it, and kept wishing that I could just give in.

And then the storm feeling was further away, no more than a matter of inches but far enough to let me breathe a little more easily. I forced my eyes open to see us entering a narrow, torch-lit area at the end of a short, narrow, delicate bridge piece, beyond which was a larger room, also torch-lit. Entering that place was impossible other than in single file, which gave the men carrying Len on a litter a good deal of trouble. Cinnan was already in the larger room, as were Aesnil and a number of female slaves, and as soon as I was carried in Aesnil gestured

and began leading the way toward a heavy, closed door. The
deeper we went into that place, the more the pain receded, the
more it dropped to a tolerable level. I found less and less of a
need to fight and struggle, even though I still hurt quite a bit. I
took a deep, shaky breath, ready to try relaxing for the first time
in hours, and instead passed out.

5

The room I awoke in was only torch-lit, but even if it had been
blazing with bright, cheery light, there wouldn't have been much
of an improvement. All four of the walls were cold, undecorated
stone, the floor uncarpeted stone, the ceiling dimly seen stone.
Aside from the narrow pile of furs I lay on, one small table and a
couple of torch sconces, the room was entirely bare. I shivered
as I looked around at it, wondering if it was a cell rather than a
room, wondering if the heavy wooden door was locked. I couldn't
remember how I had gotten there, or why someone would lock
my in a cell. I moved around under the fur covering me,
realizing I was naked, growing more and more upset—until the
door opened, admitting a female slave carrying a tray. The naked
slave hurried to put the tray down on the small table, fell to her
knees and put her forehead to the floor, then scrambled up and
backed out of the room. I didn't know Aesnil stood by the door
waiting for the slave to leave until I saw her, the bright red of
her gown an incongruous sight in the drab of that room. She closed
the door firmly behind the hurrying slave, moved gracefully to the
tray that had been left, chose one of the bowls, then brought it
over to me.

"I am pleased to see that you have recovered," she said,
handing me the bowl with a warm smile. "You must now eat to
regain your strength, and then you will be completely whole
again."

I took the bowl automatically, still trying to remember what
had happened, and then I realized that my shield was closed. Not
knowing any better I opened it—then slammed it closed again
against the shock of more than atmospheric static.

"How long have I been here?" I gasped, putting one shaky hand to my head as memory came flooding back. "How long a time do those storms continue?"

"The new day has begun," she answered, looking at me narrowly in the dim torchlight. "How are you able to know that the storms continue? Ah, but of course. You are able to feel them. I believe I no longer envy you your powers."

"No one possessed of sanity and sense would envy me my powers," I came back, looking around for a place to put the bowl she had given me. "There is little pleasure in being sought for no more than their use."

"Do not put your food aside!" she said sharply, taking the bowl back before I could get rid of it. Your strength will not return without it and your strength will be necessary if we are to escape from here!"

"Escape?" I echoed, staring at her with the frustration of not being able to read her. "Have you gone insane after all? How would it be possible to escape, and to where would we run? Are we to float through these walls? And what of your position here? You cannot be *Chama* if you are no longer present."

"I no longer *am Chama*!" she spat, squeezing the bowl between her hands as her lovely face twisted with grief. "I have publicly renounced the position, and will not take it up again no matter the doings of Cinnan! He believes I may be forced to his will, yet his beliefs will prove to be mistaken! One who has been a *Chama* will never be a slave!"

She looked down at the bowl in her hands, seemingly ready to throw it violently away from her, but then she realized what she was about to do. I could almost see her grabbing her fury and forcing it back down, establishing control over it before stepping closer and sitting down on the bed furs next to me. Her movements were still jerky as she took the small scoop out of the bowl, scraped off the excess cereal grain against the side of the bowl, then stabbed at my face with the scoop. I was so startled I opened my mouth, and found myself being fed the cereal grain I hadn't really wanted.

"The man is insufferable," she muttered, barely giving me a chance to swallow before stabbing at me with the scoop again. "He beats me and uses my body as though I were a slave, then demands that I behave as a *Chama*! When I refused to continue with the farce and informed the *dendayy* of my decision, he dared to give me as host-gift to the beast who holds you! I refuse to allow this state of affairs to continue, therefore shall we escape together."

"You still have not told my how we are to escape from this place," I said as fast as I could before the next scoopful came at me.

"This fortress was built by my family," she answered, grim satisfaction accompanying the sharp, angry movements of her hand. "For one of the blood, there is more than a single exit from it. We will await the end of the storms, and then we will depart. Do you fear to go with me?"

She stopped feeding me for the moment, but I still hesitated before answering her. I wanted very much to be away from that place, but—all alone on Rimilia, with no one but another woman like myself? Where would we go? Would I live to see my embassy again? What would we do if we were captured by strangers, men who decided they wanted us? Did I have the nerve to face Rimilia on my own?

"I do fear to accompany you," I said at last, feeling more of the throbbing headache that had diminished so much from the day before. "You find yourself filled with the same anger which fills me, and yet—I fear the world beyond these walls and you do not. That I have even greater fear of the doings within these walls is happenstance. I do fear to accompany you, yet I shall do so."

"Ah, Terril, it seems it is best that I shall no longer be *Chama*," she sighed, putting her hand on my arm. "Your lot must truly be worse than mine due to aid you gave me, yet I spent not a single moment in thought concerning what was to become of you. I must see to it that your reluctance to remain grows much greater than your reluctance to depart. In such a way will departure please the both of us."

She reached forward to hug me briefly, smiled in a sympathetic way as she got to her feet, then returned the bowl to the tray and left the room. I stared after her, wondering what she could possibly have been talking about, then shrugged to myself to dismiss the question. Aesnil always had been somewhat on the strange side, and it wasn't likely that she'd change. What she'd said meant nothing at all, and I would be foolish if I wasted time thinking about it.

Or so I idiotically believed, until the door opened again to reveal Tammad. I could see the anger in his eyes even in the torchlight, especially when he came closer to look down at me. He informed me coldly that the *Chama* Aesnil had told him that I was much better, but had refused all her attempts to make me eat something. She also said she intended arguing with me, but had suddenly found herself perfectly willing to drop the subject and leave. She didn't understand why that had happened, but the barbarian did—and was furious about it. I was so shocked I couldn't say a word, and then I was beyond shock and stumbling into panic. I babbled and tried to back away as the barbarian's hands began to unbuckle his swordbelt, but there was nowhere to go and he wasn't interested in listening to anything I had to say. He caught me easily before I could run and then beat me with the swordbelt, ignoring my screams that Aesnil was lying just as he ignored my begging that he stop. He punished me hard for something I hadn't done, then forced almost everything on the tray down my throat. When he left his anger hadn't diminished much, but mine was already growing.

I'd never been angry after being punished before, and the anger had a strange effect on the pain the barbarian had given me. I squirmed around belly down on the furs I'd been left on, feeling the flaming ache in my body and hating the barbarian more with every throb. He'd had no right doing that to me, not after I'd told him Aesnil was lying. He just didn't *care* whether or not it was the truth, not if it meant he had to pass on strapping me. He enjoyed beating me, I knew he did, and I hated him more with every passing minute. Once I was gone he'd have to find someone else to beat, and I hoped he would choose someone who had more courage than I. It would serve him right if the woman he chose stole his dagger and plunged it into his body in revenge, ending his pleasure and his life together. I put my head down to the fur as the tears ran down my cheeks, knowing it would serve him right.

I was left alone in that cell of a room for hours, long enough to brood to my heart's content. When the door finally opened and the same slave female came in with another tray, I ignored her and looked for Aesnil. The *Chama* stepped into the room in the same quiet way she had that morning, waited until the slave had left with the emptied first tray, then closed the door firmly and smiled.

"I am pleased to see that you ate well earlier," she said as she approached me, her eyes moving over what she could see of me. "Your strength will now be sure to return, and as quickly as we require it."

"Perhaps even more quickly than that," I growled, beginning to turn under the fur. I fully intended getting up to thank her properly for what she had done, but I discovered immediately that I still hurt too much to move as easily as I wanted to. I swallowed a gasp against the stiffened protest of my body, then

slumped back in defeat. On that world, I couldn't even get my
own back from a woman like myself.

"How badly were you beaten?" Aesnil demanded, stepping
closer with her eyes narrowed. "What sort of man would give
you such hurt merely for failing to take sustenance?"

"I was not beaten for failing to take sustenance," I told her,
closing my eyes against her ridiculous outrage. "I was beaten for
attempting to control you, a doing which was absolutely forbidden me. Please accept my thanks for increasing my reluctance to
remain here."

"I—was unaware of this," she stumbled, her voice sounding
guilty and filled with confusion. "I merely sought a reason as to
why I, myself, failed to command you to your food. Are you in
great pain?"

"Certainly not," I answered, keeping my eyes closed. "I
remain unmoving solely through lack of interest in motion. You
will, of course, forgive me for not rising in your presence."

"Terril, you must believe that I did not know he would beat
you in such a way," she whispered, coming close to take my
arm in both of her hands. "When he forced me to his use he
seemed so gentle, so different from Cinnan. Though I fought
him he gave me no pain, and even attempted to bring a smile to
my lips. I thought he would do no more than punish you lightly,
if at all, and be certain that you ate as I wished you to. I will seek
him out and speak the truth to him, no matter that Cinnan will
then give me what you were given. I will not have you suffer
innocently for a doing that was mine, not even though I am no
longer *Chama*. Once I *was Chama*, and I will never forget."

I watched her get to her feet and head resolutely for the door,
and couldn't control the urge to peek. Opening my shield was
still somewhat painful, but it didn't take long to confirm Aesnil's
intentions. She meant to do what she said she would, and that
was all I needed to know.

"Wait," I called, and her reluctance when she stopped and
turned back to me was real. "Speaking the truth now will do no
more than delay our departure," I said, knowing my voice
carried conviction. "Should you wish to make amends for what
you have done, do not delay our departure."

She hesitated, clearly struggling within herself, trying to decide between what was right and what was desirable. She seemed
to have begun changing from the arrogant brat I'd known only a
couple of days earlier, but I doubted if she saw the change in
herself as yet. She was beginning to think about others, beginning to step out of the limelight now and then. She hesitated

another moment, still unsure, then slowly returned to the side of my bed to sit down.

"As it is your wish, I will not speak of what I have done," she grudged, not sounding happy about it. "Although I fear Cinnan's anger, I will not lie to save myself from him, and this failure to speak feels much like a lie. The storms without have begun to lose their fury, and it is believed they will be gone by dark. Will you be able to travel by dark?"

"If necessary, I will crawl," I assured her, shifting to get more comfortable on the furs. "How will you find yourself able to return here at dark? Will Cinnan not demand that you remain in your apartments and see to his needs?"

"I foresaw the problem and have already seen to it," she answered with a headshake. "When you and that other were first brought here, I informed Cinnan that tradition demanded the presence of one of the blood here in the fortress as long as strangers were to be found within. He knows little of my family's traditions, and allowed the thing after only a brief hesitation. To see to his needs he must visit me here, which he has not failed to do. In his absence he leaves a guard at the foot of the bridge, thinking me in such a way penned within. A pity he will soon be disillusioned."

"What of this other you speak of?" I asked, partly to distract her from the bitterness I could see in her eyes, partly to find out how Len was doing. "Has he regained consciousness as yet? Has the pain lessened its hold upon him?"

"He fares at least as well as you," she answered, taking a deep breath. "He has regained his senses, and complains that the storms have not yet ceased. Also, he allows the slave who brings his tray to feed him. Though I have not been officially declared slave, you must allow me to do the same for you. Should your strength fail through lack of sustenance, it may well mean the end of both of us; we depart together, so shall we remain together, for I will not abandon you."

Even without opening my shield, I could feel the truth and determination in what she said. It was possible she was trying to make up for what she had done to everyone else by being loyal and straight with me, but her reasons didn't really matter much. When someone offers you absolute loyalty without asking more than a little in return, it's very difficult to refuse.

"Very well," I said with a sigh, not sure how far willingness would take me. "I will attempt to build my strength as you wish."

Aesnil smiled encouragingly and went for the first bowl, and I managed to eat more than I thought I could. Being beaten doesn't do much for the digestion, but being angry rather than frightened and shaky seems to compensate for that. I ate everything I could stuff down, more than I wanted but less than Aesnil wanted, then finally called a halt. It wouldn't help either one of us if I threw up everything I'd swallowed, and she seemed to understand that. She put back the last bowl with only a small amount of reluctance, helped me finish the last of the light wine she'd had brought, then left me alone. I moved around on the bed furs trying to get comfortable, thinking I'd earned some more undisturbed brooding time, but it turned out I was mistaken. Not five minutes later I became aware of the presence of someone else in the room, and when I twisted around I saw Tammad standing just inside the doorway.

"The *Chama* tells me that this time you have obediently eaten nearly all that was brought you," he said, slowly stepping farther into the room. "It pleases me that you were obedient."

I stared at him very briefly then turned completely away, unwilling to hear anything he had to say, unwilling even to look at him. There was silence for short while, and then he was standing directly behind me.

"*Wenda*, I came to see how you fared," he said, sounding as calm and contained as he always did. "Though the strapping you had was well earned, it may perhaps have been a trifle—harsh. I would know what pain you continue to have."

I bit back the urge to be sarcastic and just kept quiet, knowing well enough that sarcasm wasn't called for. I usually reserved sarcasm for people I could like, and the barbarian didn't qualify.

"*Wenda*, I hear no words from you," he said after a moment, his tone showing nothing of the touch of annoyance I was sure was in his mind. "I asked after what pain you felt."

When I still didn't answer, his hand went to the fur covering me and pulled it aside. I could imagine from his silence what he was seeing, knowing damned well what it felt like. He'd been furious when he'd beaten me, and my back hurt even when I did no more than breathe. Between the leather swordbelt and the strength of his anger, my back must have been a fascinating sight.

"I—feared as much," he said at last, his voice nearly a whisper as he gently replaced the fur. "How great a fool a man is, who loses himself to anger when his intention is merely to punish. Come and let me hold you, *hama*, and swear that I will never again be such a fool. Open your mind and share the pain with me, for I have earned that and more."

He put his hands to my shoulders, waiting for me to turn and be held, but I didn't want to be held by him. I wanted to be left alone to wipe away the damp film hanging in front of my eyes, to finally make myself understand how really alone I was on that world. I hated being so alone, but it was all I'd ever be.

"*Hama*, do not hold yourself so far from me," he whispered, the tips of his fingers just touching my shoulders. "Never will I love another as I love you, this you must believe though you disbelieve all else you have ever heard. Never have I wished pain for you, yet pain is all I bring. Turn to my arms so that I may hold you close, and swear that I will never bring you such pain again."

I lay still in the furs, my eyes closed, feeling the pain he spoke of even without repeating it in my mind. I couldn't stand any more, not without collapsing or going insane, and not moving was the easiest of all impossible options. He waited a very long time behind me, not saying another word, but even the worst of tortures has to end. When I heard the door close I knew he was gone, and I cried as hard as I ever had in my life.

I slept for a while after the sobs finally left me, jerking awake only once in the grip of a bad dream. Once it was gone I couldn't remember what it had been about, but I was nearly afraid to go back to sleep. When I finally woke all the way another tray was being brought into the room, but this time the slave was alone. I bit back the urge to ask her where the *Chama* was, waited until she'd left, then gingerly opened my shield. The static-pain I'd felt from the storm was gone, letting me open my mind wide to stretch after what seemed like years of confinement. It felt good to spread out, but that was all I accomplished. If Aesnil was within range of my mind, she was either unconscious or dead.

I moved my body even more gingerly than I had my mind, this time finding pain but a lot less than I thought I would. I got up and walked and stretched, cursing the barbarian with every twinge, wondering if it was too early to begin worrying about Aesnil. I wasn't quite sure whether dark had already fallen outside, but if it hadn't it couldn't be far off. Had she changed her plans, been delayed—or gotten caught? There was absolutely no way of telling until and unless the ax fell on me as well, a method of gaining answers I would have preferred avoiding. The bare stone floor under my feet made me shiver, so I hurried back to the bed furs and lay down again, determined not to borrow trouble. Time enough to decide something had gone wrong if morning came and Aesnil still hadn't shown up. A pity I hadn't thought to ask her where her bolt-hole was when I'd had the chance.

Subjective time is always a burden, even when pain isn't involved. It either creeps or flies, depending on what you're involved in, depending on how distracted or bored or anxious you are. I shifted around all over the bed furs, got up and walked to the tray of food, decided I had no appetite worth mentioning, walked back to the bed furs again, then nearly tore my hair. Despite the fact that time was creeping, it *had* been passing; what sort of crisis could possibly be keeping Aesnil?

When the door to the room finally opened, I had to stifle a gasp as I whirled around. I'd been so distracted with worrying that it could have been anyone barging in, but it was only Aesnil. She slipped inside and closed the door quickly and quietly, then turned to me as she leaned against it.

"There was an unforseen delay," she panted, pushing back her long blond hair with her free hand. The other hand clutched a bundle of cloth, and it was clear she'd been hurrying.

"What was the cause of the delay?" I asked, waiting for my heart to stop pounding. "Does someone suspect what we are about to attempt?"

"No," she answered, shaking her head as she swallowed large draughts of air. "No, we are not suspected. It was simply that—Cinnan came to me before returning to his apartments in the outer palace."

She walked over to the bed furs and sat down on them, dropping her bundle as she shook her head to clear the damp hair from her face. She wasn't saying anything else aloud, but her mind was clamoring and whirling so wildly she should have been shouting or screaming or jumping around. I stood it for as long as I could—about thirty seconds—then went to sit down next to her.

"What disturbs you so deeply?" I asked, ready to put an arm around her. "What has Cinnan done that affects you so strongly?"

"He has done nothing—and much," she stumbled, turning painfully confused eyes to me. "When he came to visit me, it was as though he cared for me. He made no demands, found no fault with my actions, sought no vengeance at the expense of my dignity. Though I had no wish to be held by him, he took me in his arms and spoke gently of love, a thing he had never spoken of before. I had thought he had banded me solely out of a sense of duty, and I had greatly feared being bound to one who felt no more than duty toward me. When he touched his lips to mine it was as though a spell had been cast upon me, turning my flesh to liquid and destroying my will to resist him. When he took my body I was overwhelmed, so thoroughly that I was unable to stir for some time after he left me. Now—now I am here."

"And considerably more reluctant to depart than earlier," I commented, finally able to resolve some part of her emotions. "You now wish to remain with him, to learn more of his intentions and feelings. He is no longer the man you thoug᠁ to run from."

"Yes, I now wish to remain yet I may not do so." she whispered, looking down at her lap while misery flared in her mind. "The thought has come to me that his love has been professed merely to insure the presence of a *Chama*, one who will rule as the laws of the land demand. Would his duty not then be properly seen to, without difficulty and without disgrace? While deep within my body he laughingly called me small girl-child, yet he errs in believing me a child. I am not a child, and will not be gulled as easily as a child. I will leave Grelana, and never again return."

She somehow managed to keep the tears out of her eyes, but I could see them plainly in her mind. I gave in to the urge to put an arm around her shoulders, then patted her awkwardly.

"Aesnil, should you wish the truth, I am able to give it to you," I said, automatically trying to soothe the misery in her mind. "That Cinnan feels love for you is beyond doubt, for he has spoken to me of his feelings and I was able to verify them. You may believe him without fear of being gulled."

"I cannot believe him!" she cried, twisting away from my arm as her mind twisted away from my comfort. "How may I believe him?"

"For what reason can you not?" I countered, seeing her agitation even in her back. "Is it not part of my power to know such things? Have I not assured you of the truth of his words?"

"And what of his actions?" she demanded, whirling back to face me. "Have I not also the truth of his actions? Was he not the one returned me to my apartments from the *vendra ralle*, already aching from the strapping he had given me, only to rip my gown from me as though I were a slave? Was he not the one who then forced the degradation of slavery upon me, demanding that I bow to him and serve him and beg his use of my body? When I angrily refused he strapped me again, beating me till I was unable to deny him. These are not the actions of a man who feels love, Terril, and it is for that reason that I cannot believe you."

She took her gaze away from me and went back to the bundle

she had brought, wiping angrily at her eyes with the back of her hand. I closed my lips again without speaking further, knowing from the shut-tight feel of her mind that she would refuse to listen to anything else on that subject. That she refused to believe the truism that angry men do vengeful things, I could understand; the thought was highly disturbing to any woman who had to deal with them—after getting them angry. What I couldn't understand was her refusal to believe what *I* had to say. I could see it all so much more clearly and unemotionally than she; why didn't she believe me?

"We must hurry if we are to make good our escape," Aesnil said, immediately banishing all questions on belief from my mind. "I have stolen clothing for us, for gowns will not do upon the journey we undertake. The fit will not be perfect, yet it matters little as we cannot hope to do better."

I didn't understand her comment until I saw the clothing, and then I understood only too well. She had brought two sets of the clothing her guard wore, loose, wide-sleeved shirts and baggy trousers, with wide leather belts to cinch them. The only thing she hadn't brought was the sort of heavy sandals the men wore, undoubtedly for the obvious reason. Clothing can be forced into fitting; leather sandals can't be. It took another minute to realize a second obvious thing, which made me revise my opinion on how unselfish the *Chama* was growing: Aesnil already wore a pair of sandals, her own. The only one who would be going barefoot was me.

Ten minutes later saw us both in the new clothing, and to say the fit wasn't perfect was at least an accurate description—as far as it went. Considering the size of Rimilian men, we didn't have to be wearing the clothes of the largest of them for us to feel we were wrapped in tents. The brown and yellow shirt I wore came down to just past my knees, making it almost unnecessary to lug on the brown pants. If it hadn't been for the red leather belt—supplied with extra buckle holes all the way around its circumference—I couldn't have walked more than a step and a half without being hobbled. Aesnil's outfit was blue and gray with blue pants, but even her extra inch or so of height didn't make it better than mine. We rolled and tied sleeves and trouser legs with strips of leather, then decided not to waste any more time. If the outfits came apart we could fix them later, somewhere where there was less risk of getting caught.

When it actually came down to leaving the fortress, I was somewhat disappointed. I suppose I'd expected sliding walls with fiendishly clever release levers, but I must admit rock makes a poor medium for sliding. The bolt hole we used was just that, a narrow, wooden trapdoor in the far corner of the room, painted and disguised to look just like the rock of the rest of the floor. The trapdoor groaned slightly when we raised it, but the lack of hinges meant it didn't need regular oiling to keep it usable. The door rested on a built-in ledge at the proper point below floor level, and just below the ledge were three torches, tied to metal stakes driven into the rock on three sides. The fourth side contained a wooden ladder, and I hoped it was as strong as it looked. It disappeared far down into unlit depths, a place I wanted to reach at a pace of one rung at a time. I was in something of a hurry to leave that fortress room, but not in *that* much of a hurry.

While Aesnil untied two of the torches and went to light them from the room's torch, I looked around to see if we'd left any clues showing that we'd left the palace. The only thing I found was Aesnil's discarded red gown, and knew immediately that it couldn't be left behind. If there'd been a window I would have thrown it out, but lacking a window I decided the escape tunnel would have to do. After wadding it into a ball I threw it down, half expecting to hear it hit bottom as if it were a rock. I still hadn't heard anything when Aesnil came over with the two lit torches, and then it was time to go.

Aesnil lowered herself through the trapdoor first, reached up to take one of the torches I was holding, then began a slow descent. When she was far enough down I took my turn, putting the torch down on the bare stone floor just long enough to find the top of the ladder with my feet. We'd decided Aesnil would go first to lead the way, but that left me with the job of reclosing the trapdoor. I immediately discovered that I needed one hand to hold a ladder rung, one hand to hold the torch, and one or two hands to pull the wooden cover back into place. I was seriously considering the acrobatics of draping one leg over a rung and holding the torch in my teeth when I saw an horizontal torch bracket set into the stone beneath one set of the stakes the torch had been tied to. With a sigh of relief I used the bracket, fought the wooden door back onto its ledge, then reclaimed the torch. The hardest part of the descent was behind ?, and for the first time in a long time I felt like singing.

It's embarrassing to look back on that night and ask myself if I really was that innocent, or if I had just been suffering from a severe case of wishful thinking. My urge to sing lasted all of five minutes, just long enough to let me appreciate the necessary routine for descending that ladder. The narrow, enclosed space

was hot and airless, making it more than necessary that the torch
be kept as far away from me as possible. Its orange and yellow
flickering illuminated the rough gray stone walls and dark brown
ladder, but it also started the sweat rolling down my forehead
into my eyes and made my hair feel singed. I tried resting my
torch hand on the highest rung above my head that I could reach,
but that put the torch too close to the ladder and made me
nervous. If the ladder caught on fire Aesnil and I were both
dead, and in a place it was unlikely anyone would ever find us.
Being dead is bad enough, but being dead and unmourned
somehow makes it seem worse. The torch had to be *held* up,
with my arm unbraced.

The arm not burdened with a torch had trouble of its own,
needing to steady me on the ladder as my feet climbed down.
My body seemed to tend *away* from the ladder, making it
necessary that I hold on with my free hand, not simply guide
myself with it. While stepping down to the next rung there was
little difficulty other than strain; moving the hand down to a new
position quickly became a race, to see if I would be able to
secure the new position before my body swung too far back from
the ladder. Early on I almost missed, and thereafter the race
became much more absorbing.

As if the other problems weren't bad enough, the ladder itself
was a problem. Considering the fact that it had undoubtedly been
built by the men of that world, it had also undoubtedly been built
for them. Stepping down from one rung to the next was an
exercise in body stretching, a leg below, an arm above. The
squarely cut rungs were solid enough to hold a man's weight, but
after a couple of minutes the shape of them began hurting my
bare feet. Add to that the fact that the trouser legs of my stylish
new outfit didn't take long before beginning to escape the confines of their leather ties, and we have almost all of an exciting,
fun-filled picture. The last major point left out of it was that
Aesnil was having the same trouble I had, which slowed her
descent. If I hadn't kept a regular watch on her progress, I would
have lowered myself right onto her torch, instead of merely
struggling through the smoke from it.

Subjectively speaking, how long the descent really took is
impossible to know. It seemed three or four lifetimes before my
groping lower foot found rock instead of ladder-rung, and I nearly
cursed Aesnil for not giving me the good news sooner—until I
saw her. She had moved only two steps away from the ladder
bottom into a narrow tunnel before dropping to the rock floor,
her head and back against the rock wall, her eyes closed, her

torch forgotten on the rock beside her. I knew exactly how she felt, but I managed to put my torch into a bracket set in the wall before doing the same. I was soaked with sweat and nearly exhausted, but I didn't want us to be left in the dark in a place like that.

It took at least twenty minutes before we were able to force ourselves on our way again. If we hadn't been filled so full with the need to escape, we'd probably still be there, breathing hard and moaning at the aches in our arms and legs and backs. Aesnil stirred first, sending me her intention without words, forcing me into following her example. I wouldn't have admitted it out loud, but if there hadn't been the ladder to contend with, I might have considered turning back.

The narrow tunnel we began following went on a long way, but other than that it posed no problem. We passed three other wooden ladders descending out of rough square holes in the ceiling, but found no other idiots struggling down them. I'd long since begun wondering how good an idea we'd had, but couldn't argue the fact that there were no viable alternatives. If we weren't to be forced into someone else's idea of what was right, we had to go our own way. The tunnel was narrow and dark before and behind us, the torches smoked just enough to be annoying, and the sweat poured into the heavy cloth sacks we were draped in; nevertheless we kept going, and finally reached an area that was noticeably cooler.

"Ah, we will soon be free of these confines," Aesnil said, stopping to wipe at her forehead with the back of her hand. "The exit undoubtedly lies only a short distance ahead of us."

"There is another thing which lies directly ahead of us," I said, keeping my voice low as I put a restraining hand on her arm. "I feel the presence of a number of minds, and they seem to be male."

"They could not have found us!" she cried, but softly as fear flooded her mind. She'd been projecting so much fear going down that ladder, I was surprised she had any left. I thought my own quota had just about been used up, but I suppose there's such a thing as reserves.

"Their minds hold nothing resembling a desire to search for and find," I soothed her, wondering what they were doing there if they weren't looking for us. "Let us advance cautiously, and see what we might see."

Her soft, shaky agreement came quickly, but once again we had to do things the hard way. We couldn't take the chance of anyone seeing our torches so we had to leave them there, sputter-

ing on the rock floor, and go ahead without them. We edged
slowly along one wall, seeing nothing in the deep darkness all
about, but we didn't have all that far to go. The tunnel ended at a
blank face of rock with a single fold in it, and once we'd
negotiated the fold we saw dark, cloudy skies and heard the
sound of night creatures.

"See them there, about their campfire," Aesnil whispered,
squeezing my shoulder from behind. "How many do you make
them to be?"

"Five," I told her, positive about the number even though
they were too far away to be probed. We seemed to have exited in
the woods, a short way up a rocky slope. The men were camped
at least fifty feet away, farther into the woods and below us to
the left.

"They should not be there, camped and taking their ease,"
Aesnil whispered angrily, compressing my shoulder even more.
"They are undoubtedly the wood patrol, meant to move about
singly and remain unseen. What if enemies came to attack?"

"Then they would surely be the ones who were attacked
first," I whispered back, reaching up to loosen her hold on my
shoulder. "Is it your intention to march forward and remonstrate
with them?"

"Certainly not," she answered, sounding outraged even in a
whisper. "I have scarcely put myself through rigor and danger
merely to remonstrate with inept guardsmen. We must avoid
them at all costs."

"I think not," I disagreed, looking back at the cheery campfire.
"Their *seetarr* are tied not far from them, and riding is much
preferable to walking. That is, if our destination is not too near
to require mounts."

"Our destination is not near at all," she said, also looking
toward the camp. "I had not considered the possibility of
obtaining mounts, for it seemed unlikely that we would. Now that
the possibility presents itself, we would be foolish to fail to take
advantage of it."

"Then, by all means, let us not be foolish," I said, and began
moving forward, away from the rock fold. Aesnil followed along
behind me, her mind extremely pleased, her attention on walking
softly and carefully.

There were a good number of dark shapes on the slope all
around us, boulders and stones and rocks and pebbles. The
overcast sky must have hidden us from observation as we made
our cautious way down the slope, moving from cover to cover,

but otherwise wasn't much of a help. It was difficult seeing things even directly in our path, and the pebbles and silt kept making us lose our footing. The night air had started out being cool and damp, but by the time we reached the foot of the slope we were covered with sweat again.

I left Aesnil behind a boulder and moved forward into the woods alone, my mind questing all about against detection or attack, at the same time trying to ignore what my feet felt like. Going down that slope had hurt, but I didn't have time to sit and clutch them and cry the way I wanted to. Babies had no business being out on their own, without someone to comfort their tears. If I wanted to be on my own, and I was sure I did, I had to forget about tears.

It took time and effort getting within twenty feet of the five men without being detected, but cheating helped. I was scarcely so capable in the woods that they were likely to miss my presence once I was near enough, so I watched their minds very carefully. As soon as the first one noticed something, I fed him a combined dose of conviction-regarding-identification and relaxed dismissal. The two emotions worked to tell the man that I was a harmless night prowler, and lack of attack reinforced the belief. I was noticed three times and instantly dismissed as not being worth bothering about, and then I had reached the position I wanted.

The men were totally relaxed and enjoying themselves, but I picked up the definite impression that they were there for a relatively brief rest stop, not permanently settled in. Their campfire had been built against the damp of the night and the aftermath of the rains, and they were handing around a large skin of what had to be *drishnak*, the spiced wine *l'lendaa* liked so much. The evening breeze brought the smell of it to me, wrinkling my nose, but that was one time I was pleased to see the horrible stuff. I could tell from the way they drank, carefully rationing themselves, that they probably intended the supply to last the rest of the night at least; happily for Aesnil and myself, that intention was subject to change.

Careful to project to all five men at once, I began by sending unconcern and the feeling that there was no need to hurry, that they had all the time in the world. Once those thoughts were firmly established I went after the one who was being passed the skin, making him worried about the amount of *drishnak* left and concerned that he might miss his share. The worry and concern were too generalized to convey such specific thoughts, but the wineskin in his hands and the unconcern about everything else tended to establish a focus. The man took two long pulls, more than he had at any other time, then reluctantly passed the skin on to his right. I passed on along with the skin, and tackled the second man in the same way.

I may dislike *drishnak* intensely, but there's no faulting the way it works. The amount the skin contained would have been enough to teeter twice their number of men; having only five of them to work on it put them all out cold even before the skin was empty. When the last mind slid down the well into oblivion, I stood up from behind the bushes I'd crouched near, stretched the newest aches out of my back and shoulders, then signaled to Aesnil to join me. She approached with caution, curiosity and worry intermingled, peered at the five motionless bodies, then laughed her tinkling laugh.

"Truly, Terril, your match does not exist," she said, turning away from the campfire to hug me briefly but warmly. "We may now take two of their *seetarr* and depart."

"We may take two of the *seetarr*," I said, "but we may not depart as yet. To leave these men here, in such a way, would surely be to leave them to their deaths. We must somehow protect them from predators."

"How are *we* to protect *l'lendaa*?" she demanded, impatiently. "Are we to stand over them with swords in our hands till they wake? They are sure to be grateful then, and strap us no more then till midday. Do not be foolish, Terril."

"There must be a way," I insisted, looking around, and then my attention was caught by the five *seetarr*. The big black animals were tied to a line strung between two trees, their reins fastened tight but their legs unhobbled. I'd checked them briefly earlier to make sure there were two who would accept new riders, and had found only one of the five was so attached to his present rider that even his thoughts didn't stray far from the man. *Seetarr* are more than just dumb animals, their intelligence higher than most Rimilians know. Aesnil and I couldn't have stood over the men and protected them even if we'd wanted to, but that didn't mean no one else could.

I crossed the small camp and headed directly for the *seetarr*, swerving only to avoid the unconscious men. Now that I'd thought of something I wanted to get it done as soon as possible and then continue with our escape, hopefully before I became exhausted. I was already tired, already feeling what I'd done to the men, and I didn't have all that much left. Whatever I did would have to be done before I reached the bottom of the barrel.

I quickly untied the two *seetarr* I'd chosen as mounts, and urged them to follow me back to where I'd left Aesnil. It took a certain amount of clambering and scrambling before we were in the saddles, but climbing up was necessary; making the *seetarr* kneel would have wasted my strength. Then I turned back to the other three. The two who had no attachment to their riders made no resistance to the suggestion that they pull off the line and take themselves for a walk. Rope and reins snapped in any number of directions as two moved and one stood still, underscoring the puzzlement in the mind of the last to remain. I touched his mind and merged with the puzzlement, then changed it to determination as I brought his attention to the five men. When his concern appeared I increased it, then urged him to come closer and stand in a position above the unmoving bodies. By that time he knew there was something wrong, and wouldn't have left his position of protection unless taken from it by his rider. I wiped at the sweat on my face with a sleeve, got the proper direction from Aesnil, set our *seetarr* off on their way, then slumped forward to rest.

We rode through the dark woods for hours, Aesnil silent, me half-dozing, before it occurred to either one of us that we hadn't brought any food along. The only thing on our minds had been escaping from captivity, and I couldn't help but rant silently against the stupidity we'd shown. Granted we were both relatively new to escaping, but I should have thought of it even if Aesnil hadn't. I remembered the well-filled tray I'd been sent but hadn't touched, thought about how easy taking most if it along would have been, and could have kicked myself. I was too used to traveling with the men of that world, *l'lendaa* who had no trouble hunting for what they wanted to eat. I stirred in the hard, uncomfortable leather saddle and looked over toward the dark shape of Aesnil, riding in discomfort to my right. As *Chama* she had gone out on occasional hunting parties, but I was willing to bet she hadn't done any of the hunting herself. The realization of hunger didn't breed the determination to do something about it in her, a sure sign she had only gone along for the ride. She had said we had a long way to go; if it was too long a way, we might find that we'd escaped relative safety and comfort for the freedom of disaster and death.

Nervousness to be out of the vicinity of the palace kept me quiet until daybreak, but once the sun began to rise over the mountainous and upward trending country we rode through, I had to insist on stopping for a while. I still hurt from the beating the barbarian had given me, and the saddle I'd been in for hours hadn't helped any. Aesnil was nearly as uncomfortable as I was, but the growing light had brought recognition to her of where we were, and *she* insisted that we ride on a little farther before stopping. Since she seemed to know what she was doing I reluctantly agreed, and followed along through woods that turned from black to green as though by magic, the rising sun already beginning to warm the damp. The *seetarr* picked their way through the trees until we reached a pebbled road, followed the road upward for about another half mile, then let themselves be guided off the road to the right, behind a number of giant boulders that lay at the foot of the craggy rockface that rose high on that side of the road. Grelana had turned out to be a small country tucked into the skirts of a moderately small mountain range, and now we were heading up higher into those mountains. I preferred the mountains to the desert that lay on the other side of Grelana, but for some reason climbing higher into them was making me uneasy. I thought about it as we pulled the *seetarr* to a halt behind the boulders on a flat, rocky area that almost seemed swept, and decided that the lack of food was what was making me uneasy. I didn't seem to think much about food unless there wasn't any there not to think about.

"We may rest here awhile." Aesnil announced, then raised her arm to point beyond three or four boulders that lay closer to the rockface. "There is a small spring over there, from which we may drink to heal our thirst. A pity we lacked the foresight to bring along the emptied *drishnak* skin, which might have been filled instead with water. There are sure to be other springs ahead of us, yet I know only a few of them."

I looked at her sharply as she began dismounting from the *seetar*, wondering if she was blaming me for having forgotten the skin, but her mind held only vague accusation. She was unconcerned over everything except having gotten where we currently were, and was pleased over that, extremely pleased. She slid to the ground with no more than a grunt for the stiffness she felt, still too relieved to really be bothered by it, feeling a lot more chipper than I felt. It had also occurred to me to wonder what the *seetarr* were going to eat, and I was tired of asking myself such depressing questions. We had defied the *l'lendaa* who had claimed us and had made good our escape; why couldn't I be like Aesnil and simply be pleased with the accomplishment? I sighed deeply then tackled the movement necessary for dismounting, not looking forward to it; I hurt too much for it to be anything but unpleasant.

It took Aesnil's help before I was able to lower myself all the way to the rocky ground. She tsked and fussed over the pain I felt, seriously concerned, and immediately insisted that I lie down for a while. I was in no condition to argue with her imperious commands, and merely waited while she struggled to untie the rolled sleeping furs from the back of my *seetar*, then watched her spread them next to a boulder. It didn't occur to me to be thankful that those furs were there until much later; it didn't seem that men out on a brief night patrol would need them, but I certainly did. If I'd realized sooner they were there, I would have used them to cushion myself from the saddle. I lowered myself to one of the furs and stretched out on my left side, then sighed with the comfort of it as Aesnil covered me with the second. It would soon be too warm for the covering fur, but right then it felt good. Aesnil chose one corner of the furs to sit down on, toward my feet, and I looked over at her.

"You seem quite pleased to have arrived here," I observed, watching her gather her long blond hair away from her face as she stretched. She looked ridiculous in the shirt and trousers she wore, and seemed as uncomfortable in them as I was; their one redeeming feature seemed to be that as awkward and uncomfortable as they were, they were better than gowns would have been.

"Indeed am I pleased," she smiled, beginning to take off one sandal. "We have begun the journey to lasting freedom, the journey which may even return my country to me. These are things which cannot fail to please me."

"To what lasting freedom do you refer?" I asked, more than aware of the excitement that filled her. "Where do we go, that you speak of having your country returned to you?"

"We travel to the land of Vediaster, whose ambassador I recently received," she laughed, rubbing at her foot, "Their country lies beyond this mountain, and is governed solely by females. Even their *l'lendaa* are female. Should I promise them their choice of captives as slaves, they may well return with me to attack Grelana. Male slaves bring high prices in Vediaster, and the first to be sold there will be my council of *dendayy*."

She laughed softly, inordinately pleased with the idea, her thoughts taking on the sort of movement which usually indicated fantasizing. I was glad she'd taken her attention away from me, as I wasn't sure how well pleased she would have been with my expression. I'd been there when Aesnil had received the ambassador from Vediaster, a big, unpleasant-looking woman who had brought a matched set of male slaves as one of her gifts, handsome twin men who had been so filled with fear and true servility that it had nearly made me ill. I don't know where I'd

thought Aesnil was heading us, but it had never occurred to me
that it might be a place like Vediaster. I wouldn't have trusted
women like them, but it wasn't surprising that Aesnil did. They
were her only hope of getting her country back on her own
terms, and she was far too desperate to question her actions. If
we manged to survive until we got there, I'd have to be sure to
leave as soon as possible. All other considerations aside, the last
thing I needed was to be caught up in the middle of a war.

"I may perhaps keep Cinnan as my own slave," Aesnil
mused, still half-fantasizing. "He has great skill in pleasing a
woman's body, though his manner is far too brash. How did you
find him?"

Her eyes came to me with the question, her curiosity genuine
despite its mildness. Caught unawares, all I could do was stare in
confusion, not knowing what to say. When she saw the pink in
my cheeks, her amusement came out in tinkling laughter.

"For what reason do you feel embarrassment, girl?" she
asked, back to raising her hair up off her neck. "You have
known far more men than I, yet I feel no embarrassment
discussing their various qualities. Did you find Cinnan awkward
and inept?"

"N-no," I stumbled, somehow even more embarrassed at her
amusement. "He was . . . adequate to the task."

"Adequate to the task!" She laughed, slapping her knee.
"Indeed is he adequate. His manhood was so thick and adequate
that I thought it likely I would die from the pleasure of it. His
manner of use is somewhat different from that of him who
claims *you*, he called Tammand. He, too, is more than adequate,
and I found myself helpless to resist his demands. Cinnan,
though, is far more exciting than Tammad. Tammad, I think,
would quickly bore me as a slave."

"I could not imagine holding that beast as a slave," I
muttered, still uncomfortable with the conversation. "How might
I ever approach him, with fury and pain blazing from his mind as
he struggled in his bonds? How would it ever be possible to
sleep, knowing he might break free of his chains and come
seeking me? I believe I would be even more eager to run from
him as a slave than I am to run from him while he remains
free."

"You fear him," Aesnil said, and the amusement was gone
from her as she stared at me. "You fear him so deeply that you
cannot even consider holding him in chains. I spit on one such as
he, who gives such fear through pain as he has done. You are well
rid of him, Terril, well free."

In anger she rose to her feet, holding one sandal, and began to walk toward the place she had earlier pointed to, where water might be found. As I watched her take her anger further away, I tried to consider her statement objectively. Was it true that I feared the barbarian as Aesnil believed? I knew I couldn't seem to face him when he was angry with me, and I knew how panic-stricken I grew at the prospect of being punished by him, but those two considerations paled to nothing when I thought about trying to keep him as a slave. I knew I hated him, so why *shouldn't* I find pleasure in the thought of chaining him up with metal the way he had chained me up with strength? The only logical answer was that I *did* fear him, even more deeply than I hated him, but it wasn't something he had done to me. The world of Rimilia had proven my cowardice to me any number of times, and he had merely noted the fact and used it. That I hated him for helping to show me my cowardice didn't mean I blamed him for causing something that had been there all the time. I turned slowly in the fur until I was face down, then tried to do something about the pain I felt. Cowards don't like pain, and I was no exception.

I didn't realize I'd drifted off to sleep until Aesnil woke me, excited over what she had found. She'd begun searching the *seetarr* in the hopes of finding something which would hold water, and had succeeded. Each *seetar* had a good-sized water skin in its leather saddlebags—right next to an unbelievable amount of leaf-wrapped food. The food was enough to last at least three or four days, the leaf wrappings certain to keep it mostly unspoiled during that time.

"Clearly, those *l'lendaa* were not the woods patrol," Aesnil summed up, replacing the food she had pulled out to show me. "Perhaps they were passing through the woods, and not of my guardsmen at all. Had I disregarded the wishes of the Council and commanded that all members of my guard be properly clothed, rather than merely those who served about the palace, it would be possible to know for certain."

I distracted her sharp-edged anger by suggesting that we eat some of the food she'd found, then made sure not to ask why she found those shirts and trousers so attractive. The sun couldn't have been up more than two or three hours and was partially obscured by clouds to boot, but I was already sweating in the sacks hanging on me even without the fur that had orginally covered me. Aesnil's hair looked damp and stuck together, but there wasn't a word out of her about being uncomfortable; as well as I was beginning to know her, I didn't expcet any such words in the future, either.

As soon as we finished eating, refilled the water skins, and fed the *seetarr*, we resumed our journey. The small amount of sleep I'd had gave me back some of my strength, but it wasn't likely to last long in the heat of the day riding a *seetar*. Aesnil wasn't allowing herself to acknowledge the exhaustion she felt, and again I had the impression that she was pushing herself to reach a particular destination. The depression that had settled on me didn't seem to let up, and it took me a long while before I understood why Aesnil had the determination I seemed to have lost. Aesnil was running *to* something, but all I was doing was running *away* from something. I had nowhere to go and no purpose awaiting me when I got there, nothing that promised to solve all my problems if I just reached one particular goal. I had run to keep myself from being sold like a slave, but that was beginning to look as though it had been a major mistake. Now that I had my freedom, I didn't know what to do with it.

We continued moving most of the day, stopping briefly only once to stuff down some food. Aesnil was just about ready to drop—with me not far behind her—when we reached the place she'd been heading us toward. The dulled afternoon sunshine showed us a tiny but fast-moving stream beneath a few thin shade trees, about twenty-five feet from the mouth of a cave. I checked the area carefully for signs of life before we dismounted, paying special attention to the cave. Nothing but insects and bird life came through, which made Aesnil and me laugh giddily with relief. We had no weapons to defend ourselves with, and if anything native to the area had argued our presence, we would have had to move on. We took ourselves into the cave in record time, bringing the *seetarr* along to make sure we didn't lose them to restlessness or predators, then dragged brush in front of the cave entrance to keep everything out and the *seetarr* in. The brush didn't strike me as being much of a hindrance to the exit of the *seetarr* if they really wanted to go, so I made the effort to impress the command to stay in their minds before dragging my furs off the saddle and arranging them on the cave floor. Aesnil had already collapsed into hers, their softness and the pleasant cool of the cave dragging her immediately down to sleep. Her example was the best one I'd seen in a long time, and I lost no time in following it.

When we awoke again it was still dark out, but that didn't mean we turned over and went back to sleep. We had to assume there was pursuit behind us, even if the pursuit was only one of a number of search parties, beating the bush of the countryside trying to flush us out. We led the *seetarr* out of the cave, got us all fed and watered, then began traveling again.

It was a number of hours before the sun came up, and I spent the time we moved along the road stretching my mind. Everything in the dark seemed so quiet and deserted to Aesnil, peaceful and empty except for the sound of our *seetarr's* hooves, clopping evenly against the stones of the road. To my mind the dark was anything but peaceful, with predators and prey hunting and fleeing throughout the woods we rode near. A cough sounded not far away to our left, registering in Aesnil's awareness but immediately ignored, registering in the *seetarr's* awareness and bringing them alert for further sounds like that. The cough had come from a night hunter in the woods, standing with bloody feet over the kill it had just made, hearing our passage and immediately prepared to challenge us if we tried to approach its spoils. I had felt the kill when it had been made, the shock and terror of the victim as its throat was slashed out, the keen, gnawing satisfaction of the hunter as it knew victory, the fading of the shocked mind force as life faded and drained away. I'd shuddered at the raw savagery of the scene as it came to me, sickened but in some manner also fascinated. How did that predator develop the emotions that let it kill without regret? What told it its survival was so important that it had the right to take other lives in order to continue its own? And what kept its victim from fighting back, from trying to do more for its own survival than merely running? What if its victim did fight back; how would its emotions be affected then? Would it be angry, outraged, shocked—intimidated? Would it fight anyway, or would it turn tail and run? The answers to those questions would be totally useless in any frame of reference I would care to find myself, but something inside me still wanted to know. It was an itch that couldn't be scratched, and probably never would be.

The night prowlers settled down for the day and the day prowlers took their place, but moving along the road atop the giant black *seetarr* kept Aesnil and me safe. The sun had been up three or four hours when we came upon a branching in the road, one arm leading off to the right, steeper-looking than the main road and turning higher into the mountains.

"That road would also take us to our destination," Aesnil observed, giving it a brief glance as we passed by it. "It was used by all before the construction of the bridge across the abyss, yet is it considerably longer and more arduous than the bridge road, which halves the distance. We will reach the bridge well before dark at our current pace, therefore will we cross before seeking a place of rest. When we reach Vediaster, we shall allow ourselves proper rest.''

But not before, I thought to myself, feeling her eagerness and determination. I, myself, was beginning to feel annoyed, but I didn't know why. I didn't begrudge Aesnil her shining purpose, but it was possible her continued ''we'' was beginning to rub me the wrong way. Her attitude wasn't simply a matter of friendship or concern over what would become of me; her thoughts became somehow proprietary when she said ''we,'' and I didn't care for it. If she was thinking about owning me again the way she had when she was still actively *Chama*, she was in for a rude shock.

We rode on another couple of hours, sweating in the heat, eyes slitted against the peek-a-boo glare of the sun every time it came out from behind the high-floating clouds. Since Aesnil hadn't said anything about the road branching again I was surprised when the second branching appeared, also off to the right but this time going level if not dropping. As unexpected as it seemed there were trees around this second road, and it looked a decent place to stop and have lunch. Keeping to a saddle so long had me feeling as though I'd been switched, but when I made the suggestion Aesnil's reaction surprised me even more than the sudden appearance of the branching had.

''We may not stop here,'' she said at once, her voice even despite the agitated jumping of her mind. ''That road holds difficulty and danger for us, for it leads to the holding of enemies of mine. We will continue ahead, and will take our sustenance only when well away from here.''

Even if I'd wanted to argue with her words, I couldn't very well argue with the fear she felt. I could tell she wasn't simply being high-handed, so I sighed and gave in again. If it had been anything but fear motivating her I wouldn't have, but fear is too strong to ignore.

Lunch break was hardly long enough to let me stretch the kinks out of my back before we were mounted and moving on again. Aesnil had developed a heavy anxiety to reach and cross the bridge, and the longer it went on the better chance it had of giving me a headache or forcing me to shield. I had begun thinking about going my own way as soon as we were out of the mountains, and the more I thought about it, the better it sounded. I still hadn't decided on a definite place to go, but once I was alone I could stop to think about it. The one thing I really wanted was to get off that planet, but I didn't yet know how I could accomplish that. Maybe thinking about it would give me an answer, so undisturbed thinking time was the first order of business. Having something of a plan, if not a true purpose, raised my spirits, making me feel better despite the ever-increasing saddle-ache.

If I was feeling happier, Aesnil was suddenly feeling considerably worse. The road went on and on, bearing ever so slightly to the right, and then we reached a curve, rounded it—and came upon the abyss Aesnil had mentioned. It was no more than twenty feet ahead of us, the road disappearing over its near edge, better than sixty feet of emptiness gleaming in the sun before the far edge appeared, the road then beginning again. I gasped at the unexpected sight, but Aesnil moaned with true pain.

"The bridge!" she cried, undecided whether to wring her hands or tear her hair. "What has happened to the bridge?"

I dismounted without answering her, then walked closer to the abyss to get a better look. A wind blew in over the openness, flapping my clothes and sending my hair backward, but it wasn't strong enough to drive me back before I peeked over the edge. There, just below me, was what was left of the bridge, a tangle of charred and broken wood, rope, vines and boards, all of it much too short to reach to the other side of the dizzying drop. It didn't look as though it had been all that sturdy to begin with, the sight keeping me from summoning up the sort of knife-edged disappointment Aesnil was feeling.

"It appears to have burned," I called back to Aesnil, fighting with my hair as I turned away from the chasm. "Are there those about who would have burned it?"

"No," she choked, fighting with tears which became more obvious the closer I got. "It must have been the storms recently past, the lines of fire thrown from the skies. Once before this happened, bringing about the need to rebuild the bridge once the storm season was done. It had not occurred to me it would happen a second time, when my need for the bridge was so urgent. What are we to do?"

The tears were rolling freely down her cheeks by then, her desolation so strong I winced. She'd gone ahead with her plans as though nothing in the world could stop her, and now that nature had gotten in her way she wasn't prepared to cope. It was the reaction of someone who hadn't often been denied whatever it was she'd wanted, and it annoyed me.

"As we are ill-equipped to fly over the abyss, we would do well retracing our steps," I answered, getting ready to remount even though I didn't want to. "Though the alternate route to our destination is longer, it seems we have little choice."

"Yes, yes, the alternate route," she gulped, wiping at her tears as new hope welled within her. "We will surely grow a bit hungry before we arrive in Vediaster by that route, yet will we arrive there. Let us continue on at once."

She backed up her *seetar* then turned it to go back the way we'd come, moving slowly despite the return of her anxiety to allow me time to catch up to her. I followed suit on my own *seetar*, but not because I was that anxious to be moving on again. Being that close to such a deep chasm bothered me, but once we were far enough away I intended calling a halt. I needed time to sleep and rest my body, more time than I'd recently been allowed. It would help us very little if we avoided all pursuit, only to fall over dead from pushing ourselves too hard.

Going back took us down rather than up, and the *seetarr* showed their enjoyment of the change by increasing their pace. I stood the bouncing, jarring motion as long as I could, then called out to Aesnil that it was time we stopped. I could see in her mind that she heard me, but there was no other positive ackowledgment from her aside from that. Instead she kicked her *seetar* to increase its pace even further, pulling away ahead as though she were intent on winning a race. If I'd had any intelligence I would have let her go on alone and be damned, but what she'd done had gotten me mad. If we were going to part company then rather than later, I had a few words I wanted to say first. I jiggled the reins of my own mount to let it know I wanted to go faster, and began chasing after the former *Chama* of Grelana.

Since I'd come to Rimilia I'd spent more time on *seetarr* than I'd ever been interested in, but only rarely as the sole passenger and the one doing the steering. *Seetarr* are so calm and manageable in a walk or slow trot that they tend to lull whatever normal caution one possesses, making one believe that they will be the same at any pace. I discovered my mistake only when it was too late, only when the *seetar* I rode gleefully picked up more speed than I had anticipated it would, now bent on the game of catching up to its companion. I had time enough to grab on to its mane and saddle with one hand each when the first headlong jolting began, and thereafter didn't even have the time to gasp.

As I'd noticed on other occasions, terror has the ability to freeze both body and mind without the least difficulty. Plunging down a mountain road at breakneck speed in mid-afternoon light appeared to be an excellent source of terror, and if I hadn't been entirely convulsed into a death grip to keep from falling off, I probably would have screamed myself blue. The woods and mountainside flashed past in a blur that made my eyes water, the jouncing rattling my teeth and bones so thoroughly that I couldn't even appreciate the cooled air flowing by. In a distant way I became aware of the fact that Aesnil's mount had also speeded up, which convinced me she must be crazy. Anyone who traveled at that speed voluntarily on a *seetar had* to be crazy!

I don't know how long it took before I realized that Aesnil wasn't any more a voluntary passenger than I was. She might have started the speed escalation, but it hadn't been her choice to continue it. Our *seetarr* were having fun playing a game after spending so long in dull routine, and I finally understood why the barbarian had never wanted me to ride one on my own. It was clearly in the nature of the beast to do things like that, especially to riders who hadn't the strength and experience to stop them. I can't say the realization made me any less terrified, but along with the thoughtless fear anger appeared, easing the grip on my mind just enough to let me do more than quiver and shake. With a calm deliberation I wasn't feeling, I reached out first to Aesnil's mount and ordered it to slow and stop, then did the same to mine. The *seetarr* felt the beginnings of rage in me and reluctantly obeyed, slowing carefully until they came to a full stop, one beside the other. The miserable beasts were scarcely even breathing hard, but Aesnil was gulping in deep, desperate swallows of air, and I was having trouble unclenching my hands from mane and saddle. I felt as battered and bruised as I had after the barbarian had beaten me, but as soon as I could I twisted out of the saddle and dropped to the ground. The pebbles of the road hurt the bottoms of my feet, and my legs felt as though they were made of raincloud; nevertheless I staggered across to the grass of the forest, lowered myself, then leaned back against a tree with a groan.

"Once again I owe you my thanks," Aesnil croaked, dismounting stiffly and with as much pain as I had. "Had you not stopped this thoughtless beast, it would undoubtedly have taken my life. I had not the strength to cling to it much longer,"

"How good of you to give me your thanks," I croaked back, watching her totter to the grass and collapse on it. "Had you given me your consideration instead, your thanks would have been unnecessary. The beast you ride is not alone in thoughtlessness."

"How dare you speak to me in such a manner," she huffed, trying for outrage but managing no more than a weak glare. She lay in the grass holding herself up on one elbow, her head still hanging despite the attempted glare. "Though I am no longer *Chama* I will be again, therefore do I demand respect from those about me who serve my will."

"Respect may not be demanded," I told her, letting some cold enter my voice. "To obtain it one must earn it, and be willing to give it to others as well. A true leader would know this, and know also the difference between a companion and a servant. Was this the reason you saw so carefully to my escape along with your own? So that I might *serve* you?"

"It is a great privilege to serve a *Chama*," she answered, but the attempted belligerence was gone, replaced by traces of confusion and hesitancy which also showed in the slight widening of her pretty blue eyes. "To what other would I allow such a privilege, if not she who served me once and was given pain for the doing?"

"I want none of privileges such as that!" I answered harshly. "I am not a slave, to be given the privilege of *serving*! I shall serve you now no more than I did previously, which is not at all! No more than my own purposes were served them, and the pain I received no more than the fruits of my own foolishness! To aid one who cares for no more than the use he might put you to is a foolishness I will not allow myself with *you*! More than enough that I allowed it with another."

I turned away from her then and blocked her off with my shield, not trusting myself not to strike at her out of anger. All her help and solicitous concern had in reality been self-directed, all for her own benefit and none for mine. I was nothing but a handy tool to her, something to be rescued from savage, uncaring hands, cleaned carefully, then tucked away in a traveling bag against future need. It wasn't as though it hadn't happened before or that I hadn't suspected it; my anger stemmed from the fact that I was so damned *sick* of it!

"You aided his escape from the *ralle*, and still he beat you as he did?" Aesnil asked after a long moment, now close behind me. "He hopes, then, to force you to aid him by giving you pain. It had not seemed to me that he was so cruel and without feeling, yet he is undoubtedly no other thing. Were you to serve *me* instead, I would not give you pain, for I value your powers too highly. Surely you would prefer my service to his?"

Aesnil hovered on her knees behind my right shoulder, waiting with what she considered patience for my answer. I sat cross-legged next to the tree, looking down, suddenly filled with waves of almost overpowering confusion. He knew damned well he couldn't force me to work for him by giving me pain, so why *had* he punished me like that? He never hesitated to punish me when I did something he didn't approve of, and that made no sense! He should have been pampering me and giving me everything I wanted, just the way Aesnil was offering to do. And I still didn't understand about his offering me to those other *l'lendaa*. Unless he was doing it only to threaten me into toeing the line, he couldn't be serious about it.

"Have you heard my words, Terril?" Aesnil prodded gently. "Would you not prefer my service to his?"

I turned my head and opened my mouth to tell her exactly what I thought of her service, but never got to say the words. I saw her go pale and heard her gasp at exactly the same time that I felt the startled upset of the *seetarr*. It was only then that I became aware of the other mind traces, the ones that I would have been aware of much sooner if I hadn't had my shield closed. I jerked my head back to the left and saw them then, nine low, dark shadows with eyes still gleaming from the deeper shade of the forest. They had crept close to where we sat, and now they were grinning and growling, baring fangs in anticipation of the feast before them.

"A pack of *virenjj*," Aesnil whispered, her throat almost closed with terror. "We are done!"

No, I thought to myself, still feeling the rising anger she'd started in me, and then I shouted, "No!" and projected that anger toward the nine slinking shapes. I could feel their minds wince at the touch of the projection and then they snarled, viciously rejecting the denial I'd sent. They were hunters and we were prey, and it was the way of the world for the first to take the second.

I wonder if it's possible to explain in words how I had grown to feel about being a perpetual victim. I'd been kidnapped and beaten on that world, attacked, embarrassed, shamed, denied and forced to act against my will. I'd been too close to death and also too far from it, and all the fury and frustration from all of those things surfaced in me right then, driving away the fear any sane person would have felt, and leaving behind nothing but refusal. The *virenjj* snarled again, baring their fangs and preparing to move in, and I raised up on my knees and clenched my fists, determined to go down fighting.

They'd rejected my denial, but glee and eagerness for them to come closer was harder for them to ignore. They felt the emotions clearly and hesitated, not understanding why I felt that way. They were familiar with traps and beasts who hunted *them*, but I didn't smell like a trap, just like a victim. One of those in the forefront cried out with a high-pitched howl, rejecting my suggestion, and began launching himself toward Aesnil and me.

The terror Aesnil had been putting out all along crescendoed then, and I shunted it through to the attacking beast in one great wallop, hitting it harder than with a physical blow, then added my own strength of projection and sent it toward the other eight. The one who had begun its attack howled hideously and twisted in the air, maddened by the terror and no longer aware of its original intent, spitting and screaming in all directions. The rest of the pack screamed and clawed at the frenzied one, filled with heavy fear and swirling confusion. They none of them understood what was going on, and their uncertainty was my cue to press harder.

Deeper uncertainty and fearful mistrust soon had each member of the pack striking out in all directions, back-biting and being back-bitten as the madness spread among them. Hate and envy laced into their minds, turning their screams and howls deafening, drenching me with sweat as I struggled with the effort of reaching them all. Nine of them there were, each requiring a special balance to their madness, each swirling about the trees, slashing and tearing at its fellows. My breathing came even faster than theirs did, dizziness fighting to overwhelm my struggle, and then, distantly, I became aware of Aesnil pulling at my arm and shoulder, whispering urgently that we had to run. It was hard understanding why we had to run, harder yet to pull my mind away from the nine I was so closely linked to, but Aesnil was insisting and I couldn't think clearly. I let her pull me to my feet and away from the bedlam, back toward the road, then felt her shock when she realized the two *seetarr* were nowhere in sight. To my vague surprise the shock faded immediately and then we were running, down the road and away from death and savagery.

I was able to keep going until all sounds of pain and fury were lost behind us, but after that I just had to stop. I stumbled and pulled at the grip Aesnil still had on me, almost throwing the two of us down, forcing her to slow and pull at me again. Instead of increasing my pace as she wanted, I went to my knees, holding up one hand to show that I was done. Mentally and physically I had nothing left, and all the wishing in the world couldn't change that.

"Terril, you *must* continue to run with me," Aesnil panted, pulling ineffectually at my arm. "We may not yet be safe from those beasts, and we must try to find the *seetarr*. Without them and the food they carry, we will never reach Vediaster!"

"I . . . cannot," I gasped, looking up at her sweat-stained face and greasy, disarranged hair. "I cannot go . . . another step . . . though all the beasts . . . in the world . . . come behind me. Should you feel it possible that . . . the *seetarr* may be caught . . . you must go on . . . without me.".

"Leave you?" she demanded, her pretty face twisting in outrage "Here, where you may fall prey to the first beast to chance across you? Where you might die from lack of a companion? Never would I do such a thing, never!"

I hadn't the breath or strength to argue with her, and I didn't even know if she was right or wrong. I hung my head, wanting nothing more than to collapse the rest of the way to the road surface, and only then did I become aware of the sound. It sounded something like calm thunder with pebbles in it, quickly growing louder, and Aesnil twisted her head around to look down the road toward the curve. That was the direction the sound was coming from, and she identified it long before I would have.

"Riders!" she gasped, paling under the flush our running had put in her cheeks. "We must hide or they will see us!"

I felt the same clutch at my heart that she undoubtedly did and tried to get to my feet again, but it was absolutely impossible, not even with Aesnil pulling at my arm. I shook my head even as I leaned on my left hand, the road pebbles cutting into my palm, trying to make Aesnil understand that more running was beyond me. She continued tugging at me for another minute, casting wild glances back at the curve, and then the first riders appeared around it, moving at a considerably faster pace than we had when coming up. Aesnil made a low sound of misery and let go of my arm, threw one last frantic glance at the riders, then ran for the shelter of the trees.

The *l'lendaa* coming up the road seemed surprised to see us, but surprise rarely keeps a Rimilian warrior from acting. While most of the seven or eight riders began slowing down, one of them leaned forward on his *seetar* and sent the beast flashing forward into the woods, clearly after Aesnil. I tried to put up a wall of repulsion in the mind of his *seetar*, hoping to make it shy away from the chase, but I couldn't even detect its mind, let alone influence it. It moved faster than anything that large had a right to move, and a brief moment later Aesnil's scream came, showing the chase was ended. By then the others had reached me and were dismounting, and I didn't have the heart even to look at them.

"It is a *wenda*," came a startled male voice, a voice I had never heard before. "What does a *wenda* do here, all alone and unprotected?"

"Two *wendaa*," said a second voice, and I could hear the approach of another set of *seetar* hooves. "Never has a *l'lenda* grown hair the length of that second one."

"Two *wendaa*, dressed like members of the *Chama*'s guard," said the first. "Where might they have come from, and where might they be going?"

"It seems clear their destination was the *Chama*'s palace," the second one answered. "For what other reason would they dress themselves so?"

The man looking at me so intently was as blond and blue-eyed as all Rimilians were, but he was also a total stranger. He wore a plain brown *haddin* and swordbelt just as the others did, but they were all strangers. It took me a short while to understand that we were caught but not caught, and by then the last rider had arrived and had put. She looked furious and afraid, but her eyes darted from one face to the next, her slight confusion showing that the men were strangers to her as well. The man holding my face looked up at Aesnil with the same sort of inspection he had given me, then he shifted his attention to the last man who was then dismounting.

"This one is four-banded," he said, indicating me with a short movement of his head. "What of the little bird who attempted flight?"

"She is five-banded," answered the other with a grin, looking down at Aesnil. "Had she not been, I might not have returned so soon."

All the men laughed at that, causing Aesnil to flinch and back a step, and the one before me snorted.

"You show fear at a mere jest, girl," he said, the sternness in his tone capturing Aesnil's attention immediately. "Were we the sort to do other than jest upon the matter, you would suffer far more than slight discomfort. What do you do on this road unprotected, with your sister so near to collapse that she was unable to follow you? Do you seek your deaths?"

"What we do here is our own concern," Aesnil answered, her chin high despite the obvious quiver in her voice. "By what right do you detain us?"

"Right?" the man exploded, rising to his full height to look down at the faintly trembling girl in front of him. "There is no question of right here, only a question of responsibility! It is the responsibility of any man to assure the safety of *wendaa*, whether they be his own or another's! Were my *wenda* to be found wandering this road, for whatever reason, I would most certainly wish her to be returned to me, so that I might strap her soundly for placing herself in jeopardy rather than speaking to me of her unhappiness. We will do the same for the *l'lendaa* to whom the two of you belong, for we cannot leave you here. Tell us their names and where they may be found."

"Why must you refuse to understand that we have no wish for your protection and assistance?" Aesnil demanded, trembling harder. "Leave us as you found us, and no others need know!"

"We would know," the man returned in a remorseless tone, continuing to stare down at her. "From where do you come?"

Aesnil turned away from him and raised her chin high, giving him the only answer she could. When he looked at me I simply dropped my head, not about to give up after what we'd gone through. We might end up right back where we'd started, but not through anything *we'd* done. I heard a hiss of exasperation escape from the man, his annoyance so strong I actually felt a shadow of it, and then the first man stepped closer to him.

"There can be but one place they come from, *denday*," he said, his voice tinged with the same annoyance. "As the bridge spanning the pass downed in the storm, they must surely have come from Gerleth."

"Indeed," answered the one who led them, satisfaction showing in his voice at the way Aesnil had started in upset at the mention of Gerleth. The name meant something to me as well, but I couldn't quite remember what. "As we now ride home to Gerleth, it will be a simple matter to take them with us. Once there, their *l'lendaa* should not be difficult to discover."

"I, myself, will be curious to see the one to whom *she* belongs," said the first man, pointing to me. "A *wenda* such as that, dark-haired and green-eyed, and no more than four-banded? Perhaps he will accept an offer for her."

"Perhaps he will," allowed the second man, also looking down at me. "Yet surely not before he punishes her for her foolishness. Let us continue on now, for the day grows no longer."

The one identified as their leader turned back to his *seetar*, leaving Aesnil to the rider who had caught her and me to the *l'lenda* who was anxious to meet my owner. Aesnil kicked and fought as she was lifted to the *l'lenda*'s saddle, but all I could do was think about it. The broad, well-muscled *l'lenda* lifted me from the road with no effort at all, laughed softly as I moved feebly in protest, then boosted me up to his saddle.

"Were you not so fatigued, I believe you would prove yourself to be even more spirited than that other," he murmured as he quickly mounted behind me. "I will be sure to speak with him to whom you belong, for spirit holds a great attraction for me."

He put his arm around my waist as we began moving up the road again, and I thought about where we could be going to keep from thinking about what attracted the men of that world. Everything seemed to attract them, as long as the everything was female and still breathing. Aesnil and I were a couple of wrecks, dirty, wrinkled, unkempt, sweaty and exhausted, but that didn't seem to matter to the Rimilian male libido. We were female and alive, and therefore attractive.

I was so tired, I stared at the suddenly appearing branch road with surprise, wondering how I could have missed it on the way up. I didn't recognize it until we had turned off onto it, and Aesnil had tried slipping out of the grip of the man holding her. The branch road led downward and widened, and only when the direction had finally come through to me did I remember the road Aesnil had identified as leading to the lands of enemies of hers. It was the second branch road we had passed on the way up, and between the downgrade plunge we had taken on *seetar*back and the wild, thoughtless rout we had indulged in after encountering the *virenjj*, I hadn't known we'd passed it a second time. The *l'lenda* holding me tightened his grip, pulling me against his chest, but I still lacked the strength to do more than stir. Enemies of Aesnil would be enemies of mine, and that wasn't the best of times to be taken to them. I'd need hours of sleep before I had my strength back, and I could only pray that I would get it before the first encounter.

The road ran down and around the mountainside away from the direction in which we'd been going, and we rode on for a short while with no one speaking and nothing untoward happening. I fell into a light sleep against the chest of my *l'lenda*, something that pleased him so much I could feel the faint tendrils of the emotion in his mind. One minute we were moving sedately along in the late afternoon heat, me nodding, and then we were pulling up short to keep from running into a large group of men coming the other way around a curve at a much faster pace. The second group also slowed immediately, and the leader of our group made a sound of recognition.

"Well met!" he called, urging his *seetar* ahead to the van of the second group. "It was my intention to stop at the palace, and now I need not take the time. Ferran, as commander of the palace guard, you are aware of much that occurs in our towns. Has there been word spread about concerning the disappearance of two *wendaa*, one four-banded and the other five-banded? We encountered these two on the road above, alone and unprotected.''

"Missing *wendaa*?" the man addressed as Ferran frowned, looking toward Aesnil and me. "No, Hiddar, I have heard of no such thing, nor do I know of a man in our towns who possesses a *wenda* such as that. Her dark hair and green eyes would have been spoken of by every man who saw her. You must excuse us now, for we ride with purpose and in haste.''

"Hold," came another voice from the middle of the second group, stopping the man Hiddar as he was about to gesture his men out of the way. "What is this of a dark-haired, green-eyed *wenda*?"

The voice that had spoken had somehow sounded familiar, but the *denday* Hiddar spoke again before I could place it.

"We have found a dark-haired *wenda* on the road above, accompanied by a *wenda* less distinctive yet none the less striking," Hiddar answered, craning his neck around to see into the mass of men. "Do you know of these two? Who speaks?"

"I speak," said the ticklingly familiar voice, and the men began moving aside to let him through. "I am Dallan, *drin* of Gerleth, and I do indeed know of those two. The dark-haired one is she whom I intend banding, and other is my dearly beloved cousin.''

I could see him clearly then, his eyes directly on me, but I still couldn't believe what I was seeing. In front of me was Daldrin, my servant-slave from Aesnil's palace, now called Dallan, Prince of Gerleth!

6

I had been awake for some time, but I hadn't been able to get out of the wide, comfortable pile of bed furs. After a good long night of restful, peaceful sleep I was no longer tired or hurting much, but I still hadn't been able to get up. The reason for my laziness was a thin silver collar and chain, one end of which was let into the smooth stone wall above my bed, the other end of which was around my throat. I'd pulled at the stupid thing, trying to force it open, but I'd seemed to have run out of luck. I was chained right where I was wanted, and there wasn't much chance of getting loose.

I moved in annoyance to the accompaniment of chain tinkling, looking around the room again. It was a wide, bright room, but the combination of stateliness and barbarism made it incongruously unreal. The walls and ceiling were of a beautiful, polished marble, the tall, ribbed windows to the right gracefully matching their dignified presence. What didn't match quite as well were the multicolored silks hanging on those walls and around those windows, the thick fur carpeting dyed a bright red, the piles of multicolored cushions, the small, carved-wood tables. The imposed decor spoke of the sort of people who had imposed it, the sort of people who imposed their will on everything they touched.

I turned onto my stomach in the bed, feeling the soft, golden brown fur against my bare body, angrily knocking aside the silver chain. I might have been exhausted the night before, but I had no trouble remembering what had happened once we'd run into Daldrin—or Dallan, as his name really was. Aesnil and I had been handed over to the *drin* and his guardsmen without a murmur, no more than disappointment coming from the *l'lenda* who had been holding me, in reaction. The Prince himself had condescended to take me on his own *seetar*, and the men who had found us laughed when I'd tried hitting him in the face with my fists, then had ridden away. Aesnil had been silent and woodenly numb when she'd been given to the man Ferran to ride with, but she'd continued to hold her head high with a martyred look, like someone awaiting inescapable execution. Dallan, holding onto my wrists, had stared at her until the men who had found us were gone from sight and hearing, and then he had grinned.

"Greetings, Cousin," he'd said, his amusement dry. "I'd had no idea you meant visiting here, else I would have arranged a proper greeting. Your loveliness and graciousness warms us as always."

Aesnil had gone pale at the first sight of him, and her color still hadn't come back. She'd stared into thin air while he'd been talking to her, and didn't move or change expression when he'd done.

"I hear no matching words of greeting from you, Cousin," Dallan had pressed, his tone still mild. "Such surliness is not to be understood—save that discomfort may be at the root of it. Of course! Excuse me, Cousin, for not having seen it and seen to it the sooner. Ferran, my cousin fairly swoons in this oppressive heat. Remove that cloth covering her legs, and allow her a breath of air.''

"No!" Aesnil had shrieked, losing her silence and pallor together, but yelling and struggling hadn't helped her. Despite her screams and very evident embarrassment, her trousers were pulled off and tossed away. The shirt she wore came down to the middle of her thighs, but its presence hadn't been the comfort it should have been. Her legs were long and lovely, and the laughter of the men all around us seemed to acknowledge that fact, making her blush even more deeply. Ferran had set her astride his saddle again and held her before him, and Dallan had chuckled when she'd leaned forward away from the man with a gasp.

"Much better," he'd nodded, not missing the way she was then avoiding everyone's eyes, rather than ignoring them, and then he'd looked down at me. "What has befallen you, *wenda*?" he'd asked, a frown replacing his amusement. "There has been so little of struggle and words from you, that I might have mistaken you for another. Are you ill?"

"I am no more than weary," I'd told him, moving my wrists in his hand as I'd looked up into his eyes. "Weariness passes much sooner than illness, therefore you would be wise to release us immediately. To wait till my weariness has passed would be foolishness."

"Perhaps." He'd nodded, pursing his lips to hide his faint grin. "And then again, perhaps not. In any event, we shall surely see. At the moment, we return to my home."

They'd all turned their *seetarr* around then, but I'd missed the grand home-coming. Once we'd started moving I'd been attacked by waves of sleepiness, driving in at me from all directions. I'd tried resisting them but Dallan had been holding me to his chest, trying to make me as comfortable as possible. Unfortunately for me he'd succeeded, and the last thing I remembered seeing was a deeply embarrassed Aesnil, trying to keep her nearly bare bottom away from the grinning man who held her.

I turned to my right side in the bed furs, this time ignoring the chain, sending my mind out again as far as I could reach. I'd searched for Aesnil's mind trace right after I'd awakened, but it hadn't seemed to be anywhere in range. There were plenty of other mind traces out there, male and female alike, but all of them were from strangers. I gave it up in disgust, wondering if she was in the same place I was, wondering what was happening to her, then I began wondering what would happen to me.

Dallan and I hadn't parted enemies, but we hadn't exactly been friends either. I knew he wanted me, but he also had certain things to get even for; maybe if he decided he wanted me badly enough he'd forget about getting even, and I'd have a chance to work on him.

Five minutes later, all the worrying and planning I'd been doing was abruptly terminated by the opening of the door in a wall. If I'd been paying attention I would have known Dallan was close by, and his abrupt entrance wouldn't have surprised me. I grabbed the fur covering me and pulled it up to my chin, and he chuckled as he closed the door behind him and came closer to put down the tray he was carrying onto a small table near the bed furs. I still wasn't used to seeing him wearing the dark red *haddin* of a free man, and the sword hanging at his side was equally disconcerting.

"I am pleased to see that you have recovered from your weariness," he said, grinning as he removed his swordbelt and put it aside. "When I placed you in those furs last darkness, you made no effort to hide your loveliness."

"I was not awake!" I snapped, feeling the heat move into my cheeks. I felt like an idiot for blushing, but I couldn't seem to help it. When the men of that world looked at a woman, there was nothing of the casual glance about it.

"I am aware of that." He nodded, stopping at the side of the bed furs to look down at me. "Had you not been so soundly asleep—and so clearly in need of that sleep—you would not have found yourself alone in the furs."

"You have not the right to touch me," I said, feeling myself move back from that unwavering blue stare. "We aided each other when we both had need of aid, yet that need is no longer with us. Unchain me and return my clothing, and allow me to be on my way."

"Your way has led you here, and will not lead from this place again," he said, his mind warm as he spoke the words. "It was somehow clear to me from the first that your *l'lenda* would be unable to hold you, yet I shall find no similar difficulty. When you are banded as mine, *wenda*, you will not run from me."

"And is this the manner in which you mean to hold me?" I demanded, raising a section of the chain to shake it at him. "I am not a slave to be bound so, and will take great pleasure in proving the fact to you!"

I began reaching toward him with my mind, angry enough to do to him what I'd done to those *virenjj*, but he must have been expecting the move. He suddenly came up with a blood-curdling scream that sounded like, "Hai-yah!" startling me out of my skin, at the same time diving at me. When his arms closed around me I did some screaming myself, not to mention kicking and struggling, but that didn't stop him from pulling the covering fur away. I don't know what I expected him to do then, hurt me, possibly, but controlling me was more what he had in mind. As soon as he touched me I should have known what he was after; unfortunately for the sake of thinking, I was too busy gasping and trying to get loose.

"Ah, I see you remember my touch, *wenda*," he said, holding me down with his body as his hand worked between my thighs. "I, too, recall certain things, and therefore have no need of chains with which to hold you. Force me from you, *wenda*, cause me to lose my desire for you as you once did."

His tone was mocking then, knowing as he did that he had already rattled me out of the control I needed for projection. His body was hard and warm against mine, his mind growling low in pleasure, his free hand coiling in my hair. I tried to ignore what he was doing to me and pull together the necessary calm the control required, but it was patently impossible. My body had been trained to respond immediately to those Rimilian beasts, and I hadn't been given the time to forget that training. My hands closed on biceps like metal as I shuddered and closed my eyes, and Dallan laughed low, then pulled my head back by the hair so that his lips could reach my throat.

"You cannot force me from you for I know the means to control you," he murmured, ignoring the way my fingernails dug into his arms. "Also, I believe I know another thing. Why do you travel in company with the *Chama* Aesnil? She is able to give you no assistance, no more than unnecessary hindrance and distraction. For what reason did you continue all this way with her?"

"Please, no more!" I whispered, unable to control my writhing. "Daldrin, please, I beg you!"

"I am Dallen," he answered with vast amusement, "a man who knows full well your recent intentions toward him. You melt to my touch, *wenda*, yet shall you continue in dire straits for a time, as a beginning to your punishment. You may now answer my question."

"I . . . I merely followed Aesnil," I gasped, understanding nothing of what he wanted, only what he was doing to me. "She is fam-familiar with this area as I am not. I could not have regained my freedom without her."

"Mere excuses," he snorted, staring down at me. "Your

having secured mounts and food for the both of you would surely have repaid whatever debt to her you stood in. Yes, I have spoken both with her and with the *denday* who found you and she. I am told that Aesnil would surely have escaped into the forest, had she not spent so long a time attempting to take you with her. My cousin was more difficult to extract information from, yet a strapping and the promise of another succeeded in loosening her tongue. She had refused to leave you for you had twice given her her life back, when it was all but lost. I believe there is a bond between the two of you, one you are incapable of ignoring even should my cousin fail to honor it. Is this not so?''

"Yes, yes!" I wept, trying to toss my head back and forth despite the unmoving fist in my hair. Of course I knew Aesnil would still be free if she hadn't wasted time trying to take me with her. Her actions might have been caused by fear on her part of trying to reach Vediaster alone—or she might have begun feeling something like real concern for me. If I hadn't been all used up I would have known which it was—and I couldn't forget about it until I found out one way or the other for sure.

"And so I thought," he breathed, satisfaction flaring in his mind. "In that event, I am able to use a lesson learned from my beloved cousin herself. I will release you from the chain and allow you to return to yourself—yet does Aesnil's well being depend upon your refraining from the use of your powers. Should you use them and I am affected, others, watching, will know of it and see to Aesnil. Do you understand the words I speak?''

"Yes, I understand!" I sobbed, but not only from what he was doing to me. He had trapped me, damn him, trapped me!

"Excellent," he chuckled, pulling my head back by the hair again. "Now the following days will be filled with pleasure rather than strife." He lowered his lips to mine and kissed me hard, opened the collar around my throat and tossed it away, then finally let me go. It was as though I'd been holding a live electrical wire, and had only just managed to release it: the immediate shock was gone, but my nervous system was still remembering the current that had been forced through it. I lay slumped on the furs, unable to move, my mind still whirling as fast as my blood.

It took a few minutes before I was able to force myself up on one elbow, and by that time Daldrin—Dallan—had moved the tray of food closer to the bed and was stretched out along the edge of the furs, nibbling some dried fruit and moving his eyes over me. Just because he was controlling what he felt from having touched me didn't mean he wasn't feeling it, and the jarring of his emotions began upsetting me all over again. I reached a slow hand over toward the fur he'd thrown aside earlier, but he didn't miss the movement.

"No," he said, putting no special emphasis into the word. "You have not my permission to cover your loveliness again."

"What do you intend doing with me?" I demanded, more than annoyed that he'd treat me that way. "Are you merely going to sit there and stare at me from this day on?"

"You could not have forgotten me this soon, *wenda*," he grinned, reaching a hand out to run one finger over my calf. "Best you remember that the foul mood your need instills in you may bring punishment rather than an easing of that need. Guard your words carefully when you speak to me, else I shall recall them when the time has come to see to previous matters which stand between us. I shall not warn you again."

The amusement didn't leave his face, but his eyes and mind had hardened in a way that was clearer than any threat. I still didn't like the way he was treating me, but I swallowed down what I was feeling and tried again.

"I would know what you mean to do with me," I said, wishing I didn't have to ignore the urge to pull my leg out of his reach. "Am I now your prisoner—as Aesnil is?"

"My cousin is not my prisoner." He laughed, taking another mouthful of dried fruit. "She has been made a slave in this house, as I was in hers. I believe the experience will do much for her, teaching her the fate she bestowed so unthinkingly upon others. As for you, my little bird, you will be taught obedience."

My expression must surely have told him what I thought about that, as he laughed aloud when he saw it.

"No, it will not be nearly as difficult a task as you think to make it," he said, sitting up and twisting around to put his feet on the floor. "We will begin with seeing to your feeding, go on to having you bathed, and then your lessons will begin. Come here."

I hesitated over moving closer to him, but I really had very little choice in the matter. Aesnil *had* wasted her opportunity to get clear of the riders who were about to find us, and I couldn't very well thank her by deserting her in return. If there was a loophole in Dallan's trap, I'd have to wait there until I found it. Slowly, with a reluctance the man didn't miss, I moved myself across the furs until I was right behind him, tending neither to the right nor the left. It seemed the safest place to be just then, but when he twisted first right and then left and still couldn't reach me easily, he experienced a flash of annoyance that ended my safety. He twisted around once more, all the way to his right, hooked me with one unreasonably large and muscled arm, then pulled me over into his lap.

"I care little for the manner in which you obey even the simplest of commands," he growled, the annoyance still with him and trying to grow stronger. "Now, rather than see to your own feeding, you may put your arms about me."

He was getting too close to anger for me to hesitate even long enough to ask him *why* I was to put my arms about him, but once I had done it I no longer had to ask. He was broad and hard, tanned and strong, and in order to put my arms even part way around him I had to lean very close, my chest against his. Even before I'd left Central I couldn't have been that close to a man like Dallan without feeling something, and I'd been yanked out of the Centran culture and forcibly adjusted to a much lustier one. His skin was firm and warm under my hands, the hair on his chest cushioned and caressed my breasts, and I was suddenly—strongly—reminded of what he had just been doing to me.

"You may not draw back again." he said, obviously reading the intention in my thoughts as he looked down at me. "Though your discomfort is as keen as I had hoped it would be, *I* find the posture most pleasant. You will take your food in silence, and consider what lack of proper obedience has brought you."

He reached past my shoulder for a bowl on the tray, brought it back, then began feeding me. Though I really did need food at that point, I barely noticed that the dish was that thick cereal grain mixed with dried and sweetened fruit. Dallan was feeling a good deal of pleasure from being held by me, and even his muted, controlled emotions were helping to make me dizzy and more than uncomfortable. My bottom rested on his bare thighs, my arms and hands touched his sides and back, his arm movements caused his chest to rub against mine; before very many minutes had passed, I was reduced to squirming. Dallan the free man chuckled heartily at that, and did nothing about it but continued to feed me.

By the time the food was all down my throat, I was well on the way to being intimidated. Dallan continued to feel pleasure from the way our bodies touched, but despite the growing frustration and desperation I could feel within *me*, his emotions and bodily urgings remained easily under his control. In spite of the fact that Rimilian men rarely denied themselves anything, they seemed to be capable of the most cold-blooded self-denial I had ever seen—when it suited them. For some reason it suited Dallan to refrain from touching me any further, most likely because of the punishment he had spoken of. I was being punished for not obeying him to his satisfaction, and in a way I had not expected. The worst part of it was that I didn't know how long he would leave me like that, and the uncertainty was making my mind and body more anxious to obey him no matter what my intellect thought about it.

Once my feeding was over, I was made to stand up so that Dallan might do the same. I was beyond knowing what to expect next, so his taking my arm and starting for the door came as a surprise. We were nearly there before I gasped and tried to pull back, wasting the time and effort, but happily I'd been mistaken regarding his intention. He wasn't dragging me naked into a public corridor as I'd thought when I saw the door, but into the next room of what later proved to be a suite of rooms. The next room was a bathing chamber, more pleasant than Aesnil's in that it had windows, and once we were through the doorway, my captor stopped to look down at me.

"These serving *wendaa* will see that you are properly bathed," he said, indicating the three women in the room. "Obey them without complaint, for they have already been made aware of my wishes. I will await you within the inner chamber."

He gave my bottom a smack to send me forward another step or two, then turned and went back into the room we'd come out of, closing the door behind him. I looked again at the three women waiting for me, seeing that they'd risen from the nest of cushions they'd been sitting among. None of them was the size of the men of that world, but all three of them were considerably larger than I, broad, solid women who were shapely enough, but thick rather than slender. They wore *imadd* and *caldinn*, the long-sleeved blouses and ankle-length skirts that most Rimilian woman wore, but rather than being brightly colored, theirs were solid white. They all had their long blond hair twisted close and tied back short, and even as I watched they untied the leather ties of their sleeves and pushed the slit sleeves back behind them, then tied one leather tie of each sleeve together at the back of their waists. Their arms were then both bare and free, and the sleeves were completely out of the way. It was fairly clear the women were not slaves, but they were looking at me as though I might be. I could feel my body stiffening in resentment at their appraisal, but that only amused them. In their own minds, they knew they were comfortably dressed and I wasn't.

"Come, *weerees*, and let us see to you," one of the three said, beginning to lead the other two toward me. "The *drin*

Dallan would have you clean and sweet-smelling for his pleasure, and so shall he have you. Has he used you as yet?"

"What business is that of yours?" I snapped, outraged by her question and deeply stung by the name she'd called me. *Weerees* meant adorable little girl or cuddly toy, and was a pet name for a child—or an insult for a grown woman. I *felt* insulted, but there was nothing I could do about it.

"I do not ask for my own amusement, *weerees*," the woman answered, stopping before me to look down into my eyes with an insolent twinkle in hers. "Should it be that he has not yet used you, we will take care not to tread too heavily upon your . . . sensibilities."

The other two joined the first one in laughter, all three of them getting a great deal of amusement out of embarrassing me; the one thing I didn't understand was why they were doing it. They didn't hate me, they didn't even really dislike me; they just felt terribly superior for some reason I couldn't even begin to guess at. I looked up at the three plainly pretty faces, knowing they were partially laughing at the blush on my cheeks, and tried to hold my head up higher.

"What sensibilities I had have long since been trodden upon," I told them, my voice as cold as I could make it. "Should you feel the need to add your own touches to the general effort, I am unable to deny you. I shall merely continue in my refusal to be cowed."

I thought my speech sounded rather brave and noble, but the burst of renewed laughter from the women showed it didn't hit them the same way. Their amusement was gleeful and anticipatory yet totally without malice, and I just didn't *understand* it! My hands curled into fists as I stamped my foot, but I didn't get a chance to demand that they explain what they were laughing at. The woman in front of me gestured, and the other two put their hands on my arms.

"I am pleased to hear that you will not be cowed." The woman chuckled, looking me over in a very insolent way. "In that event, we need not be overly cautious in our handling of you. Bring her to the bath."

She turned and began leading the way across the room then, the other two pulling me along between them. This room was nearly as large as the first, with silk hung marble walls and clean marble ceiling, but only half the floor was covered with fur carpeting. The covered half was near the windows, and contained the nest of multicolored cushions the three women had been sitting among. The other half of the floor was bare marble, and held the bathing pool the women were taking me toward. The pool itself was two-sectioned and oval in shape, the larger part of the oval suitable for paddling around in, the narrower left-hand end shallow enough for soaking and washing. The two women holding me followed the third to the shallow end, ignoring the way I tried to struggle loose, doing no more than tightening their grips automatically. Their minds dismissed my displeasure as though I were a small child, unimportant and therefore ignorable. Truthfully I felt like a small child among those three, especially when I was peremptorily manhandled over the edge of the pool and into the water.

"We shall see to it that you shine for the *drin, weerees*," the first woman said, watching as I was plunked down into a sitting position amidst a large splash. "It is the least we may do for one so backward as to intend defying a *l'lenda*. When he has done with you, you may look back upon our kindness with keen memory and longing, for he, himself, will find little kindness for you."

She nodded to the other two, then got to her knees beside the pool to add her share of help. I kicked and struggled as I was dunked entirely under the water, came up spluttering and shaking water out of my eyes, then tried yelling when they began to soap me. The first woman used two hands, the others one each, and all my screaming and struggling didn't stop them from spreading the slick, perfumy liquid soap all over me. Somehow the humiliation of that bath was worse than what I'd felt when bathed by the male *bedinn* of the Hamarda, the male slaves of the desert tribe I'd been held by. The slaves had been rough and uncaring, but those women . . . ! It was as though I were a small child placed in their care, one whose tantrums weren't to be noticed or given in to. Their amusement continued as long as the bath did, but it didn't interfere with the efficiency of their efforts.

After being soaped three times and dunked four, then having my hair thoroughly washed, I was finally let out of the pool. I'd tried demanding that they let me take my own bath, but was told that that wasn't part of their instructions. I'd been placed in their care, and they'd be doing whatever was necessary. The topic of necessary seemed to include drying me thoroughly with large cloths and then rubbing thick lotions into my skin, lotions which seemed downright erotic in their allure. I was put on a dry cloth on the marble for the lotion spreading, and was finally told by the first woman that if I didn't stop yelling and trying to spill the lotion, I'd be given a good strapping before they went any further. I was shocked at the promise, even more shocked that the woman wasn't joking or merely threatening, but I just couldn't stand it. After what Dallan had—or rather hadn't—done to me, I couldn't bear being touched all over like that. When I began crying I was comforted in a firm, stern way, then the rest of the lotion went on.

By the time my hair had been thoroughly dried and neatly combed, my skin had absorbed the thick yellow lotion, all excess having been earlier patted away. I stood on the cloth I'd been ordered to when they'd first begun on my hair, my head down, my mind filled with misery and deep depression. I was being prepared for show again, being prettied up at the orders of and for the benefit of a man of Rimilia again. What made them think they were so damned special that they had the right to do that to me? I was a Prime of the Centran Amalgamation, an empath whose abilities were sought after by everyone who knew of them; why wasn't *I* the one with special privileges?

"*Weerees*, I see a foolish look upon your face," the first woman said, bringing me back to that hateful room. She was standing right in front of me and looking down at me, her voice carrying as much of a warning note as her narrowed eyes and annoyance-tinged mind. "It cannot be that you have not as yet learned the lesson we attempted to teach."

"Your words hold no meaning for me," I answered, my tone sullen despite everything I could do. "The sole lesson I have learned here is one already known: I would be best off far from this place."

"Perhaps." She nodded, her mind disagreeing with the voiced thought. "You, however, are *not* far from this place, therefore would you be wise to heed the teachings of another lesson. The *drin* Dallan may do with you as he pleases, therefore is it to your benefit to see that it pleases him to do other than punish you. He need not have merely had you bathed."

"His generosity overwhelms me," I answered, looking away from her toward the windows. The day was beautiful and bright and sparkling, with only a few clouds marring the loveliness.

"You are indeed a fool for failing to understand that he is no other thing than generous," the woman said, angry now. "Ever has he been more generous even than his brother, the *drin* Seddan! A woman must needs be bereft of her senses to spurn his interest and incur his wrath! Have you no concept of how many yearn to be his?"

"The number is surely beyond counting," I said with a small shrug, still looking out the window. "I, however, preferred him when he was no more than a loyal servant-slave. He was then so much more—amenable.''

"No slave is amenable," she snorted, totally out of patience. "A slave is obedient, a state awaiting a stubborn *weerees* of a *wenda*, who thinks to pit herself against a man. You will learn better, and be the better for it. Let us place her within that, and have done with it.''

Her last comment was for the other women, but it was enough to take my attention from the windows to see what she was talking about. One of the other two had just rejoined our jolly group, and was carrying a fold of sheer pink silk in her hand. It was little more than a scrap of material, short and narrow and thin, far too small to be a gown or even an *imad* or *caldin*. The first woman saw me looking at the material, and immediately radiated amusement and self-justification.

"That garment is an excellent example of the generosity of the *drin*,'' she informed me, flicking a finger toward the silk. "Had you shown yourself sufficiently repentent and eager to please the *drin*, you would not have been required to wear such a thing. For a free woman to wear the garment of a slave is a great shaming and punishment.''

I stared as the woman holding the bit of silk unfolded it and held it up, her laughter and ridicule matching that of the others, my head shaking in negation even as the other two closed with me. It seemed impossible for anyone to wear such a skimpy little thing, but once they had forced me into it I found it was more than possible. The silk was mostly skirt, tied with two thin strands at my left hip, leaving all of the outer portion of my left side and thigh bare. As if that weren't bad enough, what there was of the skirt barely reached the tops of my thighs, showing it was designed for titillation rather than coverage. From the center of the skirt's waist flowed two narrow streamers of silk, two halves of an oval, which rose to be fastened behind my neck, only incidently—and scantily—covering the very centers of my breasts. The very sheer silk did nothing to conceal me, in point of fact made me feel more naked that I had before it was put on. I fought the grips of the women, trying to free my arms so that I might tear the silk off again, but it was no use. They were stronger than I, and fully as determined.

"You had best not struggle so," the first woman chuckled, looking me over with her hands on her hips. "You have more height than the slave meant to wear that, which will undoubtedly please the *drin* greatly. Should you continue to move yourself about so, he will be more than pleased. He is after all, a *l'lenda* and a man. Bring her.''

Again her last words were for the other two woman, who smoothed my hair and straightened the silk even as they pulled me toward the door to the next room. The first woman led the way through, knowing we followed, continuing on until she reached the middle of the room. When she stopped about ten feet in front of Dallan, who sat among the cushions on the carpet fur, I expected her to speak. Instead she waited until I'd been brought directly behind her, then simply stepped aside.

I felt the man's eyes and mind as though they were physical blows, watching with numbed attention as he slowly sat straight among the cushions. His thoughts were a roiling growl of insatiable desire, the heat in his blue eyes arising from open, leaping flames. I could feel myself flinching from the roar that rolled at me from his mind, trembling but rooted to the spot. He got smoothly to his feet, cat-graceful despite the size of him, and walked toward me, the smile on his face barely noticeable below the look in his eyes. I swallowed and tried to control the trembling that had taken me, nearly crushed beneath the weight of his mind, but still couldn't keep from cringing when he stopped right in front of me and put a hand out to touch my face. I'd gone through too much with the men of that world to trust one of them, and some of the soaring pleasure in Dallan's mind faded and died.

''*Wenda*, you are lovelier than I have ever seen you,'' he said, slowly withdrawing his hand. ''Do you believe me capable of bringing harm to such loveliness, that you fear me so? Why do you cower away from the mere touch of my hand?''

''I . . . do not cower,'' I said, disgusted with the way my voice shook, looking down to avoid meeting his eyes. ''I do not fear you, therefore may you do as you will.''

Again I could feel his eyes on me, and when his hand suddenly touched my arm I jumped, automatically shrinking back toward the women who had come into the room with me. Consider my shock when I discovered they were gone, their exit so quiet and unobtrusive that I hadn't noticed it through the turmoil in my mind and the growling in Dallan's. I was all alone again and terribly vulnerable, and when a whimper escaped my throat, Dallan's arms were immediately around me.

''Terril, what ails you?'' he demanded, holding me close to the warmth and strength of his chest. ''That you lie is clear to any with eyes, for you do indeed fear me. What has brought this sudden fear to you, a thing you felt nothing of when last I saw you?''

"It . . . is not you I fear," I answered raggedly, clinging to his warmth with pathetic desperation. "It is this world that I fear, a world where I am nothing, and the men of this world, to whom I am nothing. It is they whom I fear, not you.''

"Ah," he said, his amusement strong enough to be felt and heard. "Then I am not to be feared for I am not a man of this world. Is it that you consider me from another world, or simply not a man?''

"You seek to ensnare me with words," I protested, stirring uncomfortably in his arms, relieved to know he wasn't feeling insulted. "Were you not a man, I would scarcely feel as I do when held by you. You asked the reason for my fear, and I attempted to speak of it. As you feel the need to ridicule me, I shall not speak of it again.''

"*Wenda*, you are overly sensitive." He laughed, patting my bottom through the sheer silk covering it. "I do not ridicule you, for what is foolishness to one is true fear to another. I do, however, doubt the fullness of your words rather than their content. It is neither this world nor its *l'lendaa* which you fear, and I would know the full truth of your feelings. What has been done to you that you now find yourself filled with fear?''

"Naught has been done that has not been done before," I answered, suddenly feeling the need to try pushing out of his arms. "Release me now, for I would rid myself of this terrible garment as soon as possible.''

"I think not," he said, holding me against him without effort, his eyes still on me. "The garment pleases me, and will please me for some time to come. Speak to me of what has been done to you.''

I looked up at him, seeing the determination in his eyes as well as feeling it in his mind. I'd been told that I'd wear the silk until he had the answer he wanted, but my feelings weren't something I could talk about in exchange for a simple favor.

"Then I shall ignore the garment," I shrugged, trying to make him believe my disinterest without nudging him with my mind. "I am sure to find it less terrible the longer it is upon me.''

"That remains to be seen," he said, his amusement obvious. "You may attempt to ignore the garment if you wish, yet I shall not.''

His arms were suddenly gone from around me, and then I was being drawn closer to the pile of cushions by one arm, to be left about three feet from them while Dallan went to seat himself among them. He kept his eyes on me the entire time, and once he was leaning down onto one elbow, he grinned up at me.

"I find the sight of your loveliness enhanced by that silk rather stimulating," he said, his mind putting out an increase of the growling hum that had not at any time subsided completely. "Turn about so that I may see all of you."

I stood there in front of him, feeling his eyes touch me all over, finding it impossible not to know how I looked to him. The silk which did no more than color my flesh teased his senses, luring his mind to the memory of the sensual, perfumed softness of my skin, calling to him to put his hands on me again—and then go on from there. I knew all that as well as I knew my own feelings, and I couldn't turn around in front of him, exciting him even further—I couldn't!

"Turn about, *wenda*," he repeated, his voice still soft but beginning to harden with annoyance. "Or must I go for a strap?"

His words hit me with the shock of cold water, waking me up to the memory of where I was, what sort of man I stood before. He was Rimilian, just like all the others, no different, no better. Jerkily, with more than simple reluctance, I began to turn, moving woodenly until I was facing in his direction again. I tried to keep my eyes away from him, but suddenly he rose up in front of me, filling all the space in my view from much too close a distance.

"*Wenda*, what has been done to you?" he demanded, putting his hands on my arms to keep me from moving back away from him. "The humor in you has turned to dust and ashes, leaving little more than a hollow shell. I will hear what befell you since we parted, and I will hear it now!"

I didn't understand what his complaint was, but I also couldn't resist being pulled back to the cushions with him, to sit beside him and be held up against him. I discovered that my shield had closed tight around my mind, as though I'd be protected from him that way. I laughed briefly and bitterly at myself for being a fool, but didn't send the shield back to nothingness.

"You may begin from when you told your *l'lenda* what assistance you had been to him in his escape," Dallan said, holding me close as he began stroking my hair. When I didn't answer immediately, his hand paused in its stroking and he demanded, "You *did* speak to him of it? You did not foolishly allow him to continue believing you moved in Aesnil's cause?"

"He . . . learned of it without my speaking of it," I admitted, unable to resist leaning my cheek against Dallan's chest. "If he had not, I would not have told him. I wanted naught of gratitude for services rendered."

"And is this what you received?" he prompted gently, stroking my hair. "Gratitude for services rendered?"

"He was . . . pleased that I had not betrayed him," I said, closing my eyes. "Again he professed his love for me, in such a way that I nearly believed him, and then . . . and then your parting message was brought."

"At which he grew angry," Dallan murmured, a statement rather than a question. "Was any part of his anger given to you?"

"No," I answered, remembering how my mind had cringed away from that towering rage. "His anger was for you alone, that you had dared to do and say what you had. Afterward, he five-banded me."

"I see," he said, and that was all the comment he made. "How is it, then, that you are now four-banded? You could not have removed the fifth band yourself?"

"I had no need to," I said, my voice lower than it had been. "A . . . a thing happened between us, and then he came to the decision that I would be filled with greater hapiness as the belonging of someone other than he. It was a firm decision, for he took the fifth band and made offer among Cinnan's *dendayy*, seeking one who would band me. I was pleased at his decision, yet displeased with those he offered me to, therefore did I decide to flee from the palace with Aesnil and thereafter return to my own people. They will greet me warmly upon my return, accepting me as I am, once again giving me my place among them. I will not miss this terrible world nor its heartless *l'lendaa*, nor ever think of them again."

I believed that, I really did, but Dallan's arms tightened about me as though he thought I needed comforting. He was silent for a long moment, his lips to my hair, and then he sighed.

"Ah, *wenda*; are you able to find naught save pain in your life? For what reason would a man unband one such as you? What was this . . . thing between you and this man who calls himself *l'lenda*? In what manner did you anger him?"

"In the manner most natural to one such as I," I choked, pushing away from his chest so that I might look up at him. He had immediately assumed that the fault was mine, just as everyone on that world did, and there was no reason to disillusion him. "I attempted to control his mind, to make him bend to my will, to obey me in all things! He discovered my attempt and repulsed it, then beat me for daring to touch him! I was forbidden to touch any other with my mind, and when I disobeyed I was beaten again and yet again! He finds great joy in beating me, that *l'lenda*, yet now must find another to give him joy for I am no longer there. I am here, frightening and sickening another, who will soon take his own turn at beating me! How long will you feel safety in your efforts to guard against me, eh, *l'lenda*? How long before you, too, seek to give me to another?''

I tried to pull away from him then, to get away from the pity so clear in his eyes, but he still refused to let me go. I struggled for a minute or two, blessing the fact that my shield was closed, wishing I'd also kept my eyes closed. I'd never felt pitiful in my life—until I'd come to that world.

''*Wenda*, I am neither frightened nor sickened,'' he said as soon as he'd forced me to stop struggling. ''Nor, I think, was your *l'lenda* taken so. It is clear you feel *ahresta* due to his decision to unband you yet it is patently untrue that you are unwanted and kept only out of pity. That he punished you for touching him with your mind is to be expected, for I would do the same. I believe there is more to your upset than that which you have spoken of, and it is this which must be reached before your pain may be eased. Speak now of that which truly disturbs you.''

I dragged my head up to stare at him, not believing how cold-blooded he could be about the whole thing. His mind was calm and totally under his control, completely untouched by the maelstrom in mine.

''Why do you continually defend him?'' I demanded, ignoring the question he'd asked. ''Why must every being upon this world defend his doings with me?''

''I do not defend him.'' Dallan shrugged, reaching up to smooth the hair out of my eyes. ''I merely point out the truth of his actions, as any *l'lenda* is honor-bound to do. For what reason was the decision made to unband you?''

''I know not,'' I said, lowering my head again. ''He felt some portion of my upset, and was unable to bear it. To truly know the feelings of another is no pleasant thing, and yet—''

''And yet you had thought him strong enough to bear the burden,'' Dallan finished when I didn't. ''Earlier you said he spoke of your happiness. Can it be not *his* strength but yours which concerned him? Might his thoughts not be solely for you?''

''I care not for whom his thoughts are,'' I muttered, still looking down at my hands. ''That he speaks of my happiness does not mean it concerns him. Little concerns him save his own beliefs.''

"How is this?" Dallan asked, putting his hand under my chin to raise my face to him again. "What was done that gives you such a belief?" When I simply stared at him without answering, he briefly returned the stare then said, "Perhaps you feel so because of the punishment given you. Were you never taught that punishment is given for your benefit, not the benefit of others? That a *l'lenda* bothers to give you punishment is an indication of his concern for you."

I unhooked my chin from his hand and turned my face away, sick to death of their concept of concern. If that was the way they cared, I didn't want to be cared about ever again.

"I hear no protests, therefore must there be more to the matter," Dallan decided, his voice thoughtful as his mind poked and pried at the question. "You spoke of the joy your *l'lenda* finds in beating you, and also seemed strange when I spoke of strapping you. Even now I feel you stiffening between my hands. Can it be that he lost himself to anger when punishing you? Can it be that he gave you true pain rather than the sting of a lesson properly taught.?"

I could feel the stupid tears coming to my eyes, remembering how he had hurt me over a lie. It would have been bad enough if I'd been guilty, but all that over a lie! He hadn't believed me when I'd said I was innocent, he hadn't *wanted* to believe me. It would have made his code of behavior too complicated if he had to decide between truth and lie, so he hadn't bothered. He had just hurt me and walked away, unconcerned with what he had done because he knew he could always apologize later. It must have annoyed him when his apology wasn't accepted as it always had been in the past, it must have annoyed him like hell. A pity I wasn't there for him to beat again when the annoyance got to be too much. Dallan's finger came to my cheek to wipe at the wetness there, and then he had gathered me tightly to him, to cry if I had to. I did have to, but there was nothing left to cry over.

Dallan held me for a number of minutes in silence, but when he let me go it wasn't simply to let me sit beside him again. He rose to his feet, walked to where he had left his swordbelt, got something from it, then came back.

"It was my intention to wait until another time before seeing to this," he said, sitting back down next to me among the cushions. "I have, however, been given reason to change my mind. It disturbs me to see the pain you carry, lovely *wenda*, and perhaps this will remove a portion of it."

I watched without understanding as he reached to my right wrist and opened the band there, then went on to the other three.

When all four bands were off he gathered them together and put them aside, then reached behind him. Only when I saw the new set of gleaming bronze bands did I understand, and the enlightenment was no blessing.

"Dallan, you cannot band me," I protested, trying to inch back away from him. "You know I mean to return to my people, therefore is it foolishness to. . . ."

"To make the effort," he interrupted, nodding absently as he grabbed my ankle and pulled me easily back to him. "You mean to return to your people and have ever done as you meant, therefore is it foolishness to go counter to your wishes. There are few among your people who go counter to your wishes, are there not, *wenda*?"

He glanced up as he closed the new band around my ankle, then turned his attention to my second ankle. His mind was pleased but calm, unannoyed in spite of the way he'd spoken to me. If anything he was amused, probably over the fact that some men let their women run their own lives. I kicked at him with the leg that was already banded, found myself totally ignored, then put my arms behind me when he reached for one of my wrists.

"You are no different from any of the others!" I spat, twisting away as he reached for my arm. "You speak gallantly of easing my pain, then proceed to put me in your bands despite my unwillingness! How mighty and courageous are the *l'lendaa* of Rimilia, to stand themselves firm against the begging of their *wendaa*!"

"All men require courage and might when dealing with *wendaa*," he laughed, his light eyes sparkling with amusement. "As to begging, that is heard from one such as you. Do you wish to beg me to unband you, little bird?"

"Would you do so?" I pounced immediately, willing to consider humiliating myself if it meant being free.

"I would not," he laughed, capturing my nose with two fingers, then immediately grabbing my wrist when I tried to push his hand away. "My desire is for the warmth of a *wenda*, not the scrapings and mewlings of a slave. You may indeed soon find yourself begging, little bird, yet not for freedom."

I beat at him with my fists while he put the wrist bands on, but all he did was continue to ignore me. He had pushed me flat onto the fur carpeting among the cushions and had knelt across me, making sure that beating at him was all I could do. That silly scrap of silk I was wearing was twisted all about, but that made no difference at all; as well as it covered me, it might as well have been gone entirely. When the band had snapped closed around my second wrist he suddenly looked down into my face, the smile he wore and the growling hum in his mind forcing me still. I knew that sense of possession he radiated; I had cause to know it well. It made me swallow hard and try to shrink down and away, but he just laughed and stopped me by leaning lower.

"You will not fly from me, little bird," he said, grinning at the expression on my face. "I will complete the rite of five-banding, and then you will be mine."

"Rite?" I quavered, wondering why I always had to be such a coward with these men of Rimilia. "What rite do you speak of?"

"It does not surprise me that you know nothing of the rite." He smiled, putting his hands on the carpeting to either side of me and leaning even closer. "It is all one with the balance of what has been done. Suffice it to say that it pleases me to be first."

I didn't know what he was talking about, but didn't have the time to wonder about it. His lips came quickly to mine, soft but hungry, enticing rather than demanding, taunting and teasing and impossible to escape. Once, when I turned my face away from him, his lips came to my throat instead, drawing a moan from me despite everything I could do. He was using what he'd done to me earlier, ruthlessly and with full knowledge, bringing me to the writhing point without once touching me with his hands. I could have cried when I realized I *wanted* him to touch me with his hands, but more from desolate confusion than anything else. What had those men done to me that I was no longer mistress of my own body? Why did my will crumble and my blood run hot any time one of them was too near? I moaned again and put my hands on those wide, metal-thewed arms, trying to press myself up against him, but he refused to allow that. He continued doing nothing but kiss me until I rolled about in near-madness, dying for him, and then he leaned away.

"*Wenda*, I would make you fully mine," he said softly, holding up the fifth band. "With this band I swear to defend your life with mine, to share my victories and keep sadness from you, to deny with a sword all those who would take you from me. With this band take my heart, for they are both equally yours."

He reached down then and closed it around my throat, and only then did he take me in his arms. His kisses grew fierce and his hands touched me everywhere, and it was impossible to deny him anything he wanted. I kissed his face and bit at his earlobe even as he laughed and removed his *haddin*, and

then he put me beneath him, to enter me and take his due as
my owner. It took a long time to satisfy both of us, to quench
the flames that had risen so high, but even so I still remembered,
and afterward lay with my hand to the band on my throat
and wept.

7

Dallan, the monster, refused to allow me time to brood or dwell
on should-have-beens. I had been banded as his and would think
only of him, or at least that's what I was told. I wanted to lie still
and ask the unanswering air why Tammad had never gone through
the rite of five-banding the way Dallan had, but my new owner
had other ideas. I lay curled on my left side, facing away from
him, but suddenly found myself being pulled over onto my back
so the *l'lenda* above me might look at me more easily. Angrily I
struck at his face with both fists, expecting the useless gesture
to be ignored as usual, suddenly shocked when my blows landed
against his nose and in his right eye, sending him back with a
shout of surprised pain. I sat up quickly with both hands to my
mouth, horrified at what I had done, watching as he sat and
cradled his eye and nose in his hands, a disbelieving tinge to his
thoughts. When he finally looked over at me I was already
edging away across the carpet fur, about five feet from him. I
squeaked in alarm when he began crawling after me with dark
determination in his thoughts, but shifting to crawling myself
didn't do more than delay the inevitable. As fast as I crawled, he
crawled faster, finally getting close enough to put a big hand on
my ankle. I cried out when he caught me, wishing I'd gotten to
my feet and run instead of crawling like an infant, but I knew
why I hadn't. As big as he was on all fours he was still bigger
upright, and somehow I thought it would go harder for me if I
was caught with both of us erect. How true that was I'd never
know; it was hard enough on all fours.

Dallan wasn't anywhere near furiously angry, but that didn't
mean I had the nerve to struggle when he caught me. I shook my
head desperately when he pulled me back to him, wishing I could

say it had been an accident, wishing I could say it was his fault for not protecting himself. I was trying to think of something I *could* say, afraid to imagine what he would do to me, wasting time picturing those big fists crashing into my body or face. I call imagining being severely beaten that way a waste of time simply because with *l'lendaa* such as Dallan it was. There are worse things they can do to punish insolence, and Dallan chose one of them.

With very little effort I was draped over his knees, but I wasn't held down. I felt the ridiculously tiny silk skirt being lifted away, my bottom was patted, and then the first smack came. I jumped at the sting and writhed in humiliation, feeling so miserable I wanted to cry. Dallan knew there was no need to hold me down, that I didn't have the nerve to try getting away, but that wasn't the reason why I wasn't being restrained. It was part of my punishment to have to lie face down across his lap, with nothing holding me there, simply accepting the humiliation he gave. If he had really hurt me I could have found fury to brace myself with, but he didn't hurt me. He merely punished me one smack at a time, putting enough strength into it to let me know I *was* being punished, taking it slow with the thought that we had all day. He may have all day, but after the fifth whack, I began growing desperate.

By the time it was over there were tears running down my cheeks, and not only from the ache I'd been given. The punishment had already been well begun when a knock came at the door, followed by the sound of the door being opened. In utter, chasm-deep embarrassment I began shifting out of that humiliating position, not caring what was done to me afterward as long as no one was there to witness it, but I'd forgotten the decision wasn't mine to make. Suddenly there was a fist tangled in my hair, not painful as long as I lay still, and the punishment was continuing, somewhat harder than it had been when begun. I cried out in misery when the amusement crowded at my mind, coming from the woman who had entered, the one who had been the first of the three during my bathing. She laughed aloud from behind me, gleefully approving, then moved closer.

"I bring your midday meal, *drin* Dallan, and that of your *weerees* as well," she said. "Do you wish me to serve it?"

"Not at the moment, Ladir," Dallan answered, still swinging his arm. "I now attend to a necessary chore, one which will be some time in ending. This one will serve me when I wish to be served."

"And eagerly," the woman Ladir laughed, while I moaned to

myself over that "some time in ending" comment. "The red in
her pretty, rounded seat will assure you of that. Do you wish me
to fetch a strap?"

"No." The monster chuckled as I hid my face in my hands,
blushing fit to burn out a circuit. "Should I require a strap, I will
send this one to fetch it. You may go now."

"As you will, my *Drin*," the woman answered, taking the
earlier tray with her. I was crying hard by then, more than
miserable, but the punishment continued only another minute or
two. Abruptly it stopped, and the fist was withdrawn from my
hair.

"I suddenly find myself interested in what is held by that
tray," Dallan mused, almost to himself. "Shall I continue with
what I currently do, or have I one about who will serve me
eagerly?"

"I will serve you!" I choked out immediately, willing to do
anything to get vertical again. If I'd begun feeling intimidated by
him that morning, by then the process was nearly complete.

"Excellent," he said, the laughter in his mind surrounding me
to suffocation. "Rise, then, and begin serving me."

I struggled to my feet without looking at him, hurried to the
tray to get a bowl of spiced meat strips garnished with nuts and
vegetables, then went back to the tray after delivering the bowl,
under orders to bring a goblet of wine. I held the wine goblet
while my owner ate, kneeling in front of him, my eyes and head
down, relinquishing the wine only when he wanted to sip it, or
when he was ready for the next course. It still amazed me how
much those men ate without getting fat, a thought I held to as I
stared at the beautifully decorated golden goblet in my hands. It
was painful thinking about the serving I was doing, as though I
were a slave, beaten down and terrified of what would happen if
I did something wrong. I wasn't exactly beaten down and I
wasn't exactly terrified, but I *was* so ashamed of myself that I
couldn't stand it. I was a coward for letting myself be brow-
beaten into obeying, but I couldn't face that punishment again. I
glanced up at Dallan where he sat and ate, found his eyes on me
as his mind hummed, and quickly looked down again, hating
myself even more. He couldn't have done that to me if I hadn't
let him, but I couldn't seem to find it in me to argue the point.

When Dallan was through eating it was my turn. The last
thing I wanted just then was to eat, but my preferences didn't
matter. I brought the bowl to my owner, had him approve the
dish, then stuffed it down while he watched. I was just finishing
up the third selection, some sort of fowl in a thick sauce,

wondering where I would put any more, when the bowl was taken out of my hands. I looked up to see Dallan reaching toward me, and suddenly realized that his desire had grown too strong for him to hold back. I'd been sunk so deep in my misery that I hadn't been aware of his feelings, but once he had taken me in his lap and arms I became more than aware of them. The flames washed over me as his lips took mine, his heartbeat became a pounding in my ears, the hot blood surged from his body into mine, forced from flesh to flesh as he crushed me up against him. I knew the reactions I was feeling weren't my own, but they were absolutely overpowering. I gasped once for air, trying to protect myself or fight back, but it was already too late. The fire burning within him was too wild, his hold on me too strong, for me to be able to break loose. He swept me up as easily as his arms lifted me in the air, and by the time we reached the bed furs, I was completely lost.

Hours went by that way, and I had the distinct impression Dallan was trying to make up for all the time he'd lost as a servant-slave in Aesnil's palace. At one point I told him truthfully that I had nothing left to give, that he'd taken all there was to take, but all he did was laugh and prove me wrong. I couldn't seem to resist the way he touched me—or the way he kissed me—or the way he thought when he looked at me. I'd been forced into sharing my emotions from the very first, and the man was glorying in the sensations as never before. He was enormously pleased with his new belonging, and I was beyond desperation.

I'd been napping for a short while in Dallan's arms when I was awakened by a loud knock on the door. I raised my head when Dallan called out for whoever it was to enter, but I knew who it was before he did. Ferran, commander of the guard, came in, walked four or five paces from the door, then nodded his head to Dallan.

"My *Drin*, those you alerted us to expect have arrived," he said, his mind more curious than his tone. "They await your pleasure in the courtyard."

"Good." Dallan nodded in turn, taking his arms from me as he sat up. "Offer them refreshment after their long ride, and tell them I will be with them shortly."

"At once, my *Drin*," the man agreed, turning back to the door after a single glance at me. His mind had started to growl as was usual with Rimilian men, but sight of the small-linked bronze bands I wore had changed the growl to a hum. Apparently their society found humming over a five-banded woman acceptable, while growling was not. Growling led to swordplay, and Ferran wasn't about to challenge his *drin*.

"You may arise now, *wenda*, and clothe yourself in this," Dallan said, dropping something on the bed furs as he passed them. "We have guests awaiting us, and I do not care to have them wait overlong."

He, himself, headed for his *haddin*, and when I looked at what he'd dropped on the bed, I found it to be a gown very much like the ones I'd worn in Aesnil's palace. The thing was backless and veed in front, but instead of butterfly sleeves there were full sleeves, gathered at the wrist the way *imad* sleeves were, but not with leather. Sheer silk ties closed the sleeves, of a silver matching the delicate silver of the rest of the gown. As much as I wanted to be out of the playtime outfit I was then wearing, I glanced over toward Dallan before beginning to undress. The silver gown gave me an odd feeling of foreboding, as though something very unpleasant was going to happen, but Dallan's mind gave no indication of what it could be. The Prince of Gerleth was very pleased about something, not to mention light-hearted; if there was going to be trouble, it was nothing he was expecting. I threw away the slave-rag as he began buckling on his swordbelt, and paid attention to getting myself dressed.

By the time we left the rooms. I was glad it wasn't me waiting for Dallan. He'd had himself ready in almost no time, but he called the three women back to see to my hair and reperfuming, and he hadn't hurried them. He stood and waited patiently until the job was done, watching me carefully, determined about something even though he didn't think it was a good idea. I could see that from the way he kept pushing away a fully understood doubt, but I didn't know what the idea was, or which part he was doubtful about. The teasing hints nagged at me, taking my mind off the way I was being primped and preened. The woman Ladir seemed to have caught Dallan's mood and was no longer amused, but she wasn't the only one.

The next room past the bathing room was a reception room, full of cushions and small tables, but no bed. Beyond that room was a marble corridor, and that was where we picked up our escort. Eight *l'lendaa* fell in behind us, scarcely walking in step but still guards for all of that. We walked down the long, wide corridor to its end, then stepped through airy double doors onto a wide balcony of sorts, that moved away before us to a broad set of descending steps. When I stopped to look over the balustrade with a gasp, Dallan stopped with me and gestured widely.

"The land of Gerleth," he said, referring to the miles and

miles of country I could see, way, way down below us. There were tiny towns, and tinier individual houses, and neat rows of farmland in between the towns and houses and small stands of trees. I was looking down into a mountain valley, the entire area settled and cultivated even to the foot of the slopes. The mountain had to fall away into the valley on this side only, considering the road leading to it on the other side. I wondered how long circling that valley to the far side of the mountain would have taken and then I remembered it didn't matter any longer.

"The land of Gerleth is very lovely," I said, turning away from the valley to look at Dallan. "It is now clear why you missed it so greatly."

"It is said that once a man sees it, he may never again leave it." Dallan smiled, running a gentle hand over my hair. "Possibly it will hold true for a woman as well."

His comment was an odd one, but before I could ask him what he meant he had taken my arm, heading us toward the broad stairway that led downward. He was still firmly suppressing his doubts, and as we approached the stairway I suddenly knew why. I couldn't see him as yet, but at the foot of that stairway waited Tammad.

I must have tried stopping in my tracks; the first thing I realized after discovering who was waiting was that Dallan's grip had tightened, and I was now moving forward only because I was being pulled. I really didn't want to go down those stairs, but another sudden revelation made me stop hanging back. Knowing who was waiting below told me the Dallan intended to fight Tammad for possession of me, and it was my presence at the fight that he had been unsure about. Dallan knew well enough that I could cripple his mind so badly that he would lose, but he was bringing me there anyway. Did he intend making me choose between them—or was he too proud to hide anything from me, even if he died for it? I felt the silver gown fluttering in the light breeze as we approached the top of the stairs, and also felt the new alertness in Dallan's mind. He knew I was aware of what was happening and was waiting for me to react; as far as that went, I was waiting for the same thing.

We did no more than reach the top of the stairs and start down, and every eye below was riveted on us. Tammad was there with Cinnan beside him, a dozen *l'lendaa* ranged behind them, half Tammad's and half Cinnan's. They stood in a large marbled courtyard, marbled columns and arches rising around its perimeter, more *l'lendaa* and *seetarr* visible through one of the arches. Also around the perimeter were two dozen *l'lendaa* who seemed to belong to Dallan, all armed, all alert. A large, beautiful fountain stood in the far right-hand corner of the courtyard, but no one seemed in a mood to appreciate its beauty. Anger and impatience and wariness rose up at me in waves, unseparated and undefined even when I met Tammad's gaze without looking away. There were too many minds there for his to dominate, even with the clear displeasure flickering across his features. If I hadn't expected trouble sooner, that expression alone would have kept me from being surprised. Tammad and Cinnan began walking toward us as soon as we began descending, and by the time we were at the bottom of the steps they were only five feet away and waiting for us.

"*Aldana, l'lendaa,*" Dallan greeted them pleasantly, nodding to them in a friendly fashion. "I am told you come seeking our assistance. How may we aid you?"

"You have already aided us by ending our search." Tammad answered, his voice calm and neutral, but just barely. He and Dallan had locked eyes, and Dallan's hand was no longer on my arm. "I take it you are the one called Daldrin."

"I am Dallan, *drin* of Gerleth," Dallan answered, the ghost of a smile touching his lips. "At one point and for a certain purpose, I was indeed called Daldrin. You, I take it, are he called Tammad."

"I am," the barbarian said, forcing calm on himself with enormous effort. "I have come for my *wendaa*—and she who was banded by Cinnan as well."

"My cousin Aesnil is here and well, though far from pleased with her new lot," Dallan said, sparing a quick glance for a tight-lipped Cinnan. "She receives the courtesy in my house that I received in hers, an experience she will not soon put behind her. Should he who is called Cinnan wish it, he may remain as guest in this house, to watch his *wenda* from afar or even to be served by her, as he chooses. At the proper time, he will then be able to return her to her former place."

"And what, I would know, do you consider the proper time?" Cinnan asked, giving Tammad no opportunity to speak the words he had intended.

"The proper time will be when she has learned something of humility and obedience." Dallan answered, his smile widening to a grin even though he still looked only at Tammad. "Should you decide to remain, speak to the overseer of my house at your convenience."

Cinnan nodded as though Dallan could see the gesture, but

made no move to leave Tammad's side. Now that he knew Aesnil was safe, he could afford to forget about her for a short while. Tammad's business wasn't done, and everyone there knew it.

"I have heard no words from you regarding my *wenda*," the barbarian pursued, his eyes now the blue of ice. "I will have the return of her *now*."

"Your *wenda*," Dallan mused, the grin having left him. "A man who cannot keep his *wenda* by him has not a right to the *wenda*. A man who two-bands her, then five-bands her, then four-bands her, shows little interest in her peace of mind and self-concept. As you four-banded her, name your price to the overseer of my house and he will see that you receive it. She nows stands five-banded and cherished as well, and will remain so as long as I live."

I was shaken by the strength of the disgust coming from Dallan, but not as much as by the blast of rage coming from the barbarian. The force of the rage literally staggered me, and I might have fallen if not for the hand of one of Dallan's guardsmen on my arm. Dallan, who had begun turning back toward the stairs, ready to take my arm again, must have seen me pale and knew immediately what the problem was. Rather than trying to help me in any way, he quickly turned back to Tammad, who had taken two steps forward with the very first echoes of his rage.

"No man has the right to come between another man and his *wenda*," the barbarian grated, his voice sounding like two stones rubbing together. "You know nothing of that which lies between us, nothing of what I—" His words broke off abruptly as he fought to calm himself, but the effort was useless. He was well beyond calm, and his eyes more than showed it. "It makes no matter," he continued, again having locked eyes with Dallan. "All that concerns us is that no man may give himself approval for banding save with a sword. My *wenda* has not been offered to you, nor shall she be. Return her now or face me."

"I shall not return her," Dallan answered, standing as tall in mind and body as the barbarian. "It will be my pleasure to face you."

"No," I said, practically to myself, not believing they were really going to fight. And then, because I knew they were, I shouted, "No! I will not be fought over! Do you hear me? I *refuse* to be fought over!"

I might as well have been shouting over the side of the mountain into the valley. Tammad backed off a few paces then turned toward the center of the courtyard with Dallan following right after him, both of them ignoring me as if I hadn't said a word. I began to move forward, to stand between them if necessary, but Dallan's guardsman still had his hand on my arm. The others in the courtyard were all moving back toward the pillars and arches, giving the two central figures all the room they would need, and as real as I knew the confrontation was, I still couldn't believe it. The two men were Dallan and Tammad, and they couldn't really be serious about using the swords they were drawing; they didn't really intend trying to *kill* each other!

"I have looked forward to this meeting for some time," Dallan said to Tammad with a smile, raising the sword he held. "By the rite of five-banding do I defend possession of my woman."

"There is that which is deeper and more binding than five-banding," the barbarian returned with a similar smile, also raising his sword. "The woman is mine."

Their minds were hardened metal and rock, cold and unmoving and completely determined. I was so close to true shock I could have brushed it with the silver gown I wore, tripped over it and fallen. The smiles on their faces were absolutely ghastly, lacking all humor of any sort, making me shiver so hard I nearly pulled loose from the guardsman's grip. Their polished metal swords rose glinting in the sunlight, sharp and deadly, long and graceful, handled with ease despite their weight. Tammad and Dallan, two tanned giants, the first wearing a green *haddin*, the second in dark red, both wide and strong, both determined to win or die; they faced one another with eagerness, and it had already begun.

I think it was that very eagerness that finally broke through to me, pushing off the shock with the beginnings of anger. They were *glad* to be facing one another, happy over the prospect of fighting and killing! They were both barbarians, savage beasts who were only using me as an excuse to get at one another, calmly deciding my fate for me even as they casually gambled their lives. It made me fighting mad myself, but my weapon wasn't the sword.

Without even thinking about it, I nudged the guardsman beside me with indifference, and his hand fell away from my arm. Tammad and Dallan were casually striking at one another, their blades silver lightning, each testing for an easy opening, each pleased to find none. It was a real win they were set for, the sort that had to be worked for and earned the hard way. My fists clenched as I watched them, trying to decide what to do, and then the answer came: if it was fun they wanted, it was fun they would get.

Tammad swung hard at Dallan, forcing him to duck back to keep from being hit, and the pleasure they both felt at the well-executed exchange gave me my opening. Touching them both at the same time, I changed pleasure into amusement, a shadow of it at first while Dallan immediately moved forward from his defensive retreat and attacked. Tammad caught his blade and swung it aside with his own, then had his thrust swung aside in turn. They were very well matched, these two *l'lendaa* and abruptly they were grinning at each other even as they circled, bodies set, free arm out, swords held ready. They were both well prepared to continue, but so was I.

A flurry of attacks and counters went by with blinding speed accompanied by the ring of metal; murmurs of appreciation and approval could be heard all around, drowning out the chuckling the two combatants had graduated to. If they hadn't been so deeply involved with each other they probably would have already been suspicious, but the concentration necessary for life-and-death battle leaves very little room for consideration of other things. Dallan moved in fast with a stroke toward Tammad's head, which Tammad side-stepped and blocked as they both began laughing aloud, as though in delight. Delight was part of what they felt, but not because they were delighted with the situation. I'd had to use something to distract the growing distraction *they* felt, and delight tends to have a great attraction for most people. I could see I'd have to speed things up before they broke away.

One thing I *will* have to give them: they did try. They both began swinging at each other almost wildly, as though determined to get to the bloody part of the fight no matter what anyone did to try breaking it up. If they had started just a little sooner they might have made it, but not with utter hilarity filling their minds. Their laughter turned to roaring mirth, the sort that holds you in a helpless grip, weakening your limbs and dripping tears from your eyes. Within moments they were just about convulsed with laughter, staggering around rather than circling, unable to accurately swing those monstrous swords even with two hands. Their weapons were down, their guards were down, and if I could hold off the draining tiredness a little longer, *they* would be down as well. A rumble of confused muttering had begun when their laughter had first started, rising when the mock hysteria had roared out, culminating in some of Tammad's *l'lendaa* looking in my direction. I could only hope they were unsure of all that being my fault, and doubly hoped they couldn't see the sweat on my forehead. They, better than any of the others, knew what I could do, and I was too close to success to stand the thought of their interfering. I forced myself to stand straighter under the weight of weariness, and tried to look as confused as everyone else.

"By the Sword of Gerleth, what insanity is this?" a deep voice suddenly roared, overriding the muttering and laughter alike. Tammad was down on one knee, Dallan was bent over holding his middle, both of them had dropped their swords, and both of them were laughing their heads off. The muttering stopped abruptly at the roar but not so the laughter, and that seemed to infuriate the newcomer even more.

The big man had come through one of the arches, leading ten or a dozen other newcomers. He was as blond and blue-eyed as all Rimilian males seemed to be, and though he was noticeably older there didn't seem to be an ounce of fat on him. He wore a *haddin* of the red Aesnil's gowns had been, a black leather swordbelt from which a golden hilt protruded, and one curving golden armband. Other than that he was no different from the other *l'lendaa*, except for being angrier. My grip on the two in the middle of the courtyard began to slip when he roared, and an instant's thought told me it wasn't worth recovering. I'd done what I'd hoped to do, and I didn't have all that much left after the effort; what I did have would best be conserved for any necessary later effort.

"Dallan, what is the meaning of this?" the man demanded, stalking forward to stand and glare at the two ex-combatants. "Do I see grown men before me, or small boys in need of a sound strapping for childish foolishness?"

"Father—wait—" Dallan gasped, still unable to throw off the laughter, holding one hand up toward the other man. Then he slowly lowered himself toward the ground and dropped the last few inches, stretching himself out as though exhausted. Tammad had shifted from one knee to sitting hunched over, moving as slowly as Dallan had, looking just as weary. Strong laughter is very tiring, and theirs had been close to the draining of hysterics. They were finally bringing it under control, but the damage had already been done. I stirred where I stood, knowing they would soon be able to come after me, knowing also that I didn't really care. Possibly I was too tired myself to care, but there was no confusion to the feeling. I was glad I had done what I had, and I would not have recalled the doing even if that had been possible.

"Perhaps you would now care to explain the meaning of this—this—witless exhibition," the big man said, looking down at Dallan where he lay on the marble. "I am aware of the fact that I have not seen you in some little time, yet behavior such as this. Even as boys, you and your brother engaged in little of it. Who is this *l'lenda*, and those others as well, and what do you all do here?''

"Father, this was meant to be a contest to death." Dallan panted, rolling onto his side and propping himself up with one elbow. "That it degenerated into the farce you saw was not our doing. The buffoonery was forced upon us."

"Forced?" Dallan's father echoed, frowning in obvious disbelief. "In what manner may laughter be forced on a man? And where might one be found who is capable of such a thing?"

"To find the one responsible, you need only look there," Dallan answered sourly, sitting up and turning his head in my direction. Tammad had already been looking at me for a minute or two, and I was glad I was too played out to read them at that distance. From their expressions, it was easy to see that I wouldn't have enjoyed what I read. "Her name is Terril, and I have just this day banded her," Dallan continued, his tone going grim. "This day will also see her well punished."

"She is not yours to band nor punish," Tammad interrupted, bringing Dallan's attention back to him. "The woman is mine, and I will see to her punishment when I have returned her to my bands."

"She wears my bands and will continue to do so," Dallan answered, his tone even but his back straightening. "What disposition is made of her will be made by me. Have I not made my intentions sufficiently clear?"

"As clear as mine," the barbarian returned, holding his gaze, both their hands moving together toward their swords again. Not even Dallan's father seemed prepared to stop them, and I was more than sick of it.

"Perhaps there are those about who are interested in *my* intentions," I said, stepping forward toward them before they were able to get to their feet. "I strongly feel that ignoring my intentions would be a great foolishness."

Dallan craned back as Tammad looked up, but neither one of them got to verbalize the annoyance filling their eyes. Dallan's father had had his eyes on me since Dallan had pointed me out, and he stepped forward to stand between me and them.

"I am Rellis, *Chamd* of Gerleth and lord of this house," he said, looking down at me with curiosity and annoyance. "From what land do you come, that you have not been taught proper manners, eh, *wenda*? A matter of honor between *l'lendaa* may not be interfered with, most especially not by a *wenda*."

"This is no matter of honor," I countered, ignoring the rest of what he'd said, looking up into his eyes. "I will not be used as an excuse for bloodletting, no matter how noble the thing is made to sound. That they have greater interest in facing one another than in any end result they might attain is quite clear to *me*, even should no other be able to see it. It is for this reason that I am determined that neither shall win."

"You mean to prevent the victory of one over the other?" he asked, his tone falsely astonished while his mind chuckled indulgently. "To do such a thing you must be a greater warrior than they, greater than any who has yet been known! I am truly honored to have you as guest within my house."

He had made his voice awed and respectful, indulging the little girl in her fantasies, not seeing the expressions Tammad and Dallan wore. The two mighty warriors were finally on their feet, standing to Rellis' right, anger and frustration competing for place on their faces, outrage and indignation pouring out of their minds. I was daring to trespass on warrior domains, daring to oppose their wills with mine, but I didn't care how unhappy they were. It was time someone thought of *me* first, even if I had to be the one to do it.

"They will not face each other with weapons," I said through my teeth, grating on the condescension Rellis felt so strongly, then turned my head toward the other two. "Should they find my resolve sufficiently distasteful, my life may be easily taken by them, yet not so the decision. That I will not allow to be taken from me."

"Do not speak foolishly, *wenda*!" Rellis snapped while the other two looked as though I'd struck them in the face. "No warrior would take the life of a woman, and most especially not the life of the woman he fights to possess. You cannot know wherof you speak, therefore. . . ."

"*Hama*, do you truly believe I would harm you?" Tammad interrupted, taking a step closer to me, his blue eyes seriously concerned. "Your life is mine to protect, never to take."

"No more would *I* offer you harm, woman of my heart," Dallan agreed, stepping forward to stand beside the barbarian. "You cannot think I would consider such a thing even for a moment."

"You both not only consider it, you strive to accomplish it," I said, the harshness of my feelings coloring my words, "I will not be fought for and won as though I were no more than the spoils of your war. You both covet my possession for reasons of your own; should one slay the other toward this end, its very accomplishment will negate it. You have my word that I will open my mind wide, sharing the death of whichever of you experiences it, allowing the shock of such a contact to take me as well. You disbelieve that it may be done so; then doubt me if you wish. I say there will be no victory nor victor, not of the sort you *profess* to desire.''

"Profess?" Dallan repeated, his thoughts as shocked and confused as Tammad's though his eyes and expression showed it more. Rellis didn't understand anything that was going on, but nothing in his attitude showed that he intended interrupting or interfering. He had decided to listen and wait before coming to any decisions, an attitude which surprised me. I wouldn't have expected it from a Rimilian barbarian.

"You cannot think I do not desire you, Terril," Dallan said, his voice considerably more even that mine had been. "Should your power fail to tell you this, you may judge from my actions. Surely you understand that I would not have banded you had my feelings for you not been deep.''

"Indeed does my power tell me of your feelings," I said, glancing at him briefly before looking away. "As for your actions, there are those which stand out quite clearly in my memory. I find it difficult forgetting actions such as those.''

I could almost feel him straightening where he stood, his mind filling protests of justification, but none of them reached the vocal level.

"By the Circle of Might, what have you done to her?" Tammad demanded in a growl, his fury beginning to tower again. "Should I find that you have given her pain. I shall. . . .''

"That *I* have given her pain?" Dallan interrupted with his own anger, sounds of movement showing they were turning to face one another again. "What of the pain she has had from *you*? If your arms have held her for no more than proper punishment and expressions of love, why does she seek to run from you? Has she shown you the tears of her ache, so that you might banish them and ease her? When she was held in my cousin's house, her life and sanity nearly forfeit, why did she not believe you would seek for and find her? Why does the mere thought of you bring hopelessness to the depths of her lovely eyes? You ask what I have done to her; allow me to ask the same of you!''

When Dallan was through, there was no immediate answer to his question. I could feel the silence behind me, full of jagged edges, but even more I could feel the groaning and stretching in Tammad's mind as his emotions tried to escape his control. He had forced that rigid, unyielding calm on himself almost from the first of Dallan's words, and he refused to let it break. He'd felt the strength of Dallan's bitter outrage full force, but what effect it had had on him—if any—he refused to admit even to himself.

"All you say is true," he answered at last, his voice not overly loud and certainly even enough to match his calm. "There are far too many things between the woman and myself which should not have been. And yet the greatest of my follies was my attempt to give her up, which her recent disappearance has proven without doubt. I cannot give her up and I shall not, for she is more precious to me than life itself. She is mine and will remain mine."

"She is banded as mine and will remain *mine*," Dallan returned doggedly, completing the circle of speaking-and-refusing-to-hear. My head was beginning to hurt and I was very tired, and I realized that my eyes had closed during Tammad's say, and I hadn't opened them again. Lightheadedness tiptoed up to me, whispering of how good it would feel to sit down for a while, and I really began considering it. . . .

"Enough of this," Rellis' voice came, without anger but filled with authority. Suddenly hands were on me, lifting me in a pair of strong arms, and I didn't understand what was happening. "Are the two of you so engrossed in one another that you fail to see that the woman you both seek to possess was nearly upon the ground in a faint?" he said, showing he was the one holding me. "You squabble more like children than men, and I find myself too weary to listen further. I shall see to the *wenda*, the while you pose as though you were warriors. Should you later discover some interest in the woman's well-being, you may consider joining us—should I permit it."

Holding me tightly to him, he turned then and started away, his mind faintly annoyed. I opened my eyes to see that we were heading for the stairs leading up to the palace, but I made sure not to look over his shoulder at the two we were leaving behind. They'd registered indignant outrage at his speech, but seeing Rellis walking away had bothered them even more. They hesitated no longer than necessary to glare at each other, then they were hurrying to catch up.

"Father, this is most unseemly," Dallan protested, holding his anger down out of a deeply ingrained sense of respect. "It is unheard of for another to walk off with a woman who is the object of contention!"

"It is now no longer unheard of," Rellis answered, keeping to a brisk pace as he mounted the stairs. The other two climbed behind him, and they seemed to understand he'd said all he was going to. Dallan was annoyed and fighting off anger, and Tammad was—calm above rumbling and swirling. I leaned my head against Rellis' shoulder, trying to see the funny side of being carried away from the two men who had been fighting over me, with them now scrambling along behind in an effort to keep up. Under other circumstances the situation *would* have been funny—except for the fact that Tammad and Dallan weren't prepared to give up on the idea of facing one another no matter what had been said to them, and Rellis' mind had begun to hum with interest. I should have been used to that hum from my time among the men of that planet, but I wasn't. It still had the power to frighten me no matter how bravely I talked, especially when I felt as drained and tired as I did then. I was just about helpless to protect myself, and coward that I am, the thought made me ill with fear.

It didn't take long to reach Rellis' destination. A guard opened a door, and then we were entering a large reception room with a raised dais, much like the one Aesnil had in her palace. It was all marble with red and gold silks on the walls, golden carpet fur, and red and gold cushions; I was taken to the cushions at the foot of the dais and set down among them, but not to be left alone. Rellis went to a small table which held a golden carafe and golden goblets, poured into one of the goblets, then came back to sit down beside me.

"Here, *wenda*, drink this and you will find yourself somewhat restored," he said, handing me the goblet with a smile on his handsome face. It was delicate golden wine rather than *drishnak* so I sipped at it, ignoring the metallic taste imparted by the goblet in the same way I ignored Rellis' hand at my hair. He, in turn, was ignoring Dallan and Tammad, who stood stiffly in the center of the room, Dallan the very picture of outrage. The amusement in Rellis' mind showed he was more than aware of them, but when Tammad spoke he was still surprised.

"Your purpose has, for the moment, been achieved, *Chamd* of Grelana," the barbarian said, his usual deep calm evident in his voice. "It would, however, be wise of you to avoid too great a proximity to the woman in an attempt to prolong that purpose. Her ability to interest a man is never intentionally exercised, and therefore far more potent than it otherwise would be. To believe yourself immune would be foolish self-deception."

"Would it indeed," Rellis said, looking over at the barbarian with a good deal of annoyance touching him. He resented being spoken to like that, but he'd also taken his hand from my hair after only a brief hesitation. "And who are you, *l'lenda*, to address a *Chamd* in such a manner? You are clearly not from the land hereabout."

"I am Tammad, *denday* of the city of Thriving Near the River's Bend," the barbarian responded, folding his massive arms across his chest. "Among the membership in the Circle of Might, I speak first."

"The Circle of Might," Rellis mused, the faint frown creasing his forehead matching the one Dallan wore as he stared at Tammad, "I have heard many thing concerning the leadership of the cities of the plains and forests and their Circle of Might, yet not that they had chosen one to speak first. He who occupies that position is a man to be reckoned with, for he has the *l'lendaa* of five and twenty cities at his disposal. Does your Circle now mean to ride in conquest?"

"Our Circle is far more concerned with the well-being of our cities," the barbarian said, his calm deepening. "We have been contacted by offworlders who wish to build a complex on our world, and we have demanded many gifts and concessions to allow them their desire. To halt their intentions would be impossible, therefore do we strive to protect and strengthen the peoples of our world, so that we will one day find ourselves able to face them as equals in the mysteries of their knowledge and devices. To see one portion of our world fall to them through weakness, would soon mean the rest following in turn, our cities among them. It is for that reason we mean to demand the needs and desires of all, not merely our own; to do otherwise would be to set out upon the road which leads to self-destruction."

"I salute the wisdom of your Circle," Rellis said, a hand to his face as his mind considered what he'd heard. "It would indeed benefit each of us to see our entire world strengthened, yet it would undoubtedly mean the end of our way of life. I am a warrior as my father was and my sons are; what is to be the lot of the sons of my sons and their sons after them? To see them as shopkeepers and merchants and scholars, never knowing the feel of a sword in their hands, would sour and sicken the life I have so far found so sweet."

"Such a thing need not be," Tammad said, his voice filled with understanding. "There is one world among those of the outworlders filled with those who look upon themselves as warriors. They are called Kabras, and it is to these Kabras that the *darayse* of the outworlders go when there is a battle they wish fought with their enemies, for they have neither the stomach nor the skill to face their enemies themselves. All fear these warriors called Kabras yet are they warriors in name alone, rarely finding it necessary to raise weapons as true warriors would. I have among those who follow me one of these Kabras, one who longs for true battle and who will therefore school us in the manner in which we, ourselves, may offer our swords and protection as the Kabras now do. Those of our world who wish to remain warriors will find themselves fully needed, and perhaps find the opportunity of extending our sway to worlds not our own. The Kabras have made no attempt to claim that which they win through the strength of their swordarms; what need is there for us to emulate them to so great an extent?"

"What need indeed," Rellis chuckled, delighted with the idea Tammad had grinningly presented. For my own part I was appalled, listening to them calmly discussing conquering the other more peaceful and civilized worlds of the Amalgamation. I now knew the use the barbarian intended putting Garth to, and I wished I didn't. I swallowed the last of the golden wine in a gulp, nearly choking, unintentionally bringing myself back to the attention of Rellis.

"I fail to understand what occurs here between yourself and my son," the *Chamd* said, losing most of the pleasure he'd felt. "How does it come to be that you stand in contention over this *wenda*?"

"The woman was bought by me from the outworlders," the barbarian said, moving his eyes to me where I sat holding the empty goblet.

"They are all *darayse* and did not dare refuse my demand for her, instead eagerly accepting the offer of payment I made. She left me once, thinking I no longer desired her, and it was necessary for me to follow after her and carry her back. She was allowed to do as she pleased among the *darayse* she comes from, therefore is she ïllful to a large degree as well as the possessor of a strange power. She was stolen from near my camp by savages, sold to a tribe of the Hamarda, escaped from the Hamarda, and taken up by the *Chama* of Grelana, who wished the use of her powers to serve her own ends. It was there, at the palace of the *Chama*, that your son discovered her. Though we were each of us held as slave, he in the palace, I in the *vendra ralle*, our paths never crossed. Once we had attained our freedom, however, we were also free to face one another, which we earlier attempted to do. With the woman present and unrestrained, the effort was the farce you saw."

"Held as slaves, did you say?" Rellis demanded, suddenly

outraged. "Dallan, were you truly made slave by your cousin Aesnil? What of your brother?"

"Seddan was enslaved as well," Dallan said, a tightening evident in his jawline. "I, held in the palace, faced no more than the whips and kicks of the guard. Seddan, however, was sent to the *vendra ralle*, where it was necessary that he fight in defense of his life. He was wounded in his final enounter in the *ralle*, and wounded again when we fought to regain our freedom. I lost no time in bringing him home at battle's end, and now he rests in his apartment, regaining health and strength beneath the eyes of our healers. He will again be as he was, though through no thanks to Aesnil."

"I find your tale incredible," Rellis said, staring at Dallan as his anger grew. "You and your brother were merely to have paid your respects to Aesnil, visited a short while, and then returned home. Did one or the other of you give her insult, that she had you enslaved?"

"We refused to go to our knees before her," Dallan answered grimly, his left hand resting on his sword hilt. "The gesture was demanded of us to counter the 'arrogance' we showed when first presenting ourselves before her. Seddan laughed and called her a foolish girl-child, and the next instant her guardsmen had been set upon us."

"There must be an accounting for this outrage," Rellis fumed, keeping himself from jumping to his feet only by the strongest effort of will. "I will visit her myself, and. . . ."

"Father, you need not go far." Dallan grinned, holding one hand up to calm Rellis' anger. "Aesnil and Terril fled Grelana together, and were brought here by *l'lendaa* of Gerleth who thought them *wendaa* of our land. I have returned to Aesnil the courtesy given in her house, and have declared her slave. She now labors at whatever tasks were given her, and strives to avoid the straps of those in whose charge she stands. You may remonstrate with her whenever you please, merely by summoning her from the kitchens or wherever it is she serves."

"A fate undoubtedly well earned by her." Rellis said, losing a good deal of his anger. "Your mother, had she lived, would have been greatly upset to learn of such doings from the daughter of her sister. I will speak with the girl later, after she has had an appropriate amount of punishment, and then decide when she will be returned to Grelana. A pity she has not yet been banded."

"She *has* been banded," Tammad put in, drawing Rellis' eyes again. "Cinnan awaits without, anxious for her return yet unwilling to offer you insult by demanding it. Perhaps you would do well to discuss the matter with him.''

"I will be sure to do so." Rellis nodded, leaning down among the cushions. "The question of Aesnil will be easily seen to, yet not so the matter which stands between yourself and Dallan. Is it possible it may be seen to by other means than a meeting of blades?''

"I came here solely with the intention of regaining my woman." The barbarian shrugged, deliberately keeping his eyes from Dallan. "Should it be possible to accomplish this end without the spilling of blood, so be it.''

"When I found her, the woman was four-banded," Dallan said, also speaking only to Rellis. "I was well within my rights five-banding her, a decision I will stand with. The woman is banded as mine and will remain mine.''

"Clearly an impasse," Rellis said with a sigh, then he turned his head to me. "It is easily seen why you both desire this woman, yet I have not seen her run weeping and begging to either of you. Is she convinced that one will easily best the other, or is she unsure which of you she wishes to belong to?''

"Neither," I said before anyone could answer the question for me. "As it is the truth you seek, I shall give it to you. I wish to belong to neither of them.''

"For what reason do you feel so, *wenda*?" Rellis asked gently, pretending he was unaware of the painful silence coming from the middle of the room. "Are you not aware of the desire these men feel for you, the love they wish to share with you?''

"Oh, I am more than aware of their desire," I said, just short of a bitter laugh. "He who banded me first desires the use of my power in his designs and the use of my body in the furs. He who banded me second desires the end of the pity he feels for me in the bands of another, and the addition of my power as well as my body in his furs. The things they most wish to share with me are humiliation and pain, for those are the things I find most often at their hands. They both wish the use of my power, yet they also wish to deny *me* the use of it. I will no longer allow such a thing, therefore will I belong to neither of them.''

"*Wenda*, such a decision is not yours," Rellis said, his voice still gentle to cover the pity he felt. "Surely your upset causes you to exaggerate what was done to you, for I am able to picture neither my son nor the *denday* Tammad giving unnecessary pain to a helpless woman. You must be. . . .''

"I am not helpless!" I interrupted with a shout, furiously

throwing down the goblet I held. "Unrestrained I am not helpless at all, yet I seldom find myself unrestrained! The mighty *l'lendaa* of Rimilia fear me as greatly as those of my own world, seeking to bind me as tightly as they, offering punishment nearly as harsh! I will no longer allow myself to *be* restrained, and will fight for freedom, to the death if necessary!"

"There is much of the sound of *l'lenda* to you," Rellis mused, for the most part deciding he'd better calm me down. "It is scarcely necessary for a *wenda* to fight to the death, most especially as she has no weapon to use. Best you allow us to see to this matter, for your happiness will be foremost in our minds as we contemplate our decision. I will have you taken to a room in which you may rest yourself. . . ."

"I will not be brushed aside that easily," I interrupted again, my anger building. "If I have no weapon which may be used, I assume you have no objection to my using this nonexistent weapon on you?"

"Certainly not," he agreed, annoyed but still willing to humor me. "You may use whatever weapon you. . . ."

"No!" Tammad and Dallan shouted together, both of them coming forward from the center of the room. They were feeling considerably more nervous than they looked, anticipating all sorts of calamities. They both should have known I was too tired and drained to do anything really spectacular, but their reaction was emotional rather than logical.

"I have had more than enough of interruptions!" Rellis snapped in irritation, jerking his head around to glare at Tammad and Dallan. "The girl flounders in self-delusion, and you aid her by supporting her foolishness! It is little wonder that she feels as she does, confused and unsure and deeply *ahresta*! You are each of you fully grown *l'lendaa*, and should know of the delicacy required in dealing with *wendaa*!"

I leaned back a little as he plowed on and on, refusing to let Dallan interrupt or explain, lecturing them on how men knew better when he was young, stressing how small and helpless and delicate women were. I know he thought he was defending me, but I'd been defended that way too often to be willing to swallow it again. I had his freely given permission to use my imaginary weapon on him, and although I used restraint, that's exactly what I did.

Have you ever been the victim of a psychological itch? The condition usually manifests when you're carrying two armfuls of packages with nowhere to put them down, or when you're in the middle of a large group of people where it's impossible to turn politely away. The itch is actually emotional rather that physical, a rebellion of your mind against the intolerable chaining of conditions and circumstances. It's trigger is gross rather than subtle, otherwise I couldn't have managed it just then. As Rellis continued on and on in his lecture, I was triggering that reaction in him, spreading it faster and more completely than it would have done on its own. He began by scratching absentmindedly first at his chest, then at his thigh, then at his neck; before a full five minutes had passed he was beginning to use two hands, and that was when he became consciously aware of what he was going through. He broke off in the middle of a sentence, and looked down at himself.

"By the Sword of Gerleth, what occurs here?" he demanded, watching as his hands scratched everywhere, embarrassingly even down into his *haddin*. He was beyond being able to control the sensations, and felt as though he were infested with tiny vermin. The strength of imagination is such that he could feel tiny feet walking on him even if he couldn't see them.

"Father, I feel sure you suffer from self-delusion," Dallan said, his expression uninflected despite the chuckling in his mind. "I cannot pretend I understand the method used, yet Terril was invited by you to exercise her power. It seems she has."

"The *wenda*?" Rellis said with incredulity, then turned his head to look at me. Although I was scarcely straining, I could feel the beads of sweat on my forehead from my expending the the last of my strength. It was hard, damned hard, but I wasn't about to ease up until he cried uncle.

"It cannot be," Rellis muttered, still scratching like mad. "No being is able to do this to another, invisibly and from a distance! It is madness! It is— Enough, *wenda*! I am no longer able to bear it! Enough!"

As soon as he admitted defeat I let go, both to show him that his suffering really had been my doing, and to stop voluntarily before I was forced to stop. I hadn't been able to build up my mental muscles very far, and the limitations I worked under were painful as well as frustrating. Rellis' scratching slowed immediately, quickly petering out to nothing, and he slumped to the cushions with a sigh.

"Never in my life have I felt such a thing," he muttered, then looked up at Dallan and Tammad. "Was this the reason for your failure to face one another with swords in proper manner? I doubt it would have been possible for me to hold a sword."

"The reason for our failure was somewhat different," Dallan said, glancing at Tammad with a wry expression. "We were each forced to feel the hilarity of laughter, rendering serious battle impossible. As my recent opponent has said, the woman is strong-willed.''

"And therefore should not be allowed to escape the consequences of her actions," the barbarian put in, annoyance clear in his voice. "She must be taught to use her power with discretion, as a boy is taught to keep his sword sheathed when not truly threatened. Should she fail to learn the lesson, her life will sooner or later be forfeit."

"I'd rather lose that life than be taken advantage of any longer!" I spat, not caring that Dallan and Rellis didn't understand Centran; just then I wasn't talking to them. "If you're so afraid of what I'll do to you, you can solve the problem by never coming near me again!"

I hadn't really looked at him while I'd spoken, but I still turned my head away, toward the dais behind me. I was beginning to feel that hatred again, and it was a good thing I was too tired to do any more projecting. What would have come out of my mind right then wouldn't have been as amusing as laughter or itching.

"What does she say?" Rellis asked, shifting among the cushions so that I could feel his eyes on me. "So barbaric a tongue is beyond my knowledge."

"She—disagrees with my opinions," the barbarian answered, his voice the least bit fainter than it had been. "She dislikes punishment and fears it, yet refuses to learn from it. How is a man to abandon such a one, so filled with pride and arrogance that she is unlikely to survive without protection, yet who looks upon such protection with furious insult? What is a man to do with such a one?"

"Perhaps he would be best off seeing her with another," Dallan said, his voice soft with pity rather than hard with challenge. "When there is constant pain for both members of a match, that match is best dissolved. To live with constant pain is not to live at all."

"Only through pleasure and pain does a man know that he lives," Tammad came back, his voice strengthening again. "There are things not worth the slightest twinge, and those worth the pain of agony. To truly live is to believe that when the agony ends, the pleasure will first begin."

"I feel that this discussion would be best conducted over cups of wine," Rellis said, rising to his feet. "I, myself, can surely do with more than one. You may rest here undisturbed, *wenda*, and gather yourself together before the darkness meal. We will take our drink elsewhere."

I twisted in the cushions and tried to protest, but all three of them were heading for the door, paying no further attention to me. Getting up myself proved impossible when I tried, and I slumped back into the cushions as the door clicked closed. They were going elsewhere not to drink but to decide what was going to be done with me, a topic I wouldn't be allowed a say on. I grabbed a pillow and hugged it to me angrily, then lowered my cheek to the carpet fur in misery. I hated them terribly, all of them, but they couldn't have cared less. They weren't going to turn me loose, weren't even going to demand that I make a choice. The choice would be made for me, and all I had to do was accept it. Well, I wouldn't accept it, no matter what they did to me, I wouldn't! I closed my eyes to the urging of the exhaustion I felt, beginning to think about all the things they could do to me, and fell asleep that way.

I awoke crying out, my heart hammering, my mouth dry and stale with the taste of fear. It was terror that pursued me out of the mists of sleep, and I shuddered and pressed myself against the chest I was held to, desperately needing the arms that held me tight. It had been horrible, awful, and knowing that it had just been a bad dream didn't help at all.

"*Wenda*, what has disturbed your sleep?" Rellis asked, holding me close against the shuddering. "You seemed to be in fear of your very life."

"I—cannot remember," I answered, trying unsuccessfully to bring back what had frightened me so. It was gone behind dark clouds, leaving nothing but the reaction it had caused.

"We are not prepared to take the darkness meal," Rellis said, absently stroking my hair. "Are you able to join us, or would you prefer being served here."

"I need but a moment to gather myself," I said, remembering his views on how helpless I was. Cowering in his arms was a poor way of changing his opinion, and the effects of the nightmare were already wearing off. I stirred to let him know he could let me go, but he didn't release me immediately. He held on for a minute or two, and when his arms finally did open, I could have read his reluctance even without my empathetic ability. I looked up to see his blue eyes directly on me, as frankly and openly as all men looked at women on that world, but with more than casual interest in his mind. When I didn't look away from his stare he smiled faintly, then put a hand to my face.

"It is easily seen why my son feels so strongly about having banded you," he said. "The other, Tammad, was completely correct. Your lure is greater than that of any woman I have ever met."

"You find yourself attracted to my helplessness?" I asked, moving back a bit before straightening the silver gown I still wore.

"No, hardly your helplessness," he laughed, breaking out of whatever mood had just been holding him. "As I deem myself a prudent man, I shall prudently avoid delving more deeply into the question. It would never do that I add myself to the confusion we now face."

"I had thought the matter would by now be settled," I said, watching his reactions closely. "As I cannot press my own stand till resolution is reached, I find the delay vexing."

"I need not ask what your stand will be," he said with a grin, rising from his knees to extend a hand to me. "My suggested solution would have been the same even had I not known, yet the manner of execution would have been other than it was. It now lacks only your knowledge of what is to be, and that may be seen to over the meal."

I took his hand and let him help me to my feet, but swallowed down the questions I had without asking them. His "suggested solution" sounded like nothing I would care for, but there was time to make a fuss once I heard it. Despite the fact that I felt wrinkled and mussed, I followed him out of the reception room into the corridor, up the corridor a short way, and into another room. This one was considerably smaller than the first and had no dais, but what it did have was Dallan and Tammad relaxing among the piles of red and gold cushions. The men of Gerleth seemed to like red and gold, using it so often it was beginning to get boring. The sky outside the windows had turned dark with night, but the room was well provided with candles. Five females—servants, they were, rather than slaves—either stood near trays or served the two seated men, and Rellis led me to a place opposite Tammad and Dallan and no more than four feet away from them, then gestured for service as we sat. Two pairs of eyes watched me as bowls of food were put   the small table to my right, but I decided I was too hungry to pay any attention to those eyes or the strangely roiling minds behind them. I finished a spicy fish salad, swallowed most of a thick root soup, nibbled at a few strips of grilled meat, then finally lifted my goblet of golden wine. I could tell by the odor that the men were drinking *drishnak*, but there was nothing I cared to say about that as long as I had better.

"Perhaps you would now care to discuss what is to follow," Rellis said, watching me sip at the wine. "The—ah—stand you have taken has made you very much a part of it."

"I will make no objection to listening," I answered, leaning down to a cushion with my left elbow. "What objections I have may be made afterward."

"You may voice whatever objections you wish," Rellis shrugged with a grin, also leaning down to one elbow. "That will not change the fact that you will be required to obey. My son Dallan and the *denday* Tammad, at my request, have agreed to hold their differences in abeyance until they have returned from visiting the resting place of the Sword of Gerleth. The Sword was placed deep within this mountain by the *l'lenda* Zannon many lifetimes ago, after he had wielded it in battle against his foes, winning this land for his followers. It is said that the solution to all problems may be found by those who visit the resting place of the Sword, no matter the complexity of the problem, no matter its thorniness. It is for this reason that they undertake the descent, and the way will take some time in the wending."

"I refuse to await their return to have my future decided for me," I stated, looking directly at Rellis. "Even should you chain me, I will find my way free of the bonds and then of this place, for I will no longer allow others to dictate my fate."

I was braced for anger from any or all of them, having decided that playing it fearless and firm was my only hope, but I wasn't prepared for amusement. Tammad and Dallan chuckled where they half-lay among the cushions, and the grin Rellis had worn earlier matured to an open laugh.

"*Wenda*, we none of us believed that you might be ordered nor persuaded to await their return," Rellis said, giving me the impression that I had become predictable. "By cause of your own difficulties you will accompany them, and also return with a solution. There is no other thing that may be done."

"There most certainly is!" I huffed, trying to hide the dismay I felt. "I have made the decision to return to my own people, and shall do so. There is no need whatsoever for me to accompany those two!"

"On the contrary there is great need," Rellis came back, sitting up to look at me in a sober way. "Should you be allowed so foolish a thing as the returning to people who care nothing for you, Dallan and Tammad no longer have reason to visit the resting place of the Sword. Only with your presence does their effort become meaningful."

"Only in the opinion of certain others do my people care

nothing for me," I said, casting a hate-filled glance at a calm-minded barbarian. "Also, in my opinion, the actions of those two have as yet to be meaningful. I refuse to accompany them."

"*Wenda*, you may not refuse," Rellis said, and his eyes had grown harder. "Should you think to use your powers upon us and thereafter depart in peace, be advised that my guard has been warned and formed against you. Beyond this door stand ten warriors, a bit beyond them ten others, and ten further beyond them. Should you attempt to depart they will halt you, for you cannot hope to best them all. Two *l'lendaa* have found you of interest, *l'lendaa* and not *darayse*. Though you have been raised among offworlders, you must by now know that we are not as they. You may not turn your back upon the interest of men."

I didn't have to look around to know they were all watching me, their minds guarded and alert and suspicious of how I would react. I looked instead at the door to the hall, searching for and finding the guards Rellis had spoken of, furious but helpless to do anything about it. Human minds were harder to impress than animal minds, and I doubted if I could have handled even that number of animals. I was so angry I wanted to strike out at someone or something, but all I did was put my cup of wine aside.

"No, you are not like the men of my world," I said, looking at none of them. "On my world a woman need not fear being trapped, and held against her will, and ravished without chance of reprisal. As this is your concept of *l'lenda*, allow me to say how greatly I prefer *darayse*."

Again I was prepared for one reaction and got an unexpected other. The reaction I was expecting was anger and insult, but the waves of upset suddenly rolling at me came from all of them, showing the feeling to be unanimous. They were silent during this surge, confusion keeping any words from forming, and then one of those minds pulled itself together.

"*Wenda*, you see those about you through eyes lacking understanding," the barbarian said, the sound of movement accompanying his words. "You are held against your will only when your will is capricious and unreasonable, urging you to do that which is poorly thought out. As for ravishment without reprisal, there is no such thing indulged in by true *l'lendaa*. Should a man wish to show his love and appreciation of his *wenda* he will use her as his body urges him to do, yet with no thought of ravishment. Should the *wenda* find his use to be overly energetic due to his deep love he must be told, for he would not willingly cause her anything of pain. Though duty forces him to see to her punishment when such a thing is called for, there is no desire within him to cause her true pain. Should he lose himself and bring such pain, his regret is greater than hers."

His mind was as calm as it always was, but it was trying to tell me he was apologizing again. I kept my eyes on the golden fur I sat on, still unwilling to hear his apology, totally unwilling to let anything he said touch me. His opinions, like those of Dallan and Rellis, stemmed from the position of his own viewpoint. He'd have no idea about how I saw things until he stood in my footsteps, a place he was unlikely to ever visit. I sat among the red and gold cushions on the golden carpeting, not looking at any of them, and slowly their expectant minds understood that I would not be answering Tammad's contention in words.

"Pain is at times a difficult thing to forgive," Dallan said at last into a silence that had grown almost awkward. "*Wendaa* are small and loving and soft in a man's arms, yet when they believe themselves wronged they have the strength of ten men in support of their belief. When they have truly been wronged, the strength of the pain in their hearts is greater still. A man's proper duty is to guard himself with his *wenda* above all things, for she cannot hope to match the strength of her anger. Should he fail to do so, the disappointment within her is well earned by him."

"And yet, a man is no more than a man," the barbarian answered, his voice still soft. "He, too, is able to feel disappointment, and such a feeling brought about by the woman who holds his heart is bitter indeed. When she continues to fail him that bitterness becomes impossible to contain, if only for a moment. Though he would have it otherwise, the fool in him gains control and does that which requires forgiveness. Should that forgiveness not be forthcoming, there is foolish pain to accompany resigned understanding."

"A man is indeed a fool to expect overmuch of a *wenda*," Rellis said gently to the barbarian, sympathy urging him to give advice to someone who was a virtual stranger. "*Wendaa* are for pleasant companionship, and use, and the bearing of a man's children; though loving and attentive they are shallow and delicate. Should a man wish one he may rely upon come what may, he must seek among his brothers. *Wendaa*, for all their desirability, have not the strength nor a proper concept of honor. When you have attained my age, you will know the truth I speak."

Tammad and Dallan were considering what they'd been told,

but part of their attention was on me, warily waiting for *my* reaction to what I'd heard. I know they were expecting an explosion of some sort, but Rellis' words, on top of the barbarian's, had left very little room in me for anger. It hadn't occurred to me that Tammad had beaten me more in disappointment than in anger, and I could see that Rellis was right. Tammad *had* been a fool for thinking he could rely on me, for thinking I would bring him any more than disappointment. I was a freak among normal people, sneering at them for fearing something they had every right to fear and mistrust, invading their privacy even when it wasn't a matter of self-protection. I didn't even have enough sense to keep them from knowing it was happening, as though they were too far beneath my notice to bother with. No wonder Tammad hadn't believed that Aesnil was lying; I'd tarred myself with the brush with my own hand so often before, there was no reason for him to think I hadn't done it again. I closed my eyes and lowered my head in shame, drawing my shield in tight at the same time. Nothing I did on that world was right, and I wished I were dead.

"Father, I fear you have bruised the feelings of my little bird," Dallan said, his voice trying hard to exclude the sound of pity. "Her tears are a sight I have no wish to become more familiar with, yet they now appear distressingly upon her cheeks."

"*Wenda*, forgive me if I have given you insult or pain," Rellis said immediately, resonating to a strong sense of dismay. "I should not have spoken as I did within your hearing, for my words are certain to have been misinterpreted by you. A woman has other strengths than those of a man, ones which give to her. . . ."

I rose to my feet and headed for the door, cutting off Rellis' overblown and circuitous attempt at apology. There was no need for apology, not under those particular circumstances, especially not if I didn't want to hate myself any more than I already did. I was a poking, prying, sneak of a coward, and even I couldn't stand being near me. I got the door open and hurried out into the hall, almost bumping my nose on the guards out there, but I didn't have to wade through them. Without my knowing it Rellis was right behind me, and the guards stepped back when he took my arm.

"I will now see the *wenda* to her chamber," the *Chamd* of Gerleth announced, looking around at his men. "You are to accompany us, and then guard her door."

His hand on my arm directed me up the corridor, giving me no opportunity to disagree even if I'd wanted to. It wasn't my door that was going to be guarded, but I didn't care any longer; all I cared about was being alone. The hall made no impression on me, nor the number of doors we passed, only the one we eventually stopped at. Rellis opened it and urged me through first, followed after, then closed it behind himself.

"You may consider this chamber yours, *wenda*," he said, gesturing with one arm. "Though it is rare for a banded woman to sleep any place other than at the side of him who has banded her, it is best that you do so. When your proper ownership is once again plainly established, you will no longer need to occupy empty furs."

I walked away from him and further into the small room, distantly aware of the lack of red and gold. Brown and green and tan and white were the room's colors, to be found on the silks on the walls and single window, in the fur carpeting and low pile of bed furs, in the carved wood of the single, small table, in the two candles still lit in their sconces. The room was a box compared to what I had recently grown used to, but what difference did it make? It would hold me without fuss and presumption, without the need to impress. I neither wanted nor needed to be impressed just then; what I needed was to be left alone.

"How great an ache I feel in your silence," Rellis sighed, his voice coming from directly behind me. "Should you wish to speak with one who will listen willingly, I need not depart immediately." When I didn't move even to reject his offer he sighed again, then put his hands on my arms from behind. "*Wenda*, there is one other thing I must do, and then I will leave you to the solitude you so clearly long for. Had I not agreed to this doing, my son and the *denday* Tammad would not have agreed to leaving you unclaimed for the darkness. It will be distressing, I know, yet it will continue no longer than the darkness."

I didn't know what he was talking about, but again I was given no choice. His hands on my arms steered me to the bed furs and down onto them, and then he was lifting something metallic toward me. I immediately began to struggle, but when has struggle ever gotten me anything on that world? The metal collar attached to a chain was still closed around my throat with a click, and then Rellis had the nerve to hold me to him in an effort to calm me.

"No, *wenda*, there is nothing you may do for it," he soothed, stroking my back with one hand. "It was feared by Dallan and Tammad that you would either attempt escape or seek to take your life if none were with you, therefore was the restraint agreed upon. I, myself, would have remained to spare you the need for it, yet such an action would scarcely be wise. The restraint will not be taken with your charms.''

He held me tightly up against him, stroking me slowly, outwardly calm but inwardly watching for the least sign of invitation. With my face and body against him, feeling his warmth and strength, it was difficult not showing the hint he was looking for; when it comes to Rimilian males, I've been well conditioned. But despite the conditioning I really needed to be alone, and there was only one way to guarantee that. Reaching out gently toward Rellis, I touched him with boredom.

Boredom is one of those magic emotions that can bring any number of reactions. Some people eat when they're bored, some pace, some yawn and stretch, some close their eyes for a nap, some develop an overwhelming urge to go and do. Rellis was clearly the type to react in the last way, and that's just what he did. His mind told him he was wasting his time, and after a final hug he let me go, patted my cheek gently, then got up and left the room. Once he was gone I was able to unclamp my jaw, then stretched out on the furs.

The problem of Rellis was no problem at all, not by itself and certainly not when compared to my major problem. My hand absently stroked the dark brown fur I lay on while I tried to decide if I could consider the thing unemotionally. As a creature of emotions, I finally had to admit I was touched more by them, not less, and that made everything much more difficult.

A few minutes earlier I'd been ready to blame everything that had happened squarely on myself, but that was no more true than that I was totally innocent. The barbarian had beaten me when he'd thought I'd manipulated Aesnil, and for a minute or two I'd thought he might have been justified, but that wasn't so. He'd spoken of the way I'd failed him, and maybe I had, but was it fair of him to demand what he did of me? He wanted me because of my abilities, but he didn't want those abilities exercised except at his express instructions. If my ability had been superkeen hearing, it was as though he wanted me to listen only at approved times, and ignore what I heard at any other time. How do you stop yourself from hearing? How do you turn your hearing off except at certain specified times? You can stop yourself from hearing altogether by filling your ears with cotton or wax, but how do you stop the reflex to hear without those things? It was impossible, just as impossible as not picking up emotions without shielding completely.

I moved in some discomfort on the bed fur, reluctantly willing to admit that I'd made the mistake of intruding with my abilities more than once, but not willing to admit that it was all my fault. With my newly developing powers I was like a child just beginning to learn how to walk, aware of the potential danger but too wrapped up in the bright, glittering newness of it to be cautious. I'd been punished for my intrusions, a sure-fire way of learning to be cautious if there ever was one, but too much of the punishment had been harsh beyond the need to teach, bringing resentment rather than regret. It was all part of being on that world, all part of the victim syndrome that was making me hate everything and everyone I came in contact with. I didn't want to be a victim; in fact I refused to be one, and that didn't sit well with the men of the world. I couldn't fight all of them but that was just what I was doing, and the result had been painful, to say the least. They were afraid of what I might do, and had a right to be afraid, but I had some rights, too. If they couldn't live with what I was they had no right to change me, only to let me go.

Which brought me right back to Tammad and Dallan. Dallan enjoyed using me, but the main reason for his banding me had been pity, pity for what I had gone through. Despite the way he'd humiliated me there was no viciousness in him, no driving need to give me pain in order to make himself feel like a man. He wanted me so that he could protect me from everything including myself, which was a decent motivation but nothing to build a permanent relationship on. Dallan would give up his life before he would see me hurt, but Tammad—I still couldn't decide. My thoughts became a blur when I tried to think about him, and emotions immediately rose to rule. I hated him for beating me, and for trying to hold me, and for giving me to other men, and for a dozen other reasons, but I also couldn't forget what it was like to be held in his arms. There wasn't another man anywhere, even on Rimilia, who was able to make me feel the way he did, but I didn't understand why. Why couldn't I simply hate him for what he had done to me? Why couldn't I turn my back on him and forget him? I would do that anyway when I left Rimilia, but why did the thought of doing it bring pain instead of joy? I would still escape him no matter what he'd done to bewitch me, but why did it have to be so hard?

All those unanswered questions put me in a deep black mood, and when I shifted from brooding to sleeping, it was a distinct relief.

8

All the thinking I'd done before falling asleep hadn't solved any of my problems, but waking up certainly brought me a new one. I squirmed and moaned against a hard, broad body even before my eyes opened, wondering if I was dreaming, miserable to find that I wasn't. The early morning light coming into the room showed me Rellis' face, a chuckling in his mind, his hand moving me as though I had strings. The silver gown I still partially wore was no impediment to his efforts, but when I tried to rise up to reach him, his other hand on the chain leading to the collar about my throat was a distinct impediment to mine. I moaned again and struggled to get free, and the chuckle in his mind emerged from his throat.

"So, *wenda,* you awaken to a predicament," he said, grinning down at me. "Perhaps, had you known what you would face, you would not have done as you did."

"I do not understand," I gasped, close to tears from the way he was torturing me. "What have I done?"

"In some manner you knew I was asked to comfort you last darkness," he said, giving me no rest. "It was agreed that you were to believe the choice yours, unimposed by those about you, so that you might take true comfort from the doing. It did not come to me that I had been touched by your power till I had returned to Dallan and Tammad and had seen their surprise at my too-rapid return. I would not have left your side of my own volition, therefore was I forced from you by that which I was unable to see and defend against. Do you deny this charge?"

"I wished neither your comfort nor your use!" I cried, ineffectually trying to push his hand away. "It was my right to refuse you in my own way!"

"You have no such right," he disagreed, ignoring my efforts. "You may not refuse the man chosen to ease you by those who claim you, for in so doing you spit upon their authority and shame them. Are you unable to see that you have no right to shame them?"

172

"What of my shame?" I demanded with a sob, held down by throat and thigh. "By what right do *they* shame *me*? By the right of their being *l'lendaa*? By the belief that I, merely *wenda*, have no place protesting my shaming? Am I of so little consequence that my shame may be so easily overlooked?"

"What shame do you speak of, *wenda*?" he asked, his mind truly preplexed as his brow furrowed. "What shame might there be for a *wenda* in obeying him to whom she belongs? There is no shame in use, for that is one of the purposes of *wendaa*, to be used. What other shame might there be?"

I became aware of the tears rolling down my cheeks, but only because I didn't know how to answer him. I *did* feel shame when I was forced to a *l'lenda*'s use, but I couldn't explain why in any other way than by saying it was wrong. *I* knew it was wrong but Rellis didn't, and there seemed to be no clear way for me to explain it to him.

"To be put to the use of a *l'lenda* by the decision of another is wrong," I groped, trying to make him understand. "It is not only wrong it brings great shame, and I am not alone in believing so. All my people believe the same, therefore. . . ."

"Your people!" he laughed, interrupting me with amusement. "Now do I believe I begin to see. The *darayse* of your land are unable to bring pleasure to their *wendaa*, therefore do they beseech the approval of their *wendaa* before their pitiful attempts. Should they succeed in giving pleasure, the *wenda* is praised for having done the proper thing; should they fail, which is much more likely, they condemn the *wenda* for having done a shameful thing. In fear of having their inadequacy brought to light, they deny their *wendaa* to all others, harshly condemning any use other than their own, immediately placing the weight of guilt on all who disobey them. I know their sort well, for in my youth I visited a city of such *darayse*, a city which no longer stands. The fools gave insult to true *l'lendaa*, bringing down their wrath upon them. Their *wendaa*, when taken from the place at battle's end, thought much the same as you and were not easily reached, yet—look you. As I touch you deeply, are you able to deny me?"

I gasped and tried to refuse the sensations coursing through me, but it was impossible. I would have had to have been dead to succeed, and my body told me I was definitely not dead.

"As you cannot refuse me, is your response not meant to be?" he pursued. "Where is the shame and wrongness in doing as you were born to do? Where is the shame and wrongness in giving pleasure to one approved of by him to whom you belong?

It is pleasure he, himself, cannot give, and he joys in the thought that his woman is able to do the thing for him. If they are one she, too, will find joy in giving joy, and will see no shame in the doing. It will be *her* decision to do so, and she will not need to have force used upon her. Should there be shame involved, it is surely that a *wenda* must be forced to give joy to her beloved. The thought then comes that he cannot truly be her beloved after all. Let us remove this gown.''

His hand left me then, but only to move to the silver gown so that it could be slid off me. I didn't have the strength to resist, but more than that I was caught up in the question of what he'd said. He thought I was wrong for making men force me to their use, wrong for finding shame where there was none, inconsiderate and uncaring of a man I supposedly loved. I didn't love him—them—but that wasn't the point. Did they all see it in the same way? I couldn't have been wrong right from the beginning—could I?

"You will not be clad so cumbersomely upon your journey," Rellis said, tossing away the well-worn silver gown while I still drowned in confusion. "After your punishment, I will see you clad more appropriately."

"Punishment?" I asked, trying to remember everything we'd talked about. "Do you mean to use me after all?"

"No, *wenda*, I do not mean to use you," he sighed, trying not to lose patience. "Had you not used your power I would have given you pleasure, yet you chose to do as you deemed best. Now I do as I deem best."

He put his hands on me again, and what he gave me really was punishment. He made me want him so badly I nearly died, but he didn't let me have him. I'd refused his attentions the night before, and all the begging and pleading I did made up for it not at all. He allowed me no release whatsoever, and when he was finally through with me I was well into hysterics. His hands opened the collar around my throat and made me sit up, and by the time my crying had eased up I was already into the clothing he had brought. Clothing. I looked down at myself through a film of tears, burning and unable to sit still, seeing a slightly longer, slightly fuller, version of the thing Dallan had made me wear the day before. The top of it veed down to my waist but it had a back, leaving only my arms and sides bare. When I got to my knees, the skirt reached to the middle of my thighs, and I could feel Rellis' eyes on me and the approving hum in his mind. He wanted me, I knew he did, and I couldn't make myself not beg.

"Rellis, do not leave me so," I sobbed, putting my hands out to him. "Should it be true that my actions last darkness caused shame, I have been well repaid. Do you wish me to plead for your use? I will gladly do so. Allow me to touch you and I will plead in any way you wish."

I reached toward him where he sat at the edge of the bed furs, w...hing I could use my mind instead of my hands, but even my hands weren't permitted near him. He caught my wrists between his own hands with a smile, and slowly shook his head.

"It is not *my* use you must beg," he said, raising one hand to smooth my hair. "There are two who await you who will be pleased to see you, and all you need do is ask. Which of them, I wonder, will you approach first?"

I closed my eyes and lowered my head, whimpering at the need I felt, knowing I would have to go on that way. I'd die of shame if I had to ask one of them to ease me, and I'd sooner die of need. Somehow Rellis seemed to understand my resolve, and a flash of annoyance touched his mind as he snorted.

"So you believe you will approach neither of them, do you?" he said, holding my wrists in a one-handed grip. "Do you need to be coaxed further into the fire before you have the good sense to seek water?"

"No, do not touch me again!" I choked, stretching back away from his reaching hand. "How might I approach one without giving unnecessary pain to the other? I do not wish either of them, yet begging their use is a poor way of convincing them of it."

"Do you truly expect me to believe that you wish neither of them?" he asked, annoyed but drawing his hand back again. "Had that been so, you would already have found another to face them for you. With the aid of your power, even *darayse* would have found it possible to best them. No, *wenda,* it is clear you care for them both, yet the question remains as to which of them you care for more. Undoubtedly this journey will provide the answer—as well as prove to you your inability to withdraw from them. Come now; we have delayed long enough."

He pulled me off the pile of bed furs, made me brush my hair fast, then hurried me out into the corridor by one arm. Only two sets of twenty warriors waited for us outside, and we led a parade up one corridor and down another, passing marble walls and occasional ribbed windows, the morning light managing to break through the thin, scattered clouds in the sky. I wasn't expecting to meet anyone, so when we rounded a corner and came upon a slave down on hands and knees wiping one of the marble floors with a cloth, I was startled. When we stopped not five feet from the slave, I was more than startled; the naked woman on her knees, working under the critical eye of a large *l'lenda* holding a broad strap, was none other than Aesnil. Her long blond hair was braided to keep it out of her way, and even that early in the morning she seemed exhausted.

"Well, well, Aesnil, how pleasant to see that you are being kept from boredom in my house," Rellis said, looking down at her. "How pleased you must be at the feeling of such accomplishment."

Tears welled in Aesnil's eyes and her mind filled with misery, but she didn't look up or stop wiping the floor.

"Have you no words of morning greeting, Aesnil?" Rellis pursued, his thoughts grimly pleased. "Will you not ask after my sleep in the polite manner?"

"I may not cease my task without permission, uncle," she whispered, still moving the cloth across the floor. "Should I do so I will be strapped, and made to begin again from the beginning."

"I see," Rellis said, and then moved his eyes to the guard standing over her. "How often has it been necessary to strap this slave and begin her again?" he asked.

"Two times it was necessary to strap her and begin her again, my *Chamd*," came the answer, accompanied by a grin. "It has taken all of the darkness for her to see to her task, and it is nearly done."

"And through it she has learned some measure of wisdom." Rellis nodded in approval, looking at Aesnil again. "I am pleased that you show yourself able to learn, Aesnil, for your position in this house is as unique as your position in your own house. Here you are the sole female slave beneath my roof, and must comport yourself accordingly. I am told you find great pleasure in consigning others to slavery, therefore must you relish your position more than another would. Learn well, Aesnil, and perhaps I may be persuaded to recall that we are kin."

He stood another moment looking down at her, but when I took a step forward and tried to bend and touch her, he pulled me away by one arm and resumed our trek through the corridors. Her mind had been sunk in such deep misery and humiliation that I'd had to try comforting her, but Rellis wasn't prepared to allow that. He'd tried hurrying me away before I could wreck what he considered good work, but I'd caught the flash of gratitude in Aesnil's mind, showing she knew what I'd wanted to do. I got a short lecture on not interfering with a well-earned lesson, but I ignored most of it as I sent Aesnil as much strength and support as I could. I didn't waste my breath saying anything, but if Rellis had been able to feel Aesnil's mind the way I'd felt it, he might not have considered what he was doing to her such a good idea.

Our walk took us to the end of a corridor that had a single door in it. Behind the door was a stairway leading down, but it had nothing in common with the stairway Dallan and I had used in Aesnil's palace which led to the slave quarters. This stairway was marble rather than cut out of rock, wide rather than narrow, well-lit rather than dark and dank, and guarded rather than deserted. We led our parade downward a good thirty feet or more, and finally emerged in a wide—landing or room—which held a single, metal-bound door. Two more guardsmen stood at the door, but they were being kept company by Dallan and Tammad, who had a number of leather-bound bundles at their feet. All four watched us leave the stairway, but the humming in the minds of the two men waiting for me topped everything else for quite some distance around. I didn't realize I was trying to hang back until Rellis' hand tightened on my arm, pulling me forward closer to where they stood.

"A wait proving its worth," Dallan said, moving forward one step from the door and the bundles. "Your presence will brighten the darkness, Terril."

"And perhaps warm it as well," Rellis said, thrusting me forward ahead of him. "You have taken what was necessary?"

"Indeed," Dallan nodded, gesturing back toward the leather bundles. "Enough to feed us there and back, water to drink, furs in which to sleep, a sip of *drishnak* to ease the boredom. We will be no longer than the time necessary to reach the resting place of the Sword and return."

"You will be a bit longer than that," Rellis answered, but gave Dallan no time to ask the obvious question. "As you are completely prepared, you had best depart."

"The thought has come to me that perhaps it would be best if we were to leave the woman here," the barbarian said, stopping Dallan as he bent for one of the bundles. "There is no true need for her presence, and she will surely slow our pace. This matter is one between *l'lendaa*, and not to be given over to the dabbling of *wendaa*."

Although I really didn't want to go with them, I could feel myself stiffening in resentment at the barbarian's attitude. I might not be as ridiculously big as he and Dallan, but I wasn't entirely helpless! He made me sound as competent as a two-year-old, and I resented it like hell.

"The *denday* Tammad is no doubt known for his wisdom," Rellis answered immediately, giving me no opportunity to do something stupid like insisting on going. "This is, however, a matter with which he has had little experience. If he will accept my word as to the necessity for the presence of the *wenda,* I will most humbly offer my apologies should he feel upon his return that I have been proven wrong. Is this condition acceptable?"

Tammad didn't hesitate long, but his mind tightened with vexation even as he accepted the offer so made to him. He still didn't agree with Rellis, but the only way to say so was to insult the man. Those light blue eyes touched me briefly with disapproval, and I didn't have to guess what he disapproved of. He'd reacted with a good deal of heat when he'd first looked at me in that brief mockery of a gown, but he really didn't enjoy seeing me dressed that way in public, especially not through someone else's decision. When he'd put me up for sale he hadn't minded that my gown had been just about blown away by the wind, but the situation had changed and he just didn't approve. I didn't give a damn whether he approved or not, and I couldn't resist standing just a little bit straighter.

"I will carry these," Dallan said, lifting two of the bundles by their leather strings and slipping them over his left shoulder, just above his sword hilt. "There are two for you as well, *denday* Tammad, and the carrying of the fifth may be shared between us."

Dallan's voice was calm and friendly, but his mind was enjoying the annoyance he knew the barbarian was feeling. He felt no annoyance at all, and was actually looking forward to the trip.

"I will be pleased to carry these two bundles," the barbarian agreed, picking up what seemed to be duplicates of Dallan's packs. "The last, however, need be carried by neither of us. As the woman is to accompany us, she may as well be of some use."

He lifted the fifth bundle and tossed it at me, startling me into catching it with a squeak of surprise. It was long and round and looked as though it were heavy, but once I had my arms around it, I found it to be nothing more than bulky. It weighed very little, and Rellis and Dallan chuckled at the way I'd jumped when it was thrown at me. I cast a black look at the barbarian as he turned away from me, wondering just how pleasant the trip had to be for *him*. He seemed determined to make it as hard as possible for *me,* and I wasn't above returning the favor, not with Dallan there to stand behind. As Rellis had mentioned earlier, even a man of *my* world could have won against that mighty *l'lenda* with me behind him.

The two guards turned to the large metal door, drew back the heavy metal bolt, then pulled the door open. Beyond was darkness lit with a single torch, uninviting in the extreme, but Tammad strode through the doorway into it as though he'd done it any number of times before. I was in no hurry to follow him, but Dallan took my wrist and did some striding of his own, and less than a minute later the metal door clanged closed behind us.

The area beyond the door was something like a stone terrace, with three broad steps leading further down into the darkness. The single torch on the wall was right above the terrace, flickering gently against the faint wind movement coming out of the darkness all around. We seemed to be in the heart of a mountain, and even the two giant forms to either side of me didn't do much to reduce the chill of the place. When I found myself clutching the bundle I held and searching the darkness with my mind, I decided it was time to force myself to relax. Deep darkness is dangerous only when you don't know what might be in it, and I wasn't about to let anything alive get even as close as spitting distance.

"Are there no torches we might carry to light the way?" the barbarian asked, staring down the three carved steps. "A misstep in the darkness is certain without it, not to speak of losing what trail there is."

"I am informed that torches are unnecessary," Dallan answered. "Let us proceed as far as we may, and then reconsider the question."

He hitched up the leather ties over his shoulder and started down the steps, watching both where he put his feet and the deep blackness to either side of him. I glanced back at the door that had been closed behind us, seeing the small gong hanging to its left that I'd spotted when we'd first come through. If Dallan was leading off Tammad might simply follow him, the two of them forgetting all about me. If that happened I intended staying by the door until they were far enough ahead not to worry about and then ring the gong to be let out, but I'd run out of luck the first day I'd met the barbarian. Instead of ignoring me as he had done earlier, he reached a hand out into the middle of my back and pushed me ahead of him, down the broad steps of carved rock.

A trail of sorts waited at the bottom of the steps, the rock somewhat sharper under foot than the terrace had been. Not much of the torchlight reached that far, especially with the barbarian behind me cutting off what there was. I walked as slowly as I could with one arm partially raised in front of me, aiming for the dark shadow and fascinated thoughts that were all I could see of Dallan. I couldn't imagine what he might be fascinated with, but as the seconds passed and my eyes adjusted more fully to the dark, I discovered that the walls of rock to either side of the wide trail, as well as that overhead and underfoot, glowed very faintly. The glow wasn't bright enough to make seeing easy, but it was considerably better than pitch darkness.

"Should this continue, we will have very little difficulty following the trail downward," Dallan said softly when we reached him. "Torches might well be considered an intrusion in this place."

"Should we encounter no more than the trail, the dimness will indeed be pleasantly restful," Tammad agreed, looking around himself. "As the woman is able to detect the approach of that which may be inimical, there should be little in the way of danger to halt us."

Dallan made a sound of agreement and began moving ahead again, slowly but with more confidence than he had shown earlier. I followed after immediately, giving the barbarian no chance to put his hand on me again as he'd intended. It really annoyed me that he'd so casually assigned long-distance guard duty to me right after insisting that I stay behind, and if I could have let something horrible through that would have eaten him but left me alone, I would have. I didn't know if there *was* anything horrible down there to let through, but if I came across something I'd be sure to see if there was anything I could do with it.

We followed the wide trail through the rock corridor behind Dallan for about fifteen minutes, conscious of a slight but definite downgrade and then, suddenly, the corridor ended. Beyond it was what seemed to be an immense cavern, its walls and ceiling lost in inky blackness, only the glow from the rock below our feet and some down-trending boulders left to show us the way. Dallan moved forward slowly until he stood beyond the edge of the rock corridor and then, one hand on the boulder to his left, began what seemed a considerably steeper descent. Again I followed him but with a good deal more reluctance, watching the greenish-glow I climbed on for any uneven gaps I might trip on, beginning to shiver from the increased coolness of the open, unwalled area. I could feel that sunlight and warmth had never touched that space for as long as the mountain had lived, and almost felt that I had to fend off the shadow-fingers of the rock as it tried to touch my flesh where it was bare. We had only just begun traveling through the mountain, but it was already reaching for my soul.

Being cold sometimes turns me morbid and overly imaginative, but brisk exercise takes care of that by substituting disgust. Dallan forged ahead as if he were running a foot race, Tammad came right behind me seemingly with the intention of running me down, and I, the only one there of a normal size, was caught between them and forced into a scrambling downhill rush. By the time we reached the bottom of the rock slope I was sweating, and the soles of my feet felt as though they'd been beaten. Dallan stood looking around into the darkness as he waited for us, and the barbarian passed me where I'd stopped to rub my feet and joined him.

"The trail has widened somewhat," Tammad observed, also looking around into the receding darkness where only the faint glow of the floor appeared, and that for only a short distance away. "Were you told of any markings we might follow?"

"I was given no more information than you," Dallan admitted, and then his questing thoughts centered on an idea. "However, as we know we are to descend farther into the mountain, let us search out the direction which most seems to lead downward."

"There," the barbarian said, his shadow arm pointing to the right of our descent and close to the rock wall we had come down. "The glow of the floor disappears sooner than it should."

"It does indeed," Dallan agreed, studying the area that had been pointed out to him. "Let us by all means investigate it."

Again Dallan strode away, and again I would have stayed behind if at all possible, but I didn't seem destined to be forgotten. The barbarian stood waiting for me, impatience in his mind, but I wasn't in the mood to be rushed. I'd put down the bundle I'd been carrying in order to rub my feet, and I had to retrieve it before I could follow after Dallan. Moving very slowly and deliberately I turned my back on the giant shadow six feet away, hoping he could see me well enough to understand the snub, then reached down just as slowly and deliberately for the bundle. I was sure I would be able to spot any anger in his his mind soon enough to avoid whatever unpleasantness he might consider, but it hadn't occurred to me that he might have been expecting some sort of gesture of defiance from me and was prepared for it. I was watching so carefully for anger, that he was right behind me and lifting me off the floor by an arm around my waist before I knew what was happening.

"Clearly do I recall having once instructed you regarding the offering of temptation," he said very softly as his hand came to me beneath the very short skirt. "As you seem to have forgotten the lesson, I shall repeat it in another manner."

I almost choked trying to scream, but nothing forced itself through my straining throat but mewling. He held me backwards under his left arm, letting his right hand do what it always did to me, adding to the punishment Rellis had given me earlier. I kicked wildly and clawed at the back of his leg with my left hand, dying from the fire he caused so easily, and suddenly a burst of amusement came from his mind.

"I see you have been well prepared to give warmth through the darkness," he chuckled, abruptly setting me back on my feet and crouching, but not withdrawing his hand. "I shall do nothing to ruin that preparation, for you have as yet to learn your natural place among men. Such preparation will do well in teaching it you. Take your bundle and follow the *drin* Dallan."

If I could have spoken I would have babbled that I couldn't follow Dallan, not yet, but words were beyond me. I put both of my hands on one of his broad shoulders and tried to impale myself on his hand, but he refused to allow that. He had me squatting and grasping his knee before I realized that he had no intention of easing me, and in fact had withdrawn his hand entirely. He was still punishing me for being insolent with him, punishing me more horribly than if he had raped me the way he had the first time, and I wanted to curse at him for being able to deny me his body the way I could never do with him. With soft sobs choking me I groped for my bundle, found it and pulled it to me, then forced myself erect and staggered after Dallan. I could feel the tears running down my cheeks in a steady stream, but their moisture did nothing to quench the flames in my body.

I rounded the dark curve and followed it downward as fast as I could move without falling, catching sight of Dallan's outline in no more than a minute. He moved forward more slowly than he had earlier, his mind alert as he looked around, and I was glad he couldn't really see me even when he glanced back. Thinking through the chaos in my mind was impossible, but I didn't have to think to know how much furious misery I was filled with. They all took advantage of me, every one of those oh-so-mighty *l'lendaa* of Rimilia, and if I never saw any of them again I would laugh in delight every day of a very long life. I stepped on a pebble and hurt my foot even more than it had been hurting, but that was just another thing to add to all the rest. It was all I could do to stand straight and keep moving, thanks to the punishment I'd had from those wonderful men who were so much kinder than Hamarda slave-masters.

The half-trail we were on continued to wind down and around, gradually enough to cover more horizontal distance than vertical through that faintly illuminated darkness. After we'd been walking for an endless time we reached another vast level that spread out into the darkness all around, and again the two men walked a short way ahead to see if they could pick out the next proper direction. Despite the fact that I was dark-chilled, tired from walking, and still in terrible discomfort, I waited until the two were definitely looking away, then slipped off quietly into the darkness to the left of the trail we'd come down. I stayed close to the wall and worked at getting out of sight as fast as possible, having decided more than an hour earlier to lose myself at the first opportunity, stay out of sight until they had given up and left, and then try to head back alone. There was always the possibility that I might lose myself so well that I'd never find the way back, but at that point I really didn't care. The thought of dying in the ghost-glow of the mountain's heart wasn't nearly so depressing as the thought of continuing on in the company that had been forced on me. Once I was out of sight and sound of them I sealed my heaving emotions behind the shield that would keep me from betraying myself, took a tighter grip on the bundle that had grown heavier with the passage of time, and broke into a choppy run.

I ran until I couldn't control the gasping of my breath, hurried until my legs turned to liquid, then forced myself to walk on a bit farther, holding onto the rock wall with my left hand to make sure I didn't lose it. If there had been a giant crevasse directly in my path I wouldn't have seen it, but that possibility fell more into the category of kindness than disaster. I had been too miserable to be hungry earlier, but all the exertion I'd gone through reminded me that I'd been given nothing for breakfast, and I felt hollow as well as thirsty. I stumbled over a fair-sized boulder and scraped my hand on the rock wall trying to stay erect, and while I was flatly refusing to cry over the pain, I became aware of the cave.

The gap was no more than two feet ahead of me, low enough down on the wall that I would have missed it if I'd continued on the way I'd been going—my hand would have crossed above it. I moved forward the two feet slowly, looking down at it, then abruptly cleared my shield briefly to search the space. No living minds seemed to be behind the gap, so I got down on my hands and knees and peered inside. The space was all of eight feet wide and four deep, just big enough to achieve box status, but that was fine with me. There were no deep recesses where unimaginable monsters might be hiding, just a place where I might hide. Without thinking about it any further, I crawled inside.

I put aside the leather bundle I'd been carrying, sat for a minute looking around myself, then lay down on my side, facing away from the small entrance. The rock was hard and cold and uneven, but it was better than standing up and even better than sitting. When I sat I could see myself against the surrounding greenish glow, a dark outline-figured with no details visible, with no depth or reality. It was typical of the way I felt on that planet, that I had no true reality. People looked at me and spoke to me—and abused me—without ever thinking of me as being real or being worthy of consideration. The words concerning consideration were there, but a real understanding of *me* wasn't. It was not only painful it was wearying, and I was sick of fighting the tide. I pushed aside the wildly swirling thoughts clamoring for attention I was in no condition to give them, and simply closed my eyes.

I was hoping to fall asleep and escape everything in the way of questions and decisions, but I was just too hungry and thirsty. I would have opened the bundle I'd carried, but it would have been a waste of time and effort. It wasn't heavy enough to contain either food *or* water, and I couldn't face any other disappointments just then. At least ten minutes went by while I struggled to ignore all sorts of discomfort, and then I suddenly had an odd feeling. Not knowing what it meant I opened my eyes and turned to my back to look around, and then cringed back in shock. A black outline-form was crawling through the low opening into the box-cave, but I wasn't fortunate enough for it to be an animal. It was a human beast, far worse than anything of the lower orders, and I moaned in misery, sure I knew who it was.

"*Wenda,* why did you run?" the shadow's voice demanded, and for a minute I didn't understand. Then it came to me that it was Dallan rather than Tammad, and I shuddered in uncertain, partial relief.

"How were you able to find me?" I demanded in turn, not quite as strongly, in fact in little more than a whisper. I bumped up against the back wall of the cave, surprised that I was still retreating, upset that I'd gone as far as possible, awash in every emotion of distress there is.

"There was little difficulty in finding you," he said, dismissing the incredible as unimportant even as he straightened up to his knees. "Of greater moment is the reason for your having done such a foolish thing. No matter your own beliefs, Terril, you are scarcely *l'lenda*. You may well have found yourself irretrievably lost."

His voice held the overtones of the beginnings of anger, a clear indication that his mind would have been the same if I had lowered my shield. But I hadn't lowered my shield and wasn't about to; what little control I had left would have been totally inadequate to the task of keeping me from broadcasting.

"And what if I *had* become lost?" I came back, my voice trembling as much as my body. "Perhaps I wished it so for reasons of my own. It makes little difference, for I have now been found. You have only to give me what punishment you find necessary, and we may leave this place."

"*Wenda*, your bitterness cuts with the edge of a dagger," he said, his voice softened and filled with faint hurt. "Is this the sole thing you have come to expect from those about you? Punishment for that which was done by you? I would sooner you spoke of the cause for the distress which sent you alone into the darkness, than that you wept from the punishment for it."

"And I would sooner speak to the beasts of the forests," I said, turning my face away from him. "To speak to *l'lendaa* is more useless still."

I knelt beside the back wall, my left shoulder and arm against it, my head down in utter depression. The urge to look at him with my mind was nearly overwhelming, but I forced myself to keep the shield in place. I'd been telling myself I didn't care what he did to punish me, but when he moved forward on his knees and took my arm to pull me close to him, I gasped from more than the scrape of pebbles on my knees. Coward that I was I *did* fear what he would do, and I trembled uncontrollably as he held me against his chest. His hard body and strong arms brought warmth to chase away the chill of that dark place, but his being so near also brought flare-tinged throbs to my body as the various punishments I'd been given earlier reasserted themselves. I knew he was trying to look at me even though I kept my head down, and after a minute his hand came to my face.

"Again I have the impression that I hold a woman who has been slave to men," he said, his fingers touching my cheek gently. "Once, not long after I had first been declared servant-slave by Aesnil, I and four others of my brothers in bondage were called upon to assist in the punishment of a slave wench who was guilty of insolence. Rather than simply being whipped, the wench was passed about among a number of guardsmen to be aroused, yet none were permitted to use her. All during the early part of the day was this done, she being forced to the attending of assigned tasks in the interim, her tears and distress clearly evident to those of us who watched her. When we were permitted to eat our midday gruel, it was she who was made to serve it to us. Her body was small but nicely rounded, pleasant to look upon as she knelt naked before each of us in turn, clenching her thighs as she offered the gruel. She had begged release from those who guarded us, but could not bring herself to do the same with slaves like herself. She saw us as slaves, you understand, rather than as men who were bound.

"When our gruel had been swallowed, it was then necessary to see to the foolish *wenda,* yet not until she had been made to beg her use of us. That she had no wish to do so seemed an insurmountable problem to those who stood with me, for they had too long been set to the pleasing and serving of *wendaa* and had nearly forgotten their manhood. They were eager for the use of the slave and feared what punishment would come to them were we to fail in our assigned task, yet they knew not how to achieve their goal. It was left to me to take the *wenda* in my arms, and once she knew it was a man who held her, her pleas were quickly forthcoming. When first I put my arms about her she felt much as you do now, stiff with refusal yet helpless to disobey, atremble with need and fear, knowing well the power of men yet seeking to hide herself from it. A man's power has little purpose other than to give pleasure and easing to his woman, *memabra.* Why do you not seek my assistance when you have need of it?"

"What became of the slave when you were done with her?" I asked in a whisper, ignoring his question as I ignored the way he called me his little banded one. I knew I wore his bands; how could I forget?

"She was used by those others who were servant-slaves till she wept with pain, then was she taken by the guardsmen and whipped," Dallan answered after a brief hesitation, his arms tightening around me. "You need not fear the same, *memabra,* for we keep no slaves here, and you are no slave in any event."

"I feel nothing other than slave," I whispered, discovering to my horror that I held him around, pressing my body against his. "I would look upon it as a great kindness were you to take that sword hung at your side and with it put an end to the misery of my life. I have no further strength with which to withstand the whippings of this world.''

"Never would I take your life, *wenda* mine,'' he said, his voice soothing and filled with concern as he stroked my hair. "We will put an end to some small part of your distress, and then we will speak further upon the balance of it.''

He released his bundles and reached behind me then to the bundle I'd carried, fought open one end of it, and pulled out a sleeping fur. I don't know what it was I thought I was carrying, but seeing the shadow fur over my shoulder surprised me. I began shaking my head and crying, trying to tell him I didn't need to be used, but I was lying and we both knew it. I still held him around as he spread the fur, removed his swordbelt and then put us on the fur, and when his hands raised my face to his and his lips touched mine I was glad he hadn't listened to me. He kissed me deeply without touching anything other than my face, and when I could no longer keep from moving against him he reached down and removed his *haddin,* then knelt above me. His hands went to the open sides of the short gown I wore, his lips to the sides of my breasts beyond the narrow strip of covering silk, and as I reached spasmodically for his shoulders I knew I couldn't wait any longer. I *had* to have him, right then, and for once he let himself be rushed. He spread my thighs and entered me strongly, then gave me exactly what I needed; it wasn't slow and careful, but it was very satisfying. His own satisfaction was a match to mine, but it wasn't the wildly abandoned thing he had been hoping for. I'd let my shield dissolve at some point, and I could see that easily enough, but the way he continued to hold me gave no indication of how he felt. He knew that all my problems had not been solved by a simple toss on the furs, and he didn't pretend they had been.

"I find it increasingly disturbing that I cannot see you, *wenda*,'' he said after a final kiss, again holding my face. "The tension has gone out of you, yet the unhappiness remains.''

"You believe that sight of me would enable you to cure my unhappiness?'' I asked, too far from amusement even to laugh in derision. "Then by all means let us kindle the fire.''

"The fire we kindled a few moments ago saw to some measure of it,'' he returned with a chuckle, leaning toward me so that our bodies touched again. "Perhaps a second fire would indeed be of some benefit. Speak to me now of what disturbs you.''

"What disturbs me has not changed since last we spoke of it,'' I said, squirming a bit against the way he partially pinned

me to the fur. "That it has grown worse rather than better is
scarcely surprising, for I had expected nothing else. I must leave
this world before it takes my life or sanity."

"You will allow my world to defeat you?" he asked, running
his hand down my side to my thigh. "This I cannot believe, for I
have seen you fight against that which you could not accept and
win against great odds. It is not a thing done by many *wendaa*,
and shows great courage."

"I have no courage at all," I denied with a headshake,
shifting against his weight. "I am a coward who fears all things,
and is weary unto death of that fear. I shall return to my own
world where I feel no fear."

"Yet where others feel fear of you," he said, his voice now
sober. "Where you are bound harshly by cause of that fear and
forced to live beneath unnatural restrictions. This is the world
you prefer above mine?"

"You believe I should not?" I laughed with incredulity. "There
are none there who beat me and torture me, none who take my
use without my permission, none who give my use to others
when it is they I desire, none who—"

I broke it off and turned my face away, knowing I'd said too
much—and not enough. I couldn't make myself compatible with
Rimilia in a hundred years of trying, and I felt as though I'd
already tried at least that long. Banging my head on stone walls
has never been one of my favorite pastimes.

"Perhaps it will be best if we continue this discussion when
we have returned from the resting place," Dallan said, smooth-
ing my hair once before rolling away from me and reaching for
his *haddin*. "There is little sense in agonizing over a difficulty
now, when that difficulty may no longer remain when once we
have made our visit. Should there be need later, it may be done
later."

His outline form moved slowly but deliberately, a conscious
effort against the churning in his mind. I sat up on the fur and
stared at him, wondering what was upsetting him, but didn't get
the opportunity to decide to ask. Once his *haddin* was wrapped
around him he reached for the bundles he'd carried, took one and
opened it, drank from it, then offered it to me. I'd been afraid it
would be *drishnak,* but all it was was water, clear, wet and
very satisfying. I lifted the skin and drank deeply from it the
second time, feeling it flow down my throat with almost indecent
pleasure, feeling it giving me the strength to go on a little
farther. I savored the second swallow then went for a third, and

didn't know I'd done anything other than drink until Dallan grunted.

"Werda, you had best cease that lest I become uncontrollably aroused," he said, his mind flashing deep, true discomfort. "I had not known that water would bring you such pleasure, else I would have given it to you much the sooner."

For a minute I didn't understand, and then I realized that I'd allowed my feelings at finally getting something to drink to leak from my mind. I hadn't known Dallan would interpret and react to them as he was doing, but he wasn't, after all, an empath trained to interpret correctly.

"Please accept my apologies," I said at once, making sure he got no more accidental leakages as I handed the skin back. "I had a great need of that water, so great a need that its presence made me unaware of the doings of my mind. It will not happen again."

"It is odd that it occurred this time," he said, putting the water aside and gesturing me off the fur. "We have not been so long upon our way that your need should have grown so great. Were you so concerned over our journey that you ate and drank less than what was wise at your meal before you joined us?"

His tone showed something of the annoyance in his mind as he folded the fur we'd been lying on, undoubtedly thinking I'd skipped the meal on purpose. I stood behind him near the back wall of the cave-box, understanding that he knew nothing of what his father had done, wondering if I ought to tell him. I caused enough trouble between people without doing it on purpose, but I hesitated a little too long. His mind used my silence the way it usually did, and dove straight for the truth I was trying to avoid.

"By the might of the Sword, you were given nothing!" he swore, his anger flaring out as he grabbed my bundle and began stuffing the fur into it. "This was surely my father's doing, for he has not yet learned to know you. When we have rejoined the *denday* Tammad, we will eat before continuing on."

"For what reason would your father have done such a thing?" I ventured, being careful not to touch the edges of his anger. "He does not appear to be a cruel man."

"Nor is he," Dallan said, drawing my bundle closed and then handing it to me. "It was his intention that your need for sustenance would drive you to the feet of Tammad or myself, asking to have the hunger and thirst taken from you. With this knowledge I now understand another thing, which is the reason for your great physical need. You were aroused by him before being brought to us, were you not? This double need was to have put you at the feet of him whom you truly prefered, for hunger of the body is considerably more selective than hunger of the belly. A pity my father knows nothing of the shape and size of the pride which fills you. Had he known that, he would also have known that his efforts would be in vain.''

"I see," I mumbled, watching as Dallan took his swordbelt and strapped it on, then slung his bundles over his shoulder. I felt pale remembering the way I'd acted with Tammad after he'd touched me, but that was surely only because he *had* touched me. I hadn't put myself at his feet by choice because I hated him, and the more I squeezed the bundle I held, the more I believed it.

"I will leave this place first, and then you may follow," Dallan said, getting down on all fours in front of the gap in the wall. "Wait until I call, and then come ahead."

His dark outline squirmed and crawled through the gap, disappearing quickly, and all at once I wanted out of there. I followed immediately and got down on my knees, thrust my bundle through as I heard my name being called softly, then crawled out. My bundle had been lifted out of the way, and it was something of a shock to see not one pair of legs in front of me, but two. By that time my mind had done the frantic searching it should have done much earlier, and had discovered the vast calm that never brought itself to my attention unless I looked for it. I slowly rose up from my knees in front of Dallan and Tammad, and took back the bundle that Dallan was holding without looking up at either of them.

"It seems clear that you are the victor according to our agreement," the barbarian said to Dallan, his voice as even and calm as his mind. "As you were the one who found her, you were the one to ease her distress. I would know, however, whether the easing was given with or without her consent."

"What man would find it necessary to take his *memabra* by force?" Dallan came back in a very bland way, for some reason amused. "As the woman wears my bands, it is to be expected that she would give herself freely to me."

"Of course," the barbarian answered, a good deal of his calm having turned to stiffness. "And now it would perhaps be best if we continued on our way. This delay has cost us a good deal of time."

Dallan gave immediate and solemn agreement, then put his arm about me to move us both after the barbarian, who had turned and stalked away. After a minute a large chunk of meat was thrust into my hand, and I glanced over at Dallan to see that he had taken something to eat as well. Things seemed to be coming at me in a very disjointed fashion right then, mainly because of the way my mind kept replaying the last exchange between the two men. It was clear I hadn't done as good a job of escaping from them as I had thought, since neither one had had any difficulty finding me once they took the proper direction. It was appalling to think that I couldn't avoid recapture even in the darkness of the inside of a mountain, but that wasn't the only thing bothering me. The barbarian had demanded an answer to a question from Dallan, and hadn't even noticed that the answer he'd gotten wasn't an answer at all. Dallan had stated a couple of generalities, and Tammad had stalked off into the darkness with a matching black mood forming in his mind. If I didn't know better I would have sworn he was jealous, but that was idiotic. I'd been given to enough men by him to know that there *was* no jealousy in him, at least as far as I was concerned. That was why I couldn't understand the stiffness he had developed, most especially after the way he had tortured me. I chewed at the meat chunk Dallan had given me and thought about that for a while, then pushed the entire question away from me. If the barbarian was upset at the thought of my giving myself to Dallan, for whatever reason, I couldn't be happier. If it wouldn't have been unfair to Dallan, I would have thrown myself all over him just to see the barbarian suffer even more. It was probably an ego thing with Tammad, that any woman would have the incredibly bad taste to prefer another man to him, and he surely deserved whatever suffering he did. It was scarcely likely to last beyond the time other women became available, so I hoped the suffering he did was good and painful.

When we reached the place I had left the men, we found the next downgrade and just kept going. Hour after hour passed, filled with descending and searching and more descending, the pain of scrapes and stumbles and sharp rock underfoot, the pressure of no rest stops being allowed, and the boredom of constant, faintly shining darkness. Dallan had given me more than the single meat chunk when we'd first started, but a lot of time had passed and I was hungry all over again. The barbarian had taken over the lead of our expedition and acted as though he intended going on forever, and that was the one thing that had kept *me* going. I'd sooner drop in my tracks than ask anything of him, even if I did it through Dallan. I'd either go on as long as he did or collapse from exhaustion, whichever came first. I put a hand to my aching back, wishing I could rub my feet just for a minute, then swallowed a gasp when my elbow scraped against the rock wall we were walking near. Collapsing seemed a lot more likely than continuing on to wherever the end might be, and I really didn't want to think about it.

Thanks to Dallan, I didn't have to walk on forever *or* collapse. He was the one who finally called a halt, saying that the narrow, twisting corridor of rock we were in would do as a place to stop and sleep.

"This place will allow us to be sure that we have not lost our proper direction," he said, looking up at the sheer, glowing walls all around us. "An open gallery would scarcely serve the same purpose."

"Yes, let us by all means see a purpose served," the barbarian muttered, finding a lot less interest in the walls. "I will take the furs that are mine to the far side of this fold, and you may remain here with yours. How long do you mean to sleep?"

"Until we awaken refreshed," Dallan answered with a shade too much pleasantness. "Do you feel it necessary that we stand watches?"

"No," the barbarian answered, taking the sleeping furs bundle from me so abruptly that I was startled. "I will sleep lightly against any intrusion, therefore will you be free to enjoy your— sleep. I wish you pleasure in your dreams."

He threw the bundle back to me without the two furs he had taken, nodded to Dallan, then took his surliness around the corner of stone flaring out into the trail. Dallan chuckled softly as he stood next to me watching Tammad disappear, then he gestured toward the inside of the fold on our side.

"Spread our furs beside the wall, *memabra*," he directed, speaking as softly as he had chuckled. "Our meal will be considerably more pleasant with that one elsewhere, and after we have eaten we may sleep."

The thought of being able to sit down in comfort helped me get the furs out of the bundle in record time, but there wasn't room enough next to the wall for more than one set. Because of that I began spreading Dallan's furs on the outside of the curve, just beyond the pocket near the wall, thinking he would prefer having me on the inside, where he could keep an eye on me. I should have known that I was only partially right, but exhaustion tends to make me forget the realities of life.

"Do not be foolish, *wenda*," he chided with inner amusement when he saw what I was doing. "You may double the furs, for there is room enough for both of us in there."

To prove the point he picked up the fur I'd put outside and threw it on top of the first, picked me up and tossed me into the pocket, then removed his swordbelt and climbed in after me, pinning me down in the fur. With him on top of me there was plenty of room for both of us, but it wasn't a position likely to get me a good night's sleep. I squirmed around trying to get loose, got a chuckle and a kiss for my efforts, then was allowed to sit up next to Dallan while he got the food out.

I suppose if I hadn't been so tired I wouldn't have gotten silly, but Dallan was in the mood to be silly and I caught it from him. He refused to let us each eat our own meals, instead insisting that we feed each other, but that wasn't all. He sat me in his lap for the exchange and began tickling me, enough so that I just had to tickle him back. He had very little trouble finding ticklish spots on me, but I had to search all over before I found my target. I did as much giggling as I did chewing and swallowing, and as soon as the food and water was down Dallan took a cover fur and draped it over me, insisting that I felt too much like a block of ice for him to enjoy touching me as much as he should. I *was* cold from the hours of walking through the chill of the darkness, but somehow Dallan wasn't. His body was as warm and alive as it had been in the heat of sunlight, and when he put his arms around me under the fur I couldn't help snuggling up to his chest. I was tired enough to have my eyelids begin drooping immediately, and much too tired to struggle when his hands pushed my skirt back to get it out of his way. I suppose I should have known better than to be surprised when he got an almost immediate reaction, but I'd been sure my exhaustion would be able to set up a barrier my conscious decision couldn't. Exhausted or not, his demanding hand worked me too deeply to ignore, forcing me into writhing around in his lap, sending me further into the fuzziness of near-sleep rather than drawing me away from it. His lips took mine for a long, breathless time, a time I moved through with growing need, and then he whispered that I had to remove the covering I wore. I fought in a sightless dream to take it off without losing the fur covering me, and when I finally succeeded and moved back to his chest, found that his *haddin* was gone as well. His deep excitement was a lure I couldn't refuse, and before I knew it I had straddled him and captured his desire with mine, drawing surprise from his mind and a moan of pleasure from his throat. I rode him like a novice on a runaway *seetar*, bouncing madly and unable to stop, but he was no novice when it came to knowing his own capacity. When the pressure became too great he threw me to my back, then

followed me down to direct the rest of our pleasure. I whined
and complained and tried to force him to let me go back to
where *I* directed, and got rolled over onto my side and smacked
hard on the bottom a few times for my trouble. I was too far
gone to know he was right, but my sleepiness found the tiny
punishment enough to be intimidating. I sniffled as he held me to
him and kissed me, and immediately thereafter lost myself completely to his deep stroking. There was no hurry involved that
time, and I have no idea how long it was before he let me sleep.

There was no morning, of course, but I awoke with Dallan's
arms around me and his lips against mine, giving me a good-
morning wish. I found myself melting to him most willingly,
more than happy to oblige if he wanted anything, then cringed
and stiffened against the blast of struggling calm that hit me.
Dallan, feeling my reaction, raised his head to look out of our
little nook and saw the looming bulk of Tammad. His dark
outline was considerably more calm than the calm his mind was
fighting for, and I couldn't understand his reaction. He'd even
seen me being *used* by other men without getting ruffled, so why
should Dallan's kissing me bother him so much? I didn't understand what was going through his mind, and also didn't understand Dallan's instant amusement.

"I bid you a pleasant morning, *denday* Tammad," he said,
covertly tightening his hold on me to keep me from moving
away from him as I'd immediately tried doing. "I trust your
sleep was adequate?"

"Quite adequate," the barbarian answered, paying a high
inner price for the evenness of his tone. "I have already had my
meal, and have come to see how quickly you will be prepared to
continue on."

"We have only just awakened," Dallan answered, moving his
hands on me under the covering fur so that I gasped and arched
against him. "I had intended taking a short while with my
woman before seeking sustenance, and I now see that the time
must be brief indeed. We will be with you as quickly as I see to
her."

He turned away from the barbarian and began kissing me
again, well aware of the fact that I was nearly choking on the
storm of bulging, rippling fury-calm coming at me. Dallan was
enjoying himself immensely, but from a cause other than the
usual one. I didn't know what he was up to, and I really didn't
care; I just knew what I wasn't about to be the main attraction in
his one-man show.

Blocking out Tammad's frothing and Dallan's nearness was as easy as pulling out teeth with nothing but fingers, but somehow, miraculously, I managed to do it. After that I gathered what I needed to use on Dallan, at the same time keeping all my fingers crossed tight. I had to dip into the area of nervous reactions for what I wanted, but it was the only thing I could think of that might possibly be mistaken for a natural urge. Certain tensions produce a nervousness in some people that stems from mental activity but manifests mainly as a physical response, actually forcing the body to not only feel the distress, but to actively participate in it. You don't have to have a weak bladder to feel the urge to relieve yourself if you're jumpy enough, and you don't have to be nervous to feel that way if an empath turns desperate. Dallan held me pinned to the fur with his body, his hands in my hair as his lips teased mine, his right knee already beginning to insert itself between my knees, and all I could do was pray that he hadn't yet relieved himself that morning. I brushed him with that special feeling then brushed him again, miserably aware of how quickly I was growing weak and will-less, almost convinced that I was wasting my time—and then it took him. His muscles clenched and his teeth gritted almost at the same time, and he was abruptly no longer interested in taking his time. He brushed the covering fur away and scrambled out of the nook, trotted past Tammad without a word, then disappeared back around the last fold of rock in the direction from which we'd come the night before. I lay still on the furs trying to smooth the jangle out of my own nerves, and saw Tammad's outline turn back to me again. He'd been startled by Dallan's sudden and unexpected departure, but his startlement had inexplicably turned to anger.

"So, *wenda*, once again you act to suit yourself," he said very softly, slowly moving closer to where I lay. "The rights and desires of those about you mean as little as ever, causing you not a moment's hesitation in thought. To do as you will is a thing you have ever done, and undoubtedly always shall. What a fool a man would be to think you able to grow and change—and what a fool to speak of regret for having given you the fruits of your efforts. I shall not be such a fool again."

The bitterness and disgust in his mind cut at me like a cold wind in the dead of winter, crushing me down, suffocating me. I found myself cowering back against the inner wall of the nook, clutching the cover fur to me, shivering as though it really was the dead of winter. My mind had turned too numb with fear to do anything more than quiver and shake, faint with the thought

that his hulking shadow-shape might come closer yet, sick with
terror over what he would do to me. If it had gone on another
minute I know I would have fainted, but that was when Dallan
came trotting back.

"Terril, forgive me," he said as he approached the nook, a
chuckle of amusement in his voice. "I meant no insult in leaving
so abruptly, for a man has little choice at a time such as that. It
was not—What has happened here?"

He stopped beside the barbarian to look down at me, confusion touching him, but it was nothing compared to what was in
Tammad's mind. The big barbarian had suddenly turned almost
as numb as I felt, and his shadow profile stared at Dallan.

"For what—for what reason did you leave the woman?" he
forced out at last, almost choking on the words. "Were you—ill,
or incapacitated, or—driven away?"

"I was forced, yes, but only to relieve myself," Dallan
growled, abruptly glowing with the beginnings of a monstrous
anger. "Have you grown to believe the woman capable of
affecting our bodies as well as our minds? Must all that occurs
be laid at her feet, tied to her throat, or heaped upon her head?
Do you wish me to beat her for her fear of you?"

The larger shadow jerked his head back to me, silent in the
darkness where our bodies dwelt, screaming with guilt where his
mind dwelled alone. I nearly threw up with the agony he felt and
then he was gone, running silently around the fold and up the
trail, disappearing into the darkness and taking his illness and
pain with him. I didn't know Dallan was down on his knees
beside me and holding me until Tammad had put enough rock
between us to be out of range, and then I collapsed in hysterics.
It hurt so much I thought I would break, and Dallan's words
came to me as I forced the fur against my mouth and face to
muffle my screams.

"No, *memabra,* do not weep," he growled, trying to be
soothing but sounding savage. "Had he been worthy of you he
would have proven it during my provocation of him, yet was it
the opposite that he proved. To engender such fear in a small and
helpless woman! I know not how a *l'landa* might sink so low,
yet do I know I shall not leave you alone with him again. We
will complete this journey as quickly as possible, and when we
return you need never see him again."

He held me tight trying to calm the near-insane crying I
twisted about in the grip of, but his efforts were useless while I
found it impossible to calm myself. I'd accomplished what I'd
tried to do and had touched Dallan without his knowing it, but

what about the rest of it? Tammad had been right in accusing me and Dallan wrong in coming to my defense, but how could I tell them the truth? How could I face that bitterness and disgust from Tammad again, especially after what Dallan had made him feel? And what would they do to me if they found out the truth now, knowing they'd been fooled? I still wanted to spit out the words of truth to keep them from cutting me to pieces with the sharpness of their edges, but fear closed my throat and left them deep inside to silently spill the blood of my life. I screamed into the fur with the agony of unrelieved pain, brought about by the abomination of a disease called cowardice.

It took a long while before the storm passed, and afterward I was unable to eat. Dallan helped me dress and gather the furs together, and then we went on in the direction Tammad had taken earlier. I had my shield tightly in place, hiding as cowards usually do, but I couldn't keep my eyes closed too as I would have preferred. Once we left the corridor of folded rock we entered a small gallery, black gaps of empty air surrounded by the glow of stone. Just past the middle of it toward the far end stood a dark outline, which waited until we had almost reached it before turning and disappearing through one of the wall gaps. Dallan and I also reached the downgrade and began to descend, but why any of us were doing it was beyond me. There was supposed to be a magical cure for all of our troubles at trail's end, but I don't think even Dallan believed that any longer. I had never believed it, but if I'd had to make a choice, I would have believed in the magic sooner than in the cure.

We continued on down through the winding darkness, and after another few hours it became obvious that it was a good thing Dallan had forced me to eat not long after we first started. My head had begun to ache and I wasn't feeling well, and the chill of the darkness had been working at the same time to enter my bones. I just kept walking over the pebbled rock that had begun to feel like knives under my feet, saying nothing to Dallan except for refusing more to eat. The somewhat amusing thought had come that maybe there was real magic down there after all; if I caught something terrible and died, all my problems really would be solved.

I was almost staggering by the time we reached the bottom of the last downslope. I'd been fuzzily wondering how much longer I could go on without Dallan noticing something, when I noticed something myself. At the end of the thirty-foot corridor in front of us a stronger light source than the constant, faint rock glow could be seen, and the barbarian had stopped at the corridor's

end without ranging ahead as he'd been doing. Dallan took my
arm to speed up my sore-footed progress, looking ahead rather
than at me, missing the muttering I was doing that even I
couldn't quite catch. When we got to the place where Tammad
was waiting I thought I was even more confused than I felt, but
blinking didn't chase the sight away. Another slight downslope
led to the floor of a cavern of sorts, but the cavern wasn't dark
and it wasn't empty. Wide, picture-window gaps all around the
outer walls led to open air, making the area look like a dinner
hall rather than a cavern, and what seemed to be lazy, puffy
clouds rested on the rock floor all around the depression in the
center of the room. Rising from the depression was a marble
stand, five feet high and containing two things: a golden casting
of a big man's hand closed into a fist, and the sword which was
held in the fist by the blade. The sword blade was shining silver
rather than gold, its hilt so encrusted with what seemed to be
jewels that it surely would have been painful to hold it and swing
it. The thought of pain made me groan out loud without meaning
to, and the barbarian stirred where he stood to my right as Dallan
put his arm around me in concern.

"It is the storm which gathers in the outer air that gives the
woman pain," he said so softly to Dallan that he sounded almost
diffident. "We had best hurry and stand before the Sword so that
we may return her quickly to the depths of the mountain where
she will be protected from its fury."

"Yes, let us hurry," Dallan agreed after a strange pause, as
though he had meant to say something else and had changed his
mind at the last minute. I hadn't noticed that the outside skies
were darker than they should have been by daylight, and I hadn't
realized that I was being affected by a coming storm. I wasn't
noticing or realizing much of anything right then, but hurrying
sounded smart even to me.

Dallan helped me along as the three of us started for the
Sword and its pedestal, the barbarian walking close to my right
but not touching me. I think he understood that Dallan would
probably have drawn on him if he'd tried helping me as well,
and I don't think he disagreed with the viewpoint. The barbarian
looked expressionless rather than calm, Dallan looked grim and
not at all pleased, and however I looked couldn't have been that
far from their appearances. It was the first time in more than a
day that we were able to see each other clearly, and we discovered that we hadn't been missing anything. I limped along
between them, trying to keep my thoughts lucid, but wasn't
having much luck with it. My mind was fluttering in all directions,

and the thing of most concern to me seemed to be the worry that we'd get wet passing through the grounded clouds. I stepped into the clouds with the two men because I was given no other choice, and suddenly became delighted that I wasn't getting wet. The clouds swirled around our feet and legs and waists, and had a strange, dry smell to them, making me wrinkle my nose and bringing frowns to the men. We moved two steps through them, then four, then discovered that the clouds were growing fingers. The fingers grabbed at us and held us back, trying to keep us with them even though we didn't want to stay. Dallan and Tammad slowly began to fight with the clouds, but I didn't get to see how the fight turned out. Between one breath and the next I had returned to the darkness.

9

It was a glorious day, bright with sunshine and warmth and filled with the clean air that comes after the dawn-rain. I had stayed out of sight during chore assignments, and then had left the house and hurried out of town, eager to climb the hill-mountain and stand at its top again. On its side facing our town the hill was no more than any other hill, perhaps a bit steeper but certainly no higher; on its far side, though, the hill was a true mountain, sweeping down and away through empty air for what seemed like miles. I loved standing right at its top, high, high above the tiny valley so far below, feeling the wind blow my hair about and tug at my long wraparound skirt. Standing on top of the mountain was like suddenly being alive after spending endless time in the death of town-dwelling, and I couldn't stay away from it for long without *needing* to go back. The feeling was pure compulsion, and I couldn't have resisted even if I'd wanted to.

"So you've run away again," a voice said from behind me, startling me. "Aren't you tired of being punished for not doing your chores?"

"I don't *get* punished," I said without turning, knowing who it was. *He* was after me again, and after all I'd said and done trying to discourage him.

"You *should* be punished," he said, having heard my words despite the wind's nearly blowing them away. "If you were punished you would learn not to try avoiding what has to be done, and there would be less resentment toward you from everyone else."

"They don't resent me, they're awed by me and maybe even frightened a little," I answered smugly, stretching my arms out toward the lovely, empty air. "I can fly and they can't, but they wish they could; they wish they even had the nerve to try."

"They resent you," he said with that calm certainty that always set my temper aflame. "They resent the fact that you can and they can't, and you don't even try to make them like you. You sneer at them and laugh at their shortcomings, and always make sure they know how much you can do that they can't. One day you'll get them so angry they'll hurt you."

"Perhaps then I'll need *you* to protect me," I laughed, hugging myself, knowing myself so much better than he. "Do you think you will?"

"You know I'll have to try," he said, and for some reason he sounded angry. Without warning his hand came to my arm, and I was pulled away from the top of the mountain and down a foot or so to face him. "I'll probably die right along with you, but that won't stop me from trying. Don't you care that we'll both be dead?"

"I *won't* be dead!" I spat, struggling to free myself from his grip. "They all know I'm special, and they won't dare hurt me! You're just saying that they will because you're jealous of me, because *you* can't fly! Why don't you leave me alone!"

"If *I* leave you alone, you really will be alone," he said, his light eyes sad. "There's no one else in this whole world who feels the way I do about you. Why do you think I bother, when it would be so much easier just leaving you to your fate?"

"I don't know," I said, shaking my head against his nonsense. "I don't know why you bother when I've made it so clear that I want nothing to do with you. What do you hope to gain?"

"Why must you insist that I want something?" he came back, his eyes now annoyed. "Do you think so little of yourself that everyone who shows interest in you has to be seeking some sort of gain? Isn't it possible that all I want is *you*?"

"It may be possible, but it isn't very likely," I retorted with a snort. "Untalented people interested in talented people usually want to share a special standing among the rest of the untalented that they'd never achieve on their own. If you think you're good enough to match me, try this.''

By moving suddenly I managed to pull away from him, and immediately ran toward the mountain top again. He was no more than a step behind me, but where the top of the mountain was as far as he could go, it was just the beginning of the journey for me. I plunged over the edge and let myself fall, my wings spreading out and quickly catching at the unbelievable mix of air currents. The fall became a lazy, circling soar, my arms back under my wings, my hair flaring out backward to the caress of the stream. Most of me aimed backward but ahead was where I was going, beyond anything those others had done, beyond anything they had even dreamed. I tipped away from the ladder of air and beat skyward, glorying in my strength, sending a laugh of victory down toward the tiny figure still standing on the mountain top. He could never match me, never be my equal in a million lifetimes, and I would prove it to him over and over until he had no choice but to believe it. He would learn how outrageously he overstepped himself by aspiring to *me*, and in learning he would finally go away. I didn't need him or anyone, not when I could *fly*!

I spent hours playing alone in the skies, and when I finally returned to the top of the mountain, *he* was nowhere to be found. That gave me a good deal of satisfaction, and I strolled back to town and my house with a pleased smile on my lips. The others in the house knew I'd been out flying, and their awe kept them silent as I passed, giving them their voices back to whisper only after I was no longer near. I stole food from the kitchen without my aunts knowing it, ate it among the shade trees at the back of the house, then lay down in the grass for a nap. My sisters and cousins could take care of the chores around the house, even the ones that were supposed to be mine. I had better things to do with my time.

When I awoke from my nap and returned to the house, I was furious to discover that there was one chore I couldn't avoid. It was time for my family to bring its share of the growing to the central depot, and afterward draw its share of the made things. Everyone in the family went but my mother and aunts, and even my mother's protests would have been useless against my father. My mother knew I was much too good for menial chores, but my father had never agreed with her. He called her treatment of me pampering, and saw to it that I did my chores when he was about. Happily he wasn't about much, but even his occasional appearance was more than I cared for.

The sacks containing our growing were already in the carts, but the carts had to be pushed to the center of town, and then they had to be unloaded. I sweated in the hot afternoon sun, straining at a cart that I almost seemed to be pushing alone, annoyed by the laughter and foolishness of my cousins and sisters and brothers. They considered going to the depot a holiday rather than the drudgery it was, one where they got to meet the flirt with the young members of the other families. I had no interest in meeting those others and even less in pushing the cart, but I couldn't afford to turn and walk off, or even to shirk. Although my father and uncles had stayed at the house as always, my brothers would be sure to notice what I did and report back later. My brothers were jealous of what I could do, and always made as much trouble for me as possible with our father. One day I would leave that place, and never have to be bothered by any of them again.

It took long enough to get to the depot, but once we were there the boys took over unloading the carts. My sisters and girl cousins stood around watching them and sending covert glances toward the males of other families, and I was able to melt back into the rest of the female crowd and then hurry away. I'd taken an uninterested look around when we'd stopped our carts, and had seen *him* busy unloading with his brothers. As soon as he was through he would come looking for me, and I didn't want to be where he would find me. He had nothing to offer but a place in his family, a place that would mean work and more work, a drudgery I had no intentions of becoming a part of. I could do something no one else in the whole world could do, and somehow I would see to it that my position in life was just as special.

Once I was past the edges of the crowd, it was easier to move faster. My bare feet added dust to the air that had only just been cleared from all the carts going by, and I hurried toward the circle of shops in the market area around the depot, glad the shops were always closed on depot day. No one would need very much for a couple of days after evening out, and the shop people knew it and took the time as a holiday. That meant I could circle the depot area behind the shops, and that way get back to the hill-mountain. Since the work was all done, no one would miss me except for *him*; missing me he might try to follow, but by then I'd be beyond the top of the mountain. Let him try following me *there!*

The first of the shops was no more than twenty feet away when I dragged my thoughts out of the waiting skies to notice that the area wasn't as deserted as it should have been. Three men holding thick branch-cuts stood ahead of me in front of one of the shops, and I didn't recognize any of them. By their short wraparounds and metal jewelry they certainly weren't town men, not even from the other towns that lay one or two days travel away from ours. Those town men wore long wraparounds the way our men did, and wouldn't have strung themselves with useless trinkets any more than ours would have. I didn't know why they had come to our town, but they had certainly picked a good time. The only ones around to stand against them were boys, and if their intentions were to do mischief, I pitied the town. It was, however, none of my concern, and I immediately began to turn to my left to avoid the three, but there were three others of the same sort standing *there*. Quickly turning my head to the right showed another four, and it suddenly came to me that they were more interested in *me* than in the town. The thought was somewhat unsettling, but not unduly worrying; I didn't have to go around them to get away from them.

"A good day to you, girl," one of the three directly ahead called, stepping out in front of the other two. "It's clear you're the one we've come after, and you'd be wise not trying to struggle. If you'll keep silent we'll be gone with none the wiser; if you scream and alert the others, you'll be beaten once we've got you away."

"I don't know what you're talking about," I said, beginning to feel angry and annoyed. "Not only don't I know you, I'm certainly not going anywhere with you."

"Ah, but we know you," the man said, a grin spreading on his face. "The word about a flying girl has spread for miles around, bringing disbelief to most—and interest to some. There are those willing to pay to own you, you see, and we are the ones who will sell you to them. Now come along, for we want to be well away from here by dark."

"You're crazy!" I sneered, knowing he was simple-minded as well. "I'm not going to let you take me, and I'm not certainly not going to let you sell me. I'm not even going to stay here and talk to you any longer."

The fool's eyes widened when I spread my wings, and his arm came up to guard his face and eyes when I began beating hard to rise up and away from them. The two behind him did the same, and I laughed as I began rising into the air—until the net flew over me. It came from my right where the four men had been, rose in an arc above me, and was caught by the three men to my left. I flew right into it and was dragged back down to the ground, my laughter immediately turning into screams of shock. They were using a *net* to catch me, and it wasn't fair!

I struggled in the dust of the street as the weight of the men held the net down, screaming above the snarling of the spokesman directing the others not to break anything on me. Hands tried to silence my screams through the mesh of the heavy net, but even I was beyond silencing them. I struggled insanely as the net was wrapped around me and I was dragged to my feet, and then my screams cut off as I saw the figures racing toward us. My brothers and male cousins pelted along without any of the others, led by none other than *him*. They slowed as they came within ten feet of the men who held me, and then stopped to glare at them with chins thrust out.

"Release her at once!" my eldest brother demanded, outrage and fear mixed plainly on his face. "Release her and we'll allow you to leave in place."

"You'll *allow* us to leave in peace?" the spokesman of the raiders laughed, looking around at them. "There aren't enough of you to do anything else. We'd heard that there weren't as many as a handful of people in this town who would lift a finger to help this little bird, and it looks like the rumor was true. You don't look very eager to start anything yourself, boy, so why don't you take your handful and go back to the others? If you're smart, there's no reason for anyone to get hurt."

"Except her," *he* said, stepping out in front of my brothers and cousins. "Even if everyone in this town says you can have her, *I* won't allow it. Let her go."

"You're older than the others," the leader of the raiders mused, staring at him. "You don't look like a relative, so you must be a suitor. Take my advice and find a different girl to court. This one has already been claimed."

He started to turn away, as though done with the conversation, but he was only pretending. When *he* sprang forward in attack the leader was ready and waiting, and he whirled back to strike hard with the branch-cut he carried, over and over with all his strength. Two others of the raiders joined him, and when they stepped away there was nothing but motionlessness and blood on the dust of the ground. My brothers and cousins backed away in horror, their faces pale and shocked, and after a single glance at them, the leader of the raiders gestured to his men. The net was pulled down from my face and head, a terrible metal collar almost as wide as my hand was closed around my throat, and then the net was pulled away from me completely. Two heavy chains were attached to the metal collar, and by those chains I was pulled along the street in the direction leading out of town. I held to one of the chains to keep from sprawling in the dust and tried to look back at the still, red-covered body on the ground, but all I could see behind me, too horribly close, was the bulk of the leader of the raiders.

"Once we have you far enough away, you'll be beaten for starting that," the man said, his voice low and his eyes angry. "If any of the others had decided to join that first bunch, it could have gotten ugly for us. A good thing only that one decided to jump in, and I can't say I blame him. I'm looking forward to tasting you before the others get their turns, and I probably won't stop with once. You're a good-looking piece even with those wings."

His free hand came to my wraparound, sliding in through the side slit to grope at my flesh, but the action did no more than cause a small shudder in me. I was numb through and through, so deep in shock that I didn't think I would ever climb out again. A terrible thing had happened to me and worse things were going to happen, but none of that seemed to matter. I was wrapped in so overwhelming a sense of loss that nothing else in the world mattered. I'd thought I wanted nothing to do with him, thought I'd be happiest if I never saw him again, but he'd given his life for me as he'd said he would, and I couldn't bear the thought. More than his life had been taken and more than mine, and although I didn't understand what I felt, I wanted to lie down and die because of it. He'd tried so hard and I hadn't tried at all, not even to understand the way he looked at things, and now it was too late to do anything at all. I'd never see him again even if I were freed, never see his smile or his arms opening in invitation, offering me a safe place to rest and be loved. He was gone forever, gone beyond apology or any other effort, and life was no longer worth living. The dust of the road rose up to swirl about me in clouds, causing me to cough in the collar about my throat, causing me to pull harder at the chain I held to. Hands came to pull my arms behind me and tie my wrists, but all that did was make me fall. I fell down and down into the dust of the ground, not caring that tears streamed down my cheeks; I cried as I fell through the dust of forever, and that was the way it should have been.

10

I coughed again at the strange smell that wasn't dust and tried to force my eyes open, but I was surrounded so sharply with pain that I couldn't do it. The strange dream I'd walked through had provided pain of its own, but purely physical pain surrounded me now, stabbing at me with skull-breaking insistence. I could hear the sound of thunder and felt the clawing of lightning that accompanied it, but that wasn't all that was bringing me pain; I had to see what was happening, and the need quickly turned into compulsion.

Forcing my eyes open was a major feat, but once I had accomplished it I was sure I still had to be dreaming. The first thing I saw was Tammad and Dallan, tied by the wrists and suspended by the same lengths of leather that tied them, dangling like grotesque decorations from the cave ceiling, their bound feet a good distance from the floor. Their bodies were stripped of weapons and *haddinn*, but that doesn't mean they were totally bare; whip marks clothed them in streaks of red, sharp and awful against the bronze of their skin. Although they were conscious, they made no sound, holding the deep, wracking flare of agony wrapped inside their minds. It was partly their agony that cut at me so strongly, that and the thunderstorm outside the open rock windows, and even through the pain and confusion I felt, I knew I had to do something. What that something consisted of I didn't quite know, but there was something even more important that I didn't know. I found it out, though, as soon as I tried to move.

If the men were tied vertically, the position given to me was horizontal, or at least nearly that. The awareness finally seeped through my confusion and pain that I was tied to a boulder of sorts, my head hanging back and down, my arms stretched tight and tied at the wrists beyond my head, my ankles restrained but not tightly. I could turn my head to see Tammad and Dallan hanging where someone or something had put them, and could also turn my head an equivalent amount in the opposite direction; aside from that I couldn't move. Apprehension had taken its time reaching me, but when it came it was full-blown fear; I couldn't think clearly through everything that was coming at me, but fear seemed very appropriate. What could have captured and hurt two *l'lendaa* so easily, and what was it going to do to us beyond that?

Trying to pull myself together was worse than opening my eyes had been. The more vague my thoughts and perceptions were, the less it hurt; the converse leaned on me and poked with flaming needles until I nearly gave up. I was going to have to open my mind wide to be at all effective, but that damned storm was ripping me up and throwing me away, making me shiver and sweat and hurt and cringe. I moaned and moved feebly on the jagged stone I was tied to, fighting for any corner of control I could reach, and the reason for all that madness moved into my line of sight from the right. My first thought was a hope that I was still dreaming, but unfortunately I knew I wasn't. The man was absolutely unbelievable, both in size and in appearance; larger than Tammad and Dallan by more than a little, completely naked, and dark-haired! I know I stared with my mouth open while he stood and gazed casually at his two hanging victims, then flinched involuntarily when he turned to look at me. His mind was as cold and emotionless as the barbarian's was usually calm, something that was reflected in his soulless green eyes. I didn't have to probe to reach the cold lack of emotion, and that made me shiver even through my pain.

"So you have awakened," he said in a very deep voice, obviously addressing me. "From the fear I see in your eyes, you had not thought to meet a man of our land here, in the place of these puny weaklings of *darayse*. It is a fortunate thing for the honoe of our people that I lost my way during the last storms and took shelter in these caverns. Had I not, our honor might never have been restored."

"What honor do you speak of?" I whispered, fighting to get the words out over the pain I felt. "What people do you speak of? I do not know you, nor do I know your land. Why have you done this to us?"

"Do you think me blind, that you deny our common heritage?" he snorted, his cold eyes growing even colder. "Our numbers are as yet too few, yet are they large enough for me to know you as one of our own. Though you are young and have not yet attained your full growth, you are not so young that you are ignorant of our law. It is forbidden for one of our women to give herself to these pale non-men, and yet you have done so. You must all be punished, you for having broken the law, they for having dared profane one of ours. Their punishment has already been begun; yours is yet to come.''

"You are insane!'' I husked, trying to put some strength and conviction into my voice. "I am not one of those you claim as your own, nor have I ever been! Should it be beyond you to believe this, do as you will with me—but you must release my companions. They are guiltless, and you cannot harm them further!''

"Guiltless!'' He snorted again, still without a trace of humor. "They have had you, have they not? They have humored and used your disgusting female urges to squirm, and have put you beneath them, have they not? You could not bear to obey the law and await your full growth before seeking manhood to ease you, therefore did you flee to those who would aid you in disobeying yet a further and greater law. As you were so eager for that which you were not yet to have, I shall now give you that which you are ill-equipped to receive.''

It was so difficult following the twisting of his warped arguments, that for a moment I didn't understand what he meant. My main difficulty with him was that he *was* insane, a pathologically disturbed personality that my mind cringed back from in pain and fear. Just as a healthy person would cringe back from touching the body of someone stricken with a flesh-rotting disease, so did my mind recoil from touching the sickness that rotted away his rationality and humanity. The storm flared and crashed outside, jarring me to my teeth; Dallan and Tammad fought inside themselves to throw off their pain and break free from their restraints, and all of it just made me dizzy and weak. When the monster started walking toward me I didn't understand what he intended doing, and that was undoubtedly a kindness. Once he reached me and tore away most of my shortened gown with a single, savage pull, I understood more than I cared to.

Since the first day I'd met the barbarian on Central, I'd had a lot of use from the men of Rimilia, willing or otherwise, and usually otherwise. I'd called their use rape more often than I could recall, glibly tagging the actions with the entire title when all I'd known had been a small and not all that terible corner of the reality. That dark-haired monster taught me the full meaning of the word, his mind grimly satisfied all the while, his body as uncaring about what he did as the stones of the walls around us. If I really had been an ungrown female of his people, he probably would have damaged me so badly that I might not have survived; as it was, I screamed when he forced his way into me, understanding how outrageously outsized he was only after he had done so. He brought me nothing but pain, seeking pleasure not even for himself, hurting me deliberately as a part of his twisted concept of punishment. I closed my shield tight as I screamed, fighting to keep from being overwhelmed by that savage addition to what pain I already felt, but I couldn't block out the roars and cursing from Dallan and Tammad. They twisted where they hung, straining to break free, desperately trying to pull the monster away from me by insults and challenges. The monster ignored them as he completed his task, jarring down into me with his body, twisting and pulling at my flesh with his fingers, until he was thoroughly done and had released the strength of his need. Then he withdrew as uncaringly as he'd entered, and turned to look at his two other captives.

"You dare to attempt interference when a man disciplines a woman of his own people?" he demanded of them, his deep voice nearly a rumbling growl. "As you wished for my attention, so shall you now have it."

He strode out of my line of vision but was back immediately carrying a heavy, braided whip of a sort I'd never seen before. The leather braiding of the whip was stained with reddish brown, and I didn't have to wonder where the stains came from. All I wanted to do right then was curl up and hide, but I forced myself, through waves of pain, to watch what was happening. I didn't understand how I could have opened my shield in the midst of all that was going on around me, but to my distant, confused surprised that was exactly what I had done. Watching for me involved more than just eyesight, and something in me knew that and insisted on it.

The flare of lightning and crash of thunder hid whatever sound there was as the monster released the coils of the heavy whip to snake out behind him, but they didn't hide the various reactions coming at me. Dallan was so furious he was nearly frothing, but he hadn't been able to free himself of the leather on his wrists, nor had he been able to ignore the pain he felt. He watched the whip with helpless rage, aching with the pain already given him, knowing there was no avoiding another dose of it. Tammad, too, was filled with rage, a towering rage so strong and wide there was room in his mind for nothing else. Pain, worry, concern— all were gone beneath the weight of it, buried and forgotten as though they had never been, as though they would never be again. His mighty body strained against the leather which bound him, unable to brace itself to pull effectively yet continuing to strain, as though will alone would part the leather. The monster looked at both of them, seeing Dallan's fury but nothing of

Tammad's rage, and satisfaction briefly touched his mind. He had decided which of them he would hurt again first, and in his madness believed his decision logical. His muscles bunched as his arm brought the whip cracking forward, and Dallan twisted in the leather he hung by, agony exploding in his mind in the same way that the storm exploded outside. The double crash, one outer and one inner, blinded and deafened me, and when the thunder faded the monster was speaking again.

". . . clearly shows that you have transgressed the more," he said to Dallan while swinging his arm back and striking again. "You dare to consider the girl yours, as though you might be worthy of a female of my people. One of ours will never belong to the pale *darayse* of your lands, and this you will know before you die. You will end in the agony of the lash, having learned too late how far you have overstepped yourself."

Dallan uttered a strangled roar, half very intense pain, half insanity at the helplessness of his position. The whip continued to cut at him over and over, freeing his blood to run down his body, and I strained against the leather holding me to the stone, bathed in sweat from his pain and mine, frantically trying to get loose. I'd suddenly become convinced that if I could just put my hands over my ears, I could do whatever had to be done and everything would be all right. I felt the leather cutting into my wrists without really noticing it, panting with the unsuccessful effort to free myself, close to insanity myself. I *had* to get loose but I *couldn't*, and then I gasped at what Tammad did. He had started himself swinging back and forth, not very far and not very fast, but suddenly he lashed out at the monster with both of his bound feet, and the small amount of arc he'd achieved helped him reach his target. The monster staggered when Tammad's feet struck him, missing the next stroke at Dallan and almost striking himself, and outrage dominated his mind.

"You dare!" he hissed, jerking around to the barbarian, who still swung slowly back and forth. "For that it will be you who is the first to die!"

With that his arm went back and then came forward again, sending the lash against Tammad with all his strength, immediately drawing more blood among the lines already there. The new touch of the whip joining the older streaks was more than the barbarian could stand; despite the iron control he had always shown, despite the denial he was still working for, the pain touched him and reached him and *hurt* him! That was the point that near insanity became true insanity for me.

The feel of the stone beneath my back and the clasp of leather on my wrists, the raging of the storm outside and the groaning in Dallan's semi-conscious mind, the pain and fear I felt and the terrible desperation—all faded into shadows as though a curtain had been dropped. The dark-haired monster stood spotlighted in my attention, and attention was the least of what I wanted to give him. My mind opened wide and flowed into his, thrusting aside preferences and prejudices and inclinations alike, searching for the core and essence of him. It was like wading thigh deep through dark slime and twisting putrescence, but his insanity no longer repelled me. I knew there would be a large store of buried fear lying untapped and nearly forgotten, and the monster staggered physically when I reached it, forgetting the whip in his hand as his mind began to fight mine. He seemed to know what I was after and was frantic to keep me from it, but he had no more chance against me mentally than I had against him physically. I released the fears he couldn't face, letting them flood his mind, and then I began to help them.

The monster screamed as his face paled, fear of everything in the world covering him like a second skin. His whip fell forgotten to the stone of the floor as he went to his knees, his mind surprisingly fighting back harder than it had. The phantoms surrounding and possessing him bowed his head and caused his fists to clench, closing his eyes as he continued to scream and fight. I'd been supporting his fears and keeping them free of his restraint, but rather than trying to resuppress them he was actually conquering them, just as he obviously would have if he'd faced them sooner. If I allowed him to go on much longer he'd win and be free of the fears entirely, and that would also free him to take up where he had so recently left off with that whip. That was the last thing I would allow, no matter the pity I might have felt for him under other circumstances.

Personal fears really are personal, things that others, learning of them, might well laugh at; to the individual involved, the last thing those fears are is laughable. The single footstep in the darkness which immediately becomes the nightmare ghoul you were just reading about; the total lack of light below the last step of a stair which might be a bottomless pit instead; the small, dark, distant cloud, which might be a hungry swarm of ravening insects heading right for you; the squeak of a rodent, the click of a lock, the leap of a flame, the smell of salt water, the reek of stale air. To people with deeply buried terror experiences, these are all real, possible happenings which engender the pounding pulse and thumping heart, the shivering limbs and weakened bowels, the pumping lungs and dizzied mind. The monster kneeling on the stone was nearly to the point of besting all his fears when I gave him my lot, amplified by my power and driven in unceasingly, wave after wave of fear without name, terror and horror I left him to put a face on. The chill-tingle-up-the-spine fear, the semi-paralyzed quaking fear, the breathless-need-to-scream fear, all of it full volume and roaring in. Behind the shadow curtain containing all distractions, I became aware of the increasing violence of the thunderstorm outside, but although the curtain rattled and shook I couldn't afford to let it distract me. The monster had to be slain, and I was the only one left to do it.

The dark-haired hunter-turned-victim was down on his side on the stone, mewling and cringing and gasping for breath, but still trying to fight inside. His mind darted around looking for a corner of the fear to grasp even as it searched for a place to hide, crying and crawling but still trying to resist. I couldn't afford to wonder how much strength I had left, any more than I could afford to ease up on the way I was pressing him; if I did, the battle was lost. Hand-away-from-fire fear, and falling-into-nothingness, fear, and attacked-without-warning fear, strengthened and rolling in one after the other, followed by claustrophobia fear and acrophobia fear and xenophobia fear. A shadow-curtain-failing fear snuck in before I realized it, my own fear transmitting itself to him even while I admitted deep down that it was more a certainty than a fear. The shadow curtain *was* fading even as I fought to deny it, and I knew damned well what was on the other side. Dallan's pain and Tammad's rage, the monster's suffering—and the thunderstorm. Emotion and pain as large and heavy as the mountain around us, and if I closed my shield to protect myself, the monster would break free. I heard a whimpering noise and I knew I made it, felt the pain of stone scrapes on my flesh, became aware of leather digging excruciatingly into my wrists and ankles, saw the shadow curtain flickering madly. In another minute I was going to lose it, the protection of the curtain, the battle I fought, the very fabric of my entire existence. Terror gripped me so strongly that I knew I would die of it, and when the curtain collapsed all I could do in the blinding explosion was scream hysterically with pain. I heard myself scream, and thought I heard an echo of that scream, and then there was nothing else.

11

My head hurt. It seemed as though my head had been hurting for quite some time, even before I awoke. I looked around vaguely at the small, closed-in room, sure I was still dreaming. I'd been in such pain and discomfort for so long that it didn't seem possible it could be over and done with. I didn't know where I was or what had happened to make my head hurt so, but as soon as I stirred on the pile of furs and groaned, a woman was at my side with a softly steaming bowl in her hands. She helped me sit up to sip at the bowl, let me swallow each mouthful of broth before offering more, then took the bowl away when I'd had all I could hold. By that time I was asleep again, and hadn't even realized that the scene should have felt familiar from recent repetition. The next time I awoke my head still hurt, but the mists of confusion were already fading—and I had a visitor in place of the woman I remembered. Rellis sat among the few cushions the small room boasted, sipping from a goblet that smelled as though it held *drishnak*, his eyes already on me by the time I noticed him. His smile was warm and sincere as he sat up, and he raised his goblet to me.

"Allow me to be the first to congratulate you, *wenda*," he said, a chuckle in his voice. "It has been long and long since a battle was fought under the aegis of the Sword, and you are the victor of the first battle since then. I saluted a Warrior of the Sword."

"What happened?" I asked, putting one hand to my aching head, still somewhat confused, and then I realized I'd spoken in Centran. "I cannot remember what occurred to make my head ache so," I amended, erasing his frown. "I feel as though much pain is no more than a short way behind me."

"Do not concern yourself with pain which is past," he answered gently, losing the teasing tone his voice had carried. He rose to his feet and came to stand over me, and his eyes were filled with compassion. "You now lie in an inner room of my house, where you will be somewhat protected from the present storm which rages without. Does it give you discomfort?"

I paused to think about that, realized my shield was closed so tight that nothing came through, then quickly decided against trying to open it. I didn't feel up to coping with anything beyond just lying there in the furs on my back, and there seemed to be no reason to do anything else. I shook my head in answer to Rellis' question, then looked up at him.

"Was there—another storm?" I asked, able to reach just the wispy beginnings of the memory. "I seem to recall another storm—in another place."

"The resting place of the Sword," he nodded, sipping at his *drishnak*. "There was the storm, and Dallan and Tammad—and the intruder. Are you able to recall the intruder?"

"He hurt them!" I gasped, suddenly breaking through to the swirl of insane confusion of that time, beginning to sit up in shock. "I have to help them!"

"Rest easy, *wenda*, rest easy," he soothed, crouching down and immediately putting a hand to my shoulder to gently push me back down. "I cannot know the words you speak, for you speak in your own tongue. Do you wish to be left to rest a while longer?"

"No," I said with a headshake, switching back to Rimilian, the throb in my head growing worse. "What became of the one you call intruder? Was he able to cause more harm after I—" I choked on the words, but couldn't get them out. After all my boasting and great feelings of superiority, I'd still failed.

"*Wenda*, no man is able to cause harm when he is no longer living," Rellis said, softly and gently as though he spoke to an hysterical child. "Surely you know that before the storm took you, you were able to slay him?"

"Slay him?" I said, feeling like an echo as I looked up into Rellis' face. "I know nothing of what occurred after the storm took me. Before then, he remained alive. What of Tammad and Dallan?"

"My son and the *denday* of the Circle of Might now rest from their ordeal," he answered, putting aside his goblet of *drishnak* to pick up a bowl from the small table standing nearby. "This broth continues to retain some warmth, therefore shall I assist you in drinking in the while I speak of what occurred."

He raised my shoulders from the bed of furs, held the bowl to my lips, and smiled down at me while I swallowed at the broth. I really did need it, and the warmth of it relaxed a tension in me that I hadn't been aware of having. Rellis paused only long enough to make sure I was getting what I needed of the broth, then he began speaking again.

"By tradition," he said, "those who seek the resting place of the Sword of Gerleth do so alone, or in the company of one or two others. Their experiences are the concern of none save themselves, therefore are they accorded the privacy which is their due. Had Dallan and Tammad undertaken the journey in no company other than their own, such privacy would have been theirs as well; as an unusual *wenda* accompanied them, complete privacy for them was not meant to be.

"When half the day was done, I led a number of my warriors slowly down into the mountain after your group, taking care that we did not go so swiftly that we would overtake you. I had the thought that you might take yourself from their company, you see, using your powers to remain hidden from pursuit, later emerging and attempting to retrace your steps to my house. It was clear that your journey to the resting place of the Sword was necessary, and I wished to see you complete it."

"That mist brings dreams," I said, finding no word in the Rimilian language for hallucinogens. "It forces one to consider one's life from a new focus."

"Exactly," Rellis nodded, taking back the emptied bowl and letting me lie flat again. "It was necessary that you all experience your doings along with the true reasons for having done them in the manner you had, and this was allowed you. It was not known that an intruder had entered the place of the Sword through the lower caverns in the mountain, nor that he was mad. A man is able to dream no more than once in the mists, and the intruder had surely already dreamed before your arrival. In such a way was he able to enter the mists the while Dallan and Tammad dreamed, render them helpless, then bind you as well."

"As he had already dreamed, why did he act so?" I wondered aloud, suppressing a shiver at the memory of the monster. "Surely he was shown the true meaning of his actions?"

"Of my own knowledge, this I cannot say." Rellis shrugged, settling himself cross-legged on the carpeting next to my bed furs. "It is possible, however, that his madness had blinded him to the truth, so much so that he saw naught save approval of that which he did. An honest, sincere man will at times experience doubt concerning the actions circumstances force upon him; one touched by madness will never experience such doubt.

"Be that as it may, we arrived in the corridor leading to the chamber of the Sword, only to hear screams coming from the chamber. A woman's scream followed by that of a man, his by far the more tormented. We hurried to see what occurred, and beheld the sight you were so much a part of. Dallan hung nearly lifeless by the wrists, Tammad struggled uselessly to free himself, the *wenda* Terril lay bound senseless upon a boulder, and a strange, outlandish man lay twisted yet unmoving upon the rock of the chamber floor. We knew not what had caused such strangeness, yet were we unable to rush forward in a body to halt it. The mists of dreaming stood between us, and although I, myself, had visited the resting place of the Sword in my youth, no more than two of my warriors had done the same. We three left the others to await us and hurried forward, first freeing Tammad and then turning our attention to Dallan. It was necessary that Dallan be carried back through the mists, which was done by the two *l'lendaa* who accompanied me. When I turned to offer assistance of the same sort to the *denday* Tammad, I found that he was no longer where we had left him.

"Looking about showed me that he had forced himself to his feet despite the pain he surely felt from the touch of the whip, had taken himself over to the body of the intruder, and then, after a brief pause, had made his way to your side. His blood clearly marked the trail of his movements, and I followed to look down upon the body of the intruder, seeing no wounds and no sign of blood save that left by Tammad. The face, however, was so twisted by terror that it disturbed me, yet the questions I would have asked were interrupted.

" 'He no longer lives,' Tammad informed me, bending over your form. 'The woman, however, retains some spark of life, therefore do I ask your assistance. I cannot undo the knots of the leather upon her.'

" 'My assistance is yours without asking,' I replied, moving quickly to stand beside him while drawing my dagger. 'What has occurred here, and who is that stranger? Rarely does one see a man with hair so dark. From whence does he come?'

" 'I know not,' the *denday* answered, watching as I carefully cut away the leather which bound you. 'The man was mad, and thought this *wenda* one of his people despite her denial of it. He would have slain us all had she not been able to take his life, and surely did I believe that her life was gone as well. The thunderstorm was able to better her at last, yet she, in some manner, saw to him with the end of her strength. I thought to find myself enraged that I was unable to take his life with my own hands, but instead find no more than joyous thanks that she was spared. We must take her at once to a place deeper within the mountain, where the storm will be unable to touch her further.'

" 'You cannot carry her,' I said, seeing that he was scarcely able to support himself. 'I will take her, and you must allow yourself to be assisted by my *l'lendaa*. In such a manner will we find ourselves able to bring her to safety and peace with adequate speed. Do you agree?'

"His agreement was filled with reluctance, yet was it given for your sake, *wenda*. We left the chamber of the Sword and returned you all here, and the journey was not pleasant. You cried out often as though in the grip of a fever, and each time you did so, Dallan and Tammad attempted to go to your side. It was necessary at the last to bring you ahead more quickly, so that your companions would no longer be disturbed. They sleep now due to a healing potion within them, and I was freed to await your awakening. Is there aught you require to increase your comfort. O Warrior of the Sword?''

Rellis was smiling again, but there didn't seem to be ridicule in his amusement, only gentle teasing. I shook my head to show there was nothing I wanted, and his hand reached out to smooth my hair.

"Then I will leave you to rest and restore yourself,'' he said, rising again to his feet. ''After you have slept a meal will be brought you, one more substantial than the medicated broth you have so far had. Should there be anything you require, you need only send word of it to me.''

He smiled again as he reclaimed his goblet of *drishnak*, then he turned and left the tiny room. Although my head was still hurting I felt considerably better, knowing that I hadn't completely failed after all. I'd never really know what had killed the monster, but I suspected that it had been my doing only in that I hadn't broken the connection between us before the shadow curtain had collapsed. The terrible blast had driven from my mind straight to his, unfiltered in any way that would have cushioned the shock for him. I may have been more sensitive to that sort of thing than a non-empath, but I also had more defensive reflexes; my defenses were able to cushion the blast, while there were none in his mind to do the same. I had survived the blast that had killed him, but I wasn't feeling well enough to know how good a thing that was. The medicated broth was making me sleepy again, so I gave into it without a fuss.

I wasn't awake long the next time before a woman came in carrying a tray. She smiled when she saw I was awake, then began helping me to eat what she had brought. She was dressed in white *imad* and *caldin*, what seemed to be a servant uniform in that place, and was considerably more pleasant than the women who had bathed me. She propped me up with cushions so that I would be more comfortable, and once I had finished eating left the cushions as they were simply at my request. There was no medication in the food I ate, so after she had left with the tray, I was able to spend some time thinking.

My head still throbbed faintly to my pulse, but aside from that and the tail-end of weariness, I seemed to be all right. Under normal circumstances I would have expected to be deluged with trembling memories of what the monster had done to me, but aside from a lingering urge to hide myself in shame, my mind seemed more concerned with the dream I had experienced. Pain and humiliation were old companions for me on that world; brutal nose-rubbing in embarrassing truth wasn't.

I looked down at my hands lying on the cover fur on me, seeing the bruises my wrists retained from the leather I'd fought against, feeling very small and very petty. In the dream I'd seen myself as blatantly overbearing, and while I knew the dream had exaggerated the situation to prove the point, it wasn't all that far from the mark. I'd walked around convinced that I was better than everyone around me, while the truth was I was merely different. Sure I could do a lot of things other people couldn't, but they could do things *I* couldn't; the main difference between us was that I kept beating everyone over the head with my abilities, while no one did the same to me unless I forced them to it. There wasn't a woman on the planet—not to mention most of the men—who couldn't, for example, cook better than I, but they hadn't spent their time parading themselves in front of me, telling me how superior they were. I'd waved my one unearned ability around like a flag, crowing while I strutted, insisting on special privileges because I was so special. It was a stupid, childish attitude to adopt, but I hadn't been able to see it until I saw it from the outside. Whatever drug that mist contained, it certainly had the ability to drive straight to the heart of a matter.

I stirred uncomfortably in the furs then turned onto my right side, upset by another point the dream had made. When my rescuer had died fighting to save me from the fruits of my own arrogance, I'd experienced the most complete sense of remorse that it's possible to feel. When we argue with someone who is extremely close to us, we usually assume that the person will be available later on to forgive, or condemn, or talk to, or in some other manner interact with. If that person becomes unavailable, especially through death, whatever was said or thought or felt becomes forever irretrievable and unchangeable. It's no longer possible either to ask forgiveness or grant it, either to profess love or hear it professed. The moment and person are gone, never to return; whatever regret you feel is no more than wasted effort. There had been a lot of wasted effort during my time on Rimilia, but it was no longer clear whose effort had been wasted.

I sighed as I remembered all those conversations I'd had with people, they trying to tell me how wrong I was, I maintaining an air of injured dignity no matter what they said. Was it possible that I *was* wrong, that I'd spent more time complaining than trying to understand the reasons for what was being done around and to me? I could remember feeling in the dream that I hadn't even *tried* to see and understand his way of looking at things; even if the same could be said about him, it didn't make *me* any less guilty. And I didn't have to spend any time wondering who *he* was; there was only one he whose doings and opinions held any true meaning for me.

I lost myself to deep thought for a time, letting my mind consider and argue as it wanted to, finally coming back to my surroundings with a sigh. The room was fine for uninterrupted thinking, but the better I felt, the more bored I was becoming. When Rellis had been here he'd said it was storming again, but maybe the storm had moved on since then. I was curious as to what was going on beyond that closed door, and stretching my mind was easier than hunting for clothes and going to see. All I had to do was thin the shield and peek out—but for some reason the shield didn't want to thin. I sat up in the bed furs with a frown and tried again, this time making the action more deliberate than casual, but it still didn't work. The shield whose presence I was always aware of seemed to have been replaced by a blank wall, one which was without cracks and totally immovable. My mind clawed at it and scurried around and clawed some more—but there was no way out, no tiny opening through which I could slip. I sank bank against the cushions in vast confusion, not understanding why my shield had turned so impervious—then felt the ice-fingers of shock. Any shield, no matter how how thick and impervious, would still be subject to removal by me, would still be subject to my will. If I couldn't dissolve it, even with effort, then it wasn't a shield, it was a literal blank wall. I hadn't been killed by the thunderstorm exploding in my mind, I had only been crippled—and was now no different from anyone else. No powers, no special abilities, not even a talent for

cooking. Distantly I thought I should be reacting in some way—
hysterics, insane delight, thoughts of suicide, waves of relief—
but all I felt was numb. I lay propped up on the pile of cushions
in the bed furs, aware of my bare body being held by the furs,
aware of the crackle of candle flames in the small, windowless
room, aware of the deep silence all around, both inside and out,
breathing evenly but not thinking at all.

The sound at my door took a couple of minutes to penetrate
my awareness, and when I finally looked up Dallan and the
barbarian were already inside, Tammad closing the door behind
both of them. Neither one would have taken any prizes in a
perfect-physical-health contest, but Dallan was more clearly marked
by the trail of the lash. They both seemed to have already begun
healing, but they couldn't have been free of pain yet. I stirred in
the bed furs, vaguely wondering why they had come, somehow
unsurprised to see that they both wore their swords. They may
have been half beaten to death, but if they were going to move
around, they'd do it armed.

"*Wenda*, how do you fare?" Dallan asked, his eyes concerned
as he moved forward ahead of Tammad. "My father tells us that
you seem recovered now, yet could not at first recall what had
befallen us. Are you disturbed in any manner? Do you feel
pain?"

"I feel no more than a faint headache," I answered, looking
down and away from them. "You need not have taken the bother
to come here."

"It was no bother, *memabra*," Dallan said, his voice warm
and reassuring. "May we seat ourselves among your cushions?
There are things which must be spoken of among us."

I heard them moving across the carpeting to the nest of
cushions without waiting for an answer from me, showing the
question had been pure formality. They didn't need my approval
to do anything, and they never would. In a world of cataclysmic
changes, that would never change.

"Terril, as you wear my bands, I must be the one to speak
first to you," Dallan said when he and Tammad were settled on
the carpet. "I have learned a thing from the dreams sent me in
the resting place of the Sword, and painful though it is, I must
tell you of it."

I looked over at him where he sat just a few feet away, seeing
both discomfort and determination in his light eyes. He appeared
to be holding himself straight with difficulty, and fleetingly I
wished I could ease his pain. He was determined to say what he

had to say no matter how much he hurt, and if I couldn't help him, the least I could do was let him get it said without interruption.

"The dream sent me was scarcely one of pleasure," he continued, looking away briefly before forcing himself back into eye contact with me. "In it I was a man of great power and wealth, a *l'lenda* without equal, surrounded by lovely *wendaa* without number. These *wendaa* were mine for the taking, and yet though I used them as I willed, I felt myself deeply drawn to none of them. Much time passed in this way, giving me nothing for the nothing I, myself, gave, and then I came upon another *wenda*, one who was not mine. This *wenda* was lovely and desirable, wilful and the possessor of a great power, yet above all that she was filled with a vast unhappiness. I found myself touched by her unhappiness and able to soothe it to some degree, and from this I derived even greater pleasure than her body brought me. The concern I felt for her was deep, as deep as the concern I would have felt for the sister I had never had, yet I saw this concern as love and desire for possession, refusing to admit even to myself even what I felt was scarcely to be considered as love. When one who truly loved her came seeking her, I sneeringly refused her to him, feeling much the man by doing so. I perceived it as keeping her from greater unhappiness, you see, and not as bringing greater satisfaction to myself. I concealed the truth from all by noble speeches, and also saw myself as noble. Never had I known before how low it is possible for a man to take himself with self-delusion."

"You cannot blame yourself for pitying me," I interrupted, almost feeling the air vibrate with the hurt inside him. "Finding pleasure in helping others gripped by unhappiness is no evil thing. It shows you as warm-hearted, Dallan, not callous and cold. It was not your intention to give me greater unhappiness by banding me, nor have I seen the doing in such a light. You need not berate yourself for having shown compassion."

"It was not compassion which I thought to show," he answered, still sounding upset. "In the dream I knew nothing of what I did till I found the *wenda* cold and unmoving, having wasted away from lack of the love she so cruelly had been kept from. It was impossible for me to make reparations for what I had done, and though I now know it for a dream, I feel the ache even to this moment. You must know that I mean to unband you, *memabra*; in also knowing my reasons, you must strive to feel nothing of *ahresta*."

"Such a doing scarcely comes as a shock," I sighed, leaning

back against my cushions and closing my eyes. "You have my thanks for first speaking to me of your intentions."

"Your unbanding is not my sole intention," he said, for some reason sounding stronger. "Should I do such a thing and then merely turn my back upon you, the gesture would surely be as noble as my previous actions. It has long since come to me that much of your unhappiness stems from a lack of understanding between you and your chosen, therefore shall I stand as true brother to you and speak of your hurt to him for you. Should you find it possible to speak for yourself, do not hesitate to do so; I shall remain to assist you solely where you lack the strength."

"I lack the strength for another confrontation," I said, feeling a twinge over the decision I hadn't known I'd made. "I have no chosen nor shall I ever have one, therefore would you be wise to return to your rest. You do no more here than merely waste your strength."

"Have you taken to speaking lies, *wenda*?" he demanded with a snort, his voice now sounding annoyed. "Though in the grip of great pain, my observations of the doings in the chamber of the Sword came with unexpected clarity. Well do I recall that you offered yourself in place of Tammad and myself, and well do I recall the pain you were given for having made the offer. Also do I recall the point at which you challenged and engaged the intruder, which was neither when you were given pain, nor when I was done so. It was the safety and well-being of your chosen which drove you, a truth you cannot deny."

In my memory I was suddenly back in that cave, not doing battle with that monster but being hurt by him. My mind had been looking for a way to divert my attention from what Dallan was saying, but the way it found made me sick to my stomach and ashamed. All the things I hadn't felt earlier came rolling over me, so strongly that I threw myself under the covering fur with a sob, pulled it over my head, then held my hands over my ears. Even the Hamarda, who had held me and used me as a slave, had been seeking normal pleasure; it was only a monster who would use his body to give pain, a twisted monster incapable of feeling normal pleasure. He had used me only to hurt me, and what was infinitely worse, he had done it in front of *him*. There were no tears to soothe a feeling like that, nothing but shame unending.

Less than a minute passed in the privacy of the hiding place I had made for myself, and then the fur was pulled away again, letting in the light. The darkness behind my closed eyelids wasn't enough, but I couldn't take the cover back, and my hands were pulled away from my ears. After that there was a broad chest to be held against, but the gesture brought more agony than comfort.

"*Hama*, do not be tormented by that which you have done," the barbarian said, showing that it was he who held me. "There are none about who would have condemned you had you this time let me die, I least of all. Do not fear that you will regret your goodness."

"What is it that you speak of to my sister, *denday* Tammad?" Dallan asked gently, as though he purposely stood in the background of the conversation. "It strikes me as odd that you seem to believe her actions might have been other than that which they were. For what reason should she have withheld her assistance?"

"For what reason should she have given it?" the barbarian countered, his voice so even that the bitterness barely showed. "Time and again I beat her for having used her powers on those about her; would it not have been fitting had she obeyed me at last and allowed my life to be forfeit?"

"Perhaps," Dallan murmured. "Are you filled with regret for having done her so?"

"No," Tammad growled, Unconsciously tightening his hold on me. "I regret none of it—save the one time I allowed anger to take me. It was for her own sake that I punished her, and for the love I feel for her, yet I succeeded in teaching her no more than fear. Of what worth is a man, who is able to teach no other thing than fear?"

"I see that you, too, have dreamed," Dallan said, and somehow I had the impression he was amused. "In what manner do you see that you have taught her no other thing than fear?"

"When first I claimed her she was a burning flame," the barbarian whispered, barely loud enough to hear. "Her arrogance was full, and yet the life within her was the same, bright and sharp and requiring all of a man's efforts to meet her. You saw, in the mountain, what she has now become, what I have made of her. She trembled and recoiled in fear, filled with terror at my presence; but a moment ago she hid from the sight of me, no doubt at the urging of a similar terror. Even now her eyes remain tightly closed, and she holds her body as far from mine as possible. Sooner would I have lost my life than to have done such a thing to the woman of my heart."

His words ended in an ugly croak, the sort of sound that comes from swallowing down tears. I still felt too ashamed to look at him, but the importance of my feelings dwindled when I realized how painful his were. What he believed was a lie, and I couldn't walk away with a lie left between us.

"That isn't true," I whispered, touching him gingerly for fear of hurting the open whip cuts that covered him. "It isn't you I fear, just your anger. And only when I'm guilty; only when I'm guilty."

Which is most of the time, I added bitterly to myself. I do as I please and expect to get away with it, and when I don't I find someone else to blame for what happens to me. Taking the easy way out is a life style for some people; I had never thought I'd be one of the group.

"What does she say, Tammad?" Dallan asked, and when the barbarian had translated with confusion and puzzlement in his voice, the *drin* of Gerleth chuckled. "The truth is of great importance to one such as she, my friend, and I somehow believe we have not heard the entireness of it. As you fear no more than the *denday*'s anger, my sister, and then only when guilt is yours, for what reason did you fear him in the mountain?"

"For the reason of guilt," I answered, relieved to finally get it said—no matter what they did to me. "His accusation was true, for I did indeed force you from me, despite your belief to the contrary. It was—necessary to me that I do so, no matter that you would find my reasoning foolish. To me it was more necessary than foolish."

"I see," Dallan said, his words falling in the thick silence coming from the barbarian. "And the reason for your having hidden yourself but a moment ago? Was that equally as foolish?"

I found myself adding my own oar to the silence, more than reluctant to discuss the way I felt. Is it possible for any male, especially a Rimilian male, to understand about being hurt like that? Do they ever feel anything more than outrage over their territory having been invaded, or pure confusion and puzzlement? *Can* they know what it's like, even if it should happen to them?

"Perhaps it may be considered equally as foolish," I said at last, still looking at neither of them. "It has, at any rate, nothing whatsoever to do with fear. Cowardice, perhaps, yet not fear."

"I had not realized you understood the difference between cowardice and fear," Dallan said, his tone now approving. "There are those who believe the two the same, yet this has no bearing on our true discussion. I feel certain I know the reasons behind this foolishness you speak of, which surely links two separate actions. Was it not the same thought which caused you to force me from you, and also to hide yourself at mention of the intruder? Am I mistaken in believing so?"

I couldn't quite bring myself to answer him as I slowly pushed out of the barbarian's arms to sit alone. I didn't know what point Dallan was trying to make, and I couldn't check his attitudes any longer to find out; hell, I couldn't even look him in the face. All I felt was very tired, and I wished he would finish up whatever he was doing and let me go back to resting.

"What is this belief you speak of?" the barbarian asked, his voice at least neutral if not yet returned to its usual calm. "In what way might these things be linked?"

"The matter should be as clear to you as I find it," Dallan said to the barbarian, but there was no accusation in his tone, only faint surprise. "My sister has spoken to me of the barbaric beliefs of her former people, and the torment she has felt when faced with our civilized ways. Surely, when these things were spoken of to you as well, you saw—that—"

Dallan's speech came limping to a halt, and I could just imagine the expressions surrounding me. They'd exchange information, get a good laugh out of my "backward" point of view, then hopefully go on their way and leave me alone. Without opening my eyes I groped for the covering fur I'd lost a short time earlier, found it and pulled it to me, then just sat there with two fistfuls of covering at my throat.

"I have been told of no torment faced by this woman," the barbarian said, and he *did* sound accusing. "Little has been told me concerning her beliefs, save for her belief and that of her people that she is to be allowed her will in all things. This cannot be the belief you refer to."

"Nor is it," Dallan agreed with a heavy sigh. "You are unaware, then, of her feeling that to be used by any man save he to whom she belongs is a great shame, shaming her also in the eyes of her chosen. Had I not seen her wracked by this torment with my own eyes, I would scarcely have credited it."

Again there was silence, undoubtedly cram-packed with all sorts of overtones and undertones, and then a gentle hand came to my shoulder.

"Terril, is this true?" the barbarian asked very softly. "For what reason was I not told of this sooner?"

"What need was there to speak of it?" I shrugged, studying the dark gray and red behind my closed eyelids. "Each time I was given as host-gift, I was informed that all choices in the matter belonged to another. To speak of a thing which gives shame is possible only when there is one who is willing to listen with understanding."

"And such a one was not I," he said, so flatly that I felt the weight of it. "Even *seetarr* have proven themselves filled with greater understanding than this one who calls himself *l'lenda*. I have not done as badly as at first I thought; I have done worse."

"Calmly, my friend, calmly," Dallan said as Tammad's hand left my shoulder. "You take the blame for all that has gone before on your own head, and yet the woman is not blameless. How great must be her pride, to keep her from speaking of so pressing a matter! Had she truly wished to speak with you, would you have refused to listen?"

"No," came the answer along with a very deep breath. "Had she truly attempted to speak with me, I would not have turned away from her."

"And you, *wenda*," Dallan said, switching victims. "How often have you spoken to this man of that which disturbed you? Have you *ever* spoken of how you truly felt?"

"Sure," I muttered, lowering my head as far as it would go. "Why the hell do you think I did all those terrible things to all those poor people? For the fun of it?"

"A communication I allowed anger to keep me from deciphering," the barbarian said before Dallan could ask for a translation. "And yet, how else was I to react, save with anger? Do you think me possessed of a power similar to yours, woman?"

"You always understand how everyone else feels," I whispered, trying not to let the dampness seep out of my eyes. "Why is it so impossible for you to do the same with me? Even a *seetar* sometimes gets a pat of appreciation around the reins of ownership."

"There is little to understanding the needs of others, *hama*," he said very gently, his hand coming to stroke my hair. "Where a man sees love, his vision is often blurred, and if not blurred, then distorted. For a man to see his love clearly, she must stand very still for a time; this *you* have never done for *me*."

I turned my head and opened my eyes to look at him through a different kind of blurring, seeing the strength in his broad face and light eyes. I was now willing to believe I hadn't stood still long enough to really understand his thinking, but the revelation had come too late. He was trying to waken something that had died without his knowing it.

"Standing still during beatings isn't one of my many abilities," I said, managing to come up with a small shrug. "I don't recall much else between us lately."

"You come so close, then quickly back away," he said, his light eyes showing again the calm that was so much a part of him. "Is it fear or cowardice which moves you so, *hama*? Do you keep your inner self so far from me by design, or are you merely unable to share with others that which you so often have from them? It is my fondest desire to listen with understanding to any words you speak; for what reason do you refuse to speak them?''

I stared at him for a minute, almost tempted beyond bearing, but even considering the idea was useless. It was both cowardice *and* fear that had kept me from speaking to him before that; from that point on, there would be nothing to talk about.

"Somehow, I think you'll be too busy from now on to listen to *anything* coming from me," I said, unable to look away from him. "You see, the reason that that intruder died was because he was linked directly to my mind when the thunderstorm broke through the barrier I had raised against it. I *didn't* die—or at least not all of me. Only the part you so quaintly call my 'power.' I no longer have that power—and never will again.''

The shock in Tammad's eyes was too visible to be missed, not even by Dallan, who had been sitting back out of the way of the conversation he hadn't understood. He stirred where he had remained among the cushions, then leaned forward.

"Tammad, what has happened?" he demanded, his voice sharper than it had been in some minutes. "What has she said to you?''

"She has informed me that her power is no more," the barbarian answered, his tone reaching for calm—and not making it. "The strength of that storm has taken it from her as it took the life of the intruder. *Hama*, were you injured in any other manner? How strong is the pain you feel? I will send for Lenham immediately so that he may search for damage you may not be aware of.''

He began getting to his feet from where he'd been sitting on the bed furs near me, determination tightening his jaw, and I didn't understand what he was doing. Was he hurrying away in supposed concern, only so that he could *be* away, to begin work again on more important matters? Why hadn't he simply walked out?

"You can send for Len if you like, but there's nothing he can do," I said, watching the barbarian's distraction. "There's nothing anyone can do. I've been burned out by overload, and the circuit can't be replaced.''

"I will know if there is any other damage," he maintained stubbornly, moving those outrageous blue eyes to me. "And you will speak only in this tongue, the Rimilian tongue, so that the *drin* Dallan may understand you. Speaking to me in your own tongue with another present is a great rudeness."

I glanced at Dallan, seeing how patiently he sat in the face of what really was rudeness, but felt too confused to apologize.

"I will speak in any tongue you wish," I said to the barbarian in Rimilian, letting my hand go to my still-aching head. "I will also listen in any tongue you wish; I ask only that you explain what you are about. Of what concern can any other damage possibly be? I am now a cripple, even more uesless than before, no longer fit to be a pawn in the machinations of men. I find the state filled with an unexpected peace and lack of regret, yet not all will find it so. For what reason do you continue to flurry about me?"

"Perhaps the reason is our concern for you," Dallan said as Tammad frowned. "Have you forgotten that your current state— far from useless—has come about due to your efforts on our behalf? Are you able to believe we would now abandon you?"

"Ah, you feel gratitude." I nodded, then put my head back and closed my eyes. "I had failed to consider the presence of gratitude. My questions have now been answered."

I was telling myself that disappointment was a stupid thing to feel under the circumstances, when I heard a sound next to me on the bed furs, as though someone had sat down. It didn't mean much until a hand touched my face, and I opened my eyes to see Tammad less than a foot away.

"Should you believe that it is gratitude which fills me, *wenda*, you are greatly mistaken," he said, his eyes hard and his voice tight with an unexplained anger. "A man may feel gratitude for assistance given him, yet he is able to feel no other thing than anger when his *wenda* places herself in danger and comes to harm by cause of that assistance. Once were you told that sooner would I see this *l'lenda* harmed than you, yet the lesson taught at the time was clearly not remembered. When your strength and health have been regained, I shall teach it again."

"But—but—I do not understand!" I stumbled, uncontrollably lowering myself farther under the cover fur. "You cannot have further interest in me, for I am no longer of use to you! With the absence of my power, I will be of interest to no one!"

I know I expected an increase in his anger, but suddenly his beautiful blue eyes were filled with sadness.

"Ah, *wenda*! How great must have been the pain you were given," he said with a sigh, wrapping one of his great hands around my fist on the cover fur. "To be taught that your only value lay in the power you possessed, to be taught distrust of those about you—I, too, am guilty in part of such a doing, yet are your former people more guilty by far. It will give me great pleasure to drive them to their knees for having done such a thing to my woman."

"*Your* woman?" I echoed, my head swirling with confusion as well as throbbing. "You cannot mean to keep me as your woman?"

"I mean exactly that," he said, staring at me steadily. "Despite your penchant for disobedience, despite the sharpness of your tongue and your untalented ways about a cooking fire, despite your vast and unconcealed reluctance—you are mine and shall remain mine forever."

"Reluctance," I whispered, reaching out with my free left hand to touch him with the very tips of my fingers. "My reluctance for breathing is greater. I cannot understand your desire for a cripple—and have not the courage required to believe in it."

"You need not believe in it." He shrugged, and the ghost of a grin was on his face. "I shall no longer spend breath attempting to persuade you; I shall merely continue to keep you beside me, and shall ask of belief only at the end of our lives. Should you fail to have belief in me then, I shall beat you."

I wanted to laugh at what he'd said, but instead I cried like a weepy infant. Dallan laughed, and so did Tammad, but all I could do was cry. Tammad moved closer and put his arm around me, and it was all I could do not to hurt him in a vise-grip. I wanted to crush him to me with all my strength, and for the first time understood about those episodes where he'd hurt me without meaning to. The urge was just short of compulsion level, a purely emotional reaction to the non-thinking of a mind filled with confusion. His unexpected decision hadn't solved *all* of my problems, but without the worry of the worst one, the others seemed more likely to be taken care of at another time. I was too tired to cry for very long—even happy-crying is draining—and Tammad understood immediately how I felt.

"You are weary and now must take your rest again," he said, gently disengaging my arm from around him. "You must sleep and eat and regain your strength, and then we will talk again. The *drin* Dallan, I believe, also requires further rest, and we keep him from it."

"Indeed," Dallan agreed, beginning to force himself to his feet among the cushions. "I have indeed been too long from my furs, and the healer will not be pleased. This healer has known me from the time of my boyhood, and refuses to accept my being *l'lenda* when I am in her care. Perhaps she is correct."

"I will return when you have taken your rest," Tammad said, touching my face a final time before rising from the bed furs. Neither he nor Dallan were moving as well as they usually did, which said they needed rest at least as much as I. I kept silent as they took themselves from the room, letting them go even when there was so much left to say, then closed my eyes with a deep sigh. I intended doing a lot of thinking about what has just happened, but instead fell asleep.

When I awoke there was another tray waiting for me in the care of the white-dressed woman, and with her help I ate most of what was on it. My head was still hurting faintly—something I was almost getting used to—and I was gently but firmly refused when I spoke about getting up. Every *l'lenda* on the planet seemed to have left orders about how well I was to be taken care of, and the woman seemed to know without asking that my head still hurt. I tried telling her how bored I was, and got laughed at for pretending to be a *l'lenda*. *L'lendaa* were the ones who complained about being kept idle in the furs when there were so many other things to be done; *wendaa* were wiser, and were well able to appreciate the worth of uninterrupted rest. I can't say I agreed with the viewpoint, but arguing wouldn't have gotten me very far. The woman wasn't only convinced she was right; she was also determined to do things her way whether she was right or wrong. I watched her take the tray and leave, then spent a couple of minutes wondering what I was supposed to do to keep from going crazy.

The question was answered for me in a very direct way; as if on cue the door opened again, and Tammad came in. He looked slightly less well used than he had earlier, and he smiled as he came toward me.

"Your rest appears to have taken the weariness from you, *hama*," he said. "I, too, have rested, after having sent for Lenham. My worry will find no similar rest till he has pronounced you unhurt."

"I have nothing more than a headache," I said, returning his smile as I watched him sit down on the bed furs near me. "Compared to the shape I'm usually in on this world, that's tantamount to being in the best of health."

"You seek to ease my worry," he said, his eyes bright with amusement as he reached a hand out to stroke my hair. "Perhaps I should reply that now that my worry is eased, I may think about no more than when I may beat you."

"I think I feel a relapse coming on," I said, trying to groan hollowly but laughing instead. "I must have looked very foolish back then, trying to make you believe I didn't care if you beat me. I'm too much of a coward not to care."

"It is scarcely cowardice to fear punishment at the hands of one who is larger and stronger than yourself," he said, settling himself into a one-elbow leaning position toward the foot of the bed. "Only one who is insane—or bereft of all hope—will do such a thing. Do you truly feel no sadness at the loss of your powers?"

"I can't say I don't feel—empty," I admitted, wishing he hadn't brought up the subject, but determined not to avoid it. "I've been an empath all my life, and it's on a par with an untalented person losing his or her eyesight. But I *am* glad I can't be a pawn any longer, that there won't be people chasing after me for what I can do any more. What I'd like to know is how *you* really feel about it. Even if you keep me a thousand years, you'll never have an empath in your furs again."

"Were it possible to feel joy at another's grievous loss, *hama*, joy is the sole thing I would feel," he said, putting his hand on my leg through the cover fur. "Though I found great pleasure through the presence of a woman with the power in my furs, I shall find greater pleasure in her presence without the power. I am no more than *l'lenda*, ill-equipped for coping with your power. I may face all manner of danger with a sword, yet am I unable to face one small *wenda* with the power with equal unconcern. Such a *wenda* most often seemed beyond me; though I grieve for your loss, I joy in knowing you are no longer beyond me."

"I was never beyond you," I answered softly, leaning forward to touch his hand. "I was just so lost in the hurt of uncertainty and not being wanted for myself that you couldn't find me. I didn't let *anyone* find *me*, and then I blamed them for wanting the only party they *could* find. Why didn't you ever perform the rite of five-banding?"

"*Hama*, it was not possible," he said, appearing momentarily startled at the abrupt question. "For a man to perform the rite of five-banding, his *wenda* must be fully willing and eager to wear his bands. It is possible to force willingness upon a woman by using the needs of her body, yet this course of action was unacceptable to me. I had no wish to force a willingness which did not come of its own."

"Somehow, I knew all along it was my fault," I sighed, leaning back again against the cushions. "There are so many things I don't know about this world, and your people, and you. How could I believe I knew all there was to know just because I read a report? I'm not only foolish, I'm stupid.''

"Merely ignorant," he corrected with a chuckle, patting my leg. "Happily, the ignorant may be taught whereas the stupid may not. I have attempted to teach your ignorance, and shall continue to do so till it is no more. In time you will be as civilized and knowledgeable as my people and myself.''

"You'd best watch those insults, *l'lenda*," I said, looking at him darkly. "You're not over being hurt yet, which means I just might have a chance against you. Would you like to have it said that you were beaten by a *wenda*?''

"No, *l'lenda-hama*, I would not care to have it said that I was beaten by a *wenda*," he laughed, true delight filling his eyes. "I offer my apologies for having given you insult, and shall take care that the same does not occur again.''

"Apology accepted," I grinned, then began climbing out from under the cover fur toward him. "To tell the truth, I'm greatly relieved to have your apology. To beat you would mean to give you more pain—and I would rather die than give you pain. You are not my *hamak*, you are my *sadendrak*, the one who brings life to me in all things. Life would hold no meaning for me beside another; this you must believe above all things.''

"*Sadendra*, I do believe," he said very softly, opening his arms so that I might crawl into them. "There are many things we must teach one another, to be sure that doubt will never touch our belief again. I would have you begin with your feelings concerning host-use, so that I might know at last the reason you dislike it so. Ever did I believe that you refused as a disobedience, intending me and my brothers insult. To learn that I was mistaken has given me pause.''

I lay carefully in his arms, trying not to touch his wounds, and forced myself to come out from the dark corner I was so used to hiding in. It was difficult explaining why I wanted to belong only to him, and he had just as much difficulty explaining why the more he loved me, the more he wanted to share me with his closest brothers. We both agreed to think about the other's point of view before discussing the topic again, and then he held me very close despite his wounds, in memory of what the dark-haired intruder had done to me. The sort of rape I'd been subjected to wasn't considered a sexual act by Rimilians, I learned. It was considered assault of the worst sort, and any woman who could kill a man who did such a thing was praised and regarded highly by all who heard of it. The way Tammad spoke, it was just as though he thought of me as having been cruelly and badly beaten, with no shame attached to the occurrence, nothing but sympathy and consolation coming from him. I remembered then that he and his people didn't believe it possible for a woman to keep herself from being used, and some of the lingering hurt and shame did go away. Not all of it, and not all of the memory either, but enough of it to take the terrible edge away.

We talked for hours as I lay in his arms, and not once in all that time did he make a single sexual overture. I was sure he was hurting too much to change our association from verbal to physical, and the thought disturbed me enough so that I didn't mention it. I didn't want him trying something out of a sense of duty, and thereby hurting himself all the more. When my next meal was brought there was enough for two, and I insisted on feeding the barbarian the way I'd been fed earlier by the woman. He lay propped up on cushions, taking whatever I gave him, and it's hard to say when I last felt the sort of pleasure I got from performing that silly little act. He kept his eyes on me the entire time, silent appreciation in his stare, making me glad I wore nothing that would interfere with what he wanted to see. When the meal was done we lay down together again, the emptied tray still standing where the woman in white had left it.

When the door opened a few minutes later, I thought it was the woman returning for the tray, not realizing my mistake until I heard a chuckling behind me. It was a male voice chuckling, which immediately started me diving for the cover fur, but Tammad and I were lying on it. I tugged futilely at the cover, not missing the fact that the barbarian wasn't moving at all, and the chuckling turned into out and out laughter.

"Do you mean to hide yourself from *me*, *wenda*, the man who has banded you?" Dallan's voice came, his amusement so obvious it set my teeth on edge. "You must sit as you are and allow me to look upon you, for it is my wish that you do so."

"I will be pleased to accord you your wish, if you will also accord me mine," I answered sweetly, turning about to look at him where he stood, about two feet from the bed furs. "Shall I tell you the pertinent points of my wish?"

"Do you refrain from insolence, *wenda*," the barbarian commanded mildly, adding a tug on my hair. "A man has the right to obedience from her whom he has banded."

"And yet he means to unband me, does he not?" I pounced, seeing that Dallan was still amused. "As I am not permanently banded by him, a partial insolence should be acceptable."

"Yet only with a partial obedience," Dallan put in, still grinning. "First the obedience, and only then the insolence. And perhaps it will be my decision not to unband you after all. You are, in final thought, a desirable *wenda*, one a man may easily come to love. It may well be my decision to retain you in my hands."

"Should such an event come to pass, it will then be necessary for the *drin* and myself to again face one another," the barbarian put in while I frowned at an all-too-serious Dallan. "As you are no longer able to interfere in the matter, we will this time find a satisfactory ending to the affair, one which will satisfy honor rather than the stubbornness of a sharp-tongued *wenda*. Once again the choice has become one for *l'lendaa*."

I sat on the bed with what must have been a dumbfounded expression, looking from one unsmiling Rimilian face to the other. I'd forgotten all about the fight they'd almost had, forgotten all about the fact that I still technically belonged to Dallan. If they ever decided to fight again, there was nothing I could do about it, not even threaten to let myself die with the loser. I was not only absolutely helpless, I couldn't even think of anything to *say*.

"I hear no more than a commendable silence, *wenda*," Dallan said, and I couldn't help but notice that he also looked stronger than he had earlier. "Are you no longer interested in being accorded your wish?"

I opened my mouth to answer him, meaning to say something flip about now being willing to pass on my turn at wishing, when I finally got the point they were making. It was my big mouth that had started the trouble, just as it usually did, and if I didn't learn to think before speaking, the next time I might start something I would not be able to stop. It was one thing to joke with a man in the privacy of his furs or mine, quite another to embarrass him, even mildly, in front of others. Courtesy given is courtesy asked for, and I knew well enough what I'd been asking for.

"I ask your pardon, *memabrak*," I said in a very small voice with my head down, addressing him properly as the man who had banded me. "I should not have spoken to you as I did, for the matter is truly one between *l'lendaa*, and I am not *l'lenda*. Please excuse my having intruded in so mannerless a way."

"Excellent, *wenda*, truly excellent," Dallan said, warm approval now in his voice. "To see one's error is the necessary preliminary step to correcting that error. You may now kneel at the foot of your furs the while the *denday* Tammad and I converse.''

I raised my head quickly to look at him, and his eyes said that he wasn't simply having fun with me. I was being punished for the way I'd acted, and the worst part was that I was now sure I would have had to do nothing of the sort if I'd answered him at first with courtesy. I moved to the end of the bed furs and knelt there, filled with disgust, but the entire mass was aimed only at myself. I'd earned whatever I got, and had damned well better remember it for next time.

"You are truly lovely, *memabra*," Dallan said, moving forward the two feet to stand directly in front of me. "You may retain your arms at your sides, yet do I wish to see your head held higher. You are, after all, considerably more than a slave."

His hands came to my face, raising my chin high, and then he turned and walked to the cushions scattered on the carpeting, lowering himself with less than his usual grace despite the ease of his stride. He and Tammad began talking then, about the weather—which was clearing—about the intruder in the mountain—for whom they both continued to hold a blood-grudge—and about *wendaa*. It didn't take them long to get around to discussing *me*, and although I knew they were only talking to waste time, I still ended up blushing vividly. I'd probably never get used to having normally private topics and subjects discussed so frankly and baldly in front of me, and there was nothing else I *could* do other than blush. It went on so long I was sure I'd suffer a permanent skin color change, and then the subject was abruptly changed.

"Since our return, I find myself tiring much too easily," Dallan said, stretching carefully among the cushions before rising to his feet. "As darkness has already fallen, I believe I shall seek my furs again and hope to fare better when I awake. Is it your intention to do the same, *denday* Tammad?"

"In truth, my intentions lie elsewhere, *drin* Dallan," the barbarian answered from behind me, his voice sounding lazy. "There are furs other than my own which I wish to seek, should you be of a mind to see to a small matter before your departure."

I found myself suddenly clamping my jaw shut, to make sure the wrong thing didn't get said. Tammad was asking Dallan to unband me, and Dallan was staring at me without answering! It came to me then that that was why Tammad hadn't touched me, apart from holding me in his arms. He had acknowledged the fact that I was banded as Dallan's, and therefore wasn't entitled to touch me without permission!

"It is such a small matter, *denday* Tammad," Dallan drawled, still staring down at me. "Surely it would not inconvenience you to too great an extent if I should allow it to be seen to at another time. Surely you, and this *wenda* as well, would benefit from rest as much as I."

"The decision is, of course, yours," the barbarian answered, his tone as calm and lazy as it had been. For my part, of course, I was frantic, especially when Dallan turned away from me and headed for the door. I didn't want to wear his bands one minute longer than necessary, and I was prepared to beg if I had to. That was probably what he was waiting for, to have me beg, but I didn't care. I'd do anything I had to do to be Tammad's again. For the second time I opened my mouth, this time ready with the prettiest please I could imagine—but again the words weren't spoken. Something inside my head kept insisting, "Mind your own business! Mind your own business!" "But it is my business!" I shouted silently in answer, "And more than my business! It's my life!" The voice grew still at that, refusing to argue, but I already knew what the argument would have been. It wasn't my business because the matter stood between Dallan and Tammad, and *they* didn't consider it my business. If I was ever going to start playing by their rules, that would have to be the time. I closed my mouth again and continued to kneel where I'd been put, but my chin was no longer as high as it had been.

I know I was waiting to hear the door open and close, sure that it would, and was therefore caught off guard when Dallan was suddenly beside me again. I looked up in surprise to see the grin that he wore, not understanding it or the reason he wasn't gone.

"A man seldom wishes to feel that he does a thing because another has demanded it," he said to me, reaching a hand out to stroke my hair. "When a decision is his alone, he will, if left to his own devices, consider how his decision will affect others. To wheedle or attempt to coerce him merely takes his thoughts from those others, and instills resentment within him over the attempt to intrude upon a decision which is his to make. This applies equally to those decisions which are a woman's to make, and should asleo be kept free of a man's invasions. As you have clearly learned this lesson, you need not be left to agonize. I feel sure you will not take it amiss if I say it gives me great pleasure to now unband you."

He leaned down to touch his lips to mine, and then his hands were at my wrist, removing the first of the bands. I can't say I really understood everything he'd said, but one strange thought seemed to have formed out of it: it's sometimes possible to win by losing. The concept made no sense to me, but once I had the time I'd have to think about it. Very little that Rimilians did made sense, and that odd concept might just be the key to dealing with them without constant pain. Courtesy was another key, and one that was easier to put into practice.

The last of the bands to be taken was the one around my throat, and once it was open I impulsively took Dallan's face in my hands and kissed him gently. I didn't know if doing such a thing was proper, but it was the only way I could think of to say thank you. He returned the kiss with his hand in my hair, chuckled softly when it was over, then gathered up his opened bands and left without another word. I suddenly became aware of how strange it felt to be totally unbanded, a thing I'd tried hard to achieve not too long ago, and the thought must have communicated itself to the man who sat behind me.

"You rub your wrist with a sense of freedom achieved," Tammad observed, causing me to turn my head to look at him. "It seems you have as yet to embrace our custom of banding."

"You're right," I admitted, wondering how he could look so calm while discussing what had to be a disappointment for him. "I want to be with you, but I still don't like the idea of being chained."

"Then I shall not band you," he said, sitting up away from the cushions to shrug. "I shall merely keep you in my furs and beside me, and when others appear to band one who is unclaimed, I shall face them. Perhaps not all will fight, yet many will consider it a matter of honor to face the one who challenges them. They will, of course, be blameless, yet blood will flow by cause of misunderstanding. It is a small price to pay to keep the woman of my heart from feeling herself slave."

"You're telling me I'm being selfishly inconsiderate," I said, studying the lack of accusation in his blue eyes. "I've spent so much time emoting over being 'chained' that I never had the chance to consider what would happen if I *were* unbanded. I doubt if that many would come after me with you standing beside me, but would you really fight them just to give me my way?"

"*Hama*, to *feel* free is of great importance to a man," he said, returning my gaze. "Should he be chained he will fight those chains, often unto death. Recently has it come to me that certain *wendaa* feel the same, yet their method of battle differs. A *wenda* will use harsh words and flight in an attempt to escape, and should these attempts prove unsuccessful she may lose all hope and will herself to death. It is scarcely my intention to keep you beside me so that your death may be achieved; sooner would I see the death of others.''

"Or your own," I said, knowing it to be true. "And if I were really free, I'd know it even with chains all over me. Len was right: I'm making excuses to keep from committing myself. I wish we could find a place where no one would bother us and we could do as we pleased, but I have the terrible feeling there is no such place—or if there were, it would bore you to death.'' I took a deep breath, then plunged in with eyes wide open. "*Sadendrak*, it would give me great pleasure to wear your bands. I would have all men know that I am yours alone, till the end of my days.''

"*Hama sadendra*," he laughed, opening his arms to me. "We have become one at last, and it took no more than the efforts of both of us.''

I laughed along with him as I scrambled into his arms, finally appreciating the fact that compromise took two, not one demanding and the other compromising. We'd both been guilty of that, and even as I hungrily sought Tammad's lips, I wondered how long that understanding would stay with us. The question didn't bother me long, however; Tammad ended the kiss quickly, then produced his bands from his swordbelt. He watched me carefully as he put them on me, searching for the smallest sign of reluctance, but reluctance wasn't what I was feeling. I wanted him more desperately with each passing minute, but wouldn't have rushed him through the rite of five-banding even if I knew I would burst. I savored the words as he spoke them, crying like a fool and laughing like an idiot, and then hurried to help him get rid of his swordbelt and *haddin*. He was as hungry for me as I was for him, but we'd both forgotten about his wounds. This time I'm afraid *I* hurt *him*.

12

When the new day dawned bright and fresh, I was finally able to see it. Tammad dressed himself, then wrapped me up in a fur and carried me to the room he'd been given, a large blue and white room with arched windows and adjoining bathing room. I'd tried insisting on walking so that his poor abused body wouldn't be hurt any further, and he'd cheerfully agreed—on the provision that I did it without the fur. He laughed as I glared at him while he carried me along, then I gave up on the glare to put my arms about his neck. I loved hearing him laugh—and knowing that he was happy—and was too happy myself to stay angry long over nonsense.

When we got to Tammad's room we made use of the bathing facilities, then I smeared his wounds with the salve that did such a wonderful job of healing. He was cut just about all over by the leather of that whip, and from the depth of most of the cuts he probably wouldn't have been walking at all if not for the salve. He made not a single sound as the salve went on, but the sheen of perspiration on his forehead when I was done told the story well enough. We shared a meal—which I insisted on feeding him—and then we shared a nap.

When I awoke Tammad was gone somewhere, but a green gown lay on the furs in his place, one like the silver gown Dallan had given me. I put it on with a great deal of pleasure, sure that it hadn't been the white-dressed woman who had brought it. She seemed to know how I felt without asking, and wouldn't have brought me clothing while my head still hurt. I was tired of having that constant headache, and couldn't help wondering how long it would take to go away. I didn't care for the thought of going through life with a permanent throb behind my eyes, but also had no intentions of simply lying still until it decided to abandon me. Now that I had clothing, I could divert my attention from it by wandering around the palace.

I was just about ready to concede defeat in my battle with the tie at my right wrist when the door to the room opened, ending

239

the fight in a different way. Len came in with a broad stride that he managed to stop just short of running me down, causing me to jump back with a squeak of surprise before it was clear he did intend stopping. I looked at him with the confusion I felt, wondering why he was frowning, but just staring didn't get me anywhere.

"If you intend making a habit of entering rooms like that, don't be surprised when people stop inviting you over," I said instead. "One more step and this gown would have become carpeting."

"You really didn't know I was there, did you?" he asked, staring down at me and sounding as though he were in the middle of a different conversation. "You also didn't know I intended stopping just short of you. What's making your head hurt like that?"

"Pain," I answered suddenly understanding what was happening. "Did you really think I was faking, Len? Do you believe it's that easy to just close your eyes and pretend to be blind? No, obviously you don't believe it, or you wouldn't have expected me to be peeking. Well, sorry to disappoint you, brother, but there's nothing left to peek with. The only thing I do have left is this headache."

"Terry, I'm sorry," he said, and there was tragedy in his eyes as he put out his hand to me. "I guess I was hoping you were faking instead of being convinced of it. Maybe there's something I can do."

"You can, but not for me," I smiled, taking his hand. "Dallan and Tammad are still hurting a lot more than I am, and could use a couple of sessions of pain control. I wish I could do it myself, but I—can't."

"I'll give it a try, but I've never been very good at pain control," he said as he squeezed my hand. "But first I want a closer look at you and that headache of yours. I'd like to see for myself whether or not I can do anything."

I briefly considered trying to talk him out of it, then changed my mind with a shrug. Len would not be happy until he'd poked and pried and satisfied himself that nothing could be done, and arguing would just be a waste of time. I led him over to the room's nest of cushions, we both sat, and he looked down at me with a distracted expression. I knew he was thumbing through my emotions and feelings looking for the faintest hint of a response, but I couldn't feel a thing. His touch was usually light but very masculine, but I couldn't detect his presence even with my eyes closed and every nerve in my body straining. It seemed

I'd been hoping at least as hard as he had, but sometimes hope is more reflexive than voluntary. I pushed the feeling aside with impatience, and made myself think about something else until Len was through.

"I think I understand now," Len said at last, taking a deep breath as his eyes came back in focus.

"What do you understand?" I asked, faintly curious. "How the burnout broke the circuit?"

"No," he answered, still looking sober. "There's a—gap of sorts where I used to be able to detect your ability, but that's not what I meant. I think I understand why you aren't permanently hysterical and half insane."

"I've made myself one hell of a reputation around here, haven't I?" I sighed at the thought and shook my head. "People notice only when I *don't* throw fits."

"That's not what I meant," he repeated, gesturing impatiently. "If I ever suffer burnout, you can be damned well sure I won't get over it. Not many of us would, but I think I know why you did."

"Well, I *was* a Prime," I shrugged, feeling uncomfortable. "That has to count for something."

"It doesn't count for anything except that you've lost more than most other empaths would have," he disagreed with a headshake. "Have you ever heard the ancient myth about the goddess who fell in love with a mortal? No? Well, the story tells that there was once a goddess who met a mortal man and fell in love with him. He loved her too, but he had a lot of trouble coping with a goddess, in understanding her needs and actions, and with suiting his own actions to hers. The goddess saw the trouble he was having, and knew that if something wasn't done, their love would die. She couldn't make him a god, so instead had herself turned into a mortal woman, one he had no trouble coping with. She paid a high price for his love, but afterward they did manage to live happily ever after."

"Len, are you saying I did this on purpose?" I asked, feeling a tightening all over my body. "Because if you are. . . ."

"No, no, I know you didn't do it on purpose," he interrupted, leaning forward to emphasize the intensity of his words. "I'm trying to say I think you're glad it happened. It was your empathetic abilities that stood between you and Tammad, and now that they're gone you're ready to live happily ever after. I can't really argue with a viewpoint that has let you keep your sanity, but Terry—Don't you think you're selling Tammad short? *You're* the one who thinks he can't cope with an empath, just as you were the only one who didn't believe he really loved you. I think he *could* cope—if you ever gave him the chance.''

"Don't you think this conversation is a waste of time under the current circumstances?" I asked, finding it impossible to lose the stiffness I'd developed. "It doesn't matter whether Tammad could or couldn't cope. There's nothing left for him to cope with."

"Terry, that's part of the point I'm trying to make," he answered gently, taking my hand even though I didn't want him to. "I know almost nothing about burnout, and I doubt if you know much more. What if your abilities just need encouragement to come back? What if your denial is the only thing keeping them away? They might not be as strong as they once were, but . . .''

"No!" I shouted, pulling my hand out of his grip. "They're gone for good and I don't want them back! Do you hear? I don't want them back!"

He opened his mouth to say something else, but I didn't want to hear it. I scrambled to my feet and ran to the door, threw it open, then looked wildly about. Tammad stood in the corridor only ten feet to the right, talking to some men, and he turned in surprise when I ran to him. His arms opened to make a safe place for me as they always did, and I clung to him in an effort to stop the shaking and shuddering that had for some reason descended on me. The throbbing in my head had become a pounding, but I didn't care as long as I could stand with my cheek to his chest, held in those powerful arms.

"*Hama*, what occurs here?" the barbarian asked, his voice gently puzzled. "Lenham, why has she run to me in this way?"

"She didn't care for certain parts of my conversation," Len answered as he came up, obviously having followed right after me. "There doesn't seem to be much I can do for her, except to recommend that she rest as much as possible while she still has that headache. The more active she is, the worse it gets."

"If I could just walk around, spend some time outside, I'm sure it would go away," I said, looking up into Tammad's concerned face. "Being cooped up like that is making it worse, and I thought we could. . . .''

"She needs to rest," Len insisted, his tone pure calm and sweet reason. "If she doesn't, it can only get worse."

"Then she will rest," the barbarian said, inarguable decision clear in the way he picked me up. "You may walk about when the pain has gone from you, *memabra*."

"No, please—" I began, but it was already too late to keep

him from carrying me back toward his rooms. I thought I might be able to get him to listen to me once we were alone, but hadn't counted on the sudden waves of sleepiness washing over me. The sleepiness—sent by a grinning Len—wasn't strong enough to put me out, but it did make me yawn uncontrollably, adding to the impression that rest really was what I needed. Despite my protests Tammad put me to bed, then set with me until a meat soup was brought by the woman who was dressed in white. I didn't know whose idea that was, but the soup contained that subtle sweetness that said it was medicated. Len stood looking on while Tammad fed it to me, and the last thing I saw before my eyes closed was Len's expressionless face surrounding deeply satisfied eyes.

When I awoke the room was empty, and the gown that Tammad had taken from me was gone. I spent a few minutes cursing out Len, but all that did was send ripples through the headache that was still with me. It was pretty clear Len thought he was helping me by interfering, but that didn't change the fact that I didn't *want* his help. He had no right appointing himself the one to Set Things Straight, and had no right telling me I was wrong not to want my abilities back. If I was happier as I was, who was he to tell me I should try putting things back as they had been? All my abilities had ever done was make trouble for me, and I was tired of trouble. If Len was right and they needed my encouragement to come back, then they were gone forever.

I tried getting comfortable in the bed furs, but it was only afternoon, I was all slept out, and I was *bored*. When the door to the room opened I thought it was Tammad coming back, but I was terribly wrong. Len and Garth came in instead, big, friendly smiles on their faces, and insisted on visiting with me for a while. I discovered that the sight of Garth's dark hair upset me, but that didn't make them leave. As a matter of fact, nothing I said made them leave. I knew when Len soothed my upset at the sudden memory of the intruder, but I wasn't greatful and didn't care to be manipulated that way. Len just grinned and began telling Garth how *alive* he felt when he was awakened, and Garth helped out by asking interested questions. I put my hands over my ears and buried myself under the cover fur, but was saved from suffocation by the arrival of Tammad. He didn't press me when I said I couldn't tell him what was wrong, but he didn't need the details to know that Len and Garth were responsible for the way I felt. He overrode their attempts at explanation and just sent them away, then spent a satisfyingly long time making love to me and holding me. I quickly forgot all about Len and Garth, and didn't think about them again.

Until the next day. Telling an untalented person to stay away from someone who doesn't want them around usually solves the problem, but the same can't be done with an empath. Len didn't have to be in the same room with me to reach me, and reach me he did.

The new day was as pretty as the one before had been, but I started out feeling depressed that the headache wasn't gone and went downhill from there. My depression deepened until I cried like a baby, feeling heartbroken and all alone. Then, for some reason, the depression lightened, and kept lightening until I felt bubbly and deliriously happy. I left the bed furs and danced around the room, laughing like an idiot and gigling over nothing. Tammad came in just then, and I pulled him to the bed furs, made him sit, then danced for him. He was absolutely delighted with the dance, his eyes consuming me with every movement, but when he stood up to take his swordbelt off, I suddenly realized how shy and frightened I felt. He was so big and unstoppable that I felt like a child in his presence, and I ran from him with a squeak of alarm, making him chase me all over the room. It didn't take long before he caught me, and I was carried over his shoulder back to the bed furs, where he completed the game by raping me. I didn't realize he thought it was a game until later, when it was all over and I had come to understand why I'd been acting so strangely. Len must have exhausted himself, but he'd forced me into showing Tammad I could dance, and then had gotten me raped. I couldn't tell Tammad about what Len was doing without discussing Len's theories, and I didn't want to do that. I also couldn't protect myself from Len, which was surely his purpose in doing what he did. If I got desperate enough to protect myself I'd have to try getting my shield back, which would surely bring the rest back if it were at all possible. Len was trying to make me *want* my abilities back, but his plan wouldn't work. I wouldn't want them back no matter what he did to me.

I spent the rest of the day gritting my teeth and jumping at mental shadows, but the worst thing that happened was that Tammad made me dance for him again before he would let me eat the final meal of the day. I'd spent a lot of time and energy keeping him from knowing I could dance, and while it gave me pleasure to give him pleasure, his reactions to my dancing also made me uneasy, just as I'd known they would. Tammad wasn't a civilized man who would smile politely and applaud with moderate enthusiasm when the dance was over, coming up to me to pat my shoulder and congratulate me. He lay stretched out on one elbow in the carpet fur among the cushions, his eyes following every gesture of my hands, every slide of my hips, every turn of my feet. After a few minutes I couldn't take being stared at like that any longer and turned to dance with my back to him, but that was a mistake. I suddenly found him right behind me, his hands sliding down my upstretched arms to my sides and then to my breasts and belly, his *haddin* no longer encumbering him, his appreciation already reaching for me. I gasped as he lifted me off my feet and took me down to the carpeting with him, but he didn't hurt me the way I feared he might. He kept a tenuous but adequate control of himself while he loved me, but that meant duration rather than intensity. I was given a good deal of pleasure in return for the dancing, but by the time I was able to get to the food, it was cold. Tammad made up for that by warming *me* again, and it was quite some time before we got to sleep.

When I woke up the next morning, the headache was gone.

I stood by one of the tall, ribbed windows and looked out, aware of the warm, sweet breeze but paying no attention to it. I was more aware of something else, and that something else was making me sick inside. When the throb of the headache had faded, it was as though a curtain had been lifted, showing me something that had been there all along but obscured by the throb. The shield I was used to using covered my entire mind, but what I could feel then was a smaller shield, surrounding one small part of my mind. It was most likely the gap Len had encountered, and somehow I knew that I could now thrust it aside without effort, and my abilities would be back as though they'd never been gone. They *hadn't* been gone, only recuperating from the battering they'd taken, the key to the shield hidden from me so that I couldn't expose them until they were ready to withstand use again. Instead of being legitimately blind, I had become a sighted person with eyes held closed, a pretend cripple who didn't *want* to be whole instead of a handicapped person going on despite that handicap. I expected to feel cheap and small and I did, but I was also afraid. "Once a pawn, always afraid" should have been an old saying, and it wasn't just my relationship with Tammad that I was afraid for. My abilities were the sort that would interest anyone with an urge to influence and control his fellow man, which would put me up for grabs again. I may have felt bored from all the lying around I'd done, but being the center of that sort of interest wasn't my idea of something to do to chase away boredom.

I ran a hand through my hair then rested my arm on the window edge, a moment later adding my face to my arm. I felt absolutely no urge to remove the small, thick shield and peek out, but that didn't mean I could just go ahead and pretend that my abilities weren't there. Too often their use was reflexive rather than voluntary, like blinking because of a finger poked toward an eye. Time and again over the past few days I'd caught myself trying to read someone, and if the headache had disappeared sooner I would have succeeded. Using my abilities was too much a part of me, and I'd never get away with pretending, never. And what would happen when Tammad found out? He'd told me he was happy I was no longer an empath; the last thing I wanted was for him to think I was beyond him again. Despite Len's opinions to the contrary, Tammad had admitted that he couldn't cope with an empath. What would he do if he found out he had one to cope with all over again? I didn't know, and I didn't want to find out; speaking as a professional coward, I was much better off not knowing.

I'd been hearing the sound of metal banging on metal for a number of minutes, but the noise hadn't been able to break through the agitation in my thoughts. As soon as I decided I needed something to distract me I heard it again, and this time looked out the window to see what it was. The room I stood in was on the second floor of the palace, with a wide unrailed walk on the floor below, and an exercise area perhaps ten feet below and beyond the walk. A number of *l'lendaa* had been loosening their swordarms in this area, but just then there were only two going at it, with the rest watching. I didn't understand why the two were of such interest until I realized they were Len and Garth, and that they were getting instruction from those who were watching. Garth had more familiarity with a sword than Len did, but Garth had the problem of unlearning some of what he already knew, while Len had no such obstacle standing in his way. As I watched them I also became convinced that Len was using his abilities to predict when, and to a certain extent how, Garth would strike at him, evening up the level of ability between them even more. Len slashed and ducked and Garth ducked and slashed, and it took another minute of watching before I realized that they were using practice swords, blunted weapons that they couldn't hurt each other with. Even from that distance I could see the sweat slicking their bodies, showing they'd been at it for a while. They must have been tired, but they gave no sign that they intended stopping any time in the near future.

I'd been looking at Len and Garth just to have something to look at, but suddenly it came to me that I wasn't looking at them with anything that could be described as friendly feeling. I tried to brush the animosity aside, but it was growing too thick to be brushed. Those two down there were having a grand old time, but they probably had plans for coming after me again later, as they had the day before. Under the guise of helping me they'd put me through hell, not once considering the possibility that I really was burned out for good. If I had been, Len's prodding would have been the equivalent of pulling wings off insects, an attack against the helpless that could never be resisted or countered. The more I thought about it the angrier I got, and then I remembered what they'd done to me back in Aesnil's palace. They'd turned me into a whimpering, cringing slave begging to be used, and afterward I'd sworn to get even. For all I knew Len was right about my having lost some of my ability, but right then all I wanted was revenge.

It happened so abruptly and strangely that even I was startled. I stood at the window seething as I watched the two men, seeing them run through a complex-looking series of attacks and counters that must have been pretty good. The men watching them raised their voices in congratulatory approval as the two finally lowered their weapons, and I could almost see the chests swelling on the two Amalgamation men. They gripped left hands as they spoke to each other with grins and laughter, then released each other's hand to slap each other's shoulders. They were so damned pleased with themselves that it made me furious, and I remember wishing with fists clenched tight that they would do something to make themselves look unutterably foolish in front of all those men whose good opinion they were so eager for.

And that seemed to be all it took.

I don't know whether I noticed first that the small, thick shield was gone, or that Garth and Len were acting strangely. Instead of standing tall and strong and looking like warriors, they were suddenly standing slouch-hipped and limp-wristed, emphasizing what they were saying with broad, feminine gestures and laughing in shrill giggles. They didn't seem to notice the change until the *l'lendaa* around them began to guffaw and point, and then they looked around themselves with confused lack of understanding. I could feel their emotions clearly from where I stood, as clearly as the amusement and ridicule coming from the *l'lendaa* around them. Len had thought my abilities would come back

lessened, but he couldn't have been more wrong. I felt strong
and healthy and raring to go, and that was all I needed. Tammad
was as good as lost to me, and there was nothing I could do
about it. I slipped down to the carpeting and buried my face
against my knees, drowning in an ocean of distustingly vigorous
health and mental ability.

It couldn't have been more than five minutes before the riot
burst into the room, storming and screaming from the fury in
Len's and Garth's minds. I didn't look up until they were almost
on top of me, but not because I was trying to think of a way out
of the mess. I wasn't thinking of anything at all, or if I was it
was that I didn't give a damn what those two did to me. The
happiness had lasted such a short time, but it was all I would
ever have.

"That was a damned lousy thing to do, Terry!" Len shouted
as he stomped closer, his face flushed and his eyes blazing. "Do
you know what you made us look like out there? How could you
have—"

His words broke off as his mind wrenched to a halt, angry still
but suddenly aware of what he was saying. He'd been too wild
to think about it sooner, and he was genuinely surprised—and
then immediately pleased.

"Terry, you did it!" he shouted, this time happily. "Your
abilities are back and you used them! You're not hiding your
head in the sand any more!"

"She's also not jumping up and down with joy," Garth
pointed out, his hand on Len's arm. His anger was also a lot less
than it had been, and he looked down at me with the disturbed
sobriety in his mind. "She's crying instead of crowing, and that
isn't the Terry I used to know."

"She's crying inside a lot harder," Len said, sending me the
comfort of his mind as he came closer to crouch next to me and
put his arm around my shoulders. "Terry, I can feel that you've
given up and you mustn't do that. It'll all work out, just wait and
see."

"He doesn't want an empath, Len," I whispered, feeling the
tears roll down my cheeks. "He said he doesn't, and you know
he never lies. Why did it have to come back?"

I buried my face against my knees again as Len's arm tightened around me, his mind frantically trying to keep the stricken
feeling from reaching me. Len knew as well as I that Tammad
didn't lie, and there was nothing he could say to alter the truth:
my life with Tammad was over before it had really started. Garth
came closer to reach down and stroke my hair with an empa-

thetic echo of pain in his mind, as helpless as Len to do anything to stop it.

"What do you do near my woman?" a cold voice growled angrily. I felt Len flinch as I raised my head again to see Tammad in the doorway, and then the big barbarian was coming toward us, his left palm touching his sword hilt with a sliding caress that brought a flash of fear to both Garth and Len. They'd learned enough about Rimilian swordplay to really appreciate what level Tammad stood at, which was considerably higher than any they were likely to attain in the reasonably near future.

"Tammad, we have good news," Garth began, trying for hearty good cheer in his tone instead of nervousness, but he gave up the attempt when it was immediately clear that he was being ignored. Tammad was staring at Len, and the lack of expression on his face was chilling.

"You were told, were you not, that you were not to approach Terril again?" he said to Len, the growl in his voice echoing the anger in his mind. "Now you have not only approached her and put your hands upon her without permission, you have also brought her tears. No man may bring tears to my woman and feel himself safe from my wrath, *no* man! Stand before me, Lenham, and speak quickly upon what occurs here."

I was trembling as Len took his arm back and slowly straightened out his crouch, his mind clanging with shock and fear. I felt the fear too, a reaction to the deadliness flowing coldly from Tammad's mind, a deadliness I'd felt many times before. I knew I had to explain the misunderstanding before he hurt Len, but the trembling fear that gripped me was almost physical in its hold, freezing my throat and paralyzing my will. Len straightened all the way, his eyes widening, and then he pointed a disbelieving finger at Tammad.

"You're projecting!" Len said hoarsely, the shock still bright in his mind as he stared up into Tammad's face. "I've never had it coming straight at me before, or I would have seen it sooner. No wonder you were able to stand against Terry's projections—when you're angry you're almost as strong as she is!"

"What nonsense do you speak?" the barbarian demanded, frowning at Len in annoyance at the way he was being stared at. For my part I was frozen in shock, staring up in a daze of dumbfoundedness. When the annoyance touched Tammad his anger lessened—and so did the terrible fear I'd felt! What Len said was true—Tammad was projecting!

"And you said you didn't want anything to do with empaths?" Len laughed, a wild sound to it. "I'll bet you even receive a little without knowing you're doing it. Hell, man, you have to, or you'd never be so good with people! You work with what squeezes through that cloud of calm you use as a shield, groping around blindly, but stronger than any untrained empath has the right to be! And now that I think about it, I'll bet you're not the only one. *L'lendaa* have too much control over themselves for it to be an accident. I'll bet most of you are latents!''

"So that's why I always found myself drowning in panic when you were mad at me," I blurted, rising to my feet to stare at Tammad as wide-eyed as Len had been. "You were projecting at me so strongly that I was completely blowed over. If I'd known enough to shield—but I didn't know enough, not then and not when the men of this world projected desire at me. Unshielded, I couldn't have resisted any of you in a million years. You forced me with your minds as well as your bodies— every one of you!''

"*Wenda*, I have no knowledge of what you speak," Tammad said, his mind filling with confusion and disturbance over the outrage I was showing. "Why do you look at me so—as though I am no longer the man who banded you?''

"Oh, you're the same one, all right," I said, putting my fists on my hips as I looked up at him. "The one who was so nobly proud of never having taken unfair advantage of anyone, and the one who said he couldn't cope with an empath—and the one who punished me for using my abilities. Well, what about *you*? Who punishes *you* for projecting every time you lose your temper? Which happens a lot more often than you care to admit! Well? Who gets to do the honors?''

I was too furious to really notice that he was actually backing up away from me as I advanced on him, but if I'd stopped to think about it I wouldn't have been all that surprised. I was projecting the same sort of anger at him that he usually sent toward me, and my projections were still stronger than his. I'd copied that sense of deadliness and thrown that in as well, giving him a taste of what had time and again sent me cringing back from him. He didn't cringe the way I had but he did back up, shaking his head to throw off the effects of my projection. He was damned sensitive, all right, to know so accurately when someone was projecting at him, but he didn't get anywhere until that heavy calm swirled back into his mind, blocking off most of my efforts. He used that calm as both a shield and a control on his own emotions, and once he had it in place he stopped backing up.

"That's a good question Terry just asked," Len put in, coming up to stand next to me. "The least she ever got for unauthorized projecting was a good whacking on the backside, which is a lot less than what you gave me for doing the same thing to her. Now that we've found *you* doing it, what do *you* get for it?"

"You may attempt to do to me what I did to you," Tammad told Len in a mutter, his hand to his head as he fought to throw off the lingering effects of my projection. "You need not even wait till this throbbing abandons me, should the matter touch you strongly enough. I feel no regret for what punishments I gave, for your power was exercised willfully while mine was not. Should this insanity be true."

His last sentence sent a quiver through his mind, a rippling in the calm that showed how upset he really was. He *didn't* want anything to do with empathy, especially from the inside out, and all the anger drained out of me as though it had been blotted up in a giant towel. I used pain control to soothe away the throbbing headache my projection had given him, then turned and hurried back to the windows.

"My thanks, Lenham," I heard him say with a sigh as I sank down among the cushions. "To give aid rather than seek revenge shows you to be a man of strength."

"Don't thank *me*," Len denied with a snort of amusement. "I don't have that sort of strength, character-wise *or* pain-control-wise. Don't you recognize the touch of a Prime?"

"Terril?" Tammad said, and I could almost see his incredulity even though I was facing toward the windows. "Her power has returned?"

"That's the good news I was trying to tell you about," Garth said, a bemused quality to his mind. "I didn't know then just how much news there was."

"That's what brought us up here," Len said, his tone wry. "We—ah—discovered that Terry had her ability back and came to congratulate her. You found her crying because she had the foolish idea that you wouldn't be happy to have her the way she used to be. Now wasn't it silly of her to believe you wouldn't want her."

There was no answer from Tammad to that, and I closed my eyes and put my face in my hands. That rigid calm was keeping me from seeing how he really felt the way it usually did, but I didn't have to read him to know the truth. He had told me the truth, and he didn't lie.

"Terril, *hama*, you must not weep," his voice came then, startlingly right behind me. His hand stroked my hair as he sat down next to me, and then he was pulling me to him. "There is nothing that would cause me to not desire you, this you cannot doubt. My love will not fail you.''

"You said you can't cope with an empath,'' I sobbed, throwing my arms around him as I buried my face in his chest. "You can't tell me you were lying to make me feel better, because I know you weren't. I don't want to be beyond you—I'd rather be crippled!''

"No, *hama-sadendra*, I was not lying.'' He sighed as he tightened his arms around me, and I could feel the sadness flowing through his calm. "I did indeed have difficulty coping with a woman with the power, yet this difficulty did not, in fine, cause me to turn from her. No less a thing than death could do so. Fool that I am, I should not have refrained from saying this sooner, yet I had not thought your power would return. As for being beyond me—*wenda*, should Lenham be correct, that will never again be so. Perhaps now *I* may be beyond *you*.''

"You think you're better than a trained Prime?'' I exclaimed, shocked into leaning back away from him. And then I saw his grin and heard the chuckle in his mind, and understood what he'd done. "You said that deliberately to get a rise out of me,'' I accused with a black look, then couldn't help laughing. "You're a mean, nasty beast of a barbarian, but I love you anyway. Even if you are too good for me.''

"I may perhaps be too good for you after you have aided me in the use of this—power,'' he said with a grimace, wiping the last of the tears off my cheek. "Sooner would I have no more than a woman with the power, for the difficulties are bound to be many and large.''

"We'll take care of them together,'' I reassured him, hugging him around again. I'd train him to use what he had, and somehow get back to Central to retrieve our child, and do my damnedest to help him conquer the whole damned universe, if that's what he wanted. I'd heard that Cinnan had rescued Aesnil from her slavery, and the two of them had worked things out even better than Tammad and I had. We'd probably leave Gerleth with them and go back to Grelana for the rest of Tammad's *l'lendaa*, and then we'd head back home. After that we had the Amalgamation to tackle, and I was actually looking forward to it.

"We'll take care of everything together,'' I repeated, still hugging him. "Especially getting you trained. I wouldn't want you in danger of being punished any longer than necessary.''

"Speaking of punishment,'' Len drawled, "did I mention, Tammad, how Garth and I knew Terry had regained her abilities?

You see, we were in the exercise court just below this window, and all of a sudden. . . ."

"Len, don't!" I squeaked, suddenly filled with pure panic, but it was much too late. The unreasonably large arms around me were no longer gently soft, and a cloud of anger was rolling straight through the billowing calm. I looked up to see two hard blue eyes staring down at me, and frantically shook my head. "It was an accident!" I pleaded, trying to make Tammad believe me. "I didn't do it on purpose just to get even for what they did to me! I didn't! You can't punish me for an accident!"

Damned barbarian. He did.

DAW

SHARON GREEN
takes you to high adventure on alien worlds

The Terrilian novels

☐ **THE WARRIOR WITHIN** (UE2146—$3.50)
☐ **THE WARRIOR ENCHAINED** (UE2118—$3.95)
☐ **THE WARRIOR REARMED** (UE2147—$3.50)
☐ **THE WARRIOR CHALLENGED** (UE2144—$3.50)
☐ **THE WARRIOR VICTORIOUS** (UE2264—$3.95)

Jalav: Amazon Warrior

☐ **THE CRYSTALS OF MIDA** (UE2149—$3.50)
☐ **AN OATH TO MIDA** (UE1829—$2.95)
☐ **CHOSEN OF MIDA** (UE1927—$2.95)
☐ **THE WILL OF THE GODS** (UE2039—$3.50)
☐ **TO BATTLE THE GODS** (UE2128—$3.50)

Diana Santee: Spaceways Agent

☐ **MIND GUEST** (UE1973—$3.50)
☐ **GATEWAY TO XANADU** (UE2089—$3.95)

Other Novels

☐ **THE FAR SIDE OF FOREVER** (UE2212—$3.50)
☐ **LADY BLADE, LORD FIGHTER** (UE2251—$3.50)
☐ **MISTS OF THE AGES** (September 1988) (UE2296—$3.95)
☐ **THE REBEL PRINCE** (UE2199—$3.50)

DAW

Presenting JOHN NORMAN in DAW editions . . .

DAW

NEW DIMENSIONS IN MILITARY SF

Timothy Zahn
THE BLACKCOLLAR NOVELS

The war drug—that was what Backlash was, the secret formula, so rumor said, which turned ordinary soldiers into the legendary Blackcollars, the super warriors who, decades after Earth's conquest by the alien Ryqril, remained humanity's one hope to regain its freedom.

☐ THE BLACKCOLLAR (Book 1)   (UE2168—$3.50)
☐ THE BACKLASH MISSION (Book 2)   (UE2150—$3.50)

Charles Ingrid
THE SAND WARS

He was a soldier fighting against both mankind's alien foe and the evil at the heart of the human Dominion Empire, trapped in an alien-altered suit of armor which, if worn too long, could transform him into a sand warrior—a no-longer human berserker.

☐ SOLAR KILL (Book 1)   (UE2209—$3.50)
☐ LASERTOWN BLUES (Book 2)   (UE2260—$3.50)

John Steakley
☐ **ARMOR**

Impervious body armor had been devised for the commando forces who were to be dropped onto the poisonous surface of A-9, the home world of mankind's most implacable enemy. But what of the man inside the armor? This tale of cosmic combat will stand against the best of Gordon Dickson or Poul Anderson.
                                    (UE1979—$3.95)
